ESCAPING
PRETENSE

ALSO BY DEBORAH MILLER

The Essence of Shade

ESCAPING PRETENSE

DEBORAH JEAN MILLER

Opal Stone Press

First Edition

Cover design, photography & book layout by Emilie Haney of E.A.H. Creative

Copyediting by Michael McConnell

Author photo by Marisa Miller, Focal Point Studio

ISBN: 978-0-9980489-2-5 (Paperback edition)

ISBN: 978-0-9980489-3-2 (eBook edition)

Opal Stone Press

Plymouth, Michigan

For the nearly three thousand innocent lives lost and to the heroes that emerged on that fateful day.

The most terrible poverty is loneliness, and the feeling of being unloved.

MOTHER TERESA

PART ONE

CHAPTER 1
SEPTEMBER 11, 2001, NEW YORK CITY

T *hey know.*

Pretense reread the meeting notice, the mouse slipping between damp fingers. A spark lit somewhere deep inside, an exposed wire about to ignite.

From: Thelma Barnes, HR Director
To: Pretense Abdicator
Subject: Employee Matter
Location: Simon Crawford's Office
Date/Time: 09/11/2001 @ 8:00 a.m.

Paralyzed behind her desk, she watched the gathering storm unfold. Two unfamiliar men strode down the hall toward Simon Crawford's office, followed by the confident march of Baron Rothschild. Panic wrapped its stiff arms around her. *Oh, God. Oh, God. I need to make a run for it.*

"Good morning, Pretense," said Daphne Duke, appearing in her doorway. "Are you okay? You look frazzled."

"I'm fine," she said. "Do you need something?"

"Would you like to go upstairs with Ariana and me to the café on the ninety-third floor and grab a coffee and donut?"

"I can't. Please shut the door when you leave. Thank you."

Pretense glanced at the clock. Ten minutes to eight. She fought back a rising panic as she bolted to her feet, her chair toppling behind her. She grabbed her purse and laptop bag, then rushed around her desk.

The knock came, quiet at first, followed by a brief pause, then grew louder. She scanned the tight space in a final, desperate attempt to escape the inevitable, but there was no way out. She inhaled deeply and let it all out in one sigh as she opened the door to the pear-shaped bulk of Thelma Barnes, blooming in a three-piece, tomato-red pantsuit and toting an official-looking binder.

"Good morning, Pretense. Did you receive my meeting notice?"

"Yes, I did," she said, adjusting the shoulder strap of her laptop bag. "However, I just received an emergency phone call. I need to leave right away."

Thelma's eyes smiled in a calming way. "I'm sure it can wait. Let's walk together to Mr. Crawford's office."

Her mind whirled. "I'll meet you there. I need to change out of my running shoes."

"There is no need to change. Please, set your things down and come with me."

Pretense read Thelma's resolve and shrank. "Do I need to bring anything?" she asked, her voice choked with fear.

"No. Just follow me."

When they turned the corner, Pretense noted that Simon was standing, arms crossed, outside his office. He ushered them in and closed the door.

Her legs felt like Silly Putty as she made her way to an empty chair near the door. The relentless thumping of her heart seemed to echo across the room as she clasped her hands between her legs to stop the trembling.

Simon took a seat behind his desk in front of the dramatic floor-to-ceiling windows. The South Tower of the World Trade

Center stood tall against a cloudless September sky, laying a vivid backdrop for her impending storm. Seated on either side of Simon were two men with serious faces, their eyes studying her every move. In the far corner of the room, next to Thelma, sat Baron Rothschild, staring straight ahead.

Simon shifted in his chair; a muscle twitched in his jaw as he nodded to his right. "Pretense, this is Griffin McCoy, a private investigator." He looked to his left. "And this is Agent Dick Birchwood with the New York FBI Office. Of course, you've met Baron Rothschild and Thelma." He took an obvious swallow and folded his hands on his desk, leaning in. "The reason we are here today is to discuss a very serious matter. It has been alleged that you have embezzled money from Baron Rothschild's parents, Hyman and Edna Rothschild."

Pretense's jaw unhinged as her eyes bounced around the room. "This is a joke, right?"

Simon's lips curled in. "I wish it were a joke, Pretense. I really do. But we have compelling evidence to the contrary. After Baron became suspicious of your activities, he hired Griffin McCoy to investigate. Based on Griffin's findings, he contacted the FBI, and that's when Dick took the case."

Pretense jerked her head in Baron's direction. "This is incredibly insulting. Please tell me you haven't shared this outrageous story with your parents?"

Baron looked at Pretense, his eyes drilling into her. "I didn't have the heart to tell my parents that their trusted financial adviser was stealing their money. But I plan to call them as soon as this meeting is over." He broke his gaze, his chin jutting upward.

Pretense craned her neck around Thelma, her face crimson. "How dare you accuse me of this heinous act. And you, of all people. You should be ashamed."

Thelma interrupted. "Now calm down, Pretense. Let's not get confrontational. Dick is going to discuss next steps."

Dick stood and walked to the front of Simon's desk, his

hands stuffed in his pockets. Over the next several minutes, he cited the evidence against her while Griffin nodded in agreement. Dick paused and folded his arms across his chest. "Pretense, the proof we have is very convincing. If you cooperate, maybe we can get some leniency for you. So do yourself a favor and tell us where the money is."

Pretense sat open-mouthed, her voice sprinkled with sarcasm. "I want a lawyer. I am not…"

A sudden force assaulted the building, unleashing a whoosh of gale-force wind and shattering glass across the office. Dick fell to the floor and clawed his way to the front of the desk. The building rolled like a ship on the ocean in a sea of flickering lights. Pretense leapt from her chair, seizing the doorknob while struggling to stay afoot.

"Earthquake!" Thelma shouted amidst the mayhem as the group stumbled toward the exit.

Pretense found her footing and yanked at the knob, but the door had jammed, opening to only a slim gap. Choking smoke writhed and billowed through the office, triggering the sprinkler system and sending a spray of water arching outward. An intense stench of gasoline permeated the room. "Let me try," yelled Simon, mauling the edge of the door as water rained over his head. Desperate fingers converged on the door in a futile attempt to escape.

"Pretense, move out of the way," someone yelled, but she struggled against the sparse opening. "Move out!" She ignored the command and pushed again, squeezing her lithe body through the gap like toothpaste through a tube. Just as one foot reached the other side, the building creaked and shifted again, trapping her other foot in the narrow gap. She reached down and yanked on the shoelace, pulling her leg up several times, raw fear fueling her adrenaline. With a swift jerk, her foot came out of her shoe, releasing her body and pitching her forward. She looked back. Amidst swirls of black smoke, a shock of red emerged through the narrow opening, its hand wagging wildly.

Pretense turned away and staggered down the hallway gasping for air, the sound of Thelma's shrill scream echoing in her ears.

The building was alive, belching debris in all directions. Pretense felt her way through thick, black smoke as water sloshed at her feet. She shielded her mouth against the acrid smell and fought for her bearings in search of her office, but darkness prevailed. She moved in the direction of the eighty-ninth floor stairwell, abandoning her laptop and purse, praying that whatever hell was enveloping the building would destroy her possessions. She took a few more steps and groped at her chest. The locket dangled from her neck like a garden serpent hanging from her throat.

CHAPTER 2
THREE MONTHS EARLIER

Behind the mahogany desk in the corner office overlooking the East River in Lower Manhattan sat Simon Crawford, fighting for words as sweat droplets dotted his upper lip. He adjusted his maroon silk tie, his jaw jutting outward, straining to flee through the collar of his crisp cotton shirt. "I know this is not what you expected, Pretense, but please understand that I did not base my decision solely on your work ethic. You're one of the smartest and hardest-working employees at Crawford Spectrum."

Pretense sat erect, savoring the pregnant pause and staring emotionless into his shifty eyes.

A prolonged sigh escaped. "It is your inability to connect with your co-workers."

Pretense's lips curved upward into a soft smile, her rage controlled, emotions locked. "Thank you for your honesty, Mr. Crawford." She retrieved the ballpoint pen above her ear, flipping to a page in her Franklin Planner. "Might you offer some concrete examples of this so-called lack of connection?"

Simon dragged his hands through his graying hair. "I'll give you a recent example. At the annual company outing yesterday, everyone applauded when Ariana received this year's employee award for outstanding work. You, on the other hand…"

Pretense held up her left index finger while her pen scratched across the paper. "Okay, go on."

"I overheard you making derogatory comments before leaving the event early."

She set her pen down. "To be honest, I left early for a doctor's appointment, purposefully made during the company outing so as not to interfere with my client appointments. And the comments made regarding Ariana were not without merit."

Simon shook his head, drawing his hand over his chin. "My decision has been made." He pushed his chair back and stood. "Now, if you'll excuse me, I need to prepare for this morning's staff meeting."

Pretense sat motionless, staring ahead. "Did anyone get promoted to senior financial consultant?"

"I will share that information in the staff meeting." Simon walked to his office door and held it open.

Pretense remained seated, her hands folded in her lap.

"Is there something else?" he asked.

"Yes. Just one thing. Have my clients complained about my behavior?"

Simon heaved a sigh and closed the door, leaning against it. "Your clients have great things to say about you. They're delighted with the positive returns they've received under your guidance and the level of service you provide. But again, it's not about the work. It is how you treat your fellow employees."

Pretense turned in her chair, facing him. "I see," she said, tapping her front tooth with the pen. "Just so I'm clear, allow me to recap. My clients are pleased with my performance, and the firm is delighted with my work ethic. Yet my co-workers, who, by the way, do nothing to help advance my career, sense a lack of camaraderie when it comes to frivolous office banter."

"That's not what I said."

"It's what you implied. It's apparent I don't fit in. My focus is on my work—not on the latest designer labels, hairstyles, and narrow-minded gossip." She stood and smoothed the wrinkles from her pleated, brown tweed skirt. "Thank you for your time." She brushed past the most powerful man in the company, opened the door, and walked out—her head high, her stride measured.

———

Back in her office, Pretense chucked her planner onto a chair. *Five years I've given to this firm, and I haven't had a raise since I started.* A string of sharp breaths blew through her lips as heat billowed, a furnace blazing inside. *There's no one more qualified than me. How dare he treat me with such disregard.* From the other side of the office door, she spotted Daphne Duke heading her way.

Daphne leaned against the doorframe. "Hi, Pretense. How did it go? Did you get promoted?"

Pretense's nimble fingers hammered the keyboard, her eyes avoiding Daphne's invading form. "No. And I'm not in the mood to talk."

Daphne came around behind Pretense and rested a hand on her shoulder. "I'm so sorry. I said a prayer for you."

Pretense's body stiffened as she spun in her chair, sending a stack of papers fluttering across the floor. "Do me a favor and stop praying for me."

Daphne backed away, her mouth slung open like a flytrap. "I'm just trying to be supportive."

Pretense turned and resumed her battle with the keyboard.

"Then I guess I'll see you at the staff meeting."

Pretense heard Daphne walk away.

By the time Pretense joined the group, the meeting had begun. She scanned the cramped space for an empty chair and noted an open spot on either side of Daphne. Daphne's hand shot up, waving her over.

"Thank you for joining us, Pretense," said Simon, standing at the front of the conference table. "Now, let's continue."

Pretense soon zoned out, her mind banging from office fury. She began rehashing the conversation she'd had earlier with Simon. Then she heard him speaking. "As you know, we have been interviewing candidates for the senior consultant position. The decision was not easy, but I'm pleased to announce the results. Let's give a big round of applause to Ariana Primrose, a dedicated employee and a tireless worker." Simon's grin stretched wide as he waved Ariana to the front of the room. "Come up, Ariana, and say a few words."

Ariana stood, her white teeth glimmering against pink tattooed lips, her head snapping from side to side, as she locked eyes with her bevy of supporters. After an excessive length of time passed, she spoke with the theatrical flair of a politician, each word melodic in its delivery. "I wouldn't be standing here today if it wasn't for the support I've received from each and every one of you," she said, scanning eager faces and holding her arms out as though offering a holy blessing.

"Oh, brother," Pretense muttered.

Daphne shushed her and refocused on Ariana.

Once again Pretense zoned out. She tried to think of something pleasant, like the floor splitting open and swallowing Ariana's Gucci-clad self, flinging her lifeless body eighty-nine stories below and into the Cortlandt Street subway station—never to be seen or heard from again. The rustle of chairs interrupted her dreamy fuzz. Simon had excused the group.

Daphne caught up with Pretense in the hallway. "Hey, do you want to go to Saul's Deli for lunch today? My treat."

Pretense stared at Daphne, her eyebrows gathering in as she considered the unexpected invitation. She'd much prefer to eat alone at her desk, dwelling on the day's pathetic events and studying the latest stock market fluctuations, but she couldn't turn down a free lunch. "Yeah, sure. Why not?"

Pretense and Daphne stepped into the elevator and rode down to the sprawling, glass-enclosed lobby, exiting through massive revolving doors. They made their way along West Street, passing a throng of impeccably suited professionals, rushing like a tidal wave through the streets of the Financial District. Like two misfits—Pretense tall and threadlike, Daphne short and substantial—they kept pace with the rush, each wearing an unfortunate ensemble.

When they reached Saul's Deli, they joined a mob of patrons jockeying to place orders. "Why don't you grab a table," said Daphne. "I'll get in line. What would you like?"

Pretense skimmed the menu on the black chalkboard. "I'll have the Classic Pastrami on whole wheat. Ask to see the pastrami first. If it looks too fatty, then I'll take a Turkey Reuben. And bottled water to drink." She draped her Columbo-style trench coat over the back of a chair and took a seat.

Ten minutes later, Daphne found Pretense and placed the tray on the table. "I wasn't sure about the pastrami, so I ordered you a Turkey Reuben."

Pretense reached for her sandwich, feeling awkward sitting across the shiny metal table from her co-worker, their knees almost touching in the restricted space. She tried to think of something to say as she nibbled at her sandwich. "So, do you aspire to achieve something more prestigious than that of a lobby receptionist at Crawford Spectrum?"

Daphne smiled and pushed her plate away, wiping pickle juice from her chin. "Actually, I love my job. It works for me— you know, being part-time and without all the responsibilities. God has blessed me with other gifts. Like mission work." She leaned forward, her face lit with excitement. "In a few weeks, I'm going to Malaysia with a group from my church to help build a home for street children." She opened her purse and pulled out a flyer, pushing it across the table.

Pretense glanced at the brochure and continued eating.

"My parents are having a small get-together for our church group this weekend. If you're not doing anything on Sunday, why don't you come by? You can meet some of my friends."

Pretense leaned back in her chair. "Sorry. I have plans on Sunday."

"Maybe another time. So, do you have family nearby?"

Pretense looked off, assessing the frenzied scene inside the deli, calculating her response. "Unfortunately, my parents died in a car accident when I was three. I was an only child with no known relatives. I lived in and out of foster homes until I turned eighteen." A deep sigh escaped as she studied her folded hands. "I realized I would have to fend for myself one day, so I focused on my studies and was privileged to be accepted on a full-ride scholarship to Harvard. It's always been just me."

"Oh, Pretense. I am so sorry. I can't imagine what you must have gone through. But to rise above it all and make something of yourself is truly remarkable." Daphne reached across the table for Pretense's hand.

Pretense drew away. "Thanks for lunch. We better get back. I have a client meeting at one-thirty." She stood and walked toward the door while Daphne gathered her belongings.

"Thanks for having lunch with me today," said Daphne as they walked back to the office. "It was nice getting to know you a little better. We should do this again."

Pretense picked up the pace. "Let's hurry. I can't be late for my meeting."

———

Hyman and Edna Rothschild inched, feeble and cautious, to the lobby reception desk. "Good afternoon," said Hyman. "We are here to see Pretense Abdicator."

Daphne looked up and smiled. "Hello Mr. and Mrs. Roth-schild. Please, take a seat. I'll let her know you are here."

Minutes later, Pretense appeared, stretching her open palm out to Hyman and Edna. "It's so good to see you. Please, right this way," she said, waving toward her office. "Can I get you anything? Coffee? Tea? Water?"

"Oh, you are such a sweet dear," said Edna. "I'll have tea."

Pretense held up her hand. "Don't tell me. Two lumps of sugar, no cream. And the usual for you, Mr. Rothschild? Coffee with a smidgeon of cream and no sugar?"

"You always remember," said Edna, accepting the chair Hyman had pulled out for her.

After Pretense returned with their beverages, she took a seat at her desk and pulled up the Rothschilds' financial account on the computer, angling the monitor to face them. "I know you're short on time, so let's get started. When we last met, we discussed moving a portion of your holdings into more aggressive funds. You were both concerned that our previous approach was too conservative. I think you'll be pleased." She pointed to the Year-to-Date Returns column.

Hyman grinned and turned to Edna. "That's fantastic. We should move all our money under Pretense's watchful eye. Our other investments don't perform nearly as well."

Edna patted Hyman's cheek. "Let's talk about it tonight." She turned to Pretense. "I must tell you how delighted we are with your service. In the four years we've been working together, you've always proven to be a trustworthy and savvy investor."

"I second that," said Hyman.

Pretense beamed, wishing Simon were around to hear of her greatness.

After an hour-long discussion regarding their financial portfolio, Hyman stood and helped Edna to her feet. "We need to get going, dear." He extended his hand to Pretense. "Thank you for your time. I'll call to set up another meeting after Edna and I talk."

"Oh, I almost forgot," said Edna. "The Rothschild Foundation is organizing a fundraiser next month to raise college tuition money for at-risk women. We need speakers. Based on your years in foster care and your ability to achieve a full-ride scholarship, I think you'd be an excellent spokeswoman. Would you be interested?"

"I'd be honored," she lied. "What is the date?"

After Edna provided the details, Pretense checked her planner. "That works. I'm looking forward to helping women better themselves. My heart grieves for the less fortunate."

After escorting the Rothschilds to the lobby, she went back to her office, her face buried in paperwork. By the time she wrapped up, it was after six o'clock. Aside from the cleaning crew, there was no one left in the office. Pretense stuffed her briefcase with several market analysis reports to study over the weekend, like she did every weekend since starting at Crawford Spectrum. The overfed briefcase lay propped in the chair, a bloated bag of crap. *I doubt Ariana spends weekends studying market trends.* She switched off the light and shut her office door. For once, the leather bag would spend the weekend at Crawford Spectrum.

———

The subway doors whooshed open. Pretense pushed her way through the horde of people and bolted to the exit, climbing the concrete steps that led to Forty-Second Street.

Outside, faces moved along the sidewalk with electrifying intent. She wondered about their plans. A night out with friends? Dinner with family? Hers was a solitary life focused solely on her career. As she mulled over Simon's damning words, disappointment settled like a heavy fog. Would she ever get ahead? Or continue skimping by, trying to make ends meet. Her life felt meaningless. Perhaps she needed a little something to liven up the weekend.

The bronze bells chimed when she pushed open the worn, wooden door of Stan's Market and Wine Emporium. She wandered the narrow aisle jammed with bottles, pausing in front of a shelf lined with gallon jugs of cheap Chianti. She slipped her finger through the glass loop and headed to the cash register. After making the purchase, she walked the few blocks to her apartment building.

At the top of the third-story walk-up, she jabbed the key into the lock and lugged the bottle of Chianti over to the kitchen table. The ordinary silence ceded to a ringing hum. Surprised, she glanced at the caller ID window on the phone. *MOTHER.* Her shoulders sagged as she reached for the handset.

CHAPTER 3

"What kind of daughter doesn't call her mother in over a week?"

"Hi, Mom. Sorry. I've been busy."

"Obviously. So, did you get the promotion?"

She pictured her mother's shrunken lips drawing on a Camel Non-filter cigarette, her face collapsing with each suck of air, while plumes of smoke billowed from her nostrils like an awakening volcano. "No, I didn't."

"What do you mean?"

She heard that disgusting spitting sound she made when dislodging a piece of tobacco from the tip of her tongue. "Mr. Crawford said he's impressed with my skills, but due to cost-cutting constraints all promotions are on hold."

"Well, you better look for another job. You're going to have to support yourself for the rest of your life, since I doubt you'll ever find a man to marry you. You've never been an attractive girl. And aside from your intelligence, you have nothing to offer in the way of looks or personality."

Pretense's voice sat at the bottom of her throat as the drone of her mother's oxygen tank hummed in the background. "Mom, I can't talk now. I'm getting ready to go out."

"Out? You don't have a date, do you? Have you ever been on a date?"

"I'm hanging up now."

"You're thirty. The clock is ticking."

"I'm twenty-nine. Today."

"Are you sure?"

"Yes, Mother. I just checked my driver's license—just to be certain."

"Don't you talk to me in that tone. Anyways, did you put my check in the mail? I didn't get anything from you this month. And by the way, when are you flying me out? I keep asking, and you keep avoiding the subject."

"I need to watch my money. Things are tight, but I put a check in the mail. And as I said before, my place is too small for overnight guests."

"Oh, cry me a river," she spat out between puffs. "Here I am, living in a hamster cage while my daughter is enjoying the life of Riley out in New York City. If you wanted me there, you'd sleep on the couch."

"Mom, someone's at the door. Goodbye." She placed the phone on the cradle and withdrew her moistened hand, as though the object were toxic. *I hate her.*

A beckoning meow cornered her thoughts. She bent and picked up the furry clump, snuggling her face into its neck. "Hey, Kat. Did you miss me today? You must be hungry." She set Kat down and rummaged through the pantry for a can of tuna. She dumped the contents into Kat's dish, then twisted the screw cap on the jug of Chianti and grabbed a wine glass, filling it to the rim. After a few gulps, she opened the small refrigerator and grabbed the filet mignon wrapped in butcher paper and set it on the counter to reach room temperature, then preheated the oven.

Clutching her wine glass, she strolled to the CD player and queued up Luciano Pavarotti's *Greatest Hits*. The haunting melody of "Nessun Dorma" penetrated the quiet of her tiny apartment, washing away the remnants of her mother's insults.

She refused to let that woman ruin her special day. She went into the bedroom and changed into sweat pants, then released her feral hair from the restrictive bun. After another sip of wine, she went back into the kitchen and rubbed a russet potato with olive oil and sprinkled it with a generous pinch of kosher salt before putting it into the hot oven. Time to relax.

Her head rested back against the brown, upholstered sofa, the music stilling her angry mind as the alcohol pumped through her system. Kat jumped onto the couch, rubbing up against Pretense, demanding the steady stroke of the woman's hand. The two languished in symbiotic hypnosis before she scraped herself off the sofa and went into the kitchen for a refill —Kat's loud meows following close behind. "We better eat soon," she informed Kat, weaving between Pretense's legs. Pushing Kat aside, she bent down and retrieved the black cast-iron skillet from the lower cabinet and placed it on the gas burner. Kat hissed, then bolted. Pretense shot a mock hiss Kat's way, then turned her attention to the stove.

Having reviewed several steak recipes for her birthday dinner, she learned the pan should preheat on the burner for at least five minutes before adding the meat. She cranked the black knob to its highest setting and wiped her hands on a kitchen towel, slinging the cloth over her shoulder. Then she grabbed her stemmed glass and headed toward the sofa, pausing in front of the antique mirror hanging on the plaster wall. She studied herself, musing on her mother's words. An abundance of friz-zled brown hair sat like a nest of Brill-O pads upon her head, offsetting her angular features. Her nose was, well, unfortunate. Somewhat off-center with a sharp hook. And the chipped front tooth—compliments of the wooden rolling pin her mother used as a weapon, as Mrs. Abdicator never made pie dough in her life —set her distinctive features. She brought the wine glass to her lips, turning her head from side to side, assessing her face.

With her master preoccupied, Kat skulked into the kitchen, sprang onto the countertop and crept across the Formica in search of more vittles. The sudden wail of the smoke alarm startled Kat. The fur ball shot vertically and leapt over the pan, her tail catching the blue flame. With her appendage ablaze, she tore through the living room like a rabid cheetah.

Stunned, Pretense turned and chased after Kat zipping by the front window. The nylon curtain panel caught her tail and ignited. Pretense lunged, draping Kat in the towel, wrestling the feral animal and smothering the flame. They wrestled on the floor; the towel poking and rippling like a woman's belly impregnated with a demon. *Oh no, the curtain!* Pretense rolled aside and batted at the shriveling material until the flame petered out, then she collapsed on the floor, gasping for air, her heart flogging her chest.

Seconds later, she got up and stumbled into the kitchen and shut off the burner, then removed the batteries from the smoke alarm. Kat was nowhere to be found.

By now, her appetite had waned, but doggone it, it was still her birthday. She tossed the steak into the refrigerator and belted out an aria while pouring another glass of wine. Then she sat down to her birthday dinner, a baked potato with sour cream.

———

The following morning, Pretense awoke in her bed, still wearing her sweats. The night had been a blur. Rolling to her side, she planted her feet on the floor, her brain seemingly too big for her skull, her tongue Velcroed to the roof of her mouth. With an unsteady gait, she made her way into the kitchen and put on a pot of coffee, the smell of smoke intensifying her nausea. She took in the chaotic scene. A nylon curtain panel hung three feet short of the floor, blackened and melted. A spray of red wine spattered the couch and walls, and the floor lamp lay tipped on its side, the cord draped over a potted yucca plant.

The light in the kitchen felt painfully bright. She rummaged through her purse for her sunglasses and put them on, then popped two slices of whole-wheat bread into the toaster. Somewhere inside the apartment she heard a soft meow as she sat crunching on dry toast. She looked off, disappointment permeating her meaningless, solitary self. The lost promotion. Her mother's endlessly cutting words. And last night's drunken fugue, complete with flaming feline. The shame of it all. Her head sagged to her chest, her sorry life wafted from her core.

A knock interrupted the gloom. She went to the door and peered through the peephole. *Oh, great. Nosey Mrs. Whipple.* The landlady stood on the other side, her master key aimed at the lock like a pistol, cocked and ready to fire.

Pretense opened the door as far as the chain would allow. "Good morning, Mrs. Whipple."

Mrs. Whipple glared, her thin-lipped mouth tight. "Is everything okay in there? I heard an alarm go off last night. And I heard someone rolling across the floor. I almost called the police, but then I heard loud singing. So, I figured you were okay." Her nose inched closer to the door. "Is that smoke I smell?"

"You have an amazing olfactory organ, Mrs. Whipple. Actually, I was baking cookies last night for the homeless shelter and doing floor exercises between batches. I lost track of time. It wasn't until the smoke alarm engaged that I realized I had forgotten the cookies." She placed her hand on her chest and shook her head. "I apologize for my lack of caution. It won't happen again."

Mrs. Whipple paused, scrutinizing Pretense. "Why are you wearing those dark glasses? Are you hiding a black eye? My aunt was in an abusive relationship for years. I know the signs."

Pretense whipped off her sunglasses and flung them behind her, pushing one eye then the other up to the door crack. "No shiners here."

Mrs. Whipple stumbled back. "Well, I'll leave you be. Just be careful." She scuttled down the steps, her slippers slapping against the linoleum.

Pretense shut the door and placed the dirty dishes in the sink.

Now what? With her briefcase at the office, there would be no working this weekend. Maybe she should have accepted Daphne's invitation, but she wasn't that desperate—at least not yet.

A feeling of emptiness folded over her. She felt so incredibly insignificant, floating unnoticed in a sea of humanity. Soon she would be thirty, and what had she accomplished? There were no friends and no family to speak of. She wanted to sob, but she knew she couldn't.

A childhood memory edged in—the day she'd last cried. The underground storm shelter was dark and clammy, the stench of something rotten in the musty air. "I'll let you out in eight hours," her mother had said. "If you're still crying like a baby, you'll go right back in." She shoved the suffocating thought from her mind and drifted toward the tattered sofa, plumping the throw pillows and sinking down, tucking her feet under her thighs. The warm mug of java felt soothing in her hands, as she looked around for something to occupy her mind. The leather-bound copy of Victor Hugo's *Les Misérables* lay on the coffee table. It had been awhile since she'd immersed herself in a novel. The luxury of such frivolity had been lost on her. She picked up the book and turned to the dog-eared page, recalling the scene where she'd left off. The words arrested her thoughts as she drifted away to another time and place, her mood slowly lifting, the characters in the novel her make-believe friends. Several chapters in, she read "Even the darkest night will end and the sun will rise." Her brain piqued. She reread the sentence—slower this time—absorbing each word as she read aloud. What would life look like if she clung to hope, ridding herself of all unpleasant feelings and emotions? It was up to her. Only she had control of her future. Wallowing in self-pity solved nothing. It was time to make things happen.

She slammed the book shut, unleashing a blizzard of dust, and marched into her bedroom with determined purpose. She changed into her favorite Gordon Gekko t-shirt—MONEY NEVER

Sleeps, Pal emblazoned across the front. After pulling on a pair of black tights and lacing up her running shoes, she filled Kat's dish and grabbed a lightweight jacket from the hall closet. It was time to run.

The city breathed life, the damp, spring air rejuvenating her mind. She performed her ritual stretches before setting out for the mile walk to the southeast entrance of Central Park. Minutes later, her feet were slapping the cement path as she embarked on the five-mile loop around the park, classical music piping through her earphones.

As her pace quickened, salty sweat beads rolled down her skin. She gulped in the spring air, euphoria deepening with each breath. She felt as though she were running with purpose—out of this existence and into another reality. With each rhythmic stride, pieces of a life-changing plan materialized—creeping in and gnawing like a starved rodent.

She rounded the three-mile marker, the moss-covered path turning sharply to the left. Loping through a darkened tunnel of trees, she continued along, the plot continuing to unfold. *I must reinvent myself and release all anger. I will create a kinder me.* As she neared the end of the five-mile loop, ideas surged, neurons sparking her mind. Eager to return home before the brilliant thoughts faded, she sprinted the last mile to her apartment, mounting the steps two at a time.

Winded, she opened the door, flung her jacket in no specific direction and sat at the table with her laptop. She opened a blank Word document and began pouring out her thoughts, her fingers tapping away at the keyboard—the words streaming like confetti.

When she finally looked outside the kitchen window, the sun had ducked behind towering skyscrapers, daylight draining away. Several hours had passed, but it seemed only minutes. She hadn't eaten since breakfast, yet the pains of hunger were hushed. She pushed away from the table and stood, her open hand massaging rigid neck muscles.

On the kitchen counter sat the gallon jug from last night. Before settling back down at the table, she poured a glass and then studied the carefully crafted plan. As she read through each page, a broad smile cracked her face. It felt perfect. Justified. No more agonizing over her ordinary past. No angst about the future. A chance to escape the laughing faces of those who had harmed her. She got up and paced the floor, every fiber of her being electrified with anticipation. The once insignificant Pretense Abdicator was about to become somebody.

An insatiable hunger butted in. She opened the refrigerator and grabbed the abandoned filet from last night and set it aside, along with a few stalks of asparagus and a bag of Caesar salad mix.

Twenty minutes later, she lit a candle and sat down to a celebratory meal. One chair. One plate. And somewhere inside the apartment, Kat slumbered.

CHAPTER 4

Sunlight fanned through the bedroom window, its warm reflection rousing Pretense from sleep. She stretched her arms over her head, her face brightening as she recalled the unfolding of yesterday's master plan—an organic manifesto inscribed on her brain, propelling her forward.

After making a pot of coffee and eating a light breakfast, she sat down at the kitchen table and knocked out the details. First order of business: establish a unique identity by securing the birth certificate of a deceased female who fit her criteria. After extensive online research, she discovered that thirteen states had open access to birth and death certificates. She studied the list of states and decided on New Jersey due to its proximity to New York. Once the siphoned funds were transferred into an offshore bank account under her alias, she would flee to another country and start a new life. Location: TBD.

Several hours later, she sat back and scrutinized the plan. There could be no room for error. One minor glitch and the entire plot would implode. And she would end up behind bars. But of course, that would never happen. She was much too clever. Satisfied, she shut down her laptop and called it a day.

The details could be tweaked once the plan materialized, but for now it looked good. In fact, it was foolproof.

Her mind went to the conversation with Simon. Tomorrow would be her first day at work since being denied the promotion, and she was determined to show the head cheese she had taken his feedback to heart. She'd ooze with kindness and sharpen her appearance with a wardrobe update. That'll throw everyone for a loop. She cringed at the thought of such frivolous indulgences, but the payback would rectify the cost. She looked at the clock. Still time left in the day to do a little shopping.

———

Several hours and several dollars later, Pretense lugged her bags down the sidewalk, guilt sweeping through her. She'd never spent so much money on one shopping spree, but she believed it to be an investment in her future. One last purchase. She stopped in Stan's Market for a bottle of wine and a greeting card before heading back to her apartment.

Home at last, Pretense opened the door and stepped inside, dropping her packages on the floor. Kat limped into the room. "Oh, my precious baby." She lifted the feline into her arms and snuggled its neck. "Mama missed you. Where have you been?"

Pretense carried Kat to the sofa and set the feline in her lap, inspecting the tail for signs of blistering. "I'm sure your hair will grow back, baby. I can't afford a visit to the vet—not after today." She got up and went into the kitchen and opened a can of tuna, dumping half of it in Kat's bowl and the other half on a plate for herself, then poured a glass of wine. In the back of the cupboard, she found a half-empty box of whole wheat crackers. She grabbed the box and sat down at the table and ate while visions of the new Pretense Abdicator drifted across her mind. She pictured her co-workers' reaction when she showed up at work tomorrow, strutting the office hallway in stylish clothes and sunshiny kindness. It would be hard—no, nauseating—but oh-so necessary.

Another glass of wine later, she put on Itzhak Perlman's *Greatest Hits* CD, then went into the bedroom. She removed her street clothes and changed into the new white cotton shirt, navy blazer, and matching pencil skirt. The material felt rich between her fingers and smelled of clean linen—a far cry from her usual collection of Salvation Army castoffs. After slipping on a pair of nude pantyhose, she stepped into the indigo stilettos and pivoted in front of the floor-length mirror, examining herself at various angles. The consummate professional, powerful and distinguished. She imagined herself as Martha Stewart standing before her board of directors, flinging insults at the cowering minions seated around the hand-hewn conference table fashioned from a single Vermont birch tree. She spun, taking herself in. *Watch out, Crawford. There's a new kid in town.* Pleased with her fresh look, she strutted around the apartment struggling to balance her lithe body on three-inch heels while holding her head erect.

It was a blur in her periphery. Kat launched herself at Pretense, a flying, hissing mound of fur, splaying her claws into Pretense's dense hair mass, its furry body dangling from the back of Pretense's head like a Davy Crockett coonskin cap. She whirled frantically, stumbling over a wicker laundry basket and sprawling headlong into the plaster wall. Kat shot in the opposite direction and dove under the bed. Startled and disoriented, Pretense sat up and rubbed her forehead, feeling a knot forming above her eyebrow. She removed her heels and slowly stood, inching her way into the kitchen.

An irritated knock thumped the door. She peered through the viewing hole and observed the landlady on the other side. *Crap. Not again.* She smoothed her hair back and opened the door. "Why, Mrs. Whipple, what brings you this way?"

Mrs. Whipple's mouth puckered like a crinkled raisin. "I

heard some crashing around just now. I wanted to be sure every-thing is okay. What's that on your forehead?"

Pretense ran her fingers over the bump. "Oh, that. Silly me. I just lost my balance and fell. Nothing to be concerned about."

"Are you alone in there?"

"Yes. Just me and my cat. But help me understand your ques-tion. Is there a house rule forbidding visitors?" She wasn't sure, as she'd never had visitors.

"No, of course not. Just making sure nothing suspicious is going on."

Practice kindness. "Well, thank you. I'm so very grateful to have someone like you, incessantly looking out for my best inter-ests. Now, if you'll excuse me, I need to get to bed. Busy day at work tomorrow."

"Have a good night. I'm glad you're okay."

Pretense smiled and shut the door, locking the deadbolt. *She may be a problem. Maybe I should start taking my laptop to work.*

She fell into bed early and settled into sleep with a wicked smile on her face.

Meanwhile, Kat looked down from the headboard at Pretense's nest of hair; the feline considering its options.

CHAPTER 5

The doors pinged open on the eighty-ninth floor of the North Tower. Pretense Abdicator swept out of the elevator in all her finery, eyes forward, shoulders back, gliding across the marble floor. Slung over her shoulder was a black leather case with her portable laptop tucked inside.

She entered the offices of Crawford Spectrum and flipped on the wall switch, bathing the luxurious suite in fluorescent light. Always the first to arrive, she went to her office and placed her belongings on her desk. On her way to the galley kitchen, she stopped in Ariana's office to drop off an envelope.

After putting on a pot of coffee, the clickety-clack of heels interrupted the morning calm as Ariana Primrose sauntered into the kitchen, the neutral air colliding with an explosion of Coco Chanel.

Ariana opened the cupboard and reached for a mug. "Good morning," she said, sweeping her eyes over Pretense. "You look nice today. New suit?"

"Yes. It was time for a wardrobe update." She struggled to think of something else to say, but drew the usual blank.

Ariana grabbed the container of hazelnut flavored cream from the refrigerator, pouring a spot into her cup. Her manicured nails thrummed on the granite countertop, as they both stood silent watching the slow stream of coffee trickle into the carafe. When the last drop touched down, she filled her cup, then held the carafe out to Pretense. "Let me pour you a cup. After all, you made it."

Pretense smiled. Conscious of her jagged front tooth, she pressed her lips together and offered her empty mug. "Thanks."

"What happened to your forehead?"

Pretense fingered the knot. "I don't know. I had an excruciating headache last night, and when I awoke, this showed up."

"Maybe you should have it checked out. It could be a brain tumor."

"Oh, gosh. I never considered that." *A perfect excuse to leave the office early today.* "I'll call the doctor and see if I can get an appointment. Well, have a good day." She turned and left the kitchen, heading back to her office.

Ten minutes later, Ariana appeared in her doorway, waving a pink envelope. "I read your card. Thank you, but I'm not sure how to take it." Her Ferrari-red fingernails plucked the card from the envelope, and she read aloud the inscription on the front. *"Congratulations on your new position."* She opened the card. *"I hope its vertical."*

Pretense cocked her head and frowned. "I thought it said *versatile*. You know, like your new position affords you the ability to showcase your diverse skills." She held out her hand. "Let me see it." Pretense took the card from Ariana. "You're right. Vertical." She scrunched her eyebrows together in mock confusion. "I wonder what it means."

"I suppose it means as opposed to lying down—like I slept my way to a promotion."

Pretense threw her hand over her mouth and let rip a gasp. "Good grief. I can't believe anyone would even sell a card like that. I'm horrified."

Ariana snatched the card from Pretense. "I hope it was an honest mistake."

"Of course. I bought it yesterday while my head was throbbing. I was also experiencing double vision. Please forgive me."

"Well, I'm going to trust that your intentions were well meaning. Thanks, I guess." She pivoted on her stiletto and left.

Pretense rotated her chair and powered on the computer—her grin irrepressible. She opened her email account and began drafting a note to Simon. *Do you have a few minutes to spare... preferably before noon?*

He responded immediately. *Now is a good time.*

With her Franklin Planner clutched to her breast, she headed down the hall to the corner office. Simon's eyes were buried in *The Wall Street Journal*, half a McDonald's Egg McMuffin pressed to his open mouth.

She tapped on the doorframe. "Good morning."

"Come in," said Simon, wiping his face and setting the paper aside. "New suit?"

"Yes. I went shopping this weekend. And I also did a little soul-searching—about our discussion last Friday." She took a seat and discharged a drawn-out sigh and leaned in, placing her clasped hands on his desk. "I want to apologize. Everything you said about my behavior was accurate. I was so influenced by your words, I went out and purchased *The 7 Habits of Highly Effective People*. I read the entire book over the weekend. Honestly, I couldn't put it down. One habit in particular captured my attention." She paused, recalling the quote she had found on the internet, then snapped her fingers. "Oh, yes. *Synergize! To combine the strengths of people through positive teamwork, so as to achieve goals that no one could have done alone.* Wow. That one sealed it for me." She shook her head slowly for effect, as though pondering the wonderment of it all.

"I'm so pleased, Pretense. It's difficult admitting our shortcomings." He pulled his lips in and nodded. "Thank you for taking my feedback to heart—and educating yourself on ways to improve. You have so much promise, and I envision a brilliant future for you—hopefully here at Crawford Spectrum."

A brilliant future, yes. But not here. "I am truly humbled." She placed her hand over her heart and sucked in her lower lip. "Crawford Spectrum is a wonderful company, and I'm fortunate to have you as my mentor." She pushed her chair back and stood. "Well, I won't keep you. I just wanted you to know where I stand."

Simon rose from his chair and held his hand out. Pretense accepted the handshake with a firm grip. "Thank you for your time. Oh, by the way, I need to leave early this afternoon for a doctor's appointment—for this lump on my forehead."

"Of course. It looks painful. I hope it's nothing serious."

"I hope so, too."

On the way back to her office, she stopped in the lobby. *Keep the momentum going.* "Good morning, Daphne. How was the get-together with your church group?"

Daphne's smile stretched wide and high. "Thank you for asking. It was wonderful. I wish you could have come."

"Actually, I'm sorry I didn't come. I thought about it all weekend. Maybe another time."

"What about this Sunday? We are meeting again to wrap up a few loose ends. My mom is making lasagna. It'll be fun."

About as fun as a Pap smear. "Hmm. That may work." She strummed her fingers on the desk, working up the courage to accept. "Oh, sure, why not."

Daphne's eyebrows veered north. "Really? That's great." She handed Pretense a slip of paper. "Here's my address. Three o'clock. And come with a hearty appetite."

Pretense took the paper. "I can't wait."

"I'm so happy. Hey, is that a new suit? You look nice today. But you always look nice."

"Yes, and thank you. Thought I'd update my wardrobe."

"That's what I need to do. We should go shopping together."

Whoa. Back off, Elmer. Stop behaving like a glue stick. "Sure. Oh, before I forget, I need to leave around one o'clock for a doctor's appointment. If anyone calls, let them know I'll return their call in the morning."

"Is everything okay? I see you have a bump on your forehead."

Pretense touched the knob. "I woke up with a terrible headache and this protrusion. Hopefully, the doctor will know."

Ariana clipped across the floor, feigning importance, her heels pounding the tile surface like a jackhammer. She stopped at Daphne's desk. "Daphne, I need you to make dinner reservations for me and my client today at Wild Blue. Then I need five copies of the Brogan spreadsheet printed on legal size paper, landscape, not portrait, with the margins set at point seven-five. And the main conference room table needs bottled water assembled at the far end in billiard rack formation; you know how I like it. Please take care of that, right away."

Daphne smiled. "Good morning, Ariana. I'll get right on it."

Pretense stared after Ariana as she marched down the hall. "Is she always that curt?"

Daphne laughed. "She means well. She's just very busy. Well, I'd better get to work."

———

After meeting with her clients, Pretense Googled directions to the Office of Vital Statistics in Trenton, New Jersey, then shut down her computer and left for the day. The train ride from New York Penn Station to New Jersey Trenton Station took just under an hour. Then she set out on foot for the fifteen-minute walk to her destination, rehearsing the plan to uncover a death notice of a female whose birth date and ethnicity matched that of her own. Preferably someone who died young, before receiving a social security number, and someone born in a state other than New Jersey, since most states do not cross-reference birth and death information.

Arriving at the nondescript building, she breezed through the front door, the new suit bolstering her charade. A soft panic rose as she worked her face into a charming smile, then she approached the front desk.

A silver-haired woman looked up. "May I help you?"

"Yes. Can you point me in the direction of the death records?"

"Down the hall and to your right."

That was easy. After locating the room, she took a seat in front of a computer and pulled out a notepad and pen from her laptop bag. Given her birth year was 1972, she needed someone born between 1970 and 1974. And someone who died before reaching her fifth birthday. She started her search of death records in 1970. Next, 1971. Nothing. She continued digging. Minutes turned into hours, her bloodshot eyes burning from screen strain. Then halfway down the page, in the year 1977, she appeared. Voyant, Claire. Born in 1973, meaning she died at the age of four. She took a sip of air and leaned in. Claire was just one year younger than her own age. She jotted down the information. The actual death certificate would provide more detail.

A tap on her shoulder broke her concentration. "Excuse me, Miss," said the silver-haired lady from the front desk. "We are closing in ten minutes."

Pretense checked her watch, surprised by the time. "Thank you." She shoved her notebook into the laptop bag and left the building, her mission incomplete.

———

After returning to her apartment, she changed into a pair of gray sweats and stirred up a dish of Ramen noodles, allocating a third to Kat. They settled into contentment, the sounds of purrs and slurps filling the air. Then she flipped open her laptop and Googled *"1977 Claire Voyant death New Jersey."* As she scrolled the results, she came upon a newspaper article dated June 25, 1977:

Vacationing Family of Four Killed in Car Crash—*Trenton, New Jersey. All four members of the Voyant family died on Wednesday evening when their 1976 Dodge van skidded off the road during a rainstorm and hit a tree at high speed. The Voyant family was traveling from their home in Palm Springs, California. Authorities identified family members as 36-year-old Robert Voyant, Beth Voyant, 35, and their children: a boy, Timothy Voyant, 8, and a girl, Claire Voyant, 4.*

Alongside the article was a photo of the Voyant family. They were Caucasian. A ping of sadness quickly faded, leaving her limp with excitement. After researching states with open access birth certificates, she noted California in the listing. She sat back, marveling at her good fortune. Everything she needed was at her fingertips—parents' names, siblings, and place of birth. Her mind spun like a pinwheel. *California, here I come.*

CHAPTER 6

On Tuesday morning, she dressed in a crimson-colored sheath dress and paired it with a black, button-down blazer. After brushing her frizzled fuzz, she smeared oil serum into her hands and rubbed it through the unruly mass, gathering it back into a tight ponytail and twisting it into a bun. As she stood perched in front of the bathroom mirror, she leaned in and inspected yesterday's lump. Almost gone. She pulled the adhesive strip off the Band-Aid and pressed it over the spot where the knob once lived then grabbed her laptop bag and left the apartment.

———

An hour later, she was at her desk catching up on yesterday's emails.

"Good morning," said Daphne, standing inside her office door. "What did the doctor say?"

"They did a biopsy. I'm waiting for the results."

"I'll keep you in my prayers." She handed Pretense a pink slip of paper. "While you were out, Mr. Rothschild called. He'd like you to call back. Are you still coming over Sunday?"

"Indeed, I am. I can't wait to meet your friends and family."

After Daphne left, Pretense picked up the phone and dialed the Rothschilds' number.

"Hello, Pretense. I called to schedule a follow-up meeting. Edna and I would like to discuss moving money from our other investment accounts into Crawford Spectrum."

"That's splendid news. I'm looking at my schedule now. Will Thursday at two o'clock work?"

"Perfect. We will see you then."

Pretense hung up and leaned back in her chair, pondering her next move. If the amount were substantial, there would be no need to engage her other clients in the scheme. The fewer people involved, the better. And she must establish a new identity as soon as possible. The trip to California must happen asap. She sprang from her chair and headed down the hall to Simon's office. His door was ajar. Before knocking, she peeked inside and noticed Ariana poised next to Simon in front of a wall-mounted chalkboard. With his right hand, he scribbled an ROI calculation, his left hand cupping Ariana's backside. *Married Mr. Crawford and one-night Ariana?* Pretense blew out an exaggerated sneeze and hobbled against the door, thrusting it open. Simon's hand dropped, squirreling into his pants pocket.

"I'm sorry to interrupt," said Pretense. "When you have a few minutes, can you call me?"

A shaky smile buffeted his lips. "I'm available now. We were just wrapping up." He turned to Ariana. "Thanks for your input."

"No problem." Ariana glided past Pretense and sauntered down the hall.

"Have a seat," said Simon. "How did the doctor appointment go?"

"Biopsy," she said, pointing to the bandage and settling into the chair. "No results yet." She scooched her chair forward. "I know this is short notice, but I'd like to take next week off. I can reschedule my client meetings, so nothing will fall by the wayside. And I'll be reachable on my cell phone."

"This is surprising," said Simon, hoisting his eyebrows. "In the five years you have been here, you've never taken more than a few days off. I think you're overdue. I trust your client's needs will be met. Are you doing anything fun?"

"I wish. A good friend of mine is dying. They've given her two weeks. She wants me to help her get her affairs in order."

"I'm sorry to hear that." He shook his head. "She's fortunate to have a friend like you."

"Thank you," said Pretense, a limp smile gracing her lips. "Well, I should get back to work."

"Can you swing over and let Thelma know I approved your vacation? She'll need to enter it into the database."

"Sure." She stood and left his office.

A large green and white plaque hung on the door of Thelma's office. *Welcome to Human Resources—The Department with the Personnel Touch."*

"Good morning, Thelma," said Pretense. "Mr. Crawford asked me to stop by and let you know he approved a vacation for me next week."

Thelma peeked over wire-rim spectacles clinging to the tip of her nose. Her crisp, lilac suit was garnished with a ruffled white blouse exploding from her jacket lapels. "Come in, Pretense. What a lovely dress. Is that new?"

"Yes, thank you. Do you have a minute to chat?"

"Sure. Shut the door and take a seat. So, you'll be out all next week?"

"Yes, Mr. Crawford seemed fine with the brief notice," she said, dropping into the chair and smoothing her dress. "I'd like to talk about my performance. Mr. Crawford explained to me last week why I didn't get promoted. For the record, I want you to know that I've taken his feedback to heart, and I'm taking steps to improve."

Thelma sat taller in her chair. "I am so pleased to hear that. It's rare when employees recognize the areas that need bolstering. Admitting that you need to improve is the first step to a successful career."

Pretense nodded in agreement. "I'm committed to turning things around. And as I'm working through this behavioral change, would you let me know if you notice anything that needs correcting? I truly value your opinion."

"Yes, of course."

Pretense gutted through a couple of questions about Thelma's children and did her best to appear interested before standing to leave. "I appreciate your help."

Back at her desk, she pulled up next week's calendar and began calling clients and rescheduling meetings. A light rap on the door preceded Ariana's tentative voice.

"Got a minute?" asked Ariana.

"Sure. What's up?"

"I've been thinking that we've never gotten to really know one another. I thought it would be nice if we had lunch together. We could go upstairs. Are you free now?"

It took a moment for the unexpected invite to register. "Sure. Sounds great." All of this unnecessary co-worker intermingling nonsense was becoming exhausting, but vital to the cause.

The women walked down the hall and stepped into the crammed elevator car, stopping at floor 107. Ariana led the way off the lift.

"Ever been here?" she asked, chewing on a glob of gum that showed itself when she spoke.

"No. I don't usually break for lunch." She looked around, taking in the plush surroundings. "This is quite extravagant."

The host showed them to a table next to full-length windows with views of the southern tip of Manhattan, where the Hudson and East rivers met. After being seated, Ariana snapped open the linen napkin and placed it in her lap. Pretense did the same.

"I say we order a glass of wine," said Ariana, scanning the wine list.

"That's a fine idea. We can celebrate your promotion." Pretense browsed the wine list, then set it down. "I'll have whatever you're having."

Ariana ordered two glasses of the 1997 Antinori Toscana Solaia. "So," she said, smacking her hand on the tablecloth, "what do you do for fun? You always seem so serious."

"Well, I jog, listen to classical music, and… *What else? Make something up…* oh, and I play the accordion."

Ariana tapped her nails on the table and pressed her lips together. "Interesting. Do you play professionally?"

"Weddings. Sometimes Polish funerals… that kind of thing. How about you? What's your idea of fun?"

"Oh, just about everything. My mom says I'm a reckless daredevil. Never one to shy away from adventure."

Like sleeping with the boss.

The server returned with their wine. Pretense grasped hold of the stem, about to knock back a slug, when Ariana held her glass up. "A toast. To new acquaintances."

Pretense raised her glass. A spreading blanket of perspiration had formed on her armpits, her sheath dress clinging to her skin. She took a hefty gulp.

Ariana removed the gum-glob from her mouth and pushed her nose inside the goblet, breathing deep before taking a sip. She swished the liquid around in her mouth, causing her cheeks to bubble like a blowfish before embarking on an ostentatious chewing maneuver. "Ahh. Lovely. Superb aniseed character and such tremendous concentration. Do you like it?"

"Oh, yes. It's extraordinary. Flavors of currants and raspberries with hints of balsamic and mint. Stunning purity and depth."

"It sounds like you know something about wine," said Ariana.

"A little. I used to date a winemaker when I spent a summer

in Napa Valley. He taught me a lot," she said, winking, "… if you know what I mean."

After placing their orders, Ariana sat back, swirling her glass. "So, Mr. Crawford tells me you are going on vacation next week."

"Word travels fast. Yes, personal business."

"I'd be more than happy to help with your clients."

"That's kind of you. But I'll be taking care of business while I'm away. I've contacted everyone, and they know how to reach me if something comes up."

"Well, the offer stands if you get in a crunch."

The server returned with their entrées. Ariana speared a lump of crabmeat from her Frutti di Mare Seafood Salad, touching the tines of the fork into a side of dressing before taking a nibble. "So, how did you manage to land the lucrative Roth-schild account?"

Pretense gulped a spoonful of French Onion soup before answering, an elastic string of cheese swaying from her lower lip. "It was a small account when it was first handed to me," she said, quickly wiping her mouth with a napkin. "But over time, Edna and Hyman put more trust in me, and it grew from there."

"Must be nice. I keep hoping for a big account to land in my lap. Maybe you can give me a few pointers."

"Me? Give *you* pointers? You seem to be doing just fine without my help. Tell me, what's *your* secret to success?"

Ariana pushed her plate aside and stroked the stem of her wineglass. "I've learned that it doesn't always matter how intel-ligent you are. It's more about intuition and likability. People like me. They always have. And I use that to my advantage." She tossed her head and scanned the room as though pursuing new converts. "You don't come off as likable. You should work on that. Trust me, the payback will do wonders for your career. I'm willing to take you under my wing."

Pretense drained her wineglass, desperate to get this lunch

over with. "Wow. You would do that? For *me*? I might take you up on the offer. Let me chew on it."

After finishing their meal, they waited for the server to bring the check. "How do you like working for Mr. Crawford?" asked Pretense.

"He's great. And a wonderful mentor. He's taught me so much about the business. What about you?"

"I agree. And he seems to take a genuine interest in his employees."

The server placed the check on the table between them. Ariana reached for it, while Pretense feigned a weak attempt to do likewise. "I'll expense this," said Ariana.

"I thought we could only expense business-related meals."

She snickered. "Mr. Crawford will approve this."

Pretense held her glass up. "Well, thank you, Crawford Spectrum."

"We should do this more often," said Ariana.

"Of course. Anytime."

Back in the safety of her workspace, she parked at her desk. She shouldn't have had that second glass of wine. She could get verbose if she wasn't careful. And she didn't trust Ariana. It felt as though she'd had an ulterior motive. She replayed the whole luncheon conversation in her head. *She must know I saw Mr. Crawford copping a feel. That could be a growth fund of its own.*

———

At home that night, she flipped open her laptop and searched for flights to Palm Springs, California. Since she had plans to visit Daphne on Sunday, she booked a flight leaving Monday morning from LaGuardia Airport, arriving at Palm Springs International Airport in the afternoon and returning the following Saturday. Plenty of time to take care of business and do a little sightseeing. With that accomplished, she closed the computer and packed it away.

Reaching underneath her chair, she gathered the coiled ball, and carried Kat to the bedroom, laying her on the pillow next to hers. After brushing her teeth, she flopped onto the bed, exhausted. The muscles in her face relaxed as the day's tension waned. Sleep came like a freefall.

CHAPTER 7

After spending the better part of Wednesday tying up loose ends before the trip to southern California, Pretense focused on today's big event—the Rothschilds. A soft tremor of guilt swept through her—so soft it barely registered. Granted, the Rothschilds were pleasant people, but they had more money than they deserved, and yet, they wanted more. At their age, how much was enough?

As she flitted around her office, she turned to see Simon standing in the doorway, his fist poised to knock. "I hear the Rothschilds are coming in today at two. Weren't they just here?"

"Yes, last week. But they had to leave early, so we are wrapping up a few details today."

"Do you mind if I sit in on the meeting?" he asked. "I'm trying to engage in more face-time with our clients, and my schedule is open until four o'clock. Let's meet in my office."

She cranked out a smile. "That would be great. I'm sure they would love having you join us, as would I. I'll bring them over when they get here."

"See you then." He turned to leave.

She checked her watch, then scrambled over and shut her office door and dialed the Rothschilds' number.

Hyman answered. "Hello, Pretense. Are we still on for this afternoon?"

"Yes, but I was wondering if we could push our meeting to four o'clock today? Something urgent came up, and I'm afraid I can't get out of it."

"That would actually work better for us. We have a luncheon today, and we worried we wouldn't make it there in time. We will see you then."

After hanging up, she walked down the hall to Simon's office and tapped on the door. "Sorry to bother you, but I just got a call from Mr. Rothschild. He asked to move our meeting to four o'clock. Will that work for you?"

"No. I told you I need to leave at four," he said, sucking in his lips. "Can you include me the next time you meet with them?"

"Yes, of course. I forgot about your schedule. Too bad. I was looking forward to having you join us."

———

Edna and Hyman Rothschild arrived in the lobby and took a seat while Daphne contacted Pretense. Simon came by on his way out. He stopped in front of them and extended a hand.

"It's good to see you both. I was hoping to join you in the meeting, but Pretense informed me about the change in time. Unfortunately, I have a conflict."

As Pretense approached the lobby, she spotted Simon speaking to the Rothschilds. She quickened her pace and flung her arm out, knocking over a dried flower arrangement. Everyone turned, while Daphne rushed over to clean up the mess.

"Sorry about the grand entrance," said Pretense. "It must be the new shoes."

She turned to the Rothschilds. "Why don't you come back to my office before I destroy the place?"

"Well, it was nice to see you," said Simon. "Hopefully, I can join you next time."

Edna and Hyman trailed Pretense down the hall and into her office. After shutting the door and settling in her chair, Pretense folded her hands on the desk. "Thank you for accommodating my schedule."

"It's not a problem," said Edna. "What happened to your forehead?"

Pretense patted the bandage. "Oh, it's nothing. I had a biopsy, but the doctor said everything looks normal. But enough about me. Based on our conversation last week, what have you decided?"

Hyman unzipped a brown leather portfolio and dipped his hand inside, dragging out a stack of statements and pushing the papers across the desk. "We have investments with several management companies, aside from Crawford Spectrum. And to be honest, we are displeased with the lackluster returns and the inadequate level of service they provide."

"That's right," said Edna. "Our son, Baron, said we mustn't put all our eggs in one basket. However, Hyman and I feel it makes the most sense. We also believe that Baron mustn't stick his nose where it doesn't belong. Isn't that right, dear?"

Hyman let out a snort. "Our son is very manipulating. He told us we are getting too old to handle our finances." He stabbed his gnarly finger in the air, redness creeping over his pallid face. "We may be old, but we possess more logic than he does when it comes to finances, and we are growing tired of his domineering behavior."

"And his money-sniffing wife, Vanka," Edna interjected, patting his hand. "Now, Hyman, don't get all worked up. You know what the doctor said about your blood pressure."

Pretense picked up the statements and looked over each one, mentally calculating. "It looks like you have about ten million, give or take. Are you suggesting we move everything over to Crawford Spectrum?"

Hyman nodded. "We are delighted with the way you have handled our funds, and we feel very comfortable putting everything into your hands. We'd like to make this happen soon, so what is the next step?"

"You need to fill out a few forms, and I can handle the rest. The process takes anywhere from one to three weeks." Pretense scrutinized them both. "Are you certain you want to do this?"

Hyman looked at Edna and answered. "We talked about it at length, and we are both sure. And as much as possible, we'd like to keep this from our son, Baron."

"Is Baron involved in your investment decisions?"

"No," Hyman answered, "but he tries to be. He's listed as the beneficiary when we both die, but that is the extent of his involvement. We have a trust and have named our estate attorney as the executor with Power of Attorney—much to Baron's dissatisfaction. He'd like for us to transfer that responsibility to him, but we don't agree."

"You see," said Edna, "Baron spends more money than he makes and has gotten into financial trouble several times. We used to help him, but we put our foot down after he hired an architect to design a doggy house, or should I say palace, for Vanka's two Portuguese Water Dogs. We would rather donate our money to causes that support those less fortunate."

Like me. "I see," said Pretense, gauging her next move. "I'd suggest we do this. Complete the paperwork today so we can get the process rolling. When the funds arrive at Crawford Spectrum, they will go into an interest-bearing, money market account while I work on an investment plan."

"We don't want to lose out on potential returns by having our money sitting in a money market account," said Hyman. "We want our dollars working for us as soon as possible."

"I understand, but I want to be sure we develop a sound investment strategy." Pretense paused, her voice dipping. "I shouldn't be telling you this, but there is an exciting opportunity on the horizon."

Hyman and Edna leaned in, straining to hear.

Pretense bit her lip, looking from Edna to Hyman. "The problem, you see, is the fund is not available through Crawford Spectrum. It's a private fund, and it has been closed to new investors. That is, until now. The returns have been phenomenal."

Hyman sat forward, his body pressed against her desk. "Tell us more."

She paused, then slumped in her chair, releasing a winded sigh. "I shouldn't have said anything. I don't know what I was thinking. I could lose my job. Can we forget we ever had this conversation?"

"We don't want to get you in trouble," said Edna. "We can contact the firm directly."

"It's not that easy. New investors have to be referred."

"Is that something you would do for us?" Hyman sat erect, licking his lips.

Edna placed a firm hand on Hyman's arm. "Maybe we shouldn't get overzealous. We've been very pleased with Crawford Spectrum funds."

"Edna is right," said Pretense. "Besides, the likelihood of being referred is marginal at best. The fund manager is very selective. Even though I have an inside contact, we should stay focused on funds that Crawford Spectrum offers. I am sorry for bringing it up. I was so excited to learn they were opening the fund to new investors, but I crossed the line."

Hyman reached across the desk and patted Pretense's hand. "You don't have to worry about us saying anything to Mr. Crawford. We will keep this conversation between us."

Pretense yanked a tissue from the Kleenex box and dabbed her forehead before settling back in her chair. "Why don't we do this. Fill out the transfer paperwork today and move everything over to Crawford Spectrum like we initially planned. I'll be out next week, but I will tell Mr. Crawford you are investing ten million into Crawford Spectrum; however, an investment strategy is in the works. How does that sound?"

Hyman looked at Edna. "What do you think, dear?"

Edna turned to Pretense. "You mentioned an inside contact. Maybe you could put your feelers out and see what our chances are of being considered. However, we don't want to put you in an uncomfortable situation."

Hyman beamed at Edna. "I like that strategy."

"Let me think about it," said Pretense. Of course, what was there to think about? She had them eating out of her hand. They spent the next hour completing the paperwork for the fund transfer.

After putting on their coats, Edna slipped her leather handbag over her arm and turned to Pretense. "Before I forget, the Rothschild Foundation fundraiser is a formal affair. If you don't have anything to wear, let me know. I can have my stylist send over some gowns."

Dread pooled in the pit of her gut. "Thank you. I'll take you up on the stylist offer." Pretense stood. "Let me walk you to the lobby."

As she approached the door, a loud thump boomed in the hallway, followed by an exasperated, "Oh no!" When they stepped out of the office, Ariana was crouched on all fours in a sea of papers, an open three-ring binder lay on its side. "I'm sorry. Let me get this out of your way," said Ariana, scooping the papers into a pile before standing. She extended her hand toward Hyman and Edna. "Hello. I'm Ariana Primrose."

After an awkward introduction, Pretense walked the Rothschilds to the lobby. "I'll call you in a week."

Pretense returned to her office and dropped into the swivel chair. She had the Rothschilds right where she wanted them, like two dogs drooling for a treat. One thing she knew for certain though, Simon would want to know why $10 million sat in a money market account, delaying lucrative fees for the firm. She'd talk to him tomorrow.

———

Back at the apartment, she flung her coat on the sofa and kicked off her shoes, startling Kat hanging on the singed curtain, her claws shredding the nylon panel into tentacle-like strips. Kat ducked to the floor and scampered under the coffee table. After changing into her sweats, she opened the refrigerator and pulled out a half-empty egg carton. She cracked three eggs into a bowl and added a generous dose of salt and pepper before whisking the ingredients together. The phone buzzed.

Her shoulders slumped as she reached for the handset. "Hi, Mom."

"Are you sitting down? Do you remember that lady who lived in the Pepto-Bismol-colored trailer two lots down—the one with those plastic flamingos stuck in the yard?"

"Lola?"

"Yeah, her. The broad that seen that fancy word, *pretense*, in that highfalutin magazine."

Before her mother could finish the well-worn story, Pretense interjected. "And you both thought the word had a certain ring to it. It was one-of-a-kind, so you named me after it."

"Yeah, well, she got out of prison in January, and you will not believe this. She has family in New York, and she's driving out there in a few months. She said I could tag along if I pay for gas and she will drop me off at your place. I can stay with you."

A sickening pall sat in her loins as she searched for words. "Didn't Lola have an affair with Hank? Isn't that why you threw him out?"

"Yeah, but that's in the past. Your father was a low-life. I was planning to dump him before the affair."

Sweat gathered in her armpits. "Hank told me he wasn't my father. Why do you always say that?"

"You believe everything that scumbag told you? You clearly didn't inherit my common sense."

"Let's not argue," said Pretense, softening her tone. "I have something to tell you, now that you've ruined my surprise. I'm looking for a larger place—one with two bedrooms and two baths. My plan was to fly you out here once I got settled and move you in with me."

Aside from the dull metallic clank of the oxygen tank, silence hung over the line.

"Did you hear me?" asked Pretense.

"I heard you," her mother responded, inhaling deep. "You wouldn't lie, would you?"

"Of course not. I'm getting a raise soon, so I can afford to move into something bigger. But I need you to be patient while I search for a new apartment. And I may need to cut back on the monthly payments to save for the deposit. I'm hoping to find something soon. When is the lease up on the trailer?"

"I just signed a new lease, but I can get out of it."

"Don't do anything yet. It may take a while to find something. I'll keep you posted. I'm sorry, but I have to let you go. I'm going out with friends. I'll call you next week."

"So, you're not sending any money?"

"I'll send what I can. I have to go. Bye, Mom."

After hanging up, she poured a glass of wine and collapsed into the kitchen chair. The tremor in her hands eased as the wine pumped through her arteries. She got up and dumped the bowl of beaten eggs into the sink and refilled her glass, taking a seat at the kitchen table. Kat jumped in her lap, her soft purr quieting Pretense's raging mind.

CHAPTER 8

On Friday, Pretense grabbed a bottled water and walked to Simon's office, her stomach churning. After several deep breaths, she knocked on his door.

"Good morning," said Simon, waving her in. "How did the meeting with the Rothschilds go?"

Pretense sat across from him, drawing her moist palms over her skirt. "Overall, I think it went well. The good news is they are transferring ten million to Crawford Spectrum; this is in addition to the two million they already have invested with us. The bad news is they are weighing different investment strategies and want to take their time before deciding. In the interim, the money will sit in a money market account. I went ahead and completed the paperwork for the transfer."

Simon sat back in his chair. "That's excellent news. It is unfortunate the money won't be invested right away. I'm sure you tried steering them in a different direction."

"Yes, of course. But I need to tread lightly. I don't want to jeopardize our relationship by appearing too aggressive."

"Fair enough. I trust your instincts. It might be a good idea to stay in touch with them while you are out next week." He fidgeted with his tie. "Would you mind if I asked Ariana to contact them—in case they have questions?"

"Yes, I do mind. To be honest, I'm surprised you would offer that suggestion."

"Don't read anything into it. I'm just trying to help."

Pretense unscrewed the cap and took several swigs of water, dousing the bonfire within. *Collect yourself.* "I'm sorry. I've grown very close to the Rothschilds over the years, and I have earned their trust. They are in a vulnerable position right now. In fact," she paused for effect, chewing her lower lip, "when you talked about sitting in on the meeting yesterday, they were hesitant. They feared you would try to put too much pressure on them."

Simon's eyebrows scrunched. "What would cause them to react that way? I've never put pressure on them."

"I think I know. According to Hyman, one of the reasons they broke ties with the other management companies is because they were too overbearing. He cited specific examples of incessant phone calls and emails, and the top brass falling all over them like hungry wolves." She let out an easy laugh. "Those were his exact words."

"I see," said Simon. "We need to treat them with kid gloves, which you've been doing—and doing very well. What about your other clients? Would you like me to hand those off to someone else so you can focus on the Rothschild account?"

"That's not a bad idea."

"I want to be sure we are supporting you in every way we can." He stood and walked her to the door. "Excellent work, Pretense. I'll remain behind the scenes, but I want you to keep me informed. We can work on a plan when you get back."

"Thank you for your support."

On the way back to her desk, she stopped in the restroom to find Ariana modelling in front of the floor-length mirror, pivoting from side to side, as though admiring the way the black cashmere sweater clung to her pencil-sharp breasts.

53

"Oh, hi," said Ariana, realizing she had an audience. "All set for your vacation?"

"As much as I can be." She set her belongings on a shelf and went into a stall.

"I told Mr. Crawford I would be happy to stay in touch with the Rothschilds while you were out," she yelled over the partition. "He thought it was an excellent idea."

Pretense flushed the toilet and strode past Ariana, stopping at the sink.

Ariana leaned against the wall next to her. "So, Mr. Crawford liked the idea of me calling on the Rothschilds." She stared at Pretense.

Pretense washed her hands, then pressed the hand dryer button. The sound of a freight train roared through the room, filling the awkward silence.

Ariana laughed.

Pretense didn't. "I just met with Mr. Crawford. You will *not* be calling the Rothschilds." She gathered her belongings and walked out the door, heading for the lobby.

While Daphne wrapped up a phone conversation, Pretense waited, flipping through a magazine.

"Are you getting ready to leave?" asked Daphne as she ended the call.

"Yes. Can you do me a favor while I'm out? I need to make sure my office door stays locked. I have some sensitive information in there and don't want it falling into the wrong hands." She handed Daphne a key.

"I sure will. Mr. Crawford has a master key in case of an emergency, but I'll make sure no one goes in there. So, I'll see you on Sunday, then."

"I'm looking forward to it."

On the way back to her office, she decided—against her better judgment—to smooth over the bathroom encounter with Ariana. *Play nice, even when it hurts.*

"I'll see you at six," she heard Simon murmur to Ariana

before turning to leave. "Oh, I thought you left already," he said to Pretense, his face blooming hot pink. "I'll see you in a week." He walked away at a manic pace.

Pretense stood in Ariana's doorway, her posture tentative. "Got a minute?"

"Come in."

"I want to apologize for my behavior earlier. I know you were just trying to be helpful. I shouldn't have reacted the way I did."

"Apology accepted," said Ariana. She unzipped her purse and pulled out a compact, assessing herself in the small mirror. "You need to relax. You are too uptight and territorial. You'll never get ahead in this business if you don't learn how to work with others." She pushed away from her desk. "Now, if you'll excuse me, I have a date tonight." She put on her coat and brushed past Pretense. "See you in a week."

Pretense stared after Ariana, her fists clenched at her side. She returned to her office, envisioning herself on a tropical beach, the warm sun melting her body, the rhythmic, briny waves slapping the shore as she downed a Pina Colada. The calming image settled her nerves. She locked her file drawers and packed up her laptop, then turned out the light.

CHAPTER 9

Thunder cracked through the darkened room, the steady pattering on the window pane rousing her from sleep. Pretense turned on her side and gazed through the open curtain, red brick buildings blurred by the driving downpour. Burrowing into the soft, warm sheets, she rolled over and dozed for another hour before dragging herself from bed, stretching her arms over her head, her mouth widening into a yawn.

She opened the closet door and hauled down the floral-patterned suitcase from the top shelf. The gaudy bag had been the only "gift" her mother had given her. She'd found it sitting in the kitchen of their cramped trailer with a red bow slapped on the front, the receipt stuck behind and a tattered sheet of paper with the writing *I xpect to be payed back when you gratuade from harvard. Mom.*

She focused and unzipped the suitcase, spreading it open on her bed. Kat jumped inside, sniffing the inside of the foreign object as Pretense rifled through her drawers pulling out t-shirts and shorts, a pair of black pants, a white blouse, running shoes, and a one-piece, skirted red polka-dot Jantzen swimsuit. She scooped Kat out of the case and tossed her on the floor; the luggage was ugly, but it wasn't a litterbox.

After gathering her dirty clothes and stuffing them into the laundry basket, she headed out of her apartment. As she approached the second floor, Mrs. Whipple appeared.

"Good morning," said Mrs. Whipple. "I wanted to let you know the maintenance man will need to access your residence sometime during the day next week. He's checking on some plumbing issues."

"Fine," said Pretense. "As you know, I have a cat. She can be temperamental around strangers. And I don't have a cage to put her in."

"No problem," said Mrs. Whipple. "I'll go in with him. I love cats, and they love me."

"I didn't know that."

"Yes. I lost little Snooky last December." Mrs. Whipple's eyes glazed over. "She was my closest companion. My heart still aches."

"I hate to ask, but I'm traveling for work next week. Would you be willing to look in on Kat?"

"Oh, I would love to," said Mrs. Whipple. "Just tell me what you need."

"Great. I leave on Monday and return Saturday. I just need you to fill her bowl and change the litter box every other day."

"I can do that. I'm happy to help."

Pretense adjusted the basket on her hip. "Well, I need to get my laundry done. Thanks for your help," she said, before descending the stairs.

———

Pretense woke on Sunday morning to a dread crawling over her body. The mere thought of spending an afternoon with Daphne's friends and family felt depressing. There had to be an easier way to appear sociable, but based on her failed attempt with Ariana, she wasn't exactly winning any popularity contests.

Pretense got dressed and boarded the subway for Central

Brooklyn. Less than an hour later, she walked to the bustling neighborhood of Park Slope in search of Daphne's address. After a short trek, she found the home in the center of a row of elegant bow-fronted brick and limestone townhouses. For some reason, she hadn't pictured Daphne living in an upscale neighborhood.

Clutching a bottle of Smirnoff vodka tucked inside a brown paper bag, she climbed the wrought iron edged steps and hesitated in front of the carved mahogany door. As she raised her hand to knock, the door swung open, and there stood Daphne, her round face breaking into an enormous smile. Behind her stood a peculiar-looking child with almond-shaped eyes.

Daphne opened her arms wide. "Come in. I'm so glad you made it."

Pretense stepped inside, pushing the brown paper bag at Daphne. "This is for you." After Daphne thanked Pretense, the child sprang forward and ambushed Pretense, locking her in a bear hug and body slamming her against the door. The bottle fell out of the bag and rolled down the herringbone parquet floor.

"Sarah, no," said Daphne, her voice firm. "What did we talk about?"

Sarah backed away, smiling. "Hi, I'm Sarah."

Pretense remained plastered against the door like a flattened cartoon character, her hand gripping the door knob, her heart knocking in her chest. She took several deep breaths before speaking, her eyes avoiding the child. "You have a lovely house," she blurted.

"Thank you," said Daphne. She kissed the top of Sarah's head. "This is my baby sister. She loves meeting new people, but she gets a little carried away sometimes." She turned to Sarah. "Honey, why don't you pick up the bottle and take it to Mom?" Sarah complied and skipped down the hall.

"Follow me and I'll introduce you to the gang," said Daphne, leading the way. "Everyone is excited to meet you."

"Attention everyone," said Daphne to a cluster of smiling faces gathered around a large kitchen island, their eyes aimed in her direction. "This is my friend from work, Pretense Abdicator." Pretense offered an awkward wave.

Mrs. Duke approached and touched Pretense's arm. "Nice to meet you, Pretense. Would you like something to drink? Punch, coffee, tea?"

"I'll have a vodka and tonic with a twist of lime."

"I'm sorry, dear," said Mrs. Duke, patting Pretense's hand. "We don't serve alcohol."

Pretense felt her face flush. "Oh, then punch will be fine." She ogled the bottle of Smirnoff on the kitchen counter. Perhaps she could sneak a splash.

Daphne came beside her with a fellow from the group, their arms intertwined. "Meet Andrew. We have been dating for over a year. We met in Bible study."

An abundance of jet-black hair hung in pointed clumps on Andrew's forehead, his face partially concealed behind an over-sized pair of black horn-rimmed glasses. "Daphne tells me you're one of the smartest employees at Crawford Spectrum."

"I try to make sure my clients are well taken care of. After all, their success is my success. What do you do, Andrew?"

"I'm the youth pastor at Brookside Bible Church. Working with kids is my passion."

The conversation derailed when Mrs. Duke announced dinner and asked everyone to take a seat.

"I'm starving," said Daphne, steering Pretense to the dining room table.

Sarah ran up beside Daphne, pulling on the arm of her sweater. "I'll sit next to Pretense."

Daphne whispered to Pretense. "I think Sarah's taken a liking to you."

"Hey, Sarah, can I sit on the other side of you?" Andrew asked, tousling her hair.

"Okay," said Sarah. "Me, Pretense, and Andrew sit together."

Pretense took a seat between Sarah and Daphne and glanced at her watch. Only forty-five minutes had passed. It seemed like days. As she raised a slice of garlic bread to her mouth, Andrew offered to say grace. She placed the bread on the plate.

Like two automatons, Sarah and Daphne grasped Pretense's hands. Sweat beads accumulated at the nape of her neck. It felt like a cult of some sort.

"Wet hand," Sarah shouted, smiling up at Pretense. She pulled Pretense's hand to her mouth and pressed a gentle kiss onto her fingers.

Pretense froze. She snuck a peek at Sarah, as Andrew said grace. The child gazed up at her, her face radiant. Pretense half-smiled, taken by Sarah's unfiltered affection. Her body thawed as she heard Andrew's voice closing in prayer.

The conversation turned to the upcoming mission trip to Malaysia. Silverware and dishes clattered, as scoops of green beans, Caesar salad, and steaming thickset squares of cheesy lasagna were portioned onto plates.

"Have you been to Asia?" Daphne asked Pretense when everyone had finished eating.

"No, I haven't had the opportunity to do much traveling."

"In Malaysia, we will partner with several churches to provide food and clothing, medicine, and learning opportunities to street children. When it comes to learning, the kids are like sponges. I've gone a few times and it's such a rewarding experience. It makes you stop and think how fortunate we are."

Pretense searched for words, but her mind drew a blank. What could she say about sacrifice—the meaningless act of giving up one's own self-interests for another person? And to actually enjoy doing it. It seemed counterintuitive to the American way.

A small hand patted Pretense's thigh. "Wanna play a game?" asked Sarah.

Pretense grinned. "I really need to get going soon. Maybe another time."

"When?" asked Sarah.

"Sarah, Pretense has to get home," said Daphne. She turned

to Pretense. "It was so nice having you over today. Too bad you have to leave so soon. I'll walk you out."

After saying goodbye to the group, Daphne escorted Pretense to the front door. Mrs. Duke appeared behind them. "Why don't you take this home with you?" said Mrs. Duke, handing her the bottle of vodka. "We appreciate your gift, but no one in the house drinks." She held her arms out and hugged Pretense, while Pretense tried using the bottle as a barrier between them. Mrs. Duke pulled away and smiled. "Come back anytime. Our door is always open."

Daphne turned to Pretense, about to embrace her, when Pretense pushed out her hand for a shake. Daphne took her hand. "Enjoy your time off. I'll see you in a week."

———

Back in the solitude of her apartment, Pretense considered the Dukes. Even Sarah, with her challenges, beamed with contentment. She wondered what a life like that would have felt like. To feel the closeness of a loving family, secure in each other's company. She walked across the room to the window and parted the drapes, watching nameless faces strolling along the sidewalk below. The window had become her connection to the outside world—her family. Pretense wondered about their lives, their relationships. Was the woman walking alone going home to an empty apartment? Or to her lover? She stepped back into the room. This was her life—for now. But that life would soon change.

CHAPTER 10

F lanked by the dramatic rise of San Jacinto Peak, Pretense gazed through the window of the Boeing 727, as the narrow-bodied jet approached the runway into Palm Springs, California. The earth lifted to her and the back wheels struck the tarmac, a fierce jolt sending her stomach into a tail-spin. The engines growled as the plane wrestled down its speed before coming to an abrupt stop.

After retrieving her luggage, she stopped at a rental car desk and was soon seated in a silver Honda Civic, the new car smell flirting with her senses. With uncontrollable giddiness, she pressed her foot to the accelerator, launching the vehicle out of the rental lot. With the windows down and the open sunroof exposing the brightest blue sky she'd ever seen, she cruised along the city street into downtown Palm Springs, the desert breeze moving her brown frizz tufts.

With two hours before check-in at the hotel, she scanned the shops lining Palm Canyon Drive and spotted a chili-pepper red Mexican restaurant with outdoor seating. After parking the car, she went in and sat at an outside table abutting the main drag. Perfect for people watching, she thought. She settled into an uneven legged metal chair and kicked off her brown loafers, wiggling her naked toes in a patch of sunlight, ingesting the warmth on her bare skin. Perhaps a pedicure tomorrow. She deserved a little pampering. Digging through her handbag, she pulled out the hotel reservation and studied the small location map.

"I'm Brian," said the waiter. "I'll be your server today. Would you like something to drink?"

"Yes, I'll have a classic margarita."

Brian returned with her drink, along with complementary chips and salsa. "Here you go, ma'am. Anything else?"

"Yes. I'm from out of town. Do you happen to know how far the Marco Hotel is from here?"

"About five minutes. Where 'bouts you from?"

"New Jersey."

"I just moved here six months ago with a buddy of mine," said Brian. "I'm from Iowa. I love it here. What brings you to Palm Springs?"

"I'm an actress." She took a large swallow from the salted rim of the glass and tossed her head back. "Mostly stage, but hoping to break into film. I'm planning to move to California."

"Awesome. I always think of actresses as being beautiful, but that's a fallacy. How many movies do you see where the entire cast is good-looking? None," he declared. "Well, can I get you anything else?"

She felt temporarily incapacitated. "No. You've done enough damage. And by the way, you're not exactly a Greek god yourself."

"Oh, please, don't take it personally. I didn't mean to offend you. I was just stating a fact. Besides, good looks are overrated."

"Gee, thanks. I feel so much better. That calls for another margarita. And make it a stiff one."

Brian returned with her second cocktail. "This one is on me."

Pretense smiled cautiously, wary of her notched tooth. She extended her hand. "My name is Claire."

"Nice to meet you, Claire. I'm not good with words. Like I

said, I'm from Iowa." A mischievous grin swept his face. "Would you like to order something from the menu? The enchiladas are great."

"I'll pass for now." She watched as he walked away, his gait as uneven as her lopsided chair. She finished her drink, then waved Brian over. "I'll take the check now."

Brian returned and set the bill on the table. "How long will you be in town?"

"Until Saturday."

"If you'd like someone to show you around, give me a call," he said, handing her a card.

"Are you trying to make up for your blunder?"

"Maybe," he said, grinning.

"Thank you for the drink." She paid her tab in cash and left the restaurant. Before heading to the hotel, she stopped at an electronics retailer and purchased a prepaid phone. She didn't want her movements traced while in California.

Back on the road, her thoughts turned to the waiter, Brian. Did he just ask her out? Or was he just a nice guy desperate for companionship? Regardless, the man expressed interest. She coasted the palm tree-lined boulevard crooning a show tune, her shrill voice spilling from the open windows, bouncing off the valley floor and dancing over the mountain range. She motored along, fearless and free.

After a restful night at the Marco Hotel, she showered and dressed in black pants and a white linen blouse. She ate breakfast in her room while reviewing the script she had prepared for today. Satisfied, she brushed her teeth and ordered a cab since she couldn't risk being seen driving a car. That would blow her trumped-up story.

The taxi dropped her off in front of the Vital Statistics Office in Palm Springs. Once inside, she located the records section and sat down at a computer terminal and began her search on each member of the Voyant family, starting with the father, Robert. The record included his social security number, birthdate, and place of birth—Riverside County. She continued searching, scribbling details in her notepad. She found the mother, Beth, and jotted down her maiden name, social security number, and date of birth. Next, the son, Timothy. And lastly, Claire. Date of birth: May 19, 1973. No social security number listed. Perfect.

After memorizing the birthdates of each member of the Voyant family, she gathered her belongings and approached the front desk. "Excuse me," she said to the woman.

"Yes?" the clerk responded, her eyes fixed on an open paperback on her desk.

"Can you tell me how I would go about getting a certified copy of my birth certificate?"

The woman continued reading for several moments. Then: "Riverside County Clerk Recorder. Call and make an appointment."

"Thank you," said Pretense. "You've been so very helpful."

On the ride to the hotel, she called the County Clerk's office and made an appointment for the following day. According to the person who answered the phone, as long as she provided the mandatory information, a certified copy of the birth certificate would be available the same day. That would give her enough time to apply for a state identification card before returning to New York.

A celebration was in order. She found a salon within walking distance of the hotel and inquired about a pedicure. The nail technician looked at her feet and took her immediately. An hour later, she had a new set of toes. Feeling full of herself, she returned to her room and shimmied into her red polka-dot bathing suit, posing in front of the full-length mirror and admiring her well-toned physique. Pleased, she pulled the tote bag from her suitcase and tossed in a book, a bottle of sunscreen, her cell phone, and a swim cap decorated with multicolored foam flower petals, then headed to the pool.

She spread a beach towel on the last empty chair in the corner and reclined back, inhaling the chlorine air, as the desert sun bathed her pasty-white body. After thirty minutes, she sat up and admired her toes, the fuchsia pink polish shimmering in the sunlight. She felt restless. Like she should be doing something ... with someone. Digging through her tote bag, she found Brian's card and dialed the number.

"Hi Brian. It's Pre ...." she hesitated. "It's Claire. We met yesterday at the restaurant."

"Hello, Claire. Good to hear from you. How is your first day going?"

"Busy. I had an audition this morning. I just got back and now I'm at the pool. I'm wondering if you'd like to come by. Maybe go for a swim?"

"I'm working now. But I get off at six. Would you like to do something tonight? I know this cool karaoke bar downtown. Drinks are half-off on Tuesdays."

She contemplated the rare invite. "I suppose, but only if I'm back by ten o'clock. I have an early morning audition, and I need my beauty rest," she said with a snort.

"Great. I'll pick you up outside your hotel at seven."

After several laps in the pool—her hair shielded by the rubber lid—Pretense returned to her room, showered and changed into her lone pair of black pants, a t-shirt, and flip-flops. She wasn't sure about the ensemble, but it would have to do. Besides, Brian didn't strike her as someone who'd show up in a three-piece suit.

At seven o'clock sharp, a cartoonish, metallic blue Suzuki X-90 pulled up to the hotel entrance. Brian stepped out and opened the passenger door. Pretense almost laughed at the odd-looking vehicle, but considering the seriousness on Brian's face, she held back. "Thanks for inviting me out," she said, as she wiggled her way into the shoe box and strapped herself in, her knees pushing up against the glove box. Brian got in and looked over at her, smiling. She coughed softly as the scent of cedar wood stormed her nostrils. "Do you mind if I roll down the window?"

"Oh, sure," he said. "You look nice tonight." He left the parking lot, zipping toward their destination in clumsy silence.

When they arrived at Roxy's Place, Brian opened her door, steering her toward the building, his hand touching the small of her back. She stiffened. After taking a seat at a small table, Brian went to the bar to order drinks. She watched him walk away, the slight limp affecting his gait. He wasn't a bad looking guy. Tall and somewhat muscular. He wore his hair short, which complemented his angular features. His ears were a little too big, but not to the degree he could take off and land. And his voice soothed—a kind of husky drawl. His boyish grin and gallant manners captured her interest.

Brian returned with two draft beers and a bowl of pretzels. "So, how was the audition today?"

The story slid off her tongue like spit from a peeved Cobra. Lying had always been her game. "Intriguing," she replied. "They want someone to play a psychotic woman who goes on a murder spree after her husband runs off with her mother."

"Wow, that's enthralling. So, say a few lines."

"Okay. This was the line spoken when the woman confronted her husband." Pretense dropped her head, as though morphing into character. When she popped back up, her face contorted, her eyes squinty and darting. "You think I'm a nutcase?" she said, stabbing her finger at Brian's chest. He shrank back. "I'm just a little peanut living in the goober shell of my mother's shadow." Her face softened as she regained her former self. "Well, how did I do?"

His eyes were like two globes spinning in their sockets. "You scared me," he said, downing his beer. "That was pretty convincing."

"Thank you," she said, grinning. "I think I impressed the director."

The emcee took the stage, announcing the first act while Brian left to replenish their beers. After spending the next hour doubled over in laughter, Pretense turned to Brian. "So, a waiter. Is that your life's ambition?"

He shot her an awkward look. "Actually, I'm a website developer. My roommate and I are hoping to start our own business. But it's been a slow start. Until things pick up, I supplement my income by waiting tables."

"What a coincidence. I've been looking for someone to help develop a website. Nothing difficult. Just a few pages about my acting experience. And something that I can maintain myself. I just need assistance getting the framework up and running. Would you be willing to help? I'd pay you of course."

"Sure, that would be great. If you're free tomorrow night, we could work on it then."

"Tomorrow is perfect," she said.

Pretense turned to the dance floor. Bombastic revelers crammed the small space, gyrating awkwardly to the overplayed tune of "Jumpin' Jack Flash" blasting from the jukebox. She hated the song and hoped Brian wasn't the struttin' type, what with his bum leg and all.

"I love this song," he said, shouting over the music. "Let's dance."

Her jaw fell. She had never boogied in public. Only alone. She waved him away and muttered a sorry.

"Oh, come on." He got up and took her arm, pulling her to the dance floor.

She stood frozen in front of him. He smiled and rolled his hips, his arms jerking up and down as though he were milking a cow. She looked around and realized how silly she looked standing there. *What the heck. I'll never see these idiots again.* In a moment of wild abandon, her legs broke into a gallop, her flip-flops slapping the wooden planks like clattering hooves.

Brian stuck his hand to the side of his mouth and yelled over the music, "Yee-haw. Giddy-up, Claire."

Sensing his delight, she kicked it into high gear. Brian raised his arm toward the ceiling and swung it in a circular motion before pitching an imaginary rope in her direction. Pretense straightened her arms at her sides and reined herself in, waddling like a penguin. The other dancers backed away, cheering them on. When the song ended, they received a round of hoots and applause. Exhausted, they collapsed in their chairs, gasping for air.

"I like your style," Brian said. "How about another beer?"

"As much as I'd love one, I really need to get back. It's after ten."

The conversation felt easy on the drive to the hotel. Brian pulled up to the front entrance and turned to her. "I had fun tonight. So, tomorrow night around seven? We can meet at my place. My address is on the card."

"Sounds great. And thanks for tonight. I had fun, too." Before things turned awkward, she pushed open the door and leapt out. "See you tomorrow."

CHAPTER 11

The following morning, Pretense dressed in her only pair of black pants, the smell of cigarette smoke prompting visual clips from the night before. A lazy smile formed on her lips, as she buttoned the wrinkled, white cotton shirt. She stood before the bathroom mirror and gathered her hair, securing it to the top of her head and jabbing bobby pins into the unruly mass. Then she pulled out the blond shag hairpiece she'd purchased in New York and arranged it atop her head, shifting it around to a flattering position. She studied herself in the mirror, then opened her makeup bag. The products hadn't been touched in over five years. Holding the eyebrow pencil steady, she feathered in small strokes, angling the tail to a point, then swiped each lid with eyeliner and applied several layers of black mascara. She moved closer to the mirror, studying her nose. She'd once seen a makeup artist on television blending dark foundation and concealer on the nose to create a slimmer line. After a few attempts, the method seemed to work. She stood back and turned her head from side to side. The perfect disguise for an identification card photo.

The cab dropped her off in front of the Riverside County Clerk Recorder building. She climbed the steps, her heart jack-hammering as she stepped through the front door of the building and gave her name at the desk.

Before long, a friendly-looking, mature woman approached. "I'm Barbara Hines. You must be Claire Voyant," she said, extending her hand.

Pretense shook her hand. "Thank you for seeing me."

"My pleasure. Come on back to my office," said Barbara, leading the way.

Pretense took a seat at the desk opposite Barbara.

"I understand you are here for a certified copy of your birth certificate. Is this a replacement?"

"No," Pretense replied, pausing and lowering her head. She nibbled at her lower lip. "My situation is rather..." she stammered. "I've never had a birth certificate. After I was born, my parents, Beth and Robert Voyant, sold everything and moved the family from Palm Springs to a commune in central California— the Brotherhood of the Moon. We lived at Spahn Ranch—where the Manson Family stayed." She sniffed nervously, awaiting Barbara's reaction. There was none. "We lived off the grid. I never attended public school. My parents taught me how to read and write. As I got older, I became more and more curious. I wanted a different life for myself, so I hitch-hiked to Palm Springs—the city of my birth. I met an elderly couple who were volunteering at a local food pantry. They offered to help me out by letting me stay with them temporarily in exchange for basic housekeeping. I've never had a real job, and I don't have a social security number. I can't drive because I can't get a driver's license without identification. It's as if I don't exist." She squeezed her lids shut and reached into her purse for a Kleenex, dabbing her eyes and blowing her nose. "Yesterday, I went to Vital Statistics and found my birth record." She pressed her palm to her chest. "It was the happiest day of my life. They suggested I come here for my birth certificate. I'm hoping you can help."

She scrunched her face, pulling her lips in. "I just want to be like a normal person."

Barbara stared at Pretense. "How old are you, Claire?"

"I'm twenty-eight."

"Do you know if your parents ever received a certified copy of your birth certificate?"

"According to my mom, they did not."

"I see. I think I can help you." She pulled down the glasses from her head and removed a manila file folder from her desk, pulling out a sheet of paper. "I need to ask you some questions."

Over the next fifteen minutes, Barbara Hines asked for details about Claire's family, as Pretense rattled off answers. After taking notes, Barbara got up. "I'll be back shortly. I'm going to do a search in our records room, and if everything matches, you should receive a certified copy of your birth certificate today."

"Thank you," said Pretense. Barbara walked out, closing the door. Alone, Pretense exhaled deeply, as though she had been holding her breath for hours. She grabbed the collar of her blouse, waving it back and forth to create air, sweat sticking to her armpits as her foot tapped the floor impatiently. She looked at her watch. She imagined Barbara returning with an FBI agent. Then she heard footsteps. The door opened and Barbara entered —alone—holding a piece of paper and donning a tight grin.

"Claire Voyant, I am pleased to present to you your certificate of birth," Barbara said, handing her the document.

Pretense carefully read through its contents. Her hand went to her mouth, her head shaking in disbelief. She stared up at Barbara. "Thank you so much. You have no idea what this means to me." *If only she knew.*

Barbara placed a hand on Pretense's shoulder. "I'm glad everything worked out. Best of luck to you, Claire."

———

Pretense took a cab to the Palm Springs Department of Motor Vehicles. Before entering the building, she called Brian.

"I need a favor."

"Sure, what's up?"

"I'm at the DMV in Palm Springs, applying for a California driver's license. Since I'll be moving here, I wanted to get the ball rolling. But I need a California mailing address. Would it be okay if I used your address? If the license comes in the mail before I move out here, perhaps you could send it to me."

"I'm okay with that, but why don't you wait to apply when you move?" Brian asked. "What's the big hurry?"

She fished for a response. "My New Jersey license expires in a few days, and I don't want to pay the renewal fee."

"Got it. Yeah, go ahead and use my address. I'll see you tonight."

After completing the ID application, the grim-faced clerk asked for her social security number and some type of verification. Pretense handed him the birth certificate and explained that she didn't have a social security number. He glanced up, then shoved a pad in front of her. "Press your thumb into the ink and transfer the print on this form," he said, pointing to a blank box. Then he asked her to stand in front of a metal contraption to have her picture taken. "Smile," he said.

She didn't. The flash went off.

"Your ID card will arrive in the mail in a few weeks." He looked over her shoulder and snapped his fingers. "Next in line."

And just like that, Claire Voyant was resurrected. Pretense leaned back in the cab, drained. She thought about her meeting tonight with Brian. One more piece of the puzzle about to lock into place.

———

Pretense pulled the Honda Civic into the parking lot and climbed the short flight of stairs in search of 2-C. She knocked on the door, wondering if Brian's roommate was home. Brian answered with a crooked smile, his arm making a sweeping motion, inviting her in.

"Did you have trouble finding the place?"

"Not at all," she said, removing her jacket and hanging it on the back of a chair. "I have another early morning audition, so I'm hoping we can finish quickly," she added, in case he had other things in mind.

"You haven't even sat down and you're talking about leaving. Can I get you anything to drink?"

"I'm good," she responded, pulling out a stack of papers from her laptop bag and looking around. They appeared to be alone. The apartment contained sparse furnishings, none matching. A green and white, crochet blanket covered the sofa, arranged on a diagonal. Perhaps a futile attempt at interior design, or placed strategically to hide something, like blood? "Can we get started?"

"Sure." Brian opened his laptop and sat at a tiny pedestal table, motioning her to join him.

"So, did you come up with a URL for your website address?" he asked.

"Yes. I'd like to go with C Katz; that's C (as in Claire) K-A-T-Z. I'm hoping it's available."

"Let's give it a try." Brian's fingers flew over the keyboard. "You're in luck. CKatz.com is available. Why C Katz?"

"Claire Katz is my stage name."

"Got it. Do you want me to purchase the domain name? You can pay with a credit card."

"I didn't bring my credit card. Can you charge it to your card? I can pay you in cash tonight."

"That'll work." After purchasing the URL, Brian recommended using a website builder service. After several hours, he created three separate tabs on the site—Home, About C Katz, and Contact Us. He demonstrated how to search for images to populate the pages, how to input text, create a logo, and how to link the Contact Us page to an email address. Pretense took notes and by the end of the evening felt comfortable completing the website on her own.

"I'm not going to charge you for my services," Brian said, after closing his laptop. "Just for my out-of-pocket costs."

"Why?" asked Pretense. "I thought you were starting your own business. You'll go bankrupt if you give away your services for free."

"My services aren't free for everyone. Just people I like."

"That's very kind of you." She averted his gaze, fumbling in her purse for her wallet, as sweat squeezed in her armpits. "Well, I should get going," she said, pushing her chair back and standing. "What do I owe for the out-of-pocket expenses?"

He told her the amount. "Do you have time for a beer?"

"No." She crossed her arms, hugging herself. "I really need to get some sleep. Early call tomorrow." She laid the cash on the table.

Brian stood and walked her to the door. "Are you free tomorrow afternoon? I'm off, and I thought maybe you'd like to do some sightseeing before you head home. We could take a ride out to Joshua Tree National Park."

Pretense weighed the invitation. She wanted to do some sightseeing, but didn't want to encourage Brian if he had other ideas. But she needed his friendship if she expected him to forward her mail. "Why not? I'm available after one o'clock. Are there hiking trails in the park?"

"Yes, but I've never hiked there. I wear a prosthesis. The terrain is too rugged for me to attempt a hike."

She scrunched her face, her eyes dawdling over his legs, as though she could see through his pants. "What happened?"

"I was a Marine during the first Persian Gulf War. I stepped on a landmine."

"Ouch! That must have hurt." *What a stupid response.* "I mean, of course it hurt—I guess it hurt. Did you feel it?"

"Yeah. The pain was horrendous. Hard to describe. One minute I was running, and the next minute I was on the ground looking at my shinbone sticking out with no foot at the end of my right leg."

"So, you only need to buy one shoe." She glanced down and noticed he wore matching shoes. Redness crept across her cheeks, as she shifted the laptop bag to her other shoulder.

"You're quite the comedian," said Brian, grinning. "I'll pick you up around one o'clock. It's a beautiful drive through the park."

"It sounds nice. See you tomorrow." As she walked to her car, she mulled over her lacking social skills. As she turned the key in the ignition, she looked back toward Brian's apartment. He stood at the door, waving. Her heart fluttered. She smiled and waved before driving off.

CHAPTER 12

The following day, Pretense contacted the Palm Springs Social Security office to inquire about a social security number for Claire Voyant and learned a photo ID was required. The last item on her to-do list now delayed until she received the state identification card. Which meant she would need to wait to open a bank account. And without a bank account, the Rothschilds' money would remain in the money market account at Crawford Spectrum. She collapsed into a chair and lowered her head, kneading the back of her neck. With several hours to kill before Brian arrived, she set out on an invigorating jog to ease the anxiety clawing at her gut.

———

"I'm looking forward to the drive through Joshua Tree," she said, as Brian pulled out of the hotel parking lot.

"I think you'll enjoy it. It was one of my first daytrips when I moved here," he said, as they headed down the freeway. "So, Claire, do you come from a large family?"

Keep it vague—less is more. "Just one brother. What about you?"

"I have two older brothers and a younger sister. They all live in Iowa near my parents. My two brothers are married with kids —three each. We're a close family. I miss being near them. What about your parents?"

"Alive and well." She shifted in her seat. "How long is the drive through Joshua Tree?"

"About fifty miles one way. We'll start at the south entrance and end up in the town of Joshua Tree."

After picking up a map from the Visitor Center, they drove north on Pinto Basin Road, then pulled into the parking lot at Cholla Cactus Garden. "Let's take a walk through the gardens," said Brian.

Pretense exited the car and headed toward the path ahead of Brian. "Wow, the cacti look so soft. Like my cat's tail."

As she reached down to pet the furry stem, she heard Brian yell. "Don't touch it!"

Pretense screamed when the cactus limb detached, sticking into her palm. "It feels like knives stabbing my skin."

"Don't move," said Brian. "And don't try to pull it off. It will only make it worse. I'm going to get some pliers out of my car."

He returned and took her hand. Instinctively, she pulled back. "Be still," he said, grabbing her wrist. He wedged the pliers underneath the spiny bulb and jerked upward. The cacti bulb flew off and landed on the ground.

Pretense inspected her skin and winced. Several pointy barbs stuck out like porcupine quills. "Is it poisonous?"

"No, just painful. I need to pull the needles out with the pliers. This will probably hurt." Brian worked slowly and methodically, extracting each needle. When he finished, he ran his thumb gently over her palm. "Does that feel sensitive?"

"Yes," she said, feeling unnerved by his touch.

"You probably have glochids under your skin. Little hair-like spines. Let's go to the car." Brian rummaged through the glove box and removed a first aid kit. He took out a roll of gauze and wrapped her hand, then took a container of white glue and dispensed several globs onto the gauze, spreading it over the injured area. "Leave this on for thirty minutes. It will help loosen the spines."

Pretense stared at Brian. "How do you know what to do?"

"I get around," said Brian with a wink. He started the car and pulled out of the parking lot, continuing the drive through the park.

"Where are the Joshua Trees?" asked Pretense.

"You'll see them when we cross into the Mojave Desert." He pulled over in front of a large rock shaped like a giant face. "This is Skull Rock. Did you bring a camera?"

"No. I never take pictures. I don't see the point." She climbed out of the car and gazed at the huge boulder, studying it from different angles. "It looks man-made."

Brian came alongside her, his hands resting on his hips. "The point in taking pictures is to capture memories. You're an odd person, Claire. Let's go back to the car and take the gauze off."

Once seated, Brian took hold of her wounded hand.

"I can do it," she said, jerking away.

He pulled her hand back and gently unrolled the gauze. When the tiny spines lifted away from her skin, he ran his thumb over the injured area. "That should do it." He sat back and studied her. "I don't understand how you can be an actress, yet have such an aversion to human contact. Or is it just me?"

"It's not you," she said, looking away. "When I'm acting, I'm someone else. I let myself go."

"So, Claire can't let herself go?" he asked.

"I thought we were going to do some sightseeing. I don't appreciate the probing questions."

Brian started the car and drove off. "Fair enough. I guess I'm curious. I find you intriguing. And somewhat mysterious. Not like other women I've met."

She stared out the car window, taking in the barren land-scape, the silence uncomfortable.

"Does Claire have a last name?" Brian asked.

"Voyant." She stabbed a stare at him.

"Clever. Clairvoyant. Like a seer. Your parents have a sense of humor."

"Let's get something to eat. My treat. I'm starving."

"I know this cool restaurant located on the property of an old movie set. If we're lucky, there'll be a live band performing."

———

It was dark when Brian pulled up to the hotel. He cut the engine and turned to her, their faces almost touching. "What time does your flight leave on Saturday?"

"Noon," she replied, pressing her body against the passenger door. "Well, thanks for everything." She gathered her purse and pulled the door handle.

"I'm free tomorrow night if you want to get together," he said, his finger tracing the steering wheel. "But I understand if you don't. A professional actress like you probably isn't interested in a one-legged Iowa farm boy like me."

"Don't say that. There's always hope."

Brian stared ahead. "Gee, thanks. Good to know."

Realizing her faux pas, Pretense threw her head back and let out a snort. "Oh, Brian. I'm kidding. I would love to get together tomorrow, but I have too much to do before I leave. I'm meeting with a realtor to look at a few apartments. I'm hoping we'll see more of each other when I move here permanently. And don't forget to call me if my state ID comes in the mail before I return." She planted a peck on his cheek. He turned to her, and took her face in his hands. She wanted to fling herself from the car, but she didn't. She sat frozen, as his lips caressed hers, gently brushing her cheeks, his breaths stroking her skin. She'd never been kissed before. She felt her body releasing and pulled away. "I should get going. Thanks for everything."

A deflated sigh escaped. He opened his door and walked

around to her side to help her out. She stood before him, nervously gazing up into his unsmiling eyes.

"I really like you, Claire."

Her breath caught. A part of her didn't want to leave, but she knew she needed to. And the sooner the better. "I'll stay in touch." She turned and walked into the hotel.

In bed that night, she stirred restlessly, a sappy emptiness pecking at her soul. She'd never met a man like Brian. A gentle man. One who made her feel safe. Someone with family values. If things were different—if she were different—maybe they could have made a life together. But that wasn't possible. She kicked aside the covers and sprang from bed, her bare feet greeting the cool tile. She paced the room, as visions from her childhood muddied her thoughts. Images of sweaty men and groping hands. Her mother splayed across the well-worn bed in a drunken stupor. Her screams unheard.

On Saturday morning, Brian headed to the local car wash and dropped two quarters into the coin operated vacuum slot. After wrestling the accordion hose, he bent down and suctioned the car floor when something caught his attention from beneath the passenger seat. He reached under the seat, his fingers grasping smooth metal. He pulled it out and turned it over in his hand, then pushed his thumbnail into the small indentation on the gold locket. The cover leapt open revealing a small photo of a cat resembling a bug-eyed gremlin with bat ears. Claire had mentioned a cat. Being the only female he'd had in his car for months, it had to be hers. He dialed her cell. No answer. Maybe he could catch her before she left the hotel for the airport.

After parking his car, he went inside and approached the hotel reception desk. "I believe a friend of mine left something in my car. I'm trying to get ahold of her."

"I can't give you her room number," said the clerk, "but I can try dialing her room. What is her name?"

"Claire Voyant. She's checking out today."

The clerk searched the computer database. "I'm sorry, but I don't have anyone registered under that name. Are you sure you have the right hotel?"

"Yes, I'm sure. I dropped her off at this hotel last night. She stayed here for a week."

"Let me try again." The clerk pecked at the keyboard. "Nothing under that name."

"Thanks for checking," said Brian. He walked back to the car, wondering if he had misunderstood the pronunciation of her last name. Maybe she booked the room under her stage name, Katz. If the locket held special meaning, she would call him. Otherwise, he would send it to her, or wait until she moved to California.

CHAPTER 13

The Manhattan sky was awash with silhouettes of grey, a blunt contrast to the piercing blue skies of Palm Springs. She thought about her time in California and about Brian. The pull on her heart caught her off guard.

"That'll be thirty-dollars," said the cabbie, jockeying for a spot in front of Pretense's building.

She paid the driver and gathered her belongings, then climbed the steps to her apartment. As she neared the second floor, Mrs. Whipple's door creaked open. Inside stood a form, its head swathed in blood-speckled gauze.

"Mrs. Whipple? Is that you?" asked Pretense, peering inside. Mrs. Whipple looked distressed, her face seemingly drawn to a point, her thin lips, pulling against the lines of a past nicotine habit, were pursed and trembling. "What happened to you?"

Mrs. Whipple's mouth labored, but no words came.

"My gosh, Mrs. Whipple, is everything okay?"

"That thing you had in your apartment..." She trailed off, grasping her wrapped skull. "That thing was an evil monstrosity masquerading as a cat."

Pretense's jaw unhinged. "What are talking about? Was?"

"It's gone, thank God."

A ball formed in her throat. "What do you mean?"

"That flying fur ball came at me, fangs bared, ears laid back, snarling and spitting. I was waiting for it to start speaking in Latin—like something out of *The Exorcist*. After it attacked me, it ran out of the apartment, and I haven't seen it since." Mrs. Whipple stumbled back against the doorframe, grabbing her chest and gasping for air.

"Kat is gone?"

"Yes. I'm just happy to be alive."

Pretense drifted away, her limbs wrestling with the stairs, her brain sputtering. Kat gone? Sure, she would have had to let her go at some point, but she wasn't ready. Not yet. She plunged the key into the lock and opened the door. Kat's odor lingered. She walked through each room, calling her name, but silence lurked. She wandered to the kitchen in a daze, noting two messages on the answering machine. She pushed the playback button.

"Pretense. It's Mom. I want to talk about moving out there. Call me." *Beep.*

"Where the hell are you? Call me!"

She sat at the kitchen table and checked her prepaid cell phone. Another message. "Hi, Claire. It's Brian. Hope you made it home safely. Hey, I found a locket in my car and was wondering if it was yours. Give me a call."

Her fingers ran down the gold chain dangling from her neck. The locket was gone. Kat was gone. She went into the bedroom and set her luggage aside, sinking into bed. She didn't want to talk to anyone. Not tonight.

The following morning, she dragged her body from bed, determined to move on. Kat had never been a part of her long-term plan. And neither was Brian. She put on a pot of coffee and dialed Brian's number, sweat tickling her armpits.

"So, you found my locket," said Pretense.

"Yeah. I tried to catch you at the hotel, but the hotel clerk said no one by the name of Claire Voyant was registered there."

Crap. "Oh yeah," she chuckled. "I checked in under my stage name, Katz."

"Didn't you need a credit card or a driver's license to prove who you are?"

"I'm an actress, remember? Anyway, regarding the locket, why don't you hold onto it until I move out there? It'll give me an excuse to see you."

"You don't need an excuse to see me," he said.

She paused, chewing on the flattery. After a few minutes of lazy chit-chat, she ended the conversation. The sound of his voice stirred up too many unwanted feelings. "I'd better let you go. I have so much to do today."

"Okay," said Brian. "Hope to see you soon."

"I hope so, too."

She took a few deep breaths. One more call. Her palms grew damp, as she dialed her mother's number. The sound of her gravelly voice came on the line, dirt spinning through a rock tumbler.

"So, the Princess decides to call her mother. What if I was in the hospital?"

"Were you?" asked Pretense, sounding a bit optimistic.

"Yes, I was. Oxygen tank blew a gasket. I couldn't breathe. Lola took me to emergency."

"Were you smoking?"

"What's it to you? Anyways, I started thinking about being alone—you know, in my fragile state and whatnot." She sniffed. "You said it would take time to find a bigger place, but I'm ready to move now."

"That won't work. The reason I'm busy is because I've been moving. In with a friend. It's temporary. Until I find a place. The lease was up on my apartment, and it was too expensive to rent month-to-month."

The sound of honking geese blew through the phone line, followed by wet, ragged hacking. After several minutes, her mother's voice crackled. "I don't believe you."

"Why would I lie? Look, I have to go. I'll call you next week."

"How will I get ahold of you? Don't you have one of those flipper phones that you carry around and hook on a belt? And why can't I get your work number? Or the name of the company you work for? Everything's a big secret."

"If you need to track me down in an emergency, I work for Berkshire Hathaway. But I can't give you my direct line. Company policy. I'll call you next week. Bye, Mom." She hung up the phone and ripped the cord from the wall.

———

Pretense flicked on the lobby lights at Crawford Spectrum, then unlocked her office door. She pushed the power button on the computer. When the screen sparked to life, she opened her email account and read through the messages, most irrelevant except for three: Simon requesting a meeting at nine a.m.; the Rothschilds would like to talk first thing Monday morning; and a cryptic message from Daphne.

Before she could dial Daphne's extension, she appeared in the doorway. "Hey, welcome back," she said. "We missed you. Hope everything went well with your friend."

"Thank you," said Pretense. "I just read your email. Why don't you shut the door and take a seat."

Daphne pulled out the chair and sat. "Oh, before I forget, this is from my sister, Sarah," she said, placing a white envelope in front of Pretense.

"Pretense" was scribbled across the front in large block letters, a happy face scrawled in the corner. Pretense opened the envelope and pulled out a sheet of paper decorated with rainbows and flowers that read "Nice to meet U. If there was 1 person left in the world to meet, I would want it to be U. Luv, Sarah." Pretense looked up at Daphne, a flush creeping up her face.

"She took a liking to you," said Daphne. "She hasn't stopped talking about you since you left." She scooched her chair forward, her voice lowering. "Anyway, regarding my message —and I'm only telling you this because you mentioned you didn't want anyone in your office. Well, last Tuesday I came by here, and the light was on and the door was ajar. I pushed it open, and Ariana was sitting at your desk, going through your file drawer. I asked if I could help with something. She seemed startled and said Mr. Crawford asked her to retrieve a file. When I casually mentioned it to Mr. Crawford, he seemed confused—like he didn't know what I was talking about." She visibly swallowed and looked around. "I just thought you should know. Please don't say anything to anyone about our conversation."

"I appreciate you telling me this," said Pretense. "I'll keep it between us."

After Daphne left, Pretense unlocked the file drawer. The Rothschild folder looked as though it had been quickly shoved back into place. She pulled it out. The unmistakable odor of Coco Chanel wafted into her nostrils. She shuffled through the papers. Nothing missing. She sat back in her chair, her mind whirling. *How did Ariana get in here, and why would she be sniffing around the Rothschild file?* Thankfully, there was nothing incriminating in the file. Pretense had been careful. She thought for a second, then reached for the phone and dialed the Rothschilds' number.

"Welcome back, Pretense," said Hyman. "Hope your time away helped clear any concerns you might have regarding our last conversation. We are anxious to hear if you made a decision regarding the private fund we spoke about."

"I'm glad to be back, and yes, I have made a decision," said Pretense. "Are you two available to meet tomorrow—somewhere neutral?"

"Certainly. Why don't we meet at our club, The Metro, say at twelve-thirty? You can get a feel of the venue for the upcoming event."

After she hung up, Pretense walked to Simon's office and rapped on the doorframe.

"Come in," said Simon. "We missed you last week. Hope your time off went well, considering the circumstances."

Pretense took a seat. "Thank you. It was a blessing to have spent time with my friend. I see the Rothschilds' funds were moved over while I was away."

"Yes. Have you spoken to them?"

"I have. This morning. We are meeting tomorrow—at their club."

"Oh? Why not here?"

"I guess meeting somewhere off-site will make them more comfortable."

Simon frowned. "It sounds like me sitting in on the meeting is not an option."

Pretense shifted in her chair. "I can handle this alone. I believe I've earned it."

"Yes, you have," he said. "But let me give you some pointers." He pulled a sheet of paper from a file and pushed it toward Pretense, directing her attention to several investment plans. "The first option would allocate ninety percent of their money into low cost S&P 500 funds and ten percent into short-term bonds. Now, I believe..."

Pretense raised her hand. "Excuse me. Before we discuss options, I'd like to hear what they have to say tomorrow."

Simon blew out a winded sigh. "As an adviser, your role is to guide them."

"I agree. But before I guide, I listen. I've been very successful with that approach. And I'm not about to shake things up now, especially given the amount of money at stake. Please trust me on this."

Simon, slumped in his seat, his fingers strumming the desk. "Your point is well-taken. I would ask that you keep me in the loop."

"Of course," she said, standing, then dropping back in her

seat. "One last thing. Did you remove the Rothschild file from my locked drawer? I looked for it this morning, but it wasn't there. It was there when I left for vacation. I need that file before I meet with them tomorrow."

Simon's face drained. "I haven't been in your office since you left. I'll look into it." He stood abruptly. "Anything else?"

"No, and thank you—for everything." Pretense left and turned down the hall toward Ariana's office and peeked inside. "I'll be right there," Pretense heard her say.

"Oh, hi," said Ariana, breezing past Pretense like a hurricane. "I can't talk right now. I have a meeting with Mr. Crawford."

"Oh, sure," said Pretense, smirking. When she returned to her office, she removed the Rothschild file from her drawer and shoved it into her laptop bag.

At the end of the day, she stopped by Simon's office to inquire about the missing file. According to him, it was nowhere to be found. And according to Daphne, Ariana had left the office in tears. Pretense savored the triumphant moment.

———

The yellow taxicab pulled up to the front entrance of the prestigious private club, The Metro. Pretense stepped out, taking in the grandeur of the white marble façade. After giving her name to the doorman, she stepped into the great central hall and climbed the stairs to the second-level dining hall. Hyman and Edna were seated at a table overlooking Central Park. Hyman stood and waved her over.

"How have the two of you been?" she asked, after taking a seat.

Edna patted her hand. "We're both doing well."

Hyman leaned forward. "Yes, and we are eager to hear what you've decided about the private fund."

Pretense smiled, her eyes shifting between the two. "I've given it a lot of thought. And the decision was not easy, but I've decided that I want to help you both." She paused, watching the growing grin on their faces. "I called my inside contact, and they are willing to accept my referral."

"That's excellent news," said Hyman. After shoveling a forkful of romaine lettuce into his mouth, Hyman wiped his face and set his napkin aside. "Let's talk about allocation. How much do you think we should invest in the private fund?"

Pretense set her fork down. "While I was away last week, I put together what I feel is the optimum plan for you both. Given the outstanding returns year after year, I would put three million into the private fund, and the other seven mil in more conservative funds available through Crawford Spectrum. But before you do anything, I want you to take a week to think this through." She handed Hyman a slip of paper. "This is the internet address for C Katz Investments. You'll find some good information on their site. But you won't find much about the fund by browsing the web. They keep things very hush-hush. Look over their website and then let's talk. And again, please keep this confidential."

"You have our word," said Hyman. He leaned back in his chair, crossing his arms. "By the way, a woman named Ariana called last week and said if we had any questions while you were out to give her a call. I told her that if we had questions, we would call you directly. Edna and I were both a little put off."

"I am so sorry," said Pretense. "Did she say anything else?"

"No, I didn't give her a chance. I just hung up."

Pretense dragged her hand over her mouth. "I don't like to gossip about my colleagues, but Ariana is close to losing her job, and I feel she is making desperate decisions. I'll talk to Mr. Crawford about it."

"Thank you, Pretense. I also want to reiterate our offer to pay you a fee for referring us to C Katz Investments."

"Absolutely not," said Pretense. "It's too risky. Not only could I lose my job if Mr. Crawford learns about the referral, but if I take a fee, the SEC can charge me with a penalty, and I may be barred from working in the industry. As it is, I'll have to come up with a compelling reason why you have decided to invest a portion of your money elsewhere."

"Tell Mr. Crawford he should be happy we are not moving the entire amount," said Hyman. "He doesn't have to know where the money is going."

Edna turned to Pretense. "Now that that's settled, let's talk about the charity event next weekend. I want to show you where you'll be speaking."

Pretense followed Hyman and Edna to the Grand Ballroom. When they pushed open the mahogany double-doors, a sweeping view of Central Park emerged through the floor-length windows, Baccarat crystal chandeliers illuminated Renaissance-style murals painted on the ceiling. Pretense stood in the middle of the room, her head tilted back as she gawked at the overstated opulence. She pictured herself standing at a podium before a garish crowd of fat cats, stuffing their faces with caviar and washing it down with bottles of Cristal champagne, while she spit out a pack of lies to an unsuspecting crowd. Her newly acquired acting skills would surely come in handy.

"Well, I should get back." She shook both of their hands. "I'm looking forward to speaking at the event. And I'll let you know when the fund is open."

On the ride back to the office, she pondered the upcoming charity event, dread taking over. Her thoughts were derailed by the buzzing cell phone. Brian's name appeared. Her insides churned. "Hey," she answered. "What's up?"

"I called to tell you an envelope arrived. From the State of California."

"Wow. That was quick."

"Do you want me to hold onto it until you move out here?"

"If you don't mind, I'd like you to send it, but I'll call you back with an address. I moved out of my place, and I'm staying with a friend until I move to California. I don't have her address with me. Can I call you later? I'm running late for an audition."

After they hung up, Pretense looked out the cab window, her mind scheming. She needed the California ID as soon as possible, but she needed an address to mail it to—one that couldn't be traced to her. *Think.* As the cab traveled through the northern tip of Manhattan, they passed a cluster of free-standing houses with driveways and front yards. In front of one home, an elderly woman walked to her mailbox. "Stop," she told the cabdriver. She wrote down the address and waited for the woman to enter her home. "Wait here a minute." She walked up the driveway and knocked on the door. When the woman answered, Pretense explained her dilemma. "I'm sorry to bother you, but a friend of mine is sending me an envelope from California and they wrote down the wrong address—your address. It should be arriving in a few days, addressed to me—Claire Voyant. Do you mind holding onto it until I come by? It's very important that I get it as soon as possible."

"Of course," said the woman. "Do you want to give me your phone number, and I will call you when it comes?"

"I don't want to put you out," she said. "I'll be in the area this weekend. I'll just stop by, if that's okay."

On the way back to her office, she called Brian and gave him the address. After the taxi dropped her in front of her office building, she rode the elevator to the eighty-ninth floor, rehearsing the story she would share with Simon Crawford.

CHAPTER 14

"How did the meeting with the Rothschilds go?" asked Simon, standing in her doorway.

"It could have gone better," said Pretense, discharging a heavy sigh. "Do you have a minute?"

"Sure." He shut the door and took a seat.

"First of all, I didn't have my file with all of my handwritten notes, so I struggled to recall some of the key points we had spoken about. But that was the least of my worries. As it turns out, Ariana called them while I was out, and they were pretty upset. Were you aware of this?"

He dragged his hand down the back of his neck. "No, I was not." He stood and paced the floor. "Did they say what she wanted?"

"Apparently, she called to ask if they needed anything. Mr. Rothschild seemed pretty agitated. Then he dropped a bomb. They are not investing the entire ten million with Crawford Spectrum. They are moving three million to another investment firm. He wouldn't tell me where, and of course, I didn't probe."

Simon stuffed his hands in his pants pockets and stared at the ceiling. "This is disappointing. Did you get a feel as to why?"

"He alluded to another opportunity. I'm just grateful they are not moving the entire amount."

"You did the right thing by not probing."

She sighed. "I'll start working on an investment strategy for the remaining funds—before they get any ideas about moving more money."

"Let's go over the plan before you present it." He walked to the door and stopped. "I don't fault you for any of this. I hope you know that."

After he left, Pretense sank in her chair. She opened her computer and pulled up an Excel spreadsheet. While reviewing her work, she heard shouting in the lobby. She got up and walked down the hall to find Ariana arched over Daphne's desk, her arms flailing in the air.

"How dare you tell Mr. Crawford," she heard Ariana say. Daphne fell back in her chair.

"What's going on?" asked Pretense. She looked at Daphne. Tears spilled down her cheeks.

"It's none of your concern," said Ariana, turning to leave.

"There are clients in the office," said Pretense. "They can hear you. And it is my concern when my fellow employees are being bullied."

Ariana ignored her and clattered down the hall. Pretense pulled a tissue from the box and handed it to Daphne. Daphne honked loudly, then looked at Pretense. "Did you tell her?"

"No," said Pretense. "But I think Mr. Crawford did." She patted Daphne's arm. "Don't worry about it. And don't let her talk to you like that. You need to stand up for yourself."

"I'm not a fighter," said Daphne.

Pretense rolled her eyes. "You need to be more assertive." She walked back to her office, anger steeping.

At home that night, she sat down at the kitchen table and thought about Ariana's antics. She was up to something, but what? She couldn't possibly know about the money scheme. Pretense moved into the living room and dropped a disc into the

CD player, then sat on the sofa, her eyes screwed shut. Brian floated through her consciousness. The nicest man she'd ever met, but her use for him complete. Restless, she went into the kitchen and removed her laptop from the bag. A white envelope skittered to the floor. She picked it up and reread the note from Sarah, then tossed it in the trash. Sarah's multicolored rainbow lay shining against a backdrop of garbage. She reached in and pulled out the paper, brushing away used coffee grounds before stuffing it back into her bag. A hopeful reminder that good people existed in the world. Too bad she wasn't one of them. She sat down at the table and powered up her laptop, then began drafting the speech for the upcoming charity event, picturing the crowd's reaction. *There won't be a dry eye in the audience.*

———

When Pretense left work on Friday, her prepaid cell phone buzzed. She looked at the screen. *Brian.* She let it go to voicemail, then listened to the message. "Hi, Claire. Just wondering if you received the mail I sent. It should have arrived by now. Give me a call." She went into the closet and retrieved a hammer from her toolbox and smashed the phone into small pieces, then distributed the parts into separate trash cans. *Sorry it didn't work out, Brian.* Afterward, she took a cab to the house she'd spotted in northern Manhattan and knocked on the door. The woman she had met earlier answered. Recognizing Pretense, she handed over an envelope addressed to Claire Voyant. Pretense apologized for the inconvenience and left. Once inside the cab, she tore open the flap and pulled out a California State identification card. The photo of a woman with blond hair and makeup bore little resemblance to herself. She pressed it against her chest and beamed. *One step closer to freedom.*

———

Back at the apartment, she cracked open a bottle of Merlot and pulled out the speech she'd written for tomorrow's charity event. Her stomach tightened. She swigged a few gulps, letting the wine seep through her body. *I can do this. I must do this.* With her face aimed at the hallway mirror, she visualized her new self. Then she paced the apartment floor rehearsing each sentence of the fabled tale, her head high as she practiced timing and enunciation. Trepidation soon turned to determination, her confidence level skyrocketing. Several hours later, she fell into bed, the speech deeply rooted in her brain.

———

The faint morning light leaked through the bedroom window as her cell phone buzzed on the nightstand. She rolled over and squinted at the screen. The Rothschilds.

"I hope I didn't wake you," said Edna, "but I wanted to let you know that the stylist is on her way over with a selection of gowns. And my hairdresser will be there at noon."

A scowl formed on her face. "Thank you so much. I'm looking forward to tonight."

"And so are we. I'm sure you'll deliver an excellent speech. Our driver will pick you up at five o'clock."

After she hung up, she sprang in and out of the shower, mopped her hair dry, and threw on a pair of sweatpants and a rumpled t-shirt. As she dumped a scoop of coffee into the filter, she heard a light rap on the door. On the other side of the peephole, an impeccably dressed woman struggled to balance an armload of garment bags. Pretense opened the door and ushered her in.

"Hi. I'm Tara, the stylist."

"Please, come in. Would you like a cup of coffee?"

"Sure," said Tara, looking around. "Do you mind if I hang these bags on the curtain rod?"

"Knock yourself out." She handed Tara a mug and gawked at

the bags hanging against the tattered curtain. "Do you expect me to try on every one of those?"

"No. But I wanted to meet you before I made a suggestion." She eyed Pretense up and down, front and back. "Based on your complexion and body shape, I have two in mind." Tara unzipped the bags. "Why don't you get undressed?"

Pretense went into the bedroom and came out wrapped in a large towel.

"You can lose the towel," said Tara. "I do this for a living."

Pretense let the towel drop, her arms covering her bare breasts, the hole in her underwear exposing a patch of pasty skin.

"You have a great figure," said Tara. "Perfectly proportioned." She pulled out a pewter-gray gown. "This is a timeless and classic piece. Try this one first."

Pretense wiggled into the floor-length evening dress, hiking it up over her bare breasts. Tara zipped the back and turned her around, her eyes inspecting from every angle. The material clung to her figure like a damp sheet, folds of stretch silk gathering at the bust, below an asymmetrical neckline.

"Turn," said Tara. "You'll have to lose the underwear. I can see your panty line." She stood back assessing Pretense. "Do you like it?"

"I love it," said Pretense, running her hand along the front of the material.

"It fits you perfectly. This is definitely the one." Tara pulled out a thick rhinestone cuff bracelet from a bag, a pair of silk stilettos, and a clutch purse. "These will complete the look. When the hairdresser arrives, tell them you want something simple. Maybe a chignon—provided your hair can be tamed. And minimal makeup. Think chic." She pulled down the remaining garment bags from the curtain rod and walked to the door. "Have fun tonight."

Pretense stepped out of the gown and returned it to the

hanger, her fingers stroking the rich silk. She stood back, ogling the dress, when came another knock.

"Hi, I'm Devon," said the man. "The hairstylist and makeup artist. Edna sent me."

"Come in," said Pretense. "I wasn't expecting a man."

"Sorry." He set down a large suitcase and pulled a chair from the kitchen table, dragging it across the floor like he owned the place. "Sit."

Pretense obeyed. Devon plunged his fingers into her hair, shaking the tangled mass. "When was the last time you had your hair styled?" he asked.

"Five years ago, maybe. I'm told I need something chic—like a chignon."

Devon stared into the jungle of packed hairballs, biting his lower lip. "I'm going to do a chemical hair straightening treatment. And some highlights to brighten it up. But first you'll need a good cut."

Several hours later, her once unruly hair was cut at her shoulders, golden highlights framing her oval face. The contrast of her smooth hair against pale skin and grey-blue eyes lent her a mysterious look. Despite her lopsided nose and broken front tooth, the transformation left her speechless. "I can't believe it's me."

"After I do your makeup, I'll style your hair." Devon reshaped her eyebrows, dusting her lids with taupe shadow and applying several layers of mascara. After dabbing on foundation, he used the same trick she had used to disguise her crooked nose, then he finished with pale pink lipstick before turning his attention to her hair. He used a tail comb to part her hair down the middle, then smoothed it behind her ears, gathering it at the nape of her neck and twisting it into a circle, securing the bun with several bobby pins. Using the end of the tail comb, he slipped it into the chignon and pulled it outward to create volume, then finished with several blasts of finishing spray. He stood back and threw his arms in the air. "Miracles do happen!"

CHAPTER 15

Pretense sat erect in the back of the limousine, her hands smoothing the silken material of her gown. She removed a compact mirror from her clutch bag, checking her hair and makeup. When the coach pulled in front of the grand ballroom, she stepped out. Hyman and Edna Rothschild were waiting in the lobby.

"Oh my," said Edna, taking both her hands. "You look absolutely stunning."

Hyman stood next to her, smiling. "Remarkable."

Edna took her arm and led her up the stately staircase. "I want to introduce you to some of my friends before the event starts. You'll be sitting at our table, along with our son, Baron, and his wife, Vanka—the money-sniffer." A tuxedoed waiter strolled by carrying a tray of champagne flutes. Edna grabbed two and handed one to Pretense. "It'll take the edge off."

"Oh, I'm not nervous," said Pretense, rolling her head back and draining the glass. She smacked her lips. "I've never had champagne. It's lovely."

"Well, be careful," said Edna. "It'll creep up on you like a pair of ill-fitting panties." Edna pitched back the glass and snapped her fingers. "Waiter, two more please."

A smile played on Pretense's lips. "How long before the event starts?"

"Thirty minutes," Edna replied. "I'll welcome everyone first, then you'll have ten minutes to deliver your speech. We can walk up together—to hold each other up. I'll take a seat on the stage and wrap up when you've finished, then you can help me down. Dinner will be served after the speech."

When the time came, Edna delivered her opening speech, while Pretense stood off to the side giving thanks to the champagne gods. After the introduction, she strolled to the podium with poise, setting her notes in front of her. She took a deep breath and looked out at the countless highborn faces. "Thank you, Mrs. Rothschild," she said, turning to Edna before addressing the audience. "It is truly an honor to be standing before you tonight. My name is Pretense Abdicator, and I was an at-risk woman." She paused, allowing her words to penetrate. "At the age of three, I entered foster care after losing my parents in a tragic accident. I bounced from home to home, never spending more than two years in one place. I felt abandoned. At a very early age, I recognized that the key ingredient to a better life was education. School became my family. It was the only place I felt at home. And then one day I met Anna at the local mall. Anna was a foster child like me. We became close —like sisters. But we were very different. Anna was burdened with beauty, and I was blessed with a hunger to learn. While I craved acceptance from teachers, Anna craved acceptance from men. Anna got pregnant. When her foster parents asked her to leave, she got into drugs, lost the baby, and eventually turned to prostitution. I, on the other hand, with the help and support of my teachers, went on to receive a full-ride scholarship to Harvard. Anna didn't have help. That was her death sentence. Anna died at the age of seventeen of a drug overdose." Pretense swiped an imaginary tear from her cheek. "We were both at-risk women. But we had differing levels of care. I stand before you today as a testament to the power of a helping hand. Education saved my life. Education could have saved Anna's life." She paused and scanned the crowd. "From the bottom of my heart, I thank you for providing a network of support so that the broken women of our society can be made whole and realize their dreams. Thank you." Pretense placed her hand on her chest and turned to Edna.

Edna stood and came alongside Pretense and whispered in her ear. "Well done. You may have managed to squeeze a few tears out of those plastic doll faces." After several minutes of vigorous applause, Edna and Pretense descended the stairs and walked to their table amidst cheers and extended hands.

"Wonderful speech," said Hyman, standing and holding a chair out for Pretense.

"Thank you," said Pretense, as she settled into a seat between Hyman and a dapper, middle-aged man.

"Pretense, this is our son, Baron, and his wife, Vanka," said Hyman.

"Nice to meet you," said Baron. "A very moving speech."

"Yes," said Vanka. "Quite compelling. I can't imagine being raised in foster care. You must have been so frightened."

"It was all I ever knew," said Pretense. "But I'm grateful for the help and support of others."

A tuxedoed waiter distributed plated dinners to the seated guests. Pretense felt relieved by the distraction. Something about Baron made her skittish. His penetrating eyes were like two drill bits boring into her. She wanted the night to end.

After dessert, a vanilla bean panna cotta with brown butter shortbread, Hyman and Edna left the table to mingle with the guests. Baron turned his full attention to Pretense. "I'm glad we have this opportunity to talk—without my parents around," he said in a hushed voice. "I understand they have recently placed a large amount of money under your management at Crawford Spectrum."

Her brain sputtered. She took a sip of water and dabbed her lips with a napkin. "I'm really not comfortable discussing my clients' financial situation. Perhaps you should speak with them directly."

"Yes, I should," said Baron. "But as they've gotten older, they've become—shall we say—more spontaneous and irresponsible. And to be honest, I'm concerned."

Pretense cleared her throat and clasped her hands on the table. "I find your parents to be incredibly sharp. More so than many of my other clients. But again, I'm not in a position to discuss this matter with you. Perhaps you should take it up with them. Now, if you'll excuse me, I really must be going." She stood.

He rose, looming over her and extending his hand. "It was nice meeting you, Pretense. I'm sure we'll be meeting again soon."

She smiled. "I hope so."

After saying goodbye to the Rothschilds and Vanka, she slid into the backseat of the limousine, her body rattling in shock. She would speak to the Rothschilds on Monday. In the meantime, she may need to expedite her plan before Baron got suspicious.

———

On Sunday morning, Pretense applied makeup, put on the blond wig she'd worn during her undercover operations in California, and took a cab to a private mailbox service in Jersey City, New Jersey. After presenting the California State ID for Claire Voyant and paying in cash for twelve months, the clerk went over the contract details. "This is your address. Mail and packages can be picked up twenty-four hours a day, seven days a week. Call ahead if you don't want to make a special trip and we'll let you know if you have mail. And lastly, unlike the United States Postal Service, we are not required to reveal the address we have on file for you. That information is completely anonymous." The clerk handed Pretense a key. "If you don't have questions, you are all set."

After thanking the clerk, Pretense flagged down a cab and instructed the driver to take her to a mailbox service in Wilton, Connecticut, to set up another mailbox under the business name of C Katz Investments. By having two unique mailing addresses, an auditable paper trail would become more difficult.

With her tasks complete, she arrived at her apartment after five o'clock. Exhausted, she climbed the stairs. As she reached the third floor, Mrs. Whipple appeared, exiting her apartment.

"Can I help you?" asked Mrs. Whipple, craning her goose neck over the stair rail. "If you're looking for Pretense, she's not home."

"It's me. Pretense." *Crap. The wig.* She patted her head and laughed. "I just returned from a masquerade party at a friend's house. I went as Diane Sawyer. You know, the news anchor."

"I didn't recognize you. You look nice."

"Thank you. I see the bandages are off. Hope you're feeling okay."

"I'm doing fine. Well, have a good night."

She breezed through the apartment door and flopped on the sofa. Thoughts bounced in her brain. So much more to do, but it would all be worth it. *In the meantime, be more careful and pay attention to the details.*

CHAPTER 16

When Pretense arrived at the office on Monday, she dialed the Rothschilds. "I'm calling to thank you both for allowing me to tell my story. I had a wonderful time at the event."

"And thank you," said Hyman. "The donations we received far exceeded our expectations."

"That's great," said Pretense. "And, I enjoyed meeting your son, Baron. After you left the table, we had an opportunity to talk. He's a very interesting man."

"He can be when he tries. What did you talk about?"

"Mostly about my role as a financial adviser. But he did say something that caught me off guard. He questioned me about the money you recently moved into Crawford Spectrum. I'm assuming you told him."

"I did not," Hyman bellowed. "How dare he bring it up to you. Hold on. Let me ask Edna if she said anything." His voice lowered. "Sometimes she has too much champagne and gets a little free with her words." Hyman placed the line on hold, then returned. "Edna didn't mention a word to Baron. I will get to the bottom of this."

"Perhaps he has a contact with someone at one of the

previous investment firms," Pretense offered. "If they shared this information, it violates client confidentiality. They could lose their certification. I suggest you make a call to those firms."

"I'll do that as soon as we hang up," said Hyman. "This infuriates me. And one more thing. We checked the website for C Katz Investments and were surprised by the year-to-date performance numbers. Do you have any idea when we can start investing?"

"I just spoke to my contact this morning. She thinks no more than a few weeks. The fund opened after one of their shareholders passed away. The fund manager is required to wait until that account is officially closed and the money is disbursed to the client's heirs before new clients can begin investing. That satisfies the limit condition of private fund investors per the Investment Company Act. I'll keep you posted."

After hanging up, she swung by the lobby.

"I love your hair," said Daphne.

"Thank you. Hey, I came by to see if you wanted to go to lunch today. I know you're leaving on your mission trip this week. Consider it a bon voyage lunch. My treat." Pretense had developed a soft spot for Daphne. But hero antics aside, she also wanted to pick her brain about Asia.

"That is so thoughtful," said Daphne. "I would love to go to lunch."

"Let's do Saul's Deli at noon."

Pretense spent the remainder of the morning in Simon's office, reviewing the Rothschild investment plan she had developed for the funds that would remain with Crawford Spectrum. As they were wrapping up, she brought up the missing file. "It baffles me that I cannot locate it anywhere. Any word?"

He blew a sigh. "Nothing." He leaned forward. "Have you noticed anything else missing from your office?"

"Not that I know of. Why?"

"Just curious. Why don't you make a quick inventory and get back to me?" His eyes tracked a clacking sound behind her. "Ariana," he called out, "I need to meet with you as soon as I'm done here, so hold on." He turned to Pretense. "Anything else?"

"Yes. I need to take tomorrow morning off for a doctor's appointment. Would you mind if I work the rest of the day from home?"

"Of course not. And let me know when you've scheduled the Rothschild meeting." He stood. Pretense left his office and passed Ariana waiting outside the door. Ariana picked her with an icy stare.

———

After nabbing a table at Saul's Deli, Pretense pushed her way to their seats toting a tray filled with pastrami sandwiches, potato salad and chocolate chip cookies. As they ate, Pretense inquired about the upcoming mission trip.

"I'm so excited," said Daphne. "The people of Malaysia are so friendly, not to mention the country's natural beauty. It feels like paradise. But there is a dark side, too. Our mission is to support the street children. It's such a rewarding experience to know that we might make a difference in a child's life."

Pretense stared at Daphne, baffled by her enthusiasm. "Can you get by without speaking the language?"

"Oh, sure. Especially in the big cities."

"Interesting," said Pretense, her mind plotting. "I've always wanted to visit Asia but never figured out where. Perhaps one of the coastal countries with a tropical climate. I'll have to do some research."

"I can bring you some of my travel books. I have one that summarizes all the countries in Asia—their customs, the climate, everything you need to know."

"That would be great. Well, we should head back."

As they exited Saul's, a balled-up man tucked into a nearby stoop unrolled, a tangled mop of greasy gray hair framing his gaunt face. His bloodshot eyes homed in on Daphne, his lips unfurling, exposing russet teeth. "That you, Daphne?" the man slurred.

Daphne turned. "Joe, I haven't seen you in a while."

"Do you have anything for me?" asked Joe, his body listing sideways.

Daphne reached in her purse and pulled out a rubber-banded stack of McDonald's gift cards, handing him one. "Here you go, Joe. How've you been?"

"Doin' okay. Can't complain. You're a good woman, Daphne."

Daphne patted his arm. "You take care of yourself, Joe." She caught up with Pretense waiting a safe distance away.

"How could you talk to that drunk?" Pretense asked. "And why give him anything? He should get a job—like the rest of us."

Daphne stopped in the middle of the sidewalk. "Don't say that. You have no idea how he got to this point. People are hurting. He could be suffering from post-traumatic stress disorder. Or maybe he has some sort of disability. Or lost his job. Or grew up in an abusive home. Whatever the case, everyone deserves compassion. We need to regard people in the light of what they suffer, not in light of what we think we know."

Pretense felt as though she had just been whacked with a bat. She stood open-mouthed, gazing into Daphne's glistening eyes, her lips working to form words. They walked back to the office in silence.

When they reached the lobby, Daphne stepped behind the reception desk. "Thanks for lunch. I hope I wasn't too harsh— you know, about Joe, the homeless man."

Pretense smiled. "No. We just see the world differently. No hard feelings. Hey, if I don't see you later today, have a wonderful trip."

"Thank you," said Daphne. "By the way, you should smile more often. It becomes you."

"And you should be more assertive. It becomes *you*."

Pretense returned to her office, shaking her head. *How can someone be so sweet? She must be snorting pixie dust.*

The message light on her desk phone flashed. She punched in her password and listened to Hyman Rothschild's voicemail, letting her know he had contacted each of the investment firms that had transferred money to Crawford Spectrum and was assured that nothing had been shared with Baron. She slumped in her chair. *So, who's the mole?*

CHAPTER 17

Pretense opened her laptop on the kitchen table and read through her work emails. After responding to several messages, she went into the bedroom, searching for a document she could alter by inserting Claire's name and the private mailing address in Jersey City. She pulled out the apartment lease agreement and brought it into the kitchen. On her computer, she replicated the font size and font type of the lease agreement, then keyed in the name "Claire Voyant" and the New Jersey mail address, then sent the document to the printer. Using a razor blade, she cut around the edges of the typed information and dabbed the cutouts with white glue, then affixed them to the lease agreement, covering her original name and address. After making a copy of the doctored agreement, she smudged the edges of the altered sections to camouflage the cutout area. Satisfied, she placed it on the table and went into the bedroom to change.

She slipped on a pair of black pants and a white blouse then applied makeup. Fearful of running into Mrs. Whipple, she stuffed the blond shag wig in her purse, along with Claire's birth certificate, the California ID card, the forged lease agreement, and the Jersey City and Wilton mailbox addresses. Then she left the apartment and hailed a cab.

Once inside the Social Security office, she waited for the next available agent. Before long, she was led into the cubicle of a stone-faced, middle-aged man. "Take a seat," he barked, his eyes studying a sheet of paper on his desk. He looked up, pulling off his glasses and pinching a flap of skin between his brows. "What can I do for you?"

"My name is Claire Voyant. I just moved here from California. I've never worked before, and my parents never applied for my social security number. I'm going to be looking for a job soon, so I'll need a number."

"I need to see some identification."

She laid the photo ID and birth certificate in front of him. He studied both, then scrutinized her. "Is this your current address?" he asked, referencing the ID card.

"No. I have a new mailing address," she said, pulling out the lease agreement and pushing it in front of him. "In Jersey City."

"You need a current photo ID with the correct address." He placed a form in front of her. "Here, fill this out and write in the new mailing address. I'll go ahead and send in the request, but in the meantime, make sure you get your ID updated."

"I will. Thank you." Pretense completed the form and handed it to the man.

He made copies of her birth certificate and ID card. "Your social security number will be mailed to you in two to three weeks."

Pretense left and took a cab to the New Jersey Department of Motor Vehicles office. After producing the required documents, she had her photo taken and received a temporary ID. "The New Jersey State identification card should arrive in the mail in two weeks," said the clerk.

After thanking the clerk, she left and took another cab to a storage unit facility located a few miles from her apartment. The driver waited while she went inside. "I need to rent a storage unit," she told the woman at the counter. "Preferably an outside, temperature-controlled unit, large enough to move around in so I can access boxes without difficulty."

The woman showed her a drive-up unit. "You'll need to provide your own padlock."

Pretense inspected the interior, visualizing her meager belongings dispersed throughout. And in case she needed to flee, she would keep a packed suitcase inside the unit. "I'd like to pay three months in advance—in cash." After signing the contract as Claire Voyant and using the Jersey City address, Pretense returned to the cab and directed the driver to drop her off in the shopping district near her apartment. She window-shopped several stores, then stopped in a public restroom and removed her wig, tossing it into a bag. She flagged down another cab.

Back in her apartment, she hauled the purchases up the stairs, dropping them on the kitchen floor. One by one, she emptied the bags, arranging the purchased items across the kitchen table. She stepped back, rolling her head against her shoulders. She picked up the prepaid phone from the pile. As she stood, she read through the voicemail instructions and took several deep breaths. With her tongue flat and relaxed on the bottom of her mouth, she drew out her words and spoke into the phone, using the high-pitched British accent she'd practiced at length. "You have reached the office of Kate Spencer, senior financial analyst at C Katz Investments. I am either on the phone or away from my desk. Please leave a message and I'll get back to you promptly. Cheers." She played back the message. Satisfied, she placed the phone in her purse.

Next, she opened the metal security box and placed the storage unit contract, the two mailbox lease agreements, Claire's birth certificate, the temporary and California State ID cards, and the doctored apartment lease contract inside. She removed the key from the large padlock she'd purchased and set it aside, then unwrapped the gold-plated, rectangular locket and flipped open the front, placing the padlock key, the security box key, and the two mailbox keys inside the locket. After snapping the lid shut, she slid the loop over her gold chain necklace and put it around her neck.

One last task before she could relax. From inside her bedroom closet, she pulled out the floral-patterned suitcase and laid it open on the kitchen floor, packing it with the newly purchased undergarments, two pairs of shoes, a purse, makeup, a flashlight, and a second blond wig—reserving the other wig for the apartment. After zipping the suitcase shut, she set it by the apartment door, along with the metal security box. She pulled out an old aluminum lawn chair and a tray table from her closet and set them next to the suitcase, then left the apartment.

Pretense jogged to a nearby car rental company and rented an economy car, then drove to her apartment, parking out front. She entered the building and tiptoed up the stairs, hoping to avoid Mrs. Whipple. She unlocked her door and scrutinized the items by the front door, hoping to make it downstairs in one trip. With sweat droplets beading on her face, she balanced the security box on top of the luggage and grabbed the suitcase handle with one hand, then looped the aluminum frame of the lawn chair over her free arm and gripped the tray table. Quietly, she locked her door and proceeded down the hall. As she neared the stairway, her foot folded like a drunken tap dancer. For a full half minute she twirled and jerked, as she careened down the flight of steps before landing in a heap against Mrs. Whipple's door. The security box sprung open, spewing its contents.

The door flew open and Mrs. Whipple, clad in an ankle-length, cotton muumuu and pink sponge rollers, splayed her hand against quivering lips. "Oh, my word. What is going on?"

Pretense lay prostrate, groaning. She rolled to her side and attempted to push herself up. Mrs. Whipple reached for her arm.

"I'm fine," said Pretense, bending to collect the scattered items.

"Let me help you," said Mrs. Whipple.

"No, but thank you." Pretense gathered the documents and placed them in the metal box, then wheeled the luggage down the stairs and out the front door.

Mrs. Whipple absently straightened a sponge curler, as she watched Pretense struggle with the door. "My God, what a strange woman you are," she breathed.

After packing the items in the trunk, she went back inside for the chair and tray table. Mrs. Whipple stood in the hall, holding the California photo ID of Claire Voyant. "Is this yours?" she asked.

Pretense abruptly reached for the card. "Yes. It's my friend's. Thanks for your help."

Frazzled, she limped to the car and drove to the storage facility, her body racked with pain, her mind spluttering with worry. If Mrs. Whipple were to notice the name on the ID card, it may prove to be a problem. But she couldn't think about that now.

When she arrived at the storage facility, she transferred the cargo into her unit before closing the storage door and securing the padlock. Then she returned the rental vehicle before hobbling home, wincing with each step.

Safe inside her apartment, she powered on her laptop and launched Word, then selected the Labels option, searching for the product code of the two-sided business card templates she'd purchased. When the layout appeared on her screen, she typed in "C Katz Investments" and uploaded the logo she'd created for the website. On the back of the business card template, she typed "Kate Spencer, Senior Financial Adviser, C Katz Investments," along with the phone number assigned to the prepaid phone, then loaded the blank template sheet into the Epson color printer. The printer spit out a page of eight professional-looking, straight-edge business cards. She picked up the sheet and snapped apart the cards, placing them in her wallet.

At last, time to celebrate. She grabbed the near-empty wine bottle and dribbled the liquid into a glass and went into the living room to relax. One more to-do item: purchase a case of wine.

CHAPTER 18

Pretense pulled out the Rothschild investment plan and scrutinized the allocation percentages. Simon had seemed pleased with the plan, but she needed to be sure everything was buttoned up before scheduling a meeting with Hyman and Edna. The quiet calm was interrupted by a scent wafting toward her nostrils. Coco Chanel had entered the building and was drifting her way.

"Good morning," said Ariana. "Do you have a minute?"

Pretense set her papers aside. "What's up?"

Ariana closed the door and took a seat, flipping her head, sections of her hair moving, some frozen in place by blasts of canned lacquer. "I spoke with Mr. Crawford. He told me there is a file missing from your office, and he asked if I had taken it. I know Daphne told you I was in your office while you were out, but there is a reason. I'm sure it's not what you think."

Pretense eyeballed Ariana, her expression indifferent. *Don't react.*

Ariana squirmed. "Do you want to know the reason?"

"Not really," said Pretense, picking up a binder and shuffling through the pages.

"Well, I want you to know. And I'm somewhat embarrassed."

115

She let out an audible sigh. "Mr. Crawford is always boasting about your investment skills and how pleased the Rothschilds are with your recommendations. So, I went into your office to review their plan—to use as a blueprint for my clients."

Liar.

"But I swear I didn't remove anything." Ariana held her palm up, like a witness about to take the stand.

Pretense put the binder aside and folded her hands on top of her desk. "How did you get into my office?"

"I took Mr. Crawford's key. He wasn't aware."

Pretense raised her eyebrows. She pictured Ariana's hand slithering into Simon's pants pocket like a tongue-flicking snake. "Why didn't you just ask him about their plan? He has access to it."

Ariana pursed her lips. "Because I wanted to impress him."

"Help me understand," said Pretense, her voice escalating. "You stole Mr. Crawford's key, broke into my office, and rummaged through confidential information in order to make an impression on him. It seems to me he's already impressed with your skills. You were the one he chose to receive the Employee Award, not me. And if that wasn't enough, a promotion. What more could you possibly want?"

Ariana's eyes darted frantically, before she dropped her head into her hands, her shoulders quaking. She came up for air, mascara juice running down her cheeks, one eyelash shifted at a ninety-degree angle. "Do you have a tissue?" she asked with a sniff, her mouth open with a bit of spittle clinging to her lip.

"Sorry, I'm out."

Ariana wiped her cheeks with her fingers, black swirls creating a watercolor painting. "I admit I was wrong." She wiped her nose along her index finger. "But. I. Did. Not. Remove. Anything."

"Look," said Pretense, "what's done is done. Let's not belabor this. If you want my help, just ask. But stay away from my clients, and stay out of my personal space. Understood?"

A strained smile appeared on her clown face. "Understood," said Ariana. "I won't take up anymore of your time." She stood to leave, then stopped. "By the way, I like your hair. It makes you look more modern."

After Ariana left, Pretense pulled a tissue from her drawer and dabbed her forehead, as she sat back pondering Ariana's motive. She didn't believe her story. And those tears. They looked real. But Pretense wasn't fooled. Ariana was a devious, manipulative woman out to make a name for herself and willing to step on anyone in the process. *A bit like me, but not as clever.*

Pretense resumed work. She scheduled the Rothschild meeting for later that week and informed Simon of the date and time. He sheepishly asked if he could step in briefly to say hello and assured her he wouldn't interfere. He seemed to have more confidence in her capabilities, which would work to her advantage once the grand scheme began to unfold.

On her way home, she stopped at Stan's Market. Her eating habits needed an overhaul—especially if she planned to enjoy good health in her fast-approaching retirement years. She grabbed a shopping cart and strolled the aisles, filling her buggy with fresh fruits and vegetables, yogurt, boneless chicken and salmon filets, and several packages of frozen Lean Cuisine. Then she steered the cart down the wine aisle, rationalizing that a glass of red wine benefited a host of ailments, including heart disease, stroke, and terminal boredom.

She pulled a 1998 Mondavi Merlot from the shelf. "I'd like to get a case of this wine delivered to my apartment," she said to the man stocking the shelves.

"I'll get a case from the back. Someone will deliver it in a few hours."

After hauling the groceries up the stairs to her apartment, she set them on the kitchen table and opened the refrigerator. It needed a good cleaning. She took a bucket of soapy water and scrubbed each shelf before putting the groceries away.

For dinner, she prepared sautéed chicken breasts with mushrooms and broccoli in a lemon butter sauce over Basmati rice. A knock interrupted. She looked out the peephole and saw a young fellow hugging a large cardboard box. She yelled through the door and asked the man to leave it outside the door. After he left—without a tip—Pretense ripped open the box and drew out a bottle and uncorked the Merlot, pouring her version of a heart-healthy serving into the large wine goblet. She took a few sips, then sat down and savored the homemade meal, feeling healthier with each bite—and more relaxed with each slurp.

Later that evening, she sat contemplating the day's events, drawing her finger over her front tooth, a reminder of the physical and mental scars her mother had caused. It had been over a week since they'd spoken, and she didn't have plans to call her again—ever. But a little voice told her to touch base. She pictured her mom hitchhiking to New York, dragging an oxygen tank down a bustling Manhattan sidewalk, shouting her name into a bullhorn. She shivered and poured another glass of wine, taking a long, deep swallow. Dampness painted her palms as she reached for her cell phone and punched in the number.

"Hello," answered a raspy voice.

"Hi, Mom. It's me. Pretense."

"Well, looky here. The royal princess awakens. Did you move?"

"That's why I'm calling. I wanted to let you know that I got laid off." Pretense waited for a response. Silence. "So, I won't be looking for a larger place. In fact, I'm thinking about moving back home—in with you. Maybe getting a job at the casino."

"I don't believe you," said her mother. "You told me you got a promotion. And now you're laid off? You're lying. Or were you lying then? I can't keep track. You've always been a liar. Ever since you were able to talk."

A deflated sigh escaped. "Well, I guess the apple doesn't fall far from the tree."

"Don't change the subject. I've been burdened by your existence for years. I could have made a life for myself if it weren't for you. All those years I spent taking care of you, making sure you came home to a home-cooked meal after school every day, and this is the thanks I get?"

"A can of Spam and a bag of pork rinds is not considered a home-cooked meal. And when did you ever take care of me? I was nothing but your meal ticket. You should be rotting in prison for what you've done to me."

"How dare—"

Pretense pressed the END CALL button and dropped the phone, covering her ears with her hands, shaking her head. The wine glass left her hand, crashing into the wall, glass shards exploding across the room. The floor welcomed her body, as she coiled into a ball, rocking back and forth.

Several hours passed before she found the strength to pull herself up, steadying her body against the wall. She went into the kitchen and returned with a broom and dust pan. After sweeping the broken glass, a jolt of adrenaline surged. She swept every inch of the apartment floor, shoving furniture aside, dropping to her knees to reach under the bed, dragging out clumps of fur balls. She grabbed a bottle of all-purpose cleaner and wiped down everything in sight—walls, pictures, tables, lamps, chairs. She kept moving, sweat dripping down her face and limbs, Molly Maid on human growth hormone. An hour later, her heart thrashed, her body dowsed in perspiration. She stripped off her clothes and stepped into the shower, the steamy droplets beating against her tired body. She grabbed the waxy soap bar, working it into a lather, the scratchy loofa scouring her skin until it turned red and tingled. She felt liberated—the frayed cord snapped in two.

CHAPTER 19

On Friday morning, she arrived at work earlier than usual, clad in a navy-blue suit and a pair of Air Max Nike running shoes. Straddling her laptop bag over her shoulder, she entered the main floor lobby and proceeded to Stairwell A. Doubting she would be able to scale eighty-nine floors in one hour, she set her goal for today at sixty minutes, then planned to take the elevator the remainder of the way to her office. It was vital to keep her body in tip-top shape through a ritual of vigorous exercise, a healthy diet, and semi-moderate alcohol consumption. At any time, she could find herself on the run, dodging bullets and leaping tall buildings in a single bound.

She began the stair ascent, walking sprightly at first, mastering two steps at a time, the Rocky Balboa theme song trumpeting her ears, egging her on. Thirty minutes in, her pace slowed, but she kept pushing, unwilling to stop. Sixty minutes and she had reached the seventy-eighth floor, her heart banging against her chest. She emerged from the stairwell with her blazer hung over one shoulder, wisps of hair scattering from her pony-tail. After riding the Sky Lobby elevator to the eighty-ninth floor, she stepped out and entered the Crawford Spectrum suite, invig-orated and ready to conquer the day. She jabbed her key in her office door, then slipped into a pair of high heels. While crunching on an apple and reading through her emails, Simon appeared.

"Good morning, Pretense." He cleared his throat and stuffed his hands in his pockets. "I know I said I wouldn't butt in on your Rothschild meeting, but I'm having second thoughts."

Her body stiffened. She dropped the apple into the trashcan and wiped her mouth with a napkin. "Have I lost your confidence?"

He pulled out a chair and sat down. "Not at all. But as the managing partner of this firm, I believe it's my responsibility to be involved when we're dealing with such a large amount of money. It has nothing to do with your capabilities."

Keep calm. "I understand. Why don't we do this: When they get here, I need to update their account profile. There's no reason for you to sit in on that. It will only take about fifteen minutes, then we can meet in your office."

He let out a long sigh and stood. "Perfect. Thanks for being open-minded. See you around ten-fifteen." He left her office.

The Rothschilds were waiting in the lobby when Pretense appeared. "It's so good to see you both."

"And you, too, dear," said Edna. "Where is that nice young lady who sits at the front desk?"

"Daphne? She's on a mission trip, but she'll be back next week."

"That's commendable," said Hyman. "We talked about going on a mission trip once."

Edna patted Hyman's arm. "But decided against it when you found out you couldn't take your golf clubs."

"I'm thinking about going with Daphne on the next mission trip," said Pretense, shutting her office door. "It's something I've always wanted to do. But enough about me." She settled into the chair and leaned forward. "Before we get started, I want to forewarn you that Mr. Crawford has asked to join us as we go through the investment plan. We obviously won't be able to discuss C Katz Investments, so I've set aside this time for just the three of us." She went into her purse and pulled out a business card, sliding it across the desk. "Kate Spencer will be your financial adviser at C Katz. She is the inside contact I told you about—a very gifted and savvy investor. You're in safe hands."

Hyman took the card and placed it in his pocket. "Thank you."

"As I mentioned, they are still awaiting clearance before any new funds can be invested. Kate will contact you directly when they get the green light. In the meantime, call her anytime with questions. I've told her all about you, and she is anxious to begin working with you."

"While we are waiting, maybe we should schedule a face-to-face meeting with Kate," said Edna.

Pretense curled her lips in. "Private funds don't work the same way. Transactions are typically handled remotely. Kate works in small satellite office in Connecticut. However, she often comes to the city to visit family. I can arrange a meeting the next time she is in town."

"We don't want to put you to any trouble," said Hyman. "You're doing enough already."

"It's not a problem." Pretense looked at her watch. "Do you have any questions before we meet with Mr. Crawford?"

"Just a comment," said Hyman. "We never did find out how Baron learned about the money transfer. It's quite bothersome to Edna and me. And don't worry about our meeting today with Mr. Crawford. Our lips are sealed regarding C Katz."

Pretense smiled. "Thank you for being discreet."

As they stepped out of Pretense's office, Ariana leaned against the wall near her door with a cell phone pressed to her ear. "That's correct, Mr. Greenfield," said Ariana, her voice notching up an octave. "How does tomorrow sound?"

Now what is she up to? Pretense stumbled into Ariana, knocking the phone out of her hand and sending it skittering across the floor landing at Hyman's feet. Pretense raced over and picked it up, speaking into the handset. "Sorry about that. Here is Ariana. Hello? Hello?" Ariana's fingers frantically reached for the phone. Pretense handed it back. "I think you've been disconnected." She turned to the Rothschilds and led them to Simon's office.

After an hour-long meeting, they wrapped up. The Rothschilds were pleased with the investment plan, and Simon allowed Pretense to do most of the talking—that is until the end. As they were getting ready to leave, his feelers came out, directed toward Hyman. "So, Pretense tells me you're moving three million into an investment fund outside of Crawford Spectrum. Can I ask which fund? We may be able to bring it in-house."

Pretense jerked back. She looked over at Hyman squirming in his chair.

Edna leaned forward and clasped her hands on the desk. "Let me be frank with you, Mr. Crawford. One of the things we appreciate about Pretense—aside from her investment skills—is her ability to perform with unobtrusive propriety. Perhaps you should take a few cues from her." She scooched her chair back and stood. "Now, if you'll excuse us, we should be going. Thank you for your time."

Hyman stood, taking Edna's arm and steering her toward the door.

Simon leapt from his chair, his feet bouncing over the floor, as he hurried to escort them out. He stopped with his hand on the door knob. "Please forgive me for being inquisitive. I shouldn't have asked. We are grateful for your business." He let out a nervous laugh. "And I'll work with Pretense to brush up on my tactfulness."

"Very well then," said Edna, shaking his hand before turning to leave.

Pretense escorted the Rothschilds to the front lobby, a wry grin smothering her face, while Simon remained in his office.

"How did I do?" Edna whispered to Pretense.

Before Pretense could answer, Hyman wrapped his arm around Edna's shoulders and pulled her close. "After sixty years of marriage, you'd think you know someone."

When they left, Pretense returned to her office, tossing around the meeting details in her head. The plan was progressing quite well. No, the plan was progressing brilliantly. The Rothschilds were onboard in keeping C Katz confidential, and Simon just got spanked by Edna. In her wildest dreams, she couldn't have imagined a greater outcome. She twirled in her swivel chair like a kid on a Tilt-A-Whirl, her salt-water taffy grin stretching across her face.

Overcome by ravenous hunger, she went into the galley kitchen and microwaved her lunch, then returned to her office to eat. While noshing on a Lean Cuisine Zucchini Lasagna and guzzling a Gatorade, Simon appeared. "I don't mean to interrupt, but I came to apologize," he said.

Pretense wiped her mouth and pushed her meal aside. "Have a seat."

A gale wind blew through his lips, as his hand shoveled his hair. "You warned me, and I didn't listen. I guess greed got in the way. From this point forward, it's your game. You call the shots. If you want me involved, I'm there. If not, I'll watch from the sidelines. Just keep me apprised."

"Don't be too hard on yourself. Three million dollars is a lot of money, and, like you, I want nothing more than to have those dollars invested here at Crawford Spectrum. But I've learned that the more pressure you put on the Rothschilds, the more they pull away. Who knows, maybe they won't be satisfied with the nameless investment company and may end up moving the money back here."

"We can only hope," said Simon. "Aside from my blunder, I think the meeting went well. They seemed pleased with the strategy." He stood. "I'll let you finish your lunch."

"Before you go, would it be okay if I bow out of this afternoon's staff meeting? I have a lot of loose ends to tie up."

"Sure. I'll have my assistant forward you the meeting minutes." He started to leave, then stopped. "Thanks for all you do. I may not always say it, but I want you to know that you are an asset to this company. You won't be overlooked during the next round of promotions."

"Thank you." She threw her hand to her chest, her lips pulled inward. "I'm touched. Truly." *Of course, I'm an asset, you idiot. I always have been. But this undervalued asset won't be around long.*

CHAPTER 20

After contacting the Jersey City mailbox office every day for the past week, mail finally arrived. Pretense applied makeup and grabbed the wig from her closet, stuffing it into her purse. She felt for the locket hanging between her breasts, then left the apartment and hailed a cab.

With her wig in place, she entered the building in Jersey City and headed toward her assigned mailbox, plunging the key into the lock and opening the metal door. Two envelopes lay inside; one from the Social Security Administration, and the other from the State of New Jersey, both addressed to Claire Voyant. She shoved the letters into her purse and left.

Once inside the cab, she tore open the first envelope and pulled out an introductory letter and a social security card, the name Claire Voyant typed below. She ripped open the second envelope and removed a New Jersey State identification card with a photo of a blond-headed woman smiling closed-mouthed into the camera. She heaved a sigh, her mind centering on the next phase of her elaborate plan.

———

Back at the apartment, Pretense flipped open her laptop. It was time to set up a shell company for C Katz Investments. After perusing numerous online articles discussing the pros and cons of forming a shell company within the United States and offshore, the British Virgin Islands caught her eye. Scrolling through the list of registering agents in the BVI, she homed in on one in particular—Global Corporate Solutions, or GCS. They not only filed the paperwork, but also assisted in setting up a business bank account. She pulled out the international prepaid phone she'd purchased and dialed the number.

"Global Corporate Solutions, Justin Moore speaking."

"Good afternoon. I'm calling to inquire about setting up a shell company in the British Virgin Islands. Is this something I can do over the phone?"

"With whom do I have the pleasure of speaking?" Justin asked.

"My name is Claire Voyant."

"Hello, Claire. The entire process can be completed by mail if you are unable to travel to our office. Where are you calling from?"

"The United States."

"Many of our clients reside in the United States."

Pretense chewed her lip. "I read on your website that you also help to set up a company bank account. Can you tell me more about that?"

"Yes, for an additional fee, we partner with several global banks. We advise you on the best location based on your business needs. But for that service, we require a face-to-face meeting. Are you able to visit our office? I have openings this week, including next Saturday. Our office is located next to a boutique hotel owned by my brother. We're about ten miles from the airport. Our clients receive discounted prices at the hotel if you mention GCS when booking your stay. And I can arrange transportation to and from the airport."

She would need a passport in Claire's name, and no telling how long that would take. "Can I call you back?"

After hanging up, she Googled "expedited passports" and discovered she could get a same day passport at the New York Passport Agency, provided she had an appointment, the proper documentation, and proof of travel within the next fourteen days. She checked flights leaving from JFK airport to the Beef Island airport. There were seats available next Friday. In order to pay in cash, she would need to make a trip to the airport.

She called Justin back and scheduled an appointment for the following Saturday, booking a room at the hotel for two nights. After hanging up, she went into her bedroom and checked the cash hidden in an envelope, taped to the bottom of a dresser drawer. Just over fifteen-hundred dollars. She grabbed the blond wig, headed out the door and flagged down a cab.

On the way to the airport, the driver stopped at the storage facility while she retrieved Claire's State ID card and birth certificate. Once inside the airport terminal, she approached the ticket counter. "I'd like to book a flight to the British Virgin Islands departing this Friday and returning Sunday."

The agent's eyes rolled up and down the screen. "I have a flight leaving Friday at noon, arriving at Beef Island Airport at 6:30 p.m. with a return flight on Sunday, arriving in the early evening."

"Can you book me on that flight?"

The clerk entered Claire's information into the database and verified her name against the State ID card. "Do you have a passport number?"

"No. I have an appointment on Monday to get an expedited passport."

"I can go ahead and book the flight, but you'll need to show your passport when you check in."

"Thank you." After paying in cash, the agent handed her a ticket.

Once home, she Googled the passport agency and read the

hours of operation. She would need to wait until Monday morning to call for an appointment. With nothing else planned for the day, she decided to go for a jog in Central Park. She hadn't run these past few weeks, but the daily stairwell climb at the office had transformed her lean body into solid muscle. She needed to keep up the momentum.

Pausing near the entrance to Central Park, she performed her routine stretch exercises, drawing each foot up behind her and pulling it toward her butt. With her hands on her hips, she lunged forward with her right foot and her shoe skated across a slippery, brown mass, her body altering in a half-split before tipping over onto a grassy knoll. An over-powering stench drifted from her shoe, as a flock of flies congregated on the awakened manure. *Crap.* She sat up, assessing the situation.

"Pretense?" said a voice.

She looked up and saw Daphne and Sarah walking toward her, waving.

"Pretense smells like poop," said Sarah, standing over Pretense and patting her head. "Poor Pretense."

"Oh, no," said Daphne. "Why don't you take off your shoe. There's a bathroom nearby. I'll go wash it off." She turned to Sarah. "Stay here with Pretense. I'll be right back."

"Thank you," said Pretense, brushing herself off and feeling oddly pleased to see them both. "Those stupid horses, crapping everywhere. They don't belong in the park."

Sarah sat on the grass next to Pretense, inching her way closer until their bodies were touching. "I'm happy you are here. I made a card for you. Did you read it?"

"Yes, I did. It was the nicest card I've ever received." In fact, the only card she'd ever received. Pretense looked down at Sarah, her small head leaning against Pretense's arm, her tiny hands gently resting on her thigh, as a gentle breeze stroked their bodies. Pretense didn't move. There was something sweet and calming about this moment. A feeling she'd never felt before. And she didn't want it to end.

"I like you." Sarah smiled up at Pretense. "Did you know God made me special?" Pretense opened her mouth to respond when Sarah sprang to her feet and ran toward Daphne walking toward them. Daphne handed Pretense the shoe.

"You didn't have to do that," said Pretense, pushing her foot into the Nike and tightening the shoelaces. "Well, I'd better head out on my jog. I'm glad I ran into you."

"We were going to grab a bite to eat. Why don't you join us?"

"Eat with us," said Sarah, taking Pretense's hand.

"Maybe another time." Pretense patted Sarah on the head, then turned to Daphne. "I'll see you on Monday. Maybe we can do lunch."

"Great. And I can tell you about my mission trip."

"Sounds good." She watched Sarah and Daphne walk away hand in hand, Sarah skipping along the path. Envy cut through her. She shook off the sentiment and set out on her solo run.

CHAPTER 21

When Pretense arrived at work on Monday, she decided to mix up her stair routine. Instead of climbing Stairwell A, she chose to test her stamina in Stairwell B and hike to the eighty-ninth floor. The change of scenery was a welcome diversion. She uncovered areas of the building she hadn't realized existed.

An hour later, she was at her desk checking emails and finalizing a status report. The unfamiliar ring pierced the silence. It had to be the prepaid phone in her purse—the one earmarked for C Katz Investments. Her heart leapt. She set her container of yogurt aside and sprang from her desk, locking the office door. She took several deep breaths before answering in a heavy British accent. "Good morning, Kate Spencer speaking."

"Hello, Kate. This is Hyman Rothschild. I was referred to you by Pretense Abdicator."

"Oh, yes. Hello, Hyman. Pretense has wonderful things to say about you. I'm excited to be working with you both."

"And we are eager to work with you. Pretense had mentioned there would be a delay before we could invest our money. Edna and I were wondering how much longer. We are excited to put our funds to work."

"I understand. It just so happens I was going to call you this afternoon. It looks like next Monday—a week from today. I do apologize for the holdup, and I thank you for your patience. It's taking a bit longer than anticipated. But while I have you on the phone, do you have time to go over a few details?"

"Oh, yes. I'll put my wife on the other line."

When Edna came on the line, Pretense asked them to confirm the investment amount.

"As of now, we plan to invest three million dollars. But if the returns are as impressive as Pretense claims, we may invest more."

Her brain sputtered while Hyman's words caught up. *More? How much more?* "Excellent. For the initial amount, my recommendation would be to make six investments of five-hundred-thousand dollars each over a period of three months. The objective is to capture the best possible returns while allowing for market fluctuations, rather than investing all at once." In truth, the idea was to fly under the radar by making several smaller deposits into her offshore bank account—soon to be established —so as not to tip off the money laundering fraud squad.

"If you feel that is the best strategy, then we agree," said Hyman.

"Very well. I would also suggest you wire transfer the funds, since the money will be invested that much sooner. However, if that is not an option, you can send a personal check."

"We will wire transfer the funds from Crawford Spectrum."

"Lovely. I will call you next Monday with the wire transfer instructions. Once your account is established, you'll begin receiving monthly statements on or around the first of each month."

After gathering the Rothschilds' personal data, Pretense asked if they would like to discuss anything else.

"Yes," said Hyman. "I'm assuming we can go online to our Crawford Spectrum account and place a wire transfer, directing the funds into the C Katz bank account. Correct?"

"I'm not familiar with Crawford Spectrum's process, but I'm sure Pretense can advise. I'll give her a ring when we hang up and discuss the best option. In the meantime, if you have any questions, do not hesitate to call."

"You've been very helpful. I look forward to your call next Monday."

After Pretense hung up, she swiveled in her chair, tapping a ballpoint pen against her chipped tooth. Sure, she would love to hang around and siphon more money; however, she needed to be careful … to move fast and get out of the country in three months. And aside from that, she did have some scruples. She didn't want to bankrupt the Rothschilds, just skim a little fat off the top. They were good people, but they had more money than they could possibly spend. She would call Hyman and advise against moving more than they initially discussed. She felt pleased with her virtuous decision.

She hung up, dialed the New York Passport Agency, and scheduled an appointment for tomorrow afternoon, then walked down the hall to Simon Crawford's office. He waved her in.

"I just wanted to remind you about my doctor appointment tomorrow afternoon. I need to leave around one o'clock."

His eyebrows furrowed. "That's fine, but I don't recall having that discussion. I usually mark it on my calendar."

"I mentioned it to you last week after our meeting with the Rothschilds. You said not to worry about the doctor appointment and the wedding on Friday."

"Friday?" He looked at his calendar, scratching his head. "Are you taking the day off?"

"Not the whole day. I told you last week that I needed to leave before noon. Is this a problem?"

"No, no. Not at all. Thank you for reminding me."

"Sure thing." She started to leave, then turned. "By the way, the Rothschilds will start moving money from the money market fund into the 'unspecified fund' sometime next week."

He pulled in his lips. "Still no idea where they are moving it to?"

"Not a clue."

On her way back to her office, she stopped in the lobby. "Good morning, Daphne. I wanted to thank you again for Saturday. That was very kind of you. How about lunch today?"

"I'd love that," said Daphne. "Too bad Sarah can't join us. She talked about you all afternoon."

Pretense smiled. "Let's leave around noon."

———

After they had finished lunch, Daphne pulled a compact camera from her purse. "Let me show you some pictures of our mission trip to Malaysia." She moved to the open chair next to Pretense and slid in close, holding out the camera viewing screen.

Pretense inched her chair away, pressing against the wall.

"This is a picture of the church we are building. And this is a group photo of everyone that went on the trip. Oh, and …"

Pretense zoned out, her mind focused on the Rothschilds and tomorrow's visit to the passport agency. She'd need to make sure she remembered her wig when she left for work tomorrow. And she must stop at the bank and get some cash for the trip on Friday.

"And this was a free day for the mission team," Daphne continued. "We went to the Perhentian Islands."

Pretense glanced at the small camera screen. An immaculate sugar-sand beach bordered a cerulean blue sea, two yellow kayaks drifting lazily upon the tranquil waters. She could almost feel the whisper of an ocean breeze against her skin, its salty breath teasing her senses. "It's gorgeous. Do people live on the island?"

"Yes, but not many. Tourists come during the day and most leave before sunset. I wanted to stay overnight, but we didn't have enough time."

Pretense studied the images as Daphne advanced through the blissfully scenic photos. She envisioned herself living on an Asian island, a tiny speck in the middle of the ocean, where she could live among the locals. She glanced at her watch. "We'd better get back to the office."

On the walk, Daphne suggested getting together over the weekend for lunch. "Sarah wanted me to ask you. She was so disappointed when you didn't go with us on Saturday."

"I'm busy this weekend. Maybe another time. Is Sarah ... you know—"

Daphne finished her sentence. "Mentally challenged? Sarah has Down syndrome. My parents were older when my mom got pregnant. They knew before she was born."

"Did your parents consider an abortion?" Pretense asked.

Daphne stopped and gasped. "No, never. We don't decide who gets to be born. I can't imagine life without her. Not a day goes by that we don't thank God for the gift of my beautiful sister."

"She's lucky to have you. You're lucky to have each other." Pretense grew quiet, trying to process the concept of unconditional love, but her mind went dark. She thought about her dismal childhood, born normal, yet never loved, while Sarah with her challenges was surrounded by love. It didn't make sense.

———

After returning to her office, Pretense shut the door and dialed the Rothschilds' number. "Hello, Hyman. I understand you spoke to Kate this morning."

"Yes. She called you?"

"Yes. She mentioned you wanted to know the process for executing a wire transfer from your money market account. Actually, it's quite simple. Once you receive the account information from Kate, you can go into your Crawford Spectrum account and make the transfer. Or, if you prefer, we can do it together."

"I'm not comfortable with computers. Would you mind helping us?"

"Of course not. But not at the office. Do you have access to a computer at the club? Or, I could come to your home."

"I hate to see you go to that trouble," said Hyman.

"You are my clients. And you've invested handsomely with our company. It's the least I can do. By the way, Kate mentioned that you might be moving additional money into C Katz."

"Yes, we wanted to talk to you about that."

"I know it's tempting, but your portfolio is designed to withstand market fluctuations. I would caution you against it. Don't put all your eggs into one basket."

"It was just a thought. If we decide to invest more, I'll discuss it with you first. Let's plan to meet next week, after we hear from Kate."

After the call, she leaned back in her chair. Instead of feeling ecstatic, she worried about the added scrutiny if they were to invest more. She must stick to her original plan and not get greedy. That could be her downfall. She would continue to steer the Rothschilds in the direction she wanted them to go, convinced they would take her advice.

One more nagging issue. She hadn't spoken with Ariana since the conversation in her office, and she needed to keep her close. Now that Ariana was back after a ten-day vacation to Bora-Bora, it would be prudent to schedule some girl time.

Ariana was perched at her desk, her honeyed brown skin like smooth caramel against a crisp, white linen blouse. Pretense knocked on the doorframe. "Welcome back. How was the vacation?"

A broad smile formed on her face, as she pushed a stack of papers aside. "I had a wonderful time. I didn't want to come home."

"I'd love to hear more, but I have a meeting. Do you want to grab a drink after work?"

Ariana looked surprised. "Sure. We can go upstairs to The Greatest Bar, if that works."

"Perfect. Meet you at five-thirty."

CHAPTER 22

T he bar was swarming with suited professionals when Pretense arrived. She found an empty stool and took a seat, looking around for Ariana. "What can I get you ma'am?" asked the bartender.

"I'll have a glass of Sauvignon Blanc." After the bartender returned with her wine, she took a few sips, assessing the crowd, their conversations swirling in a hazy cloud of smoke. A few minutes later, she spotted Ariana strutting her way.

"Sorry," Ariana said, hoisting her toned body up on the padded bar stool, her pencil skirt hiked mid-thigh. "Mr. Crawford came by and I couldn't get rid of him." She snapped her fingers and shouted over the jangle of voices. "Hey, Eric. I'll have the usual." She tossed her head back, her golden tresses bathing her shoulders like liquid sunshine.

Eric placed a tall glass in front of her. "One Long Island Iced Tea for the lady."

"You're a sweetheart," said Ariana, patting his hand.

"You're having iced tea?" asked Pretense.

"No. It looks like tea, but it's mostly liquor; tequila, rum, vodka, gin, triple sec, and a splash of cola. It's lethal." She turned to the man next to her and flaunted a smile, then took a large slurp from the straw. "I'm so glad we're getting together. Ever since that issue with the Rothschild file, I've been feeling just awful."

"Don't worry about it," said Pretense. "I'm over it. Now, tell me about your vacation in Bora Bora."

She threw her head back and gripped the bar with both hands, emitting an orgasmic sigh. "I have never been anywhere so incredibly beautiful. We stayed at a Four Seasons resort in an overwater bungalow, right in the shadow of Mount Otemanu. It was heavenly. The food was phenomenal. And the water was so clear. We even swam nude in the lagoon. It felt like we were the only two people there." She smirked and straw-slurped.

"It sounds expensive," said Pretense. "A little too rich for my blood."

"I wouldn't know." Her lips choked the plastic tube, her drink rapidly shrinking. "That was the best part. The gentleman I traveled with paid for everything." Her head lolled to one side, as her arm shot upward. "One more, Eric." She rumpled her fingers through her hair and swiveled toward Pretense, her eyelashes struggling against gravity. "Are you still nursing that wine?"

"I'm good for now." Pretense longed for another glass, but she needed to remain vigilant—especially given Ariana's diminishing state. "This is my second glass. I downed one before you got here."

Ariana howled and drew long on her straw. "You know, I like you. I used to think you were smug, but you really can be fun." She slogged her face into a lopsided grin, her eyes narrowing, as she leaned in close, almost whispering. "Rumor has it that the Rothschilds are moving money out of Crawford Spectrum and investing somewhere else. A lot of money."

Pretense remained calm. "You seem to have a fascination with my clients."

"I just like good gossip," she said, sneering. "Don't read anything into it."

"Where did you hear that rumor?" Pretense held up her hand. "Wait, let me guess. Mr. Crawford?"

"No, no," said Ariana, flapping her hand in front of her face. "He's too professional. At least when it comes to confidentiality. So, is it true?"

Pretense leaned close to Ariana and spoke in a barely audible voice. "I'll let you in on a secret. But promise, you won't tell anyone."

Ariana made the sign of the cross, drawing her thumb and forefinger across her scrunched mouth.

"You probably won't believe this." Pretense paused and took a deep breath, dragging her lips in. "Oh, I really shouldn't be telling you this. It's not appropriate." She sipped the wine and looked around.

Ariana glared at Pretense. "Come on. I won't tell anyone," she said, desperation dribbling from her voice.

Pretense enjoyed the game. She stared into her wine glass, her finger stroking the stem, her mind plotting. "They are not investing. They are donating. To a religious sect. The Children of the Sun. It's a separatist group with a vision to construct a temple in the Sahara Desert. Apparently, Hyman and Edna are long-time members and very high up in the chain of command. You won't find anything published about the group. I tried doing research. Nothing. And quite frankly, I'm surprised the Rothschilds were so open with me. But I get the feeling they might be trying to recruit me."

Ariana's eyes popped, as she smacked her hand on the bar. "Get out! That's the most ludicrous thing I've ever heard."

"I know, right? You can't make this stuff up. It's like something you'd see on *Dateline*. But you can't tell a soul. If you do, I'll deny it and you'll look like a fool." Pretense glanced at her watch. "Darn. I really need to go. I'm late for an engagement." She slid off the barstool. "I'll see you tomorrow. Remember, lips sealed."

On the subway ride home, she mulled over the conversation

with Ariana. She was obviously fishing, but for what? Pretense didn't believe she was trying to steal her clients. Simon would never let that happen. Something felt off. She filed the concern away. *Not much longer.*

———

On Tuesday, Pretense left the office in route to the New York Passport Agency. With her disguise in place, she stepped inside the building and double-checked the documents in her purse. After registering at the Information Window, she took a seat in the nearly empty waiting area, morphing into character. A quiet calm settled. She was beginning to believe she was someone else, decomposing down to her very essence and a new person emerging.

When they called her number, she went over to the assigned window. "Hello. My name is Claire Voyant. I need an expedited passport. I'll be traveling on Friday to the British Virgin Islands." She handed the woman the required paperwork.

"Hello, Claire," said the employee, methodically perusing the documents. "I see you have everything completed and in order. What is the purpose of your trip on such short notice?"

"My grandmother is in the islands visiting her ailing sister. She fell yesterday and broke her hip. Aside from her sister, I am her only living relative. It's important that I be with her when she has surgery on Saturday."

"I'm surprised the doctors are waiting that long to operate," said the woman. "My mother broke her hip and her surgeon insisted she be operated on as soon as possible."

Pretense assumed a look of concern. "I'm sorry to hear about your mother. I did speak to her doctor and asked if it was okay to wait that long, and he assured me it was. I do hope he's right. Now you have me worried." Pretense chewed at her lower lip, her breathing exaggerated.

"I'm sure she'll be fine," said the woman. "It usually takes about three full days to process an expedited passport, but I'm going to put on rush on it, based on your circumstances. You can pick it up on Thursday here at the office. We are open until six o'clock."

"Thank you so much," said Pretense.

She left the building deliriously happy. The pieces were falling into place. She felt confident about everything. And when it felt this right, it couldn't possibly go wrong.

CHAPTER 23

Pretense peered through the window of the small turboprop. It came in low, rushing toward a strip of pockmarked concrete floating in the middle of the Caribbean Sea. Her stomach lurched when the wheels slammed the runway, the tin can braking to a stop. She heaved a sigh, thankful to be on the ground—alive—with clean underwear.

After clearing Customs, she waited at the curb outside the terminal until she spotted a stocky man stepping out of a black Lincoln Town Car holding a "Claire Voyant" sign. She greeted the driver and slid into the backseat, adrenaline spiking as they drove along the shoreline with the windows cracked, the balmy tropical air twisting her hair. The fading daylight draped wispy palms against a blood-red sky, verdant mountains jutted from the sea like camel's humps. Her first time abroad, and it felt as though she had stepped into a cave of wonders.

The car came to a stop in front of a quirky, beachfront motel with an enormous black and white spotted chime dangling above a "Moore Cowbell" marquee. After retrieving her duffel bag, and confirming the driver would pick her up on Sunday, she went inside the lobby. A thirtysomething man stood behind the reception desk, his forehead swathed in a red, tie-dyed bandana, a mass of sun-bleached curls tumbling over his shoulders. "Welcome to Moore Cowbell," he said.

"Hello. I have a reservation under Claire Voyant."

"Ah, yes. My brother, Justin, sent you," he said, extending his hand. "I'm Jack Moore, the owner." He pulled a handwritten index card from a box. "It looks like you are staying two nights. I understand you'll be meeting Justin tomorrow." He smiled, baring dazzling white teeth that seemed to illuminate his shocking blue-grey eyes. "His office is two doors down to the right." He handed her a key. "You are in room sixteen. It's pretty slow this time of year, so it should be quiet. Do you need help with your bag?"

"No, I'm good," she said, taking the key. "Any restaurant recommendations?"

"My favorite is the Islander. It's within walking distance and right on the beach. The best burgers and drinks in town. They also serve healthy options, if you're into that."

"Thanks. I'll check it out."

She went outside and followed the narrow walkway through a tunnel of overgrown flowering shrubs and past a string of rooms before locating her room. The interior was tastefully decorated in black and white with a tile floor leading to an outdoor patio with a panoramic ocean view. Propped on the nightstand was a cellophane-wrapped wicker basket with a small card. *"Welcome to the islands. I look forward to our meeting tomorrow. Justin."* Inside the basket, she found a bottle of Cabernet Sauvignon, two wine glasses, and an assortment of dried fruits and nuts. She tore off the wrapping and opened the bottle, pouring a glass of wine and stepping onto the porch, inhaling the ocean's salty breath. After swilling a second glass and munching on the snacks, she decided to stay in and get a good night's rest.

She awoke the following morning to a light rapping. Stumbling from bed, she opened the door. A young woman greeted her, holding a tray. "Your breakfast, ma'am. Lemon scone and an English tea."

Pretense thanked the woman, then put on the wig and went outside, plopping onto a lawn chair, savoring the warm biscuit with clotted cream and strawberry jam while mentally rehearsing the script she'd planned for today's meeting with Justin. Squinting against the sun's reflection on the water, she spotted Jack, the motel owner, jogging down the beach, shirtless and wearing a pair of faded, blue jean cut-offs. He waved when she looked up, as though he were anticipating her attention. She waved back, curious if she were the only guest staying at the motel. An off-kilter sensation crept in. Just one more night and she'd be back in New York.

As the hour for the meeting drew near, she went into the room and changed into a floral print sundress with a light-weight cardigan sweater, pivoting before the mirror. Not too conservative. Not too showy. Pleased, she grabbed her documents and headed out the door and down the street toward Justin's office.

The red brick building looked out of place nestled between tacky souvenir shops and colorful restaurants, the smell of smoky barbeque and jerk seasoning gliding past her nostrils. She entered through a glass door, Global Corporate Solutions etched across the front. A clean-cut man, bearing a slight resemblance to Jack, appeared. He stretched out his hand. "You must be Claire Voyant. I'm Justin Moore."

"Nice to meet you, Justin. And thank you for the basket. It was a welcome sight after a long day."

"Glad you enjoyed it." He led the way down a short hallway to a cramped office. "Can I get you anything before we get started? Coffee? Tea?"

"No, thank you." Pretense took a seat at a small table and pulled out a manila folder. "How long have you been in business?"

"Twenty years. I'm originally from Florida but moved here to start my company. Then my brother, Jack, followed." He sat opposite her and pulled out a stack of paperwork. "Shall we get down to business? Anything we discuss today will be strictly confidential."

"Good to know," said Pretense, pleased with his cut-to-the-chase demeanor.

Justin thumbed through a pile of papers and pulled out a sheet, looking it over. "I ran a query on the company name you requested, C Katz Investments, and it is available. You will need to add the word Limited, Corporation, or Incorporated."

"Let's go with Inc.," said Pretense.

"Very well. The company name will be C Katz Investments, Inc.," he said, removing another page from the stack. "Because shell companies are legal entities that exist only on paper, the regulatory body of the British Virgin Islands requires that each company designate a nominee director and shareholder. This requirement prevents the public from knowing that a direct relationship exists between you and the offshore company. Your personal information will not be disclosed on the company documents and the Government record; however, you do retain full control over your company through Power of Attorney. For an additional one-thousand dollars, I can provide the name of the person that could assume the director and shareholder role. Would you like to include this service?"

Based on her research, Pretense knew these two roles were required. "Yes, please add this service."

Justin entered the data on his computer. When he finished, he pulled out another form. "Now, let's work on the company bank account. The British Virgin Islands are not ideal for hosting corporate bank accounts unless you physically live here, which is why we partner with banks in another jurisdiction—specifi-cally Singapore. I can assist you in filling out the forms and provide you with the appropriate introduction materials to my banking contact in Singapore. Global Corporate Solutions is an approved intermediary. As long as everything is airtight, which I will personally ensure, there should be no problem. The account will be set up within a few days. The bank will contact you directly with the information and will send the official documents to the address you provided in Wilton, Connecticut."

Pretense nodded. "Once the account is established, there will be a number of wire transfer deposits made over a period of three months. I'm assuming I will be able to access these funds much like my own personal bank account, correct?"

"Yes, that is correct," he answered. Justin gathered the paperwork and inserted it into a binder, sliding it across the table. "You are all set. Is there anything else I can help you with today?"

"I believe I'm good. Thank you." She paid in cash, then pushed her chair back and stood.

Justin shook her hand. "Don't hesitate to reach out if you have any questions."

Pretense left the office armed with a certificate of incorporation, an official business registration, and the Memorandum and Articles of Association for C Katz Investments, Inc. An impish glee lit her face, as she hurried back to the motel, struck by how easily everything came together. Like it was meant to be.

After packing her bag for tomorrow's flight, she tucked the binder between a pile of clothes and tossed the cardigan sweater aside. She slipped on a pair of sandals, freshened her makeup, and headed out the door in search of the Islander—Jack's restaurant recommendation.

She strolled down the street, stopping in several shops along the way. An unexpected emptiness stumbled into her brain. What would it feel like to share her life with someone—someone like Brian? Their time together in California was the closest she'd ever come to a romantic relationship. A part of her missed him.

After pawing through several bins crammed with touristy trinkets, she ended up purchasing a glass necklace with wooden beads and a straw hat of gigantic proportions. Sporting her new accessories, she headed to the Islander, feeling like an islander. The sound of steel drum music pulsed beneath her feet as she neared the restaurant, the smell of deep-fried fish taunted, a reminder that she hadn't eaten since morning. She moseyed into the weather-beaten shack and took a seat at the bar under a covered pavilion close to the water's edge. "What can I get you?" asked the bartender.

"What do you recommend?"

"How about a Pain Killer? It's an island favorite—rum, pineapple juice, cream of coconut, and orange juice."

"Sounds sinful." She slapped her palm on the bar. "A Pain Killer it is. And an order of conch fritters."

"You got it."

Pretense turned in her chair and gazed past the turquoise backdrop, her eyes fixed on a parade of moored fishing boats and yachts bobbing in the gentle swell. She leaned back and drank in the tropical air when suddenly a strong gust came off the sea, causing the brim of her straw hat to flap like a seagull. Before she could react, the hat went airborne, dipped, then somersaulted across the sand before splashing down in the water. She leapt from her stool and made a full throttle sprint in pursuit of the runaway hat. When she reached the shoreline, Jack from the hotel appeared from nowhere, chasing her wayward bonnet into the ocean. He body flopped onto the shredded-wheat mass and disappeared beneath a wave. A full minute later, he surfaced wearing the hat and a huge grin. "I take it this is yours," he said.

A goofy smile cut her face. "Yes. Thank you, Jack. I'm Claire. Not sure if you remember me, but I'm staying at your motel."

"I know who you are." His unblinking eyes traveled over her flower-patterned sundress, lingering at a burst of lavender blossoms seemingly sprouting from her breasts.

"Can I buy you a drink?" she asked, folding her arms across her front.

He removed the waterlogged headpiece and handed it to her. "I never turn down a free drink offer."

Jack followed her back to her seat. A liquid-filled mason jar, garnished with pineapple and orange slices with a sprinkle of nutmeg, waited for her. Jack sat down and waved to the bartender. "Hey, Tony, I'll have a scotch on the rocks."

"So, who's minding the shop?" asked Pretense.

"I have an assistant who works the night shift. When I first opened the motel, I worked twenty-four hours a day. Not much of a life. But things changed when business picked up." He leaned in and turned to her, his bare arm rubbing against hers. "So, Claire, you're obviously here on business or you wouldn't have met with my brother. What do you do?"

She drew on the plastic straw, nearly draining the sweet concoction, then ran her tongue across her lips. Reaching inside the glass, she plucked out the pineapple garnish, sucking the juicy wedge before tilting toward him and whispering. "I work for a Mexican drug cartel."

Jack's head snapped. He reached for his scotch and knocked back a slug. "You're pulling my leg, right?"

She smiled and turned in her chair, facing the ocean. "It's so beautiful here. Do you ever feel trapped living on an island?"

He stared slack-jawed, as though the shifting conversation hadn't registered. After a pause, he answered, "Never. I wake up every morning to a balmy breeze fluttering through the louvers, lifting the white cotton sheets from my stark-naked body."

Pretense let her eyes linger on his, her face expressionless. As Jack droned on about island life, her mind drifted as she tapped her toes to the music, her head bobbing from side to side. "I'll be right back," she said, sliding off the barstool in search of the restroom.

When she returned, a fresh drink appeared. "I took the liberty of ordering you another Pain Killer," said Jack, strumming his fingers on the bar in tune with the music. "Hey, care to dance?"

She took a sip of the drink and glided off the stool. "I'd love to." Since boogying with Brian in California, she'd been itching to give it another go. Jack took her hand and led her to the empty dance floor, then he broke away, stepping into a sort of left, right, and back rhythm in tune with the tempo, tossing his head around, his curly locks whipping through the air occasionally smacking Pretense in the face. She tried imitating his moves, but she felt stiff. Jack yelled over the vibrating drum. "Close your eyes and let your body go. Let the music guide your steps." She relaxed and gave it all she had, waving her arms over her head, her hips swinging wildly, like a savage hula dancer. Jack nodded his approval, further proof she was something to behold.

When the band went on break, they returned to their seats, their bodies slippery with sweat. Pretense drained her cocktail and turned to Jack. "I'll buy the next round." As she turned away, she felt as though she were watching a slow-motion slide show; each frame a stalled moment in time, as she floated, weightless, through a sea of underwater voices. She tried to speak, but her chin fell, words jammed in her mouth. She was tired. So unbelievably tired.

CHAPTER 24

Pretense awoke, naked on the floor.

Her jaw pinned against the cold tile, her skull exploding. She pushed herself up, collapsing into a cage of pain. As she reached to her mouth, sticky scarlet painted her fingers, the taste of metal overwhelming. The room came into focus, sunlight bleeding through the blinds. Something hairy lay next to her. A dog? She blinked. It was her blond wig. Cautiously, she raised her head and looked around. Her sundress and panties were strewn across the floor, wooden beads scattered across the tile. She urged her body onto all fours, crawling to the edge of the bed and hoisting herself up. Her legs felt wobbly and weak as she stumbled to the bathroom in dizzy confusion, clutching the porcelain sink. She splashed her face with cool tap water and looked into the mirror. A diagonal gash swept across her swollen lower lip, purple welts flanked her upper arms and thighs, and a throbbing discomfort between her legs. Her thoughts were disjointed, pieces of a jigsaw puzzle jumbled in a box. The last thing she remembered was sitting next to Jack. *Did he put something in my drink? A date rape drug?* Inhaling deeply and slowly exhaling, she tried steadying her nerves, her muscles straining until calm settled. She wanted off this island, and the sooner, the better.

She slipped on her bath robe and searched the room for her purse. It lay under the nightstand, tipped on its side. She slid open the zipper and tossed the contents aside. Her wallet and passport were there. She checked the duffel bag, burrowing under the pile of clothes. The binder lay undisturbed. Her fingers went to her neck, searching for the chain and locket. Gone. Frantic, she whipped back the bed covers, running her hand along the sheets, flinging the pillows and blanket on the floor. Down on her knees, she swept her hand under the bed, her brain colliding with her skull. The gold chain rolled against her palm. Relieved, she pulled it out. The clasp had broken, but the locket was there, the keys tucked inside. She dropped the necklace into her wallet. Whoever did this had only one thing in mind.

It was eight-thirty. The driver would be here at ten. She locked the front door and jammed a chair under the door knob, then drifted into the bathroom, sliding her robe off her shoulders and stepping into the shower. Water rained down, pelting her tender skin, her legs threatening to buckle. Gently, she patted the soapy washcloth over her body, then scrubbed her pubic area, washing away the tacky fluid. Her mind looped, visions of her childhood rushing back. Her mother's harsh voice bellowing over the shower wall, "Wash yourself real good. We don't want uninvited guests moving in." Pretense sucked in a spurt of air, exhaling through pursed lips. *Think cheerful thoughts … palm fronds swishing lazily in the breeze, crystal waters kissing the shore, three million dollars in my offshore bank account.* Several more gulps of air, and the tension slowly eased. Reporting the assault was out of the question. The attention would bring unwanted scrutiny … something the assailant must have known. She turned off the shower and stepped out, dabbing her damp skin with a terry cloth towel, then dressing in a long-sleeved shirt. After putting on her wig, she pushed her face to the mirror. A dab of concealer over the gash on her lip made it more pronounced. She found a Band-Aid in her makeup bag and affixed it over the cut, then grabbed her belongings and rushed out of the room.

Saliva thickened in her throat, as she neared the front lobby to settle her bill. If Jack was there, she'd act like nothing had happened. Her hands shook as she opened the door. Jack smiled from behind the desk.

"Good morning. I think that last Pain Killer did you in." His smile faded. "What happened to your lip?"

He appeared casual and concerned. *Maybe it wasn't him, but who?* She clenched her teeth to stop the chattering. Managing a stiff smile, she set her bag down and reached in her purse, pulling out her wallet. "I fell. What do I owe you?"

"It looks painful." He pushed the invoice across the desk.

Pretense counted out the exact amount and slid it across the counter. "I see my driver is out front." She picked up her bag and walked to the door before turning. "Thanks for last night. It was fun."

A wide-open grin cracked his face. "Come back soon."

———

The plane touched down at JFK International. When the flight attendant gave the all-clear, she pulled her bag from the overhead bin, her arms throbbing under the weight.

Once seated in the cab, she pulled off the wig. Her mind stalled on the fuzziness of the assault. She felt dirty and disgusted with herself—just like the days of her childhood. She had been here before. As the taxi idled at the stoplight, she gazed out the window, a steady mist falling over the city. A homeless man shuffled down the sidewalk, his soggy clothes a tattered mess, his life's possessions stuffed into a plastic bag slung over his shoulder. A nobody with nowhere to go. A raindrop in an ocean.

Rain sheeted down the day her mother had locked her out of

the trailer. She'd said she had "company" and told her to wait outside. She must have forgotten. Pretense dragged her damp blanket through the muddy field in search of shelter. When a policeman found her, he'd asked her age. "I'm six, sir," she'd replied. He put her in the car and drove her to the trailer and knocked on the door. Several minutes went by before her mother answered. She said she'd overslept and lost track of time. "This isn't the first incident," said the policeman. "If it happens again, I'll charge you with neglect." Her mother smiled and slithered onto the porch. "Why don't you come inside and we can work this out?" her mother had asked. "This is a warning," said the policeman. "One more time and I'll haul you in and charge you." He patted Pretense on the head before leaving. When the squad car had left, her mother's rage flared. "That ugly face of yours is begging to be punched. If I end up in jail, no one would ever take you. You're nothing but a burden. A nobody with nowhere else to go."

The cab leapt from the light, reorienting her thoughts. A blur of faces rushed along the city street—a mother's hand protectively clasped to a child's, young lovers huddled under an umbrella—people with purpose and meaning. The somebodies of life. She felt stuck in a bad dream with no one to save her but herself. But it had always been the bad dreams that fueled her determination. She would pull through this. She always did. And she would never again allow anyone to take advantage of her.

The driver pulled into the storage facility and parked in front of her unit. "Wait here," said Pretense, grabbing the duffel bag. She unlocked the padlock and pushed open the roll-up metal door, pulling it down once inside. She turned on the flashlight and unlocked the security box, placing Claire's documents inside before locking it. Then she pulled the binder containing the shell company documentation out of her duffel bag and placed it into the floral suitcase. After a quick look around, she exited the unit and secured the padlock.

Once inside her apartment, she unpacked the duffel bag and went down to the laundry room with a hamper of dirty clothes. She pulled out the floral sundress and held it up to the light. It smelled of sweat and faintly of wood. Maybe scotch? She wadded the dress into a ball and shoved it in the trash can with such force the plastic container tipped onto its side. Her breathing came in short huffs, as she willed the memory away. *Don't let it beat you. What's done is done.*

She returned to her room and set aside her work clothes for tomorrow, then studied her face in the mirror. The Band-Aid curled from her lip, exposing the unsightly wound. *I can't think about this now.* Mentally and physically exhausted, she showered and applied a glob of Neosporin to her lip, then climbed into bed. Shame surrounded her as she held the pillow to her face, shielding her from the ugliness of this world. Sleep dodged her this night.

CHAPTER 25

Pretense burst from the massive revolving door and landed in the lobby, the strap of the laptop bag tangled around her torso. Ignoring the curious stares, she gathered her wits and walked with a slant to Stairwell B, her exercise regimen top of mind. Her body ached from the attack, but she vowed to press on as though nothing had happened—like she'd always done. *Positive energy with a focus on optimum health and well-being*—her mantra.

She ascended the stairs with a sprint, pushing through the nagging discomfort. Despite her valiant efforts, her limbs gave way at the seventy-first floor. Pain seared through her muscles and her lip felt numb, as though it were feeding on Botox. She stumbled out of the stairwell and collapsed into a leather chair, gasping for air. When her breathing stabilized, she rode the elevator to the eighty-ninth floor, determined to resume her routine tomorrow.

She flicked on her office light and sank into the desk chair, then fired up her computer. Several email messages populated her inbox, most of them irrelevant. Her main focus nowadays—shanghaiing the Rothschilds' money. Everything else was a sideshow.

"Good morning, Pretense," said Daphne. "Oh, my. What happened to your lip?"

Pretense shrugged. "Oh, just a nasty cut. How was your weekend?"

Daphne bulged with fervor, her eyes rolling back, lashes flapping. "You remember Andrew, don't you—my boyfriend? Well, we went to a concert in Pennsylvania to see a Christian rock band. I was so nervous, because we've never spent the night together. Andrew booked a room with two queen beds, and we held hands in the space between us until we fell asleep. It was so romantic." She seemed to be gurgling or something.

Let me top that, kiddo. I had rough sex this weekend. Nothing more romantic than being stripped naked by a stranger and knocked to the floor. "Oh, wow, Daphne. What a perfect way to spend the weekend. It sounds heavenly."

"It was." She sucked in a gale of air. "I digress. The reason I came by was to tell you that on Friday some woman called asking for Pretense Abdicator. She said she was your mother, but I know your mother passed away. I didn't know what to say, so I told her you were out of the office." She handed Pretense a slip of paper. "She asked me to have you call her."

Pretense felt her bowels churn, a sickening bile rising in her throat. She exhaled deep and dropped her head into her hands, weaving another tale of doom. When she looked up, Daphne was wincing in anticipation. "Please, shut the door and take a seat." Pretense looked off. "Her name is Wanda. She was one of the foster parents I lived with. The state took me out of her home when ..." She placed her hand over her mouth, stuttering hiccups escaping from her fingers. Daphne looked on, her eyes brimming with tears. "The state took me when they learned I was being abused." She dropped her head again and covered her face.

"Oh, Pretense. Words cannot express my sorrow."

"It is what it is. But I need to ask a favor. Wanda is not right upstairs, if you know what I mean. She's been in and out of mental institutions, and every five years or so she manages to get in contact with me. Would you call her back and tell her that I resigned suddenly on Friday? Tell her I didn't leave forwarding information. Would you do that? And can I trust you—as a friend—to keep this confidential?"

"I will keep this confidential. You have my word. But I cannot tell her you resigned on Friday because you didn't. That would be lying."

"Right." Pretense looked off. "I'll call her."

Daphne rose from her chair and held out her arms. "Can I give you a hug?"

Pretense flinched. "Not today. I have important meetings and I don't want to wrinkle my blouse." Pretense stood and held the door open. Daphne exited.

As if I don't have enough to worry about, now I need to figure out how to get rid of Wanda. A phone rang inside her purse. She got up and closed her office door, then pulled out the two cell phones. It was the international phone. "Claire Voyant speaking."

"Hello, Ms. Voyant," said a slightly accented female voice. "This is Lan Chan calling from the PTS Bank in Singapore. You recently applied for a bank account for C Katz Investments, Inc. through our partner, Global Corporate Solutions. I'm pleased to inform you that the account has been approved. I will be sending the banking information to the Wilton, Connecticut, address you provided. You should receive it in five to ten days."

"Thank you so much," said Pretense, her grin stretching so wide, the cut on her lip broke open. She pulled a tissue from her drawer and dabbed at the lesion. "Would it be possible to receive the account information right now?"

"Of course. I am happy to do that." Lan Chan provided the information. "When you receive the paperwork in the mail, there will be instructions for setting up online banking."

"Regarding wire transfers, there will be several large deposits made over a period of three months," said Pretense. "Does PTS Bank limit the amount of a single wire transfer?"

"We do not place limits on the amount. As long as the money is from a legitimate source, it won't be a problem."

When the call ended, Pretense leaned back in her chair, her mind salivating as she smelled the aroma of $3 million sitting in her offshore bank account. Using the cell phone designated for C Katz Investments, she placed a call to Hyman Rothschild. When he answered, she slipped into a British accent. "Good afternoon, Hyman. It's Kate Spencer from C Katz Investments. I have good news. We have received clearance for you and Edna to begin investing."

"Wonderful," said Hyman. "I will work with Pretense to put through the first wire transfer of five-hundred-thousand dollars."

After providing Hyman with the offshore bank account number and other details, she hung up and waited for a call from Hyman. The desk phone rang ten minutes later. They agreed to meet tomorrow at six o'clock at the Rothschilds' penthouse on the Upper East Side.

"And come hungry," said Hyman. "We'll have our cook prepare a nice dinner."

———

At home that evening, Pretense kicked off her shoes and uncorked a bottle of wine. She plopped on the sofa and hoisted her glass into the air. "Here's to you, Claire Voyant." She took a hearty mouthful, her marred lip numb against the rim. A few more gulps later, she made the dreaded call.

"Hello," answered her mother's gruff voice bellowing into the phone, as the television screeched in the background.

"So, you found me."

"Damn straight I found you. You lied. You never worked at that Berkshire place. My friend Lola did some traversing on the

Google and up popped your name. Well, looky here, I says to myself. How many people in New York are named Pretense Abdicator? It said right there on the computer screen that you worked at Crawdad Spectrum for five years. The broad that answered the phone said you were out. So fess up."

Pretense took another slug of wine and a chaser gulp. "I'm going to say this real slow so it sinks in. I am not sending you any more money. You are not living with me in New York. I never want to see or hear from you again. And if you call me at work, I'll contact the police in New Mexico and tell them all your dirty secrets. Good riddance, Wanda."

"You little—"

Pretense pressed the END CALL button and drained the glass before pouring another. She leaned back into the sofa and held her fingers up before her eyes. Her hands were steady, her palms bone dry. And her heartbeat even, pattering softly. Something had changed. The umbilical cord had been severed. She sighed, picturing her mother circling the skies with her oxygen tank strapped to a broom, crashing into a cloud and evaporating in a puff of smoke.

CHAPTER 26

Pretense left the office and rode the subway to the Upper East Side, then walked the short distance to the address on Fifth Avenue near 81st Street. She entered the limestone building through massive mahogany doors and gave her name at the desk, then took the private elevator to the sixteenth floor. The doors opened to a vestibule with a single apartment door. She knocked and a woman greeted her and led her into a light-filled, formal living room with French doors leading out to a garden terrace overlooking Central Park. "I'll let Mr. Rothschild know you are here," said the woman.

Pretense turned in a circle, digesting the lavish surroundings, her wide eyes bounding from one priceless object to the next. Her entire apartment could fit into this one room.

"How good to see you," said Hyman. "Edna's in the kitchen with our cook, Rafaela, making sure everything is perfect. How about a glass of wine?"

"I'd love one. You have a beautiful home. Have you lived here long?"

"Twenty years. It's really too big for the two of us, but we love the location and the view."

Edna teetered into the room, balancing a silver platter of hors d'oeuvres. Several baguette slices topped with foie gras slid off the tray and onto the tapestry rug. Oblivious, she set the tray on a wine cart and went to Pretense with outstretched arms, before stopping. "That's a nasty cut on your lip."

"It looks worse than it is," said Pretense. "Just a silly accident, and it's too embarrassing to repeat."

"Well, thank you for coming and agreeing to assist with our first wire transfer." She turned to Hyman, uncorking a bottle of Bordeaux. "Hyman, dear, one never serves a Bordeaux with foie gras. Please open the bottle of Sauternes."

"Certainly, dear," said Hyman. "But what about the crackers on the rug? The Bordeaux might pair well with woven silk and wool notes."

Edna glanced down. "Oh, my. I should have had Rafaela serve the appetizers, but she was busy trussing the duck. I hope you like duck."

"I've never had duck. But I'm sure I'll love it."

After nibbling on appetizers and sipping white wine, Edna gave Pretense a tour of their two-story penthouse before dinner was served in the formal dining room. They took seats at one end of an expansive rectangular table situated beneath two ornate crystal chandeliers, dangling from a gold-leaf gilded ceiling. Rafaela brought out a platter of crispy roasted duck, along with bowls of plum applesauce, roasted Brussel sprouts, and mashed potatoes with caramelized onions. Pretense squirmed in her seat, straining to silence her growling stomach. She felt out of place among the ceremonious grandeur, but the Rothschilds seemed to enjoy her company—and she theirs. A shred of guilt pinged her brain, but she cast it aside.

Hyman raised his glass. "Here's to C Katz Investments, and to the brilliant mind of our guest tonight. May we enjoy many more working years together."

"That was a lovely toast," said Edna, passing the platter of duck to Pretense. "Now, don't be shy, dear. Eat up and put some meat on those bones."

"I'll try." Pretense shoveled a hearty helping onto her plate, determined to ease up on the wine. As they dined, she learned a great deal about the Rothschilds. They had met at Brown University in Rhode Island, and were married in the Hamptons two years later. A year after the wedding, Baron—their only child—was born. Hyman spent his entire career working in the family business, a commodities giant with operations spanning manufacturing, farming and food products and services. And Edna wasn't exactly a bottom feeder. Her father owned a very successful publishing company in New York. Between the two, they were dripping in assets.

"You've led very interesting lives," said Pretense, setting her silverware across her plate and dabbing her mouth with the linen napkin. "The meal was delicious."

Hyman stood, pushing his chair away. "It's after nine, and we don't want to keep you out late on a worknight. Are you ready to process the wire transfer?"

Pretense and Edna followed Hyman into the study. "Sit here at the desk in front of the computer," said Hyman to Pretense. "We will watch you this time, and hopefully, we'll be able to do this on our own going forward."

Pretense took a seat and pulled up the Crawford Spectrum website, then stood up. "Here, I'll let you type in your password."

Hyman sat at the desk and punched in his password using two index fingers, while Pretense looked the other way. On the third attempt, his account appeared.

"Okay, it's all yours," said Hyman, standing.

Pretense sat back down at the computer and asked Hyman for the bank account information Kate Spencer had provided. Then she completed the process for linking the Singapore bank to their account. After a series of verification steps, the offshore account was connected to the Crawford Spectrum account. "Now watch what I'm doing. You may want to write this down." She accessed the Rothschilds' money market account and processed the transfer, moving five hundred thousand dollars into the C Katz account. She wondered if the Rothschilds could hear her heart banging against her chest. She pushed away from the desk and stood. "It may take three to five days for the transfer to appear in the C Katz account. Kate will notify you when they've received the funds. Did she let you know when you should expect the first statement?"

"Yes, she did," Hyman responded. He reached over and hugged Edna. "Well, my dear, this calls for a toast. I'll ask Rafaela to bring a bottle of champagne. Pretense, please stay for a toast."

Pretense looked at her watch. It was after ten o'clock, but she had more to celebrate than they did. "I'd love a glass of champagne."

An hour later, Pretense got ready to leave.

"We've asked our driver to take you home," said Hyman. "He's waiting out front. Let's talk next week."

———

That night, she lay buried under the covers, swathed in luxury. Five-hundred-thousand dollars had just been transferred into her offshore bank account. One wire down, five to go. A rich smile broke on her face.

CHAPTER 27

Two weeks had passed since the first wire transfer. With the plan in full swing, Pretense had taken extra steps to cover her tracks. While out for a jog, she dropped by the storage facility and dropped off the credit card she'd received from the bank in Singapore. And in the event she needed to flee, she began holding back a portion of each paycheck and stashing the cash inside the storage unit. Until she officially became Claire Voyant, she didn't dare touch the money in her offshore bank account.

If everything went as projected, the Rothschilds would be processing the second transfer any day. When Pretense had called to thank them for dinner, Hyman seemed confident he could handle the remaining wires without her help. Nonetheless, she felt anxious. Her plan to leave the country in ten weeks hinged on the timely deposit of $3 million into her account.

She closed her office door and pulled out the dedicated cell phone for C Katz from her purse and punched in the Rothschilds' number. When Hyman answered, she engaged her British accent. "Hello, Hyman. Kate Spencer calling from C Katz Investments. I wanted to touch base and let you know that you should be receiving your first investment statement in a few weeks. I'm sure you'll be pleased with the returns. In the interim, is there anything I can do for you?"

"Thank you, Kate. I did check our current status on the website yesterday and was quite pleased. Edna and I were just discussing the account, and are getting ready to make the second wire transfer. I'm glad you called. We were wondering if we should take advantage of the upswing by decreasing the number of installments and increasing the amount. So instead of sending five hundred thousand this time, maybe we wire a million, then decide later how to disburse the remaining amount. What do you think?"

Neurons rapid-fired. Hyman's strategy would work to her advantage and potentially bump up her exit plan. The sooner she got out of the country, the better. She was dizzy with excitement. "I like the idea," she said. "But I want you to be comfortable with your decision. Why don't you take a day or two to decide?" Hyman agreed.

After she hung up, her desk phone rang. It was Hyman asking for Pretense's opinion. Pretense thought through her response, not wanting to sound too eager. "Well, I checked the website last night, and I must admit the returns have been impressive. But it's a gamble, as you know. I'd recommend you go with your gut instinct. Do you need help making the second transfer?"

"I should be okay. Our gut instinct is telling us to double up and invest one million dollars now. I'll let you know if we change direction. As always, thanks for your help."

Soon, she would be a millionaire—$1.5 million, to be exact. Pretense got up, her feet barely touching the ground, and burst through her office door. Ariana stumbled back and froze. "Good morning," said Pretense. "Were you waiting for me?"

"No, no," Ariana stammered. "I was walking by, and you startled me."

Pretense gave her a once over. "You seem jumpy. Is every-thing okay?"

"I'm fine. Just a lot on my mind." Her body loosened, giving way to a charming smile. "Hey, what are you doing for lunch today? We haven't talked in a while."

Pretense loathed the offer, but she needed to keep her enemies close. "I don't have any plans."

"Great. Let's grab something from the cafeteria around noon."

———

Pretense and Ariana found an open spot in the busy dining hall and set their trays on the table. While Pretense dug into her salad, Ariana picked at her sandwich, tossing her head from side to side, occasionally waving to a passerby. *Does she even know these people? They don't seem to be waving back.*

"So," said Ariana, as though suddenly aware of Pretense's presence, "how are things going with your clients?"

"Things are going well," said Pretense. "What about yours? We never talk about your clients."

She balked. "I guess we don't. I have quite a few clients, but their portfolios pale in comparison with those of the Rothschilds. I've been working with Mr. Crawford, trying to leverage my current client base as a prospecting strategy. We plan to host a client appreciation event. I'm going to ask my customers to invite their friends and relatives. It's a lot of work, but maybe one day I will land an account like the Rothschilds." She looked off, likely scouting for imaginary friends. "Speaking of the Roth-schilds, have they started donating to that cult—the one you told me about—The Children of the Moon?" she said in a whisper.

"The sun, not the moon." Pretense leaned forward and answered in a low voice. "You haven't told anyone, have you? You gave me your word."

"I would never share a friend's secret."

"I knew I could count on you. Here's what I know. A chunk of money has been transferred out of their account. I haven't asked them about it. The less I know, the better."

"Do you believe their story about the cult? I don't. Maybe they made it up to keep you from asking questions. Think about it. Who would want to get into a conversation with a religious zealot?" said Ariana, shuddering. "Certainly not me."

"Unfortunately, I do believe them. That's why I avoid the subject."

Ariana hid her reaction behind a poker face. "Interesting," she said, enunciating each syllable. "So, how big was the chunk of money?"

"I'm not at liberty to say." Pretense looked at her watch. "I should get back to work. This was nice. We should have lunch more often."

"I'm game whenever you are."

———

That evening, Pretense pulled out her laptop and brought up the Rothschilds' balance in the Crawford Spectrum money market account. One point five million remained. The second transfer went through. Her excitement dimmed as she pondered her conversation with Ariana. Pretense felt uneasy. Perhaps the best thing to do would be to flee the country now and forget about the remaining money. She would have enough to live comfortably, so why risk it? *Because I deserve it, that's why!* No, she would go the whole nine yards and take everything due her. She would have enough money to alter her appearance and open a small beachside café somewhere tropical. And Claire Voyant would live happily ever after.

With sudden determination, she double-clicked the *C Katz Monthly Statements* folder and began typing numbers into the template she'd created earlier—credible numbers that might drive the Rothschilds to further expedite their investment plan. When she finished, she updated the C Katz website, knowing that Hyman and Edna were watching it like two hawks. She gave thanks to the Money Gods for greed.

CHAPTER 28

Exiting the A Stairwell at the eighty-ninth floor, Pretense walked the short distance to the Crawford Spectrum suite. As she passed Simon Crawford's office, she heard muffled voices inside. A beam of light emerged from beneath the closed door. A female's cackle could be heard above the hum of the air-conditioning unit. *Ariana.*

Pretense headed toward the kitchen. A few minutes later, Ariana swept in. "Good morning. Looks like I beat you in today. I had an early meeting with Mr. Crawford about my upcoming client event."

"How is that going?" asked Pretense, pulling down a mug from the cupboard.

"Better than expected. So far, thirty people have RSVP'd. You're welcome to come if you like. Free drinks and dinner."

"Thanks, but I'll pass." Pretense poured a cup of coffee, steam snaking up her arm like a deadly asp. "Sorry I can't stick around and chat. I have a boatload of work to get done this morning."

When she returned to her office, a message appeared from Hyman Rothschild calling to say that after seeing the returns posted on the website, they were considering transferring another $1 million late in the week or early next week. They were going to be in the area and would like to stop in. She called them back and suggested they meet at a nearby diner. Her plan had worked.

Simon appeared at her door. "Good morning. It looks like the Rothschilds have moved more money out of the money market account. Has there been any discussion of potentially transferring more than they initially planned?"

"Honestly, I don't believe so. Hyman has been pretty upfront with me. In fact, he called this morning to say he had given my name to one of his friends from their country club. I don't think he would be handing out referrals if he wasn't pleased with Crawford Spectrum."

Simon nodded. "That is a good sign. Maybe you should invite his referral to Ariana's client event. Of course, I would ask that you attend also, since it would be your prospect."

"That's an excellent idea. I'll look at my schedule."

———

Pretense spotted Hyman and Edna sitting at a back table in the small diner. Hyman looked uncomfortably out of place amongst white t-shirted waiters wearing grease-stained aprons and shouting orders in broken English through a pass-through window behind the counter.

"Sorry about the setting," said Pretense, taking a seat.

"It's fine," said Edna. "I'm rather enjoying it. It's a nice change of pace." Hyman wrinkled his nose.

"What I get for you?" shouted the waiter, dragging a pen from behind his ear and licking the tip. The waiter took their orders, scribbling furiously on a small note pad, then snatched their menus and left.

"Friendly place," said Hyman. He clasped his hands atop the table and leaned forward. "Did you happen to look at the C Katz website today?"

"Yes," said Pretense. "I pulled it up after we spoke this morning."

"What would you do in our situation? We took your advice and went with our gut last time, but we value your opinion. We don't know Kate that well, so we wanted to talk this through with you first."

"One split salad, one soup, three waters," said the waiter, tossing their dishes like Frisbees across the plastic checkered tablecloth.

Pretense paused until the waiter had left. "If markets are trending upward, it sometimes makes sense to implement a strategic asset allocation quickly. Historically, investors who take this risk have been rewarded with positive returns over the long run. But of course, that's not always the case. If I were in your shoes, I would move one million now and the remaining five hundred thousand in two weeks." She picked up her spoon and sipped her soup.

Hyman slowly nodded. "I have to agree. Why wait? In fact, maybe we should move more money out of Crawford Spectrum and into C Katz."

Pretense wobbled, knocking her spoon off the table. As much as she wanted the money, a brash move like this would bring unwanted interrogation from Simon. "I wouldn't recommend that approach. Remember, the Crawford Spectrum allocation is more conservative, giving you a more balanced portfolio overall."

Edna reached across the table and patted Pretense's hand. "If you're worried about losing our account at Crawford Spectrum, don't be. We would speak to the higher-ups at C Katz Investments and insist they hire you as our personal adviser. We have no relationship with Kate. For all we know, she could be a robot. She hasn't done anything for us other than take our money."

"That's very kind of you, but that's not what I'm worried about. I honestly think that the allocation we've been discussing is the best strategy. And just to reassure you, Kate is a very skillful financial adviser."

"Maybe she's right, dear," said Hyman. "We will make a transfer tonight." He turned to Pretense. "Thank you for your patience with us. I know we can be a handful at times."

"Don't be ridiculous. I'm here to help, and I always have your best interests at heart." She smiled, her eyes glowing like neon dollar signs.

CHAPTER 29

The following morning, Pretense took a deep breath and pulled up the Rothschild account, her fingers quivering on the keyboard. Her eyes grew absurdly wide, as she stared at the screen. The balance in their money market account was five hundred thousand dollars, meaning her offshore bank account balance should be $2.5 million. With her arms behind her head, she leaned back, visualizing lazy days spent swimming with a rainbow of tropical fish, exploring sea caves on a kayak, strolling the food stalls while ogling fragrantly cooked vegetables and unidentified things on sticks. Maybe Thailand. Maybe Australia. The options were endless.

"Pretense. Excuse me, Pretense."

She tipped forward in her chair, her torso slamming up against her desk. "Oh, sorry, Mr. Crawford. I was just tossing around several investment strategies for my new prospect—the one I told you about—Hyman's friend Morley."

"Ah, yes. Did you invite him to the client event?"

"I did. But unfortunately, he will be in Tanzania on an African safari. But he did say he is definitely interested." She held up her thumb and forefinger, rubbing them together. "He'll be back in the country sometime in late September and will give me a call."

"That's great news. Maybe we can plan a lunch meeting for the three of us."

"Excellent. I'll call and get something on his calendar."

He turned to walk away, then pivoted. "I almost forgot. The reason I came by was to talk about office space. As you know, our VP of Operations is retiring. I'd like to move you into his office. It's a much nicer space and closer to my office."

"Won't you need that space for his replacement?"

"I'll move his replacement into your office."

Pretense thought about her loss of privacy. "I'm truly honored," she said, placing a hand to her chest. "This is so unexpected. But I would like to respectfully decline. This may sound peculiar, but I do some of my best thinking in this office. It's my Zen zone. I'm very superstitious."

He lifted an eyebrow. "I never knew that about you."

"You'd be surprised at some of the things you don't know about me."

"Well, I certainly won't do anything to disrupt your environment. If you change your mind, let me know."

"Thank you. I will."

After he left, she saw Ariana whizzing past her door with the gold chain strap of her Fendi bag crisscrossed over her body. It must be lunchtime. She could use some fresh air. She grabbed her purse and headed out.

She walked toward Hanover Square, where food trucks and carts were parked, among them Lucky Lan Thai. An opportune time to become more familiar with Thai cuisine, and the long line at the window spoke volumes. She quickly got in queue. Ten minutes later, she reached the front of the line and stepped up to the window perusing the menu posted on plexiglass. "I haven't tried the food here," she said to the Asian woman taking orders. "What would you suggest?"

"C'mon lady," said the man behind her. "Speed it up."

Pretense turned to him and smirked. "Of course." Then speaking as slowly as she possibly could, she asked about the ingredients and calorie count in each dish before settling on Drunkman Noodles. After receiving her order, she took the warm aluminum pan to a nearby park bench and savored her lunch, swimming through a maze of bold, fresh flavors and daydreaming about island life.

As she watched sidewalk faces rushing past, she spotted Ariana across the street, entering a bistro. She got up and headed toward the nearest trash receptacle, dumping her garbage, then she turned in the direction of the office but stopped. *I wonder if she's meeting someone.* She altered direction and walked across the street, lingering outside the eatery before stepping inside, pretending to examine the menu. In the far corner of the restaurant, she spotted Ariana engaged in conversation with an older man. She didn't recognize the man until he turned. Pretense froze, panic clutching its grip around her throat. Baron. Baron Rothschild.

She spun and fled through the door, possibilities flooding her brain. Maybe a freak coincidence—one of her many lovers who just so happened to be the son of Hyman and Edna. But her gut told her otherwise. Things were starting to make sense; Ariana digging through her files, the probing questions, lingering around outside her door. *What does she know?* She needed to find out before it was too late.

After returning to the office, she stopped by the lobby and asked Daphne to let her know when Ariana returned from lunch, then she walked back to her office, dread gnawing her insides. She paced the floor, chewing on a fingernail. *Think. Think.* There was no incriminating evidence in her file drawer, except the notes on the Crawford Spectrum account. And she had been careful when in Ariana's company. It had to be the hallway antics. Could she hear through the door? She tried recalling specific conversations she'd had when she'd spotted Ariana skulking outside her office. She sat down, rubbing her temples, when the desk phone rattled. Daphne was calling to inform her that Ariana had returned from lunch.

She headed down the hall to Ariana's office. The knock startled Ariana as she admired herself in a small, compact mirror.

"Hey, I was checking out the menu at Le' Bistro today," said Pretense. "I thought I saw you in the back, sitting with Baron Rothschild."

Ariana pulled her eyes away from the mirror. "You should have come over. How do you know Baron?"

"Baron is Hyman and Edna's son. I met him at a charity event."

She threw her hand to her forehead. "You're kidding."

"You never made the connection? Baron Rothschild?"

"I didn't know his last name was Rothschild. I met him a few nights ago when I was out with friends. He asked for my number. We decided to meet for lunch today."

"You do know he's married, right?"

"Married? He never mentioned a wife. Not that it matters, but thanks for the heads-up."

Pretense pushed Ariana's door shut and sat, leaning in and making a steeple with her fingers. "I'm not comfortable having one of my peers dating the son of my wealthiest client. Especially given the confidential information I've shared with you about their donations."

"As I said, my lips are sealed. But that shouldn't affect my relationship with him."

Pretense pushed her chair back and stood. "I'll speak with Mr. Crawford and get his opinion."

Ariana bolted upright. "Wait. This is none of Mr. Crawford's business."

"Oh, but I think it is his business. After all, he is part-owner of this firm."

"If you tell him, then I might have to share the story about the cult."

"If you share the story, I'll deny it."

Ariana wilted. "I won't see him again. You have my word."

Pretense stabbed a stare, then opened the door and left. Ariana was up to something, and Baron likely the driver. According to the Rothschilds, Baron was fanatical about his inheritance. But she didn't believe Simon had any involvement. Not based on Ariana's reaction. She stood in her office, her arms wrapped around herself, fingering the locket around her neck. Maybe the time to flee had come.

CHAPTER 30

Griffin McCoy leaned back in his chair and stroked his grizzled beard, his foot tapping the floor. The woman was a liar, and while that didn't make her a criminal, financial advisers didn't typically persuade clients to invest in other firms.

Baron Rothschild had come to Griffin with concerns about his parents' financial adviser. "With a name like Pretense Abdicator, I'd be concerned, too," he'd mumbled at the time. Baron hadn't wanted his parents to know about his concerns until he had proof. He had paid a woman who had worked with Pretense to keep an eye on her—a woman named Ariana Primrose. She had overheard a conversation between the Rothschilds and Pretense about a private fund not offered through Crawford Spectrum. Ariana hadn't been sure about the name of the fund, but thought it sounded like *Seacats* or *Seacast*. Baron became suspicious, and that suspicion intensified when he heard her give a speech at a charity event about her upbringing. He did some investigating and learned Pretense hadn't grown up in foster homes, as she had claimed. In fact, she lived in a trailer park in Gallup, New Mexico with her mother, Wanda, until she went away to Harvard.

Having spent over twenty-five years in the FBI, mostly in white-collar crime, Griffin was intrigued. A sizeable portion of the Rothschilds money had been set aside in a money-market account with the intent to invest elsewhere. When Ariana Primrose tried to find out where, Pretense came up with some wild story about a cult. Neither Baron nor Ariana believed the story, nor could they confirm that the money had been transferred. And Baron was hesitant to approach the partner in the firm of Crawford Spectrum until he had proof.

Griffin pulled a leather-bound notebook from his attaché case and began jotting down notes. He buzzed his secretary, Helen, and asked her to clear his schedule. According to Baron, a very generous bonus would be waiting if Griffin could wrap up his findings within two weeks.

His first task would be to determine the name of the investment firm Pretense had recommended. After spending the better part of the afternoon searching online for investment firms similar to the name Seacats or Seacast, he about gave up, ready to explore another avenue when he decided to change his search criteria, using the letter C followed by "cats" or "cast." Then he tried "kats" and "katz." Bingo. A website appeared for a C Katz Investments under the URL CKatz.com. The website appeared legitimate. The company was headquartered in Wilton, Connecticut. He dialed the phone number listed on the website, and a woman with a British accent answered—a Kate Spencer. He told the woman he was researching private funds and was interested in making an investment with C Katz. Kate briefly explained the minimum investment amount and indicated that anyone interested must first be referred. Griffin asked if he could meet with her at the office in Connecticut to learn more, but the woman declined, saying he would need a referral. She also indicated they were in the process of moving to another location and quickly ended the call. The conversation felt rushed. The woman seemed curt, something he wouldn't expect from a prestigious firm catering to wealthy investors. He called his wife and told her not to hold dinner, then left his office for the hour drive to Wilton.

He exited the freeway in Wilton, Connecticut, in search of the address listed on the website, turning down a side street and into an industrial area. A few blocks ahead, he located the building. The sign out front read THE PARCEL SPOT. It was nothing more than a mailbox service. Being a private firm by referral only, C Katz Investments may have elected not to publish its official office address on the website, but something wasn't sitting right with him.

On the drive back to the city, Griffin stopped at McDonald's and ordered a Big Mac, a large fry, and a chocolate shake. The wife wouldn't approve—not good for his high cholesterol. But steamed vegetables and poached fish every night wasn't good for his marriage. He ate in the car, enjoying the caloric delectable and flipping through his notes. The next step would be to determine the website's creator.

Griffin returned to his office after eight o'clock. He didn't like working late, but the offer of a generous bonus would help pay for the new furniture his wife had ordered. He pulled up the C Katz website and checked the footer, where developers sometimes added their credentials. Nothing. He checked a querying database, listing registered assignees of domain names. Nothing. Stymied, he called his friend Dick at the FBI. Dick answered on the first ring. After giving him crap about being semiretired and working until 10 p.m., he said he would do some digging and get back to him tomorrow. Griffin packed his briefcase and left the office.

The following morning, Dick called. "Hey, I got some information for you. A guy named Brian Hansen in Palm Springs, California, created the C Katz website. I found a phone number and the guy's address."

Griffin booked a flight leaving in the morning.

———

When the plane touched down in Palm Springs, Griffin collected keys at the rental car desk and exited the air-conditioned terminal. He removed his blazer and tie, found his rental vehicle, and set out for Hansen's. On the way, he made a detour to an In-N-Out Burger joint. He'd heard about the West Coast chain for years. From the limited menu inside the restaurant, he ordered a Double-Double, fries, and a milkshake that claimed to be made with real ice cream. He took the meal to his car and wolfed it down, his hamburger addiction temporarily sated. As he exited the parking lot, he gazed at the empty wrappers on the front seat, then made a U-turn, looping back into the lot and getting in line at the drive-thru window. He placed the same order to-go, then drove off, the perfume of grilled onions filling the car.

Brian Hansen's apartment was located on the second floor with an outside entrance. Griffin climbed the cement steps and knocked on door 2C. No answer. He went back to his vehicle and waited. As he finished his second Double-Double, a metallic blue Suzuki X-90 pulled into the parking lot. A muscular man emerged from the miniature car, unfolding to well over six feet. The man walked with a slight limp and headed to the stairway, then unlocked the door of 2C. Griffin waited five minutes, then climbed the stairs and knocked on the door.

Brian answered. "Can I help you?"

Griffin presented his card and identified himself as a private investigator. "Are you Brian Hansen?"

"Yes. What is this about?"

"If I may, I'd like to ask you some questions about a website I believe you may have created. Do you mind if I come in?"

Brian held open the door and waved him in. "Have a seat."

Griffin pulled out a notepad and sat in the chair opposite Brian. "I won't take up a lot of your time. A client of mine is interested in a site that, according to my investigation, was created by you. Are you the developer of CKatz.com?"

Brian's eyebrows rose. "Yes. I set up the basic framework for a friend, and she was going to add the content."

Griffin nodded. "My client is concerned about his elderly parents who may be planning to invest money in C Katz Investments. This client is trying to determine if the company is legitimate."

"Investing?" said Brian. "My friend is an actress. The site is named after her stage name. She wanted a website that would promote her acting experience." Brian flipped open his laptop and typed in the URL and waited while the site loaded. "To be honest, I haven't looked at it since setting it up." His eyes narrowed as he browsed the site. "Interesting."

"If I may, what is your friend's name—the actress?"

Brian's face paled. "Is she in trouble?"

"I'm not at liberty to say. And you are not required to answer my questions. But I will tell you, as a former FBI agent, that you could be considered an accessory if any wrongdoing is uncovered. I'd suggest you be as honest as you can."

Brian stood and paced the room, his hands on his hips. He sat back down and looked off. "Her name is Claire. She said she was planning to move from New Jersey to California. We hung out a few times. I spoke to her a couple of times after she left. When I last tried calling, the phone had been disconnected. I never heard from her again."

Griffin scribbled notes as Brian relayed the story about the California State identification card. "Do you have the address where you sent the card?" Griffin asked.

"I don't. I tossed it once it was sent."

"Do you happen to know Claire's last name?"

"I know Katz was her stage name." He chewed at his lower lip. "It was a funny name. I remember commenting about it, but I'm drawing a blank." He snapped his fingers. "Wait. It's Voyant. You know, like clairvoyant."

Griffin scribbled in his notebook. "Can you describe what she looked like?"

"Tall and slender—nice figure. Wild hair and a hooked nose. Plain looking, but I liked her personality. Quirky. Different from most. And a chipped front tooth. I remember thinking she might be pretty if she tried a little harder. But I guess that's what I liked about her. She didn't try too hard."

Griffin closed his notebook and stood. "You've been very helpful. If you think of anything else, you have my card." He extended his hand. "Thanks for your time." As he turned to walk away, Brian stopped him.

"I just remembered something. I found a locket in my car. When I went to her hotel to return it to her, I gave her name at the front desk. They told me no one by that name had stayed there."

Griffin noted the comment. "Thanks again." When he returned to his car, he flipped through his notes from his earlier meeting with Baron. He didn't have a photo of Pretense, but he did have a description which matched the description Brian had provided of Claire.

The next day, Griffin drove to the Palm Springs office of the Department of Motor Vehicles and spoke to a supervisor. After extensive questioning, the supervisor relented and pulled out a file labeled "Claire Voyant." Inside the manila folder was a copy of Claire's birth certificate and California State ID card with a photo. The picture was that of a blond-headed woman baring a slight resemblance to Pretense, but Griffin couldn't be sure. He was given permission to make copies.

Afterward, he drove to the Riverside County Clerk Recorder and asked to meet with Barbara Hines, the woman who had signed off on the birth certificate. Barbara remembered Claire and nodded her confirmation when shown the photo ID. "I felt sorry for the young lady," said Barbara. "She had gone through so much, what with being raised in a commune like that wacky Manson family. I was happy I could be of help."

His last stop, the Marco Hotel. He went inside and flashed his ID card at the young man working the front desk. "I need info on a guest who stayed here." Griffin provided the dates Brian had given him. "Can you tell me if this hotel booked a room under any of the following names: Claire Voyant, Claire Katz, or Pretense Abdicator."

The clerk's hands quivered, sweat peppered his upper lip. He scrolled through several screens, searching. "I think I found something. Pretense Abdicator. She—I think it's a she—booked a room on those dates. It looks like she paid in cash. I can't answer any other questions. It's my first day on the job. The manager will be here in the morning."

Griffin smiled and thanked the young man. "Excellent job, son. Thanks for your help."

CHAPTER 31

Back in New York, Griffin drove to the apartment address Baron had provided. Being early afternoon, Pretense would likely be working. He found a parking spot on the street one block down and walked to the three-story walk-up. Skimming the nameplates next to the door phone, he buzzed all but *Abdicator*. The door clicked and he entered the small vestibule.

An older woman leaned over the second-floor stairwell. "Stop right there," she said. "Do you have permission to be on this property? I'm the apartment manager, Mrs. Whipple. I heard all the buzzers go off. If you're up to no good, I have a gun, and I'm not afraid to use it."

Griffin froze and held up his hands. "Ma'am. I'm just going to slowly reach inside my breast pocket and show you my credentials. My name is Griffin McCoy. I'm a private investigator."

"Private investigator?" She beamed, raising her hand to pat tufts of hair trapped beneath a mesh hairnet. "How can I help you?"

"Do you mind if I come up and ask a few questions?"

"Certainly. I'm making tea if you'd like to join me."

"That would be nice," said Griffin, heading up the stairs. He took a seat at her kitchen table and glanced around the claustrophobic space. Vapor erupted from a large, active pot on the stove, the smell of rotten eggs seeping beneath a partially opened lid. His stomach convulsed.

"Why don't we go into the front room and sit on the davenport?" said Mrs. Whipple, wiping her hands on a frilly, floral apron. "I'll bring our tea there, where it's more comfortable."

Mrs. Whipple returned to the front room with two teacups and set them on the table. "I'm making golabki for dinner. It's my grandmother's recipe."

Griffin forced a smile. "It sounds like you are busy, so I won't keep you." He pulled out a notepad.

"Oh, it's just me for dinner. I have all day to roll the little pigeons. That's what we call stuffed cabbage in the old country. My grandmother hails from Poland."

"Well, I'm sure they are delicious. So, the reason I am here is to ask about one of your tenants. A woman named Pretense Abdicator."

She fanned herself with her hand, her eyes rolling uphill. "Strange woman, that Pretense. And quite the klutz. What has she done? Tripped over the Empire State Building?"

He grinned. "Nothing, I'm sure. The company she works for is auditing their employees. They want to keep everything confidential. Can I ask that you not discuss our visit?"

"Oh, my, yes. You know, when I was younger, I wanted to be a secret agent. Spying seems to come naturally for me." She snickered. "And I'm a huge fan of James Bond. You know," she said, tapping her finger on her chin, "you're a dead ringer for that Bond man, Sean Connery." She looked off, as though picturing herself leaping from a flaming vehicle with an AK-47 slung over her shoulder. "I'm sorry. You were saying?"

Griffin took a sip of tea. "Pretense. What can you tell me about her? Her habits? Does she seem ethical? The type of people who come and go from her apartment? Anything you can think of that might help me determine her overall standing. Basically, I am doing a character audit."

"Character?" Mrs. Whipple rolled in her lips. "Well, aside from being incredibly clumsy, she does seem to be ethical. She pays her rent timely. I never smell pot—and I would know, because I tried it once." She chortled and paused. "Friends? I don't think she has any. The only people that go to her apartment are delivery people. Basically, she's a good renter, just peculiar. And she had that damn cat. She called him Kat. 'Kat with a K,' she told me. I offered to watch the beast when she left town for a week. The thing ran away, thank God, after it attacked me." She pushed her hairnet up exposing a small scar partially obscured by a hairy mole. "See here? It nearly mauled me to death."

Griffin made a note. Kat. Katz. *Did she name the company after her cat?* "You are lucky to be alive. Do you recall the dates when she went away?"

Mrs. Whipple provided the exact dates, which matched the days Brian had said he spent with her in California.

"Now, about Pretense's habits. Did you ever notice anything out of the ordinary? Some odd behavior you hadn't noticed in the past?"

Mrs. Whipple twisted her mouth, then clicked her tongue several times. "As a matter of fact, yes. There was that time she came home wearing a blond wig, and her face was all made up. I didn't recognize her, at first. She's a homely girl, but not that day. She said she had gone to a masquerade party, which struck me as strange since she arrived home in the afternoon. Who throws a midday masquerade party?"

"How long ago was that?"

"Maybe three weeks ago. Maybe more. I can't really say." Her eyes darted from side to side. "Oh my, I've forgotten my cabbage." She stood abruptly and dashed into the kitchen. "It's probably overcooked. I'll be right there. I need to drain it."

Metal pots clattered against the stainless-steel sink, as a thick cloud of steam rolled past Griffin, bathing the windows and mirrors in a dense condensation, the stench unbearable. He grabbed his notebook and headed for the door. "Mrs. Whipple, I just realized I'm late for an appointment. I really must be going. I'll leave my card on the table. If you think of anything else, please call. Thank you for your time."

Her voice called out after him as he hightailed it down the stairs. "If you'd like some golabki, come back tomorrow about this time."

"Thank you for the offer," he yelled over his shoulder. When he reached the sidewalk, he loosened his tie and bent over, taking several deep breaths until his stomach settled. Maybe the wife's cooking wasn't that bad, after all.

When he returned to his office, a voicemail message lit his phone. "Hello, Sean Connery. I mean Mr. McCoy." He heard a snort. "This is Mrs. Whipple. I remembered something after you left. Call me if you desire."

When he returned her call, Mrs. Whipple relayed the story about a metal box Pretense had dropped in the apartment lobby. "She quickly gathered the contents, but she had overlooked something. When I picked it up, I noticed it was a California State ID with a photo of a blond woman. She said it was her friend's. If memory serves me, I think the name on the ID was Claire something, but I didn't get a good look at the last name." Griffin thanked her and apologized for not taking her up on the offer of golabki, then hung up. He could still smell cabbage lingering on his attaché case.

He stood before the wall-mounted whiteboard and jotted down his thoughts with a black marker. He had a photograph of Pretense, compliments of Baron's contact, Ariana. He taped the image to the board next to the photo ID of Claire he'd received from the California Department of Motor Vehicles. The two women looked similar. He stood back, rolling the black marker in his fingers, assessing the probable facts: *Claire Voyant and Pretense Abdicator are likely one and the same. Which means that*

Pretense is the owner of the C Katz Investments website. And according to Baron, Pretense was overheard recommending C Katz Investments to the Rothschilds. And then there were the unanswered questions: *Is Kate Spencer Pretense Abdicator, or is there another culprit in the mix? Is C Katz Investments a legitimate company, and who is the owner? Has the Rothschilds' money been transferred, and if so, how much and to where?*

Griffin called his friend Dick at the FBI and asked if he would do a voice analysis using a phone conversation he had recorded while speaking with Kate Spencer and compare it with a phone conversation with Pretense Abdicator. It took a bit of persuading, as this was an involved, and not entirely authorized, request. In the meantime, Griffin would attempt to uncover the location where C Katz was incorporated.

A public records search produced nothing. His gut told him the company was likely set up as a shell company—an area in which he had extensive experience from his days in the FBI. If that were the case, connecting Claire Voyant or Pretense Abdicator to C Katz would prove difficult, if not impossible. And the research could drag on for months, exploring every possible jurisdiction—anywhere from Delaware to Denmark—taking him well past the two-week limit for that generous bonus.

He chose a different path. Griffin asked Baron if it were possible to speak candidly to his parents. Baron declined but instead offered to contact the Rothschilds' maid, Rafaela, and offer her compensation if she would go through Hyman's office and look for materials with the C Katz name. Rafaela seemed hesitant at first, until Baron explained that he felt his parents were being conned. A few days later, Rafaela called Baron after finding a C Katz investment brochure in Hyman's desk. In addition, she recalled a woman, Pretense Abdicator, who came for dinner one night, and she was positive she overhead them discussing C Katz Investments.

Dick called later that day and confirmed that the voice analysis suggested Kate Spencer and Pretense Abdicator were the same person. Griffin advised Baron and he agreed to bring Abdicator's employer on board.

Baron arranged the meeting with Simon Crawford in Griffin's office to review the case. As Simon listened to the evidence, including the fact that Baron had used Ariana as a mole, his face drained. "I can't believe this," he said, slumping in the chair. "I trusted her. Pretense had so much promise."

"Can you tell us how much money has been transferred out of the Rothschilds' account?" Griffin asked.

"Of the three million set aside in the money market account, two point five million has been transferred." Simon stood and paced the office floor. "Baron, do your parents know about this?"

"No, and I'd rather not say anything until the FBI is brought in," Baron answered.

"FBI?" Simon drew his hand over his chin. "Is that necessary?"

"We have circumstantial evidence, but we lack direct evidence," Griffin responded. "The FBI will be able to get a search warrant on her personal computer and her apartment—something I'm not able to do. But before we get the FBI officially engaged, I have one last ace up my sleeve, but I need your help," Griffin said, turning to Simon. "It sounds like there is another five hundred thousand waiting to be transferred. What if you instructed your IT group to temporarily shut down the wire transfer system first thing tomorrow—maybe blame it on a computer bug or a security breach—and encourage clients who didn't want to wait until the system came back up to instead write a check? If the Rothschilds were to write a check, is there a way Crawford Spectrum could stop payment on the check without the Rothschilds knowing?"

"I believe I can, but I don't understand where you are going with this," said Simon.

Griffin walked over to the whiteboard and pointed to the Wilton, Connecticut mailbox address. "On the C Katz website, the only address listed is in Wilton, Connecticut—it's a mailbox service. If my hunch is correct, when Pretense informs the Rothschilds about the problem with the wire transfer system, she'll suggest they write a check. That check would likely be sent to the Wilton address, and if Pretense is involved—as we believe she is—she will physically show up at that location to retrieve the check. I'll have round-the-clock surveillance set up, snapping photos."

Baron listened, nodding his head.

"As long as she doesn't perceive there is a threat, I doubt she will flee the country immediately," said Griffin. "She will probably take a few days to tie up loose ends. That's why it is absolutely critical that we keep this under wraps and not share our conversation with anyone outside this room, including the inside contact, Ariana. The fewer people that know, the better."

Simon turned away and gazed out the window. "Let's do it." The following day, Simon sent out a company communication regarding the temporary shutdown of wire transfers. Griffin then added a team of private investigators to stake out the Wilton mailbox location, working round the clock. In the meantime, Griffin met with his friend Dick at the local FBI office and summarized the details of the case. According to Dick, if Griffin provided evidence of Pretense retrieving mail from the Wilton mailbox assigned to C Katz Investments, he would take over the case.

CHAPTER 32
PRESENT DAY - SEPTEMBER 11, 2001

Panic pulsed through Pretense's body, as she groped her way within the frantic chaos toward the A Stairwell. A quick glance over her shoulder confirmed the worst. The office door remained jammed in the same position when she squeezed through, likely trapping everyone inside; Simon, Baron, Thelma, and the FBI agent and private investigator. Her throat shrunk. She passed a cluster of frenzied figures, turning in circles, as ceiling tiles cascaded from above exposing gaping holes and dangling wires. She kept her head down to avoid being recognized, but no one seemed to care. Moving along at breakneck speed, she scaled downed partition walls and over-turned furniture, until she reached the stairwell door. Once inside, the clamor of desperate voices and the acrid stench of kerosene engulfed the congested space. Pieces of drywall were strewn along the stairs exposing heavy steel beams. With only one shoe, she tried quickening her pace, but could barely make out the luminescent stripe on each step.

Thirty minutes into the stairwell descent, a bottleneck of people inched their way forward. Two men were walking abreast, their hands interlocked, as they carried a disabled woman. Then everyone came to a complete stop.

"We can't get through," shouted a woman up ahead. "There's a wall down. It's blocking our path. Turn around and go back up."

The group switched direction, but Pretense and another man continued downward. When they reached the obstruction, the man used his body as a brace, and held it aloft while Pretense slid underneath. After she reached the other side, she found two discarded briefcases and wedged them under the blockage, while the man pushed his way under. They continued at a faster pace until they came upon another section of collapsed wall. They mounted the unsteady barrier and were helped down by a group of people on the other side. As she forged ahead, light filled the stairway, illuminating the floor number marked on the stairwell door. Number thirty. A deflated sigh escaped. She assumed she was farther down. Fresh terror crept up within her, her heart staggering in her chest. "Keep it together," she chanted. "You can do this." A few floors down, the steps became slick with water and fuel, the rubber sole of her lone running shoe skidding on the surface. She pulled off the shoe and tossed it aside, moving as fast as her legs would allow until another road-block appeared. A column of firefighters was ascending the stairs, loaded down with equipment.

"Keep moving down," one of them said, breathing heavily. "The stairway is open all the way down."

She hugged the wall to let them pass, staring into the resolute faces of men and women—young and old, black and white—all risking their lives to save others. A lump formed in her throat. Nothing seemed real.

As she moved down the stairs, the building quaked, then a roaring force blew open the stairwell doors, filling the space with flying debris, almost knocking her to the ground. She clung to the handrail and looked back. The heavy steel doors were flapping like cardboard, then the lights flickered and went out. Water flooded the stairwell. She picked up the pace, sloshing through ankle-deep liquid, thankful for the daily stair routine which had prepared her for this very day, as though written in a script.

An hour later, she was standing in the first-floor lobby covered in ash, the overhead sprinklers soaking her dusty clothing. The once opulent space was now in shambles. She took in the unimaginable scene; elevators had been blown apart and melted beyond recognition, chandeliers and marble wall tiles were littered across the floor, and the windows had all been blown out. She waded through water pouring from the ceiling and moved toward a blown-out window, passing two charred figures bobbing against a wall. A hysterical woman pointed at the bodies, screaming, "A fireball came down the elevator shaft. They blew out of the elevator!"

Pretense choked back a rising stream of vomit, as a police officer shouted. "Move people! Get out now!"

When she stumbled outside, people were rushing down the street covered in white ash. Pamplona during The Running of the Bulls. She merged into the frenzied crowd when suddenly she heard a loud rumble, like a derailed train coming up behind her. She turned. The tower collapsed onto itself like a thumb puppet. A large, black cloud rolled down the street like a gigantic bowling ball. As death marched toward her, she covered her face with her hand and kept running, the trained will of her muscles taking her beyond what she thought capable. Debris sliced into the soles of her feet.

"The South Tower collapsed!" she heard someone say. When she looked back, the North Tower was still standing, engulfed in flames, black smoke rising against a perfect blue sky. She turned away and kept going until she came upon a crowd and stopped.

"Were you in one of the towers?" asked a woman next to her, as she took in the sight of Pretense, shock stamped on her face.

"The North Tower. It must have been a bomb."

"It was two planes. Two passenger planes," said the woman, tears spilling down her face. Then her eyes bulged. "Oh my, God. The other building is coming down!" The woman ran off, as Pretense stood paralyzed, watching the North Tower disintegrate into a pile of dust. Like a mindless zombie, she turned and started walking in no particular direction. A man on a corner handed out bottled water. Paramedics attended the injured. Two reporters yelled after her, jockeying for an interview. With her head down, she kept moving until she could no longer move. Several hours had passed when she came upon an open pizza parlor and wandered inside. Two middle-aged women rushed to her aid. "Sit down, and let us help you," one said. "You must have been in one of the towers. Can we take you somewhere?"

Pretense dropped into the chair, unable to speak. A waiter came with a stack of wet towels, dabbing her ghost-like face until her skin appeared through the chalky mask. One woman bent down and took off her shoes. "Here, honey, put these on. I think they'll fit." Pretense extended her bleeding, bare feet, as the woman placed a running shoe over each foot.

"Here, eat something," said the waiter, setting a pizza on the table before her.

Pretense picked up a slice and set it back down. "Bathroom?" she heard herself say.

One of the women escorted her to the restroom. "Take as long as you need."

When the door closed, Pretense looked in the mirror. Her hair looked prematurely gray, her clothes covered in thick, white ash. She splashed water on her face, drinking in the clear liquid, then she went into the stall. When she finished, she remained on the toilet, too frightened to move. She heard a light rap on the door.

"I'm sorry to disturb you, but do you need help?"

"I need a minute," Pretense answered. She felt around her neck for the locket, surprised it was still there. *I can't go back to the apartment. I'll book a flight out tomorrow.* She opened the stall door and looked in the mirror, wishing she hadn't washed away the mask.

When she stepped out of the restroom, a woman waited by

the door. She took Pretense's arm and led her back to the table. "What is your name?" she asked.

"Jane," Pretense responded. "I must go." She moved to the front door. The waiter thrust a pizza box and a bag with two bottled waters into her hand. She thanked everyone, then left, heading in the direction of her temporary shelter.

CHAPTER 33

Exhausted, her brain choked with chaotic thoughts, Pretense reached the storage facility on foot and pulled out the locket, nudging her thumbnail into the notch. It sprang open, the three keys tucked within. She unlocked the padlock, then rolled up the heavy metal door and entered the darkened cavern. Feeling around inside her suitcase, she found the flashlight and turned it on, then pushed the door down, leaving it slightly ajar to let in fresh air. She set up the aluminum lawn chair and tray table in the middle of the cement floor. The aroma of spicy pizza wafted, her stomach crying to be fed. She lifted the cardboard flap. The cold slices were scattered with burnt pepperoni, their edges curled in like mini cups of orange grease pools. She devoured the entire pie, her raging hunger quenched.

After she ate, she pulled a washcloth from the suitcase, then removed her clothing and wetted her bare skin with bottled water, wiping away the powdered ash before changing into clean clothes. She shut off the flashlight and sank into the lawn chair, bleary-eyed, the soles of her feet throbbing. Her head snapped back and forth, as she drifted in and out of consciousness, random snapshots floating aimlessly behind her eyelids. Without warning, the weight of the day came crushing down like an errant wrecking ball; the dreadful meeting, Thelma's screams, burning towers, dead bodies. She sat erect, her body drenched in sweat. She shook her head, as though trying to reset her brain after a bad dream. But it wasn't a dream.

———

Daylight crept along the floor from beneath the steel door, urging her to move. Every bone ached, as she pulled herself up and dragged her body over to the suitcase, familiarizing herself with its contents. An empty purse lay buried in the bottom, along with the metal box. She opened the box and retrieved the cash, the credit card tied to the bank in Singapore, and the identification documents for Claire Voyant, stuffing the items inside the purse.

The check she had retrieved from the Wilton, Connecticut mailbox lay at the bottom of the metal box. According to Simon and private investigator, Griffin McCoy, the check was a ruse, meant to expose the perpetrator. She tore the paper into tiny pieces, then put on the blond wig, a pair of sunglasses, and a baseball hat before locking the storage unit and hailing a cab.

The taxi traveled along the silent streets, the acrid smell of smoke and ash hanging in the air, a reminder of yesterday's horror. The once bustling city was now a war zone, teeming with shell-shocked people, the familiar sprint gone from their steps. The driver dropped her off in front of an upscale hotel near Central Park. She went inside the building and strode past the desk clerk, then headed down the hallway and into a restroom. After washing her body with paper towels and brushing her teeth, she returned to the lobby. A discarded copy of *The New York Times* lay abandoned on a side table. She picked it up and scanned the headline. "U.S. Attacked. Hijacked Jets Destroy

Twin Towers and Hit Pentagon in Day of Terror." She read the article. The first plane had struck the North Tower, destroying floors ninety-three through ninety-nine. It was assumed no one above the ninety-second floor made it out alive. A sickening pall welled up inside, blood draining from her face. She recalled the conversation she'd had with Daphne before the meeting. *She asked me to go upstairs with her and Ariana to the café on the ninety-third floor.*

Pretense dropped the newspaper and rushed to the restroom, making it inside a stall before emptying her stomach of yesterday's pizza. After settling herself down, she left the hotel and entered a small shop, purchasing a prepaid cell phone. Then she called the airline. The ticket agent explained that all flights were grounded for the next few days, but she was able to reserve a first-class ticket to Singapore, leaving in three days, which meant a few more nights in the storage facility.

———

The day before her flight, she gathered her possessions from the storage unit and tossed the lawn chair and tray table into a dumpster, then hailed a cab to JFK International Airport. Increased security was everywhere as the driver pulled curbside and dropped her off. The eerie scene left her feeling vulnerable. She thought about leaving—maybe renting a car and driving to California—but she needed to get out of the country.

Once inside the nearly deserted airport, she headed toward the TWA Hotel in the terminal and booked a room. It would be her last night in the United States, never to return home again. With hours to kill before her flight, she contacted Lan Chan at the PTS Bank in Singapore and let her know she'd be arriving in a few days to review her account. After scheduling time to meet with Lan, she asked for a plastic surgeon and dentist referral.

"My uncle is a plastic surgeon," said Lan. "And I can give

you the number to my dentist. I've been with him since I was twelve."

After scheduling the two appointments, she ordered room service. When dinner arrived, she poured a glass of wine and stood before the mirror, offering a toast. "To the end of Pretense Abdicator. May she rest in peace."

PART TWO

CHAPTER 34

After an exhaustive check-in screening, and another round at the gate prior to boarding, Pretense passed the test. Before long, she was escorted to her seat in first-class on the upper deck of the 747. The small number of passengers glanced around nervously, scrutinizing each other for signs of suspicious behavior.

"Would you care for a glass of champagne, Ms. Voyant?" asked the flight attendant.

"Yes, please," Pretense responded, anxious for something to calm her nerves.

"Ladies and gentlemen, we have been cleared for take-off. Please buckle your seatbelts." She glanced at the vacant seat next to her, then sank into the cushy leather headrest and closed her eyes.

Hours into the flight, a young woman and a small child came out of the restroom, heading down the aisle toward Pretense. The child reminded Pretense of Daphne's sister, Sarah.

"Mommy, does frozen poop fall from the sky when the toilet is flushed?" asked the child. The mother shushed her, as the girl ran down the aisle and stopped at Pretense's row, struggling to climb into the empty seat. "I wanna sit here."

"No, honey," said the mother. "We have to sit in our seats." As the mother tried steering the child away, the little girl grabbed Pretense's arm and began wailing. "I'm so sorry," said the woman, contending with her daughter.

"It's okay if she wants to sit here," said Pretense, stunned by her own words.

"That's very kind of you," said the woman. "I'm just two rows back." She hesitated, as though pondering risks. She turned to the child. "Emily, you can sit here for a little while, but only if you promise to leave when I say so."

"I promise, Mommy."

"Are you sure you don't mind?" the woman asked.

"I'm positive," said Pretense. "I could use the company."

When the woman left, Pretense turned to Emily. The child smiled up at Pretense, the corners of her eyes crinkling.

"What's your name?" Emily asked.

"Claire," Pretense responded. "How old are you?"

"I'm six. Did you hear the toilet flush? It almost sucked my butt off."

Pretense laughed. "Yes, the toilet is very scary."

The flight attendant came by with a tray of warm chocolate chip cookies. Emily grabbed two and started to shove one into her mouth.

Pretense took her hand. "Why don't we wait until we ask your mother if it's okay." She took a napkin and wrapped the cookies inside and set them on Emily's lap. "Do you like being on an airplane?"

"It's okay. I'm going to meet my grandma. Do you have a grandma?"

"I'm sure I have a grandma somewhere, but I never met her." Pretense considered her dysfunctional life. Her mother never spoke of family or about her own upbringing. When Pretense once broached the subject, her mother told her she grew up in a rainforest and was raised by wild animals.

"Do you want to meet her?" asked Emily.

206

"I suppose. But it's too late now."

Emily asked a few more ominous questions, then she went silent, her eyelids opening and closing like those of a reptile. She cuddled closer to Pretense and, before long, fell asleep. Pretense studied the child, culling images of Daphne and her sister strolling hand in hand through Central Park, the intensity of their bond distinct.

She choked back the memory and gazed out the small window and into the ominous dark black sky, wing lights blinking against infinite space. *Oh, Daphne, where are you now,* she wondered? Daphne believed in heaven, a place more glorious than anything we could ever hope or imagine, she once said. But Pretense thought Daphne a hopeless optimist, clinging to the far-fetched belief in the hereafter. The end of this life is simply the reversal of birth. Nothing more. End of story.

Her thoughts turned to the Rothschilds' money—now her money—sitting in a Singapore account under an alias. The thrill had gone. Emptiness folded over her as she stared into the black sky on the other side of the window. A pool of tears filled her eyes, then coursed down her cheeks. She squeezed her lids shut, trying to dam the flow. *What's wrong with me? I haven't cried since I was a child.*

"Excuse me," said Emily's mother. "I see she's fallen asleep. I was going to take her to her seat."

"Oh, don't worry," said Pretense, swiping her face. "She's no bother."

"That's very kind of you." Her brows grew together. "Is everything okay?"

Pretense smiled. "Yes. I'm just feeling emotional."

"I understand," said the woman. "Our world will never be the same."

———

After successfully clearing Customs at Changi Airport, she collected her bag and scanned the crowd. A man holding a "Claire Voyant" sign stood by the door.

"Welcome to Singapore," he said in perfect English, taking her suitcase when she approached. She followed him out of the air-conditioned terminal and into a hot blast of Singaporean humidity, her linen pants and t-shirt clinging to her skin like a wet drape. He loaded her luggage into the trunk as she settled into the backseat. They drove through the downtown area, leaving behind the pristine, cosmopolitan city-state and entering the lush grounds of the Shangri-La Hotel, her home for the next two weeks.

When the bellhop unlocked her room door, the grandeur of the garden-view suite seized her breath. After tipping the young man, she opened the sliding glass doors and stepped out onto the spacious balcony, bright purple bougainvillea spilling from everywhere. The floral-scented air danced with the aroma of the sea. Singapore was more beautiful than she had imagined. She lingered on the balcony for some time before going back inside the room and unpacking her bag, eager for a shower.

After showering, she skimmed the in-room directory, looking for dining options within the hotel. It had been awhile since she'd had a decent meal. Excited to sample the local cuisine, she dressed and grabbed her purse, but before she made it to the door, her body gave out. Too exhausted to move, she flopped on the bed and sank into a nightmarish sleep of burning bodies and crumbling buildings. When she woke after midnight, she undressed and burrowed under the sheets, her plans for a night out on hold.

————

The following morning, Pretense left the hotel for PTS Bank, located within one of the many towering skyscrapers dotting the Downtown Core. After entering the diamond-shaped atrium, she located the office of Lan Chan. A thirtysomething woman came from behind her desk extending a delicate hand.

"It's so nice to meet you, Claire. Please, take a seat. Are you enjoying our city?"

"Yes, it's absolutely beautiful," said Pretense. After a few minutes of courtesy small talk, Pretense steered the conversation. "I would like to close the business account for C Katz Investments and transfer the funds into a personal, interest-bearing account. Can you tell me what options are available?"

"I would recommend our private banking solution." Lan explained the suite of tailored services and the strict confidentiality rules governing this type of investment. "To qualify, a minimum of two million dollars is required. Since you meet that requirement, we could transfer the bulk of your money today. But I would suggest leaving a small amount in the business account—say ten thousand—in case you need that account in the future." After carefully reviewing Lan's recommendation, Pretense agreed and completed the paperwork, then left for her next appointment.

———

Dr. Terrence Tay studied Pretense's bone structure, declaring her an excellent candidate for rhinoplasty surgery. When she had made the consultation appointment, the office penciled in a surgery date within three days, provided Dr. Tay agreed to perform the operation. "I will align your nose to create facial balance and correct proportion. And I will remove the dorsal hump by shaving down the bony cartilaginous portions of the bump," he said as he waggled her nose from side to side like a joystick. "The result will be natural in appearance and will complement facial harmony. I will see you in three days."

She left the doctor's office and took a cab to the next appointment. After the dentist examined her teeth, he recommended a porcelain veneer to repair her chipped front tooth. And for a small fee, the dentist would contact the dental lab to expedite the veneer making process. Her new tooth would be ready in a few days.

With the day's engagements completed, she strolled the shops along the main avenue and stopped in a trendy-looking hair salon. Hours later, Dasha stood behind the black, swivel chair, placing his hands on Pretense's shoulders and talking into the large mirror. "What do you think?"

"It's perfect," said Pretense. "It's exactly what I wanted."

With everything accomplished, Pretense returned to the hotel to change. But after showering, her limbs felt like concrete blocks. *It must be jet lag.* She sank into the soft mattress and pulled the luxurious pillow to her face, her eyes drifting shut; blissfully unaware of her surroundings.

And then the nightmares invaded.

CHAPTER 35

Pretense woke the following morning exhausted, as though she had spent the night at war with herself. She dragged her body from bed and staggered to the shower, determined to take in the sights of Singapore. After dousing her skin in sunscreen, she dressed in a linen, sleeveless shirt, and a loose-fitting skirt. Grateful her wig-wearing days were over, she tousled her mussy, blond hair. The layers were cut fuller at the crown and tapered into choppy, feathered ends, lending her a carefree, bohemian look. One last glance in the mirror, then she left the room, ready to dive into the culture.

An hour later, she was back in the air-conditioned hotel room, peeling off her clothes and stepping into the shower, the cool water soothing her sunburnt skin. After wrapping herself in a towel, she collapsed onto the bed, her plan for an epicurean feast on hold. It was only mid-afternoon, but the idea of going anywhere seemed daunting. She lay motionless for some time as uncertainty invaded her thoughts. She now had everything she wanted—money, freedom, a chance to start over, but yet she felt empty, like a wealthy nomad with no real purpose in life. *Why didn't I die in the towers?* Tears welled on her lower lids, spilling onto the pillow before her eyes grew heavy, and she drifted off to another place.

She was alone in a house—a mansion—perched on a gilded throne, her body dripping in precious stones. An elderly servant wobbled into the room, struggling to balance a teetering crystal decanter on a silver platter when it toppled to the floor. The woman began to whimper, as she lowered her feeble body, crawling on hands and knees, pursuing the runaway carafe. She turned to Pretense with a pained look on her face. It was the face of Edna Rothschild.

Pretense sprang upright, fully awake and soaking wet. She rolled out of bed and opened the sliding glass door and stepped onto the balcony, sinking into a chair. An easy breeze tousled her hair, as she inhaled the temperate air, the night sky shimmering with a million stars. She looked up, imagining a lit room above the sky, its light seeping through tiny pinholes in the floor. What existed up there, beyond the sky, beyond the universe? She pulled her legs to her chest, her chin resting on her knees, lost in thought, guilt snaking in. Maybe she should return to New York, turn herself in, beg the Rothschilds' forgiveness, and pay her dues. Hyman and Edna had always treated her with genuine kindness. More so than anyone she had ever met, aside from Daphne. She pictured their horrified faces when they'd learned of the scheme. Or maybe they didn't know—yet. Baron had said he hadn't told them. She went back inside the room and climbed into bed, nestling deep within the covers and fell asleep with a whisper of hopefulness in her heart.

———

The next day, she left the dentist's office sporting a new front tooth. She ran her tongue over the porcelain surface, astounded by the smooth texture, as she strolled the busy sidewalk trying to contain her smile. With her spirits uplifted, she continued down the street in search of a taxi.

The cab driver dropped her off near Marina Bay. The Singapore guidebook claimed some of the freshest and cheapest food could be found at hawker centers, described as large food courts with stalls serving local dishes. Her stomach rumbled, as she strolled along Satay Street, eyeing thingamajigs on a stick, the aroma of barbeque smoke clouding the air. She happened upon a busy stall and ordered a small satay set, consisting of grilled lamb, beef, and chicken, a side of cucumbers and onions, and assorted dipping sauces. Toting the Styrofoam container and lime drink to a long, empty bench table, she sat down and plunged a lamb and beef stick into a bowl of chili sauce, nibbling the chunks of tender meat and licking her fingers.

"Excuse me," said a middle-aged man. "Do you mind if my wife and I join you?"

Pretense wiped her face with a napkin and sipped the lime juice. "Not at all."

"Are you from the States?" the woman asked.

"Yes. And you?"

"We're from Michigan. It's our first time in Singapore. She extended her hand. "I'm Sherry O'Brien. And this is my husband, Pat."

Pretense shook their hands. "I'm Claire. Are you folks here on vacation?"

"Yes. Pat wanted to go to Ireland, but I wanted something more exotic."

"Like Ireland isn't exotic," said Pat. "Where bouts you from, Claire?"

"Southern California."

"Oh, yeah? We used to live in southern California. What part?"

"Palm Springs," Pretense responded.

"Small world," said Pat. "I grew up in Palm Springs. I worked at the Riverside County Clerk's Office for thirty years until I retired, and we moved to Michigan."

Pretense stiffened. She had broken her golden rule—never

reveal too much. She scooped up her disposable plate and stood. "Well, I'd like to stay and chat, but I have to get going. It was nice meeting you."

"You, too," said Sherry. "Where are you staying?"

"With some friends," said Pretense. "Not far from here. Enjoy your trip." Pretense left, disappointed that her first evening out had failed.

She returned to her room and grabbed a paperback, then went out onto the balcony. *Is this how my life is going to be? Always looking over my shoulder?* She read several chapters, then put the book aside. As she leaned over the balcony, breathing in the night air, she spotted a couple below strolling along the illuminated garden path. It was the couple she had met at the food court, the O'Brien's. They must be staying at the same hotel. With just over a week left in Singapore, she resolved to spend the remainder of her time hidden inside her room.

———

The day of her surgery, she left the hotel, uneasy about the procedure and paranoid she would run into Sherry and Pat from the food court. She pulled a straw hat down over her eyes and hurried through the lobby to the waiting limo out front. Once inside the vehicle, she struck a deal with the driver; he would pose as her emergency contact and would remain in the waiting room until her release.

After checking in, she changed into a hospital gown. The anesthesiologist administered something through an IV. Three hours later, she awakened in the recovery room, woozy and confused, her nose wrapped in bandages. Dr. Tay came to her bedside and declared the surgery a success. After giving her a list of do's and don'ts, he told her to return in one week.

———

The following days slipped past with minor pain and discomfort. Aside from some bruising and swelling, she felt back to her old self. At the post-op appointment, Dr. Tay removed the bandages and handed her a mirror. "It will take a good six months before your nose has lost all of its swelling and up to two years before the tip has full definition. But from what I see today, I think you will be very pleased."

When Pretense looked in the mirror, a huge grin formed on her face. Her nose appeared perfectly aligned, the sharp hook unhitched. She turned her head from side to side, overwhelmed by her appearance. "I love it. It's better than I had imagined."

"I'm happy it worked out." Dr. Tay handed her a business card. "Here is the contact information for the plastic surgeon I told you about in Thailand. Since you'll be leaving tomorrow, I'd like you to follow up with him every few months."

Pretense left the clinic armed with a new sense of self. Amazing what a little plastic surgery can do to lift a girl's spirits.

CHAPTER 36

Before leaving Singapore, Pretense applied for a Thailand tourist visa, allowing her to stay in the country for up to sixty days. She chose the island of Koh Samui in the Gulf of Thailand as her temporary home due to its laidback vibe, and in terms of accessibility, not the easiest to reach.

After collecting her bag at the island airport located in the Gulf of Siam, she cleared Customs, then took a shuttle to a small, family-run resort on Maenam Beach. The property was exactly what she had envisioned, located on the North Coast of Koh Samui, a quieter, less commercialized section of the island with views across the sea toward the neighboring isle of Koh Pha-Ngan.

She wheeled her bag into the charming lobby of the resort. A blond thirtysomething woman with bronze skin and teeth whiter than a porcelain toilet greeted Pretense. "G'day. Welcome to Moonbeam Bungalows. How can I help you?" asked the woman in a thick Aussie accent.

"I have a reservation. Claire Voyant."

The woman thumbed through a stack of index cards. "Ah, yes. Nice to meet you, Claire," she said, extending her hand.

"My name is Kerry Tiput. I'm the owner, along with my husband, Denzel. It looks like you reserved one of our beach-front cottages for a week."

Once the check-in process was complete, Kerry led Pretense along a paved, garden walkway past a string of picturesque cottages leading to a sandy beach. "Here you are," said Kerry, stepping onto a private patio set in caramel-colored sand, just steps from the water's edge. "It's private here on the end. We are fully booked, but the guests are mainly singles and couples. Overall, it's very quiet." A blast of cool air escaped the Thai-inspired room when Kerry unlocked the door. A mosquito-netted, king-sized bed sat atop a raised platform. Off to the side was a kitchenette and a well-appointed bathroom with a walk-in, rainfall shower.

"It's lovely," said Pretense. "How long have you owned the resort?"

"Fifteen years. My husband is a Thai national. I met him while on holiday from Australia almost twenty-years ago, and I never left. Some holiday." She threw her head back and laughed without measure. "Where are you from?"

"California. I'm hoping to stay in Thailand a few months. I plan on checking into short-term rentals tomorrow."

"The easiest way to scout out properties is to rent a motor-bike and drive around the island. Many owners post FOR RENT signs. If you're interested, we rent motorbikes by the day." Her expression dampened. "It's just awful what happened in New York. Do you know anyone who lives there?"

"Fortunately, no. I left the United States right after it happened. I just wanted to get away." Images clattered in her mind as an icy chill snaked down her spine. "I see there is a restaurant on the property. Do you own that as well?"

"Denzel's uncle owns the restaurant. Excellent food. And there are some great bars and shops along the beach. Some people say it's too quiet here, but I love the tranquility. Well, I'll let you get settled. Let me know if you need anything." She flashed a toothy grin and left.

Pretense unpacked and changed into a flowy sarong, sleeveless t-shirt, and open-toed sandals. She pushed her face up to the oval mirror, cocking her head from side to side. The swelling on her nose was practically gone. She tousled her hair and left the bungalow in search of local cuisine.

Pulling off her sandals, she strolled down the beach, the sugar cane sand squishing between her toes. A paved walkway led to a street with several food stalls, the scent of exotic spices laced the warm, tropical breeze. She stopped at a stall and ordered Kao Pad, then carried her meal to a cluster of empty plastic chairs set up on the beach. The sun was dipping low by the time she finished eating. She walked back along the shore to her bungalow and sat on her patio, eager to witness her first Thailand sunset.

She inhaled the unrivaled beauty of the island, listening to the gentle sound of waves lapping at the shore as palm fronds swished in the warm breeze. Across the sea, lights twinkled from neighboring Koh Pha-Ngan.

She woke after midnight, slouched on the dew-covered patio chair. She dragged her body into the room and flopped across the bed in her sarong and t-shirt, too exhausted to change.

The night terrors began: the Rothschilds on her heels, the FBI bearing down, the towering inferno. She awoke before sunrise with tears burning her eyes and shame searing her heart. After several hours of doleful reflection, she got up and wandered around the room, familiarizing herself with the layout. A wicker basket in the kitchenette held an array of herbal tea packets. She made herself a cup, then sat down at the desk and opened the drawer. Inside, she found a hardcover book, *Buddhism for Beginners*, a user's guide to Buddhist basics written in English. Perhaps a previous guest left the book. She had heard that Theravada Buddhism was the predominant philosophy in Thailand. As she sipped the hot tea, she leafed through the pages, reading about "The Four Noble Truths" and "The Noble Eightfold Path," then she put the book aside and showered.

———

Kerry was arranging a bouquet of flowers and humming a tune when Pretense entered the lobby.

"Good morning," said Pretense. "I'd like to rent a motorbike."

"Sure," said Kerry, leading Pretense outside to an area with several scooters lined up on an angle. "How was your first night?"

"It was wonderful," said Pretense, distracted by the colorful machines. "I've never ridden one of these things. They look intimidating."

"Ahh, Claire, it's pretty simple," said Kerry, grabbing the handlebars of a hot pink machine and steering it out of the pack. She handed Pretense a map of the island and provided a cursory lesson on motorbike safety, then handed Pretense a helmet. "Now, hop on, and off you go."

Aside from running over an orange safety cone and nearly taking out a street side clothing rack, she had managed quite well. She zigged and zagged through the busy streets and side roads of the island, absorbing the lay of the land, passing several FOR RENT signs along the way, and making note of a few properties.

On the ride back to the resort, she rounded a bend and came upon a gargantuan, glimmering golden Buddha raised upon a platform as though rising from the sea. She steered the motor-bike toward the small rocky island and parked, then walked the causeway connected to the main island. At the base of the Buddha, several tiers of steps rose skyward to the imposing statue. Ready for a challenge, Pretense began the ascent up the endless wall of steps until she reached the top, winded and flushed from the oppressive heat. How could she be so out of shape after all the stairs she had climbed while working at Crawford Spectrum? She spotted a nearby bench and collapsed, reveling in the quiet solitude of the sacred site.

After gathering her strength, she descended the steps and reached the bottom where she noticed several people receiving some type of blessing. Eager to experience the sacred ritual, she went into an area where monks were seated cross-legged on a raised platform and placed a small donation in a basket, then stood before a monk, unsure what to do. Should she remain standing, lay prostrate, perform a tribal dance? She looked to her left. A woman was kneeling, her head down, her hands clasped together. Pretense dropped to her knees and assumed position. The monk's lips moved, chanting some type of prayer. Then he reached for a nearby bowl and dipped a brush inside, flinging it in her direction, spraying her with beads of water. When he finished, he motioned her forward and tied a white string around her left wrist, wishing her protection and good health, then instructed her to keep the Sai Sin thread on her wrist for three days.

She walked back to her scooter, fingering the sacred bracelet. An aura of lightness shrouded her being as she hopped back on her scooter and headed for the resort. When she pulled into the lot, she found Kerry outside. Kerry waved and smiled. "Find anything to rent?"

Pretense parked and climbed off. "Not sure, but I got a good look at the island and spotted several potential areas."

"That's great," said Kerry. "Hey, do you have plans tonight? It's not often that I meet single, English-speaking women at the resort. Maybe we can grab a bite and a drink. Denzel is on night duty, so I'm free."

"Sounds wonderful," said Pretense, trying not to sound desperate. "I can be ready in an hour."

Kerry and Pretense arrived at the Wild Monkey Tavern in Fisherman's Village and sat at a beachside table. After they ordered drinks, Kerry opened up about life in Thailand. She was homesick for Australia, and her marriage was faltering. The responsibility of owning a resort had become overwhelming, and they had no time for each other—they were drifting apart. Kerry looked off, a flicker of sadness creeping over her face. She sipped her cocktail. "Well, enough about me. So, tell me about you, Claire."

Pretense tapped her fingers on the table, pausing, sick of the endless but necessary lies. "When I lived in California, I was dating a guy—Brian—but it didn't work out. I needed a change —a big change. A chance to see the world." Somewhat true. "The terrorist attacks sealed it for me. I decided to start a new life in another country. I have no family. My parents died when I was young, and I inherited a little nest egg, which will get me through for a few years." Full-on lie. "I'm hoping to open a business, so I'm traveling around, trying to figure out where to plant roots." She took a sip of beer, her stomach howling for food. "Should we order something to eat? I'm famished."

Kerry recommended the special, Kao Phad Poo. After placing their orders, Kerry leaned across the table, her hands folded. "I have a proposition for you. Denzel and I are looking for a partner. Someone to assume half the responsibility so we can spend more time on our marriage—maybe start a family. If it worked out, we could come to some agreement. Maybe offer free room and board for a few months on a trial basis while we show you the ropes. I'd, of course, have to talk to Denzel. I don't expect you to answer me now, but give it some thought."

Pretense was captivated, but cautious. "It sounds interesting. Give me a few days to think it over."

"Absolutely. It's a big decision."

The waitress set their dishes in front of them. Pretense devoured the plate of fried rice, the smell of garlic and onions wafting through the air. "The food in Thailand is superb."

"I never get tired of it," said Kerry. "How about another drink?"

After their meal, they lingered over drinks, the conversation unbroken, their laughter free and easy, like two long-lost friends catching up after years apart. Pretense felt at home, as though she were meant to be in this land of gentleness and grace.

"I had fun tonight," said Kerry when they arrived back at the bungalows. "You remind me of my best friend back in Australia and how much I miss her." She looked away, as though embarrassed. "Well, see you tomorrow."

"I had a great time. And I'm looking forward to meeting Denzel."

She walked back to her room, soaking up Kerry's words—the potential partnership, the comment about her best friend. She changed into a thin nightgown, swiped a toothbrush across her teeth, then crawled under the covers, feeling at home.

CHAPTER 37

If only.

Pretense lay in bed the following morning, wishing she were someone else. Someone good and pure, like Daphne. Sure, she had a new name, but every place she went, Pretense Abdicator was there. She opened the desk drawer and pulled out the Buddhism book, flipping to where she had left off. Suffering, she read, is trying to gain something one doesn't have, and the way out of suffering is to develop habits of principled behavior, thought, and meditation. She chewed on the theory, her mind hanging on the plethora of lies she'd told, the money she had embezzled from two innocent people. She shut the book and went into the bathroom to shower. *How do I detach myself from the grip of sin? It will always be there, weighing on my mind. Buddhism is not meant for people like me.*

After dressing, she went into the lobby in search of Kerry. A handsome, dark haired man came out from behind the counter, his eyes smiling. "You must be Claire. I'm Denzel, Kerry's husband."

Pretense shook his hand. "Nice to meet you, Denzel."

"How do you like Thailand?"

"From the little I've seen, I love it. Have you lived here all your life?"

"Pretty much. I studied business at Arizona State University. I thought about moving there, but decided to come back home and take over my family's resort. And then I met Kerry."

"Did I just hear my name?" asked Kerry, sweeping into the lobby carrying a basket of fresh cut flowers. "I see you've met Claire. I told Denzel all about you last night. And about my proposition."

Denzel looked at Kerry with mocking eyes. "Kerry likes to get right to the point. I'm sure she caught you off guard. But I understand you're going to think about it."

Pretense grinned. "Yes, I was flattered by the offer. I've dreamt of owning a tropical resort, but I lack the experience."

"Kerry tells me you're from California. What did you do there?"

"I was self-employed. I managed the books for a few small companies … not very exciting."

"Your finance background will be helpful," said Denzel. "If you are considering the offer, a two-month trial period would give us a chance to feel each other out, but of course, you would need to apply for a special visa and a work permit. If, after the trial period, it didn't work out, then you've lost nothing but your time, and you've gained the experience you lack." Denzel glanced at Kerry and winked.

Kerry's face lit, as though her marriage had just been saved. "We are eager to hear what you decide, but no rush. So, what's on the agenda today?"

"I'm going scuba diving—for the first time. I booked a tour with a professional guide."

"Wonderful," said Kerry. "Stay safe, and we'll see you when you get back."

———

After discovering a love of scuba diving, Pretense considered opening a dive shop, but her mind stayed glued to the offer from Kerry and Denzel. It felt odd making a connection so quickly to two strangers, but something clicked between them. The business proposition seemed frighteningly appealing.

Pretense mulled over the pros and cons. On the plus side, she could learn everything she needed to know about running a resort. And having a partner would lessen the cash outlay and time commitment required to run a business—especially a partner like Denzel, well-versed in the business laws and regulations of Thailand. On the flip side, she was an impostor and would open herself up to unwanted scrutiny. It wasn't worth the risk.

She would move forward with the trial-run, but insist that she not receive any type of compensation. That way, she could avoid applying for a special work permit. After two months, she would back out of the deal. They didn't need to know that part. It would give her time to gain the experience she needed, and Kerry and Denzel would benefit from her services. It was a win-win.

Kerry and Denzel were ecstatic when she told them of her decision, and they quickly put her to work operating the front desk and motorbike rentals, maintaining the property, marketing the resort, and shopping for supplies. Pretense loved every facet of the business. In her free time, she offered to assist at the restaurant, and Denzel's Uncle Sunan was more than happy to oblige. With so much to learn in two months, she planned to make the most of each opportunity.

During her first week on the job, Pretense went to the busy town of Chaweng to run a few errands. While in town, she rented a P.O. Box and visited an affiliate bank of the PTS Bank in Singapore where she withdrew money and verified her balance. Then she contacted Lan Chan at the Singapore bank to update her contact information. With personal business out of the way, she went in search of the market.

On a busy street corner, she spotted a little Thai girl of about five, holding a cluster of wilted jasmine flowers, her pink lace dress tattered and worn, her bare feet caked with mud. Beneath a mass of dark, tangled hair, the child's eyes stalked Pretense as she passed by, her lips curling into a shy smile. Pretense kept walking as the child skipped after her, tugging at the hem of Pretense's skirt. When Pretense turned, the girl handed her a floppy stem. Pretense crouched, taking the gift and placing a five-baht coin into her outstretched palm. The little girl reached up and cautiously touched Pretense's hair, her tiny fingers gliding over the blond layers. "Suay," she said, then ran off. Pretense stared after her, wondering who watched over her. She looked around, but no one seemed concerned. *Who leaves a small child alone wandering the streets—aside from my mother?*

After purchasing the items on Kerry's list, she hopped on the scooter and drove back to the resort. When Pretense pulled into the lot, Kerry was outside, wearing a large floppy hat, tending to several potted orchids lining the front entrance.

"Here, let me give you a hand with those bags," said Kerry, wiping her hands on her skirt. "Did you have trouble finding the market?"

"Not at all," said Pretense, grabbing the last sack from the carrier. Her face turned grim. "On my way to the market, I saw an adorable little girl selling flowers. She looked abandoned—all alone, standing on a busy street corner."

Kerry paused. "It's the ugly side of paradise. Rumor has it, there are a few street children in that area of the island, some of them trafficked for sex." She swallowed deep. "It's been a problem on mainland Thailand for years, and just recently we started seeing it here. But there is good news. A local nonprofit, Beacon of Hope, just partnered with a Christian church in this area. They provide shelter to children, along with education and medical care. I'm hopeful things will change."

Pretense drank a gulp of air and slowly exhaled, tempering

her emotions. "When you say *few*, how many children are you talking about?"

"I really can't say. Denzel and I are planning to visit the church and offer a donation, but we haven't found the time. Now that you're here, maybe you and I could pay a visit one day next week."

"I would love that," said Pretense. "That is if Denzel doesn't mind."

Kerry laughed. "He can go another time. Hey, if you're not doing anything for dinner, you are welcome to come over."

"Thank you, but I'll pass. I'm looking forward to an early night."

"Maybe another time. Oh, and Claire, I just want you to know how much we appreciate having you here. Whether or not you decide to stay, you've made a positive impact. And I will forever treasure our friendship."

Pretense stiffened, the words penetrating. Friendship? She liked the sound of it. She smiled and uttered a simple, "Ditto," then turned to leave. As she turned, she felt the blood drain from her face as her legs buckled, the floor swaying beneath her. And then darkness.

When she regained consciousness, Kerry was crouched beside her, patting her face with a damp towel. "Claire. Claire, are you okay?"

Pretense moaned, trying to focus. "What happened?"

"You fainted. Maybe I should take you to the hospital."

"No, no," she mumbled. "I'm okay." She sat up and looked around. With Kerry's help, she stood and smoothed her hair, taking a seat in a nearby chair.

"Why don't you stay put for a few minutes?" said Kerry. "I want to make sure you're okay."

Pretense nodded. "I don't know what happened. I've been feeling fatigued since leaving the States. I'm thinking it's the humidity."

"I don't mean to be blunt, but you mentioned breaking up

with a guy named Brian before you left. Any chance you could be pregnant?"

"Pregnant?" She let out a small gasp, then answered with a shake of her head. "We were careful," she whispered. In truth, she had never slept with Brian. Images of that night in the Virgin Islands pushed in like a mudslide. *When was my last period?* She'd never been regular and seldom paid attention to her menstrual cycle. Her mind sparked a desperate calculation. It had been over eight weeks since that night, and she didn't recall having a period since. With all that had transpired, it had been the least of her worries.

The sound of Kerry's voice jerked her back. "Hey, you look far away. Are you absolutely sure you're not pregnant?"

"I don't think so," she said, nibbling her bottom lip.

"You're not convinced. Why don't you go into town tomorrow and pick up a home pregnancy test?"

She managed a wooden nod. Her eyes were empty pools. She stood and ambled to the door in a fog. "Maybe I'll do that. I need to lie down."

CHAPTER 38

What if?

The morning got off with her mind in a funk. Pretense had never considered the possibility. Angry with herself for not being more careful that night in the British Virgin Islands, she hauled her tired butt out of bed and dragged her body into the shower, the water awakening dead limbs. Working the soap into a lather, her hands slid over her belly, her fingers probing for life. Was it her imagination, or did her stomach appear bloated? After rinsing off, she stepped out of the shower and stood naked before the mirror, turning from side to side. Nothing looked out of the ordinary, she convinced herself. She breathed a sigh of relief, then dressed and left the bungalow. Insidious worry held her.

When Pretense climbed onto the scooter, Kerry ran out and handed her a shopping list. "While you're in town, do you mind picking up a few things?"

"Not at all. And thanks for your support."

"No worries, mate," Kerry said. "Everything will work out in the end."

Pretense forced a limp smile before motoring out of the lot. When she reached town, she parked the scooter and walked toward the market. The child she had seen yesterday stood on the same corner, selling what looked to be the same wilted flowers. Pretense stopped next to a building, observing. A few tourists came by, taking pictures of the child and handing her money. The girl dropped the coins into a small pouch strapped to her waist and looked around.

From behind a parked Jeep, a tall man appeared and approached the girl. He looked European, with bronze skin and strong, chiseled features, his jet-black hair slicked back in a low ponytail. He stooped next to the child, his dark brows furrowed, as he spoke to the girl, his mannerisms gentle, but coaxing. The girl smiled up at him. When he stood, she took his hand, and they headed for the Jeep.

Without thinking, Pretense burst from her spot and ran across the street. "Hey, what are you doing? Do you know that girl?"

The man stopped and turned, his left brow arched. "Do *you* know this girl?" he asked in English, bearing a slight Spanish accent.

Pretense took a step back, gazing into his unwavering and expectant eyes. Redness bled across her face as she tried coaxing her mouth to speak, her eyelashes flapping like pigeons in flight. She placed her hands on her hips, her chin jutting out. "I do not know this girl. And you?"

The girl looked up at Pretense, a huge grin taking over her face. "Suay."

"Yes, she is very pretty," said the man, winking at Pretense. He stretched out his hand. "My name is Pedro Garcia. I'm the pastor at Crossroads Church. We work with Beacon of Hope to rescue at-risk street children. So, to answer your question, I do know this girl."

Pastor? Her face bloomed like an overripe tomato. "Nice to meet you, Pedro," she said, shaking his hand. "I'm Claire Voyant, a concerned bystander. I've heard about the street children."

"I wish everyone were a concerned bystander." He turned to the child, patting the top of her head. "This is Maya."

Pretense looked down at Maya, her hand tucked inside Pedro's, her grin contagious.

"As you can see, Maya sells flowers." He looked down at Maya pulling his hand, distracted by a stray dog roaming the street. His eyes narrowed, his voice softened. "Her mother, Kwang, uses Maya to make extra money—to support her drug addiction. We've tried to help her mother by offering counseling, but her needs have destroyed her ability to think in a rational way. Children around here are vulnerable to trafficking. I do what I can to keep them off the street."

"Can't you turn her mother in to the authorities?"

"Unfortunately, children in Thailand have few rights. We are trying to convince Kwang to let us keep Maya at our shelter until things improve for her. We came very close a few months ago, but she changed her mind." He tousled Maya's hair. "We suspect her mother's dealer is involved in a network that recruits children. That's how they operate. They get parents hooked, then they offer to exchange their children for their addictions."

Pretense swallowed deep, taming a sickening bile threatening in her throat. "What are you going to do with Maya now?"

"I'm taking her to the shelter. Then one of our staff members will pay a visit to her mother and let her know where Maya is. Sometimes she comes right away, other times not so quick. We do what we can while we can. The rest is in God's hands."

Pretense scrunched her face. *What a curious man. And what an odd thing to say.* "I admire the work you are doing. I've heard of Beacon of Hope. In fact, a friend of mine is planning to visit and make a donation. She invited me to come along."

"That's very kind. We are in desperate need of money. My church is housed on the same property. If you come by, be sure to say hello. I'm usually there." His eyes hung on Pretense. "Well, we should be going. Come, Maya."

Pretense gazed freely as they crossed the busy road. He turned and waved. She waved back and headed to the market.

After gathering the items on Kerry's list, she browsed the aisles and located the home pregnancy test kit. She read the instructions on the box. *Results available in ten minutes.* Dread fluttered her stomach. She hurried back to the bungalow.

"Did you get it?" asked Kerry, when Pretense parked the scooter.

"Yes. I'm not looking forward to taking the test."

"Do you want me to be there with you?"

"No, I'll be fine," Pretense said, waving her hand. "I'll take the test in the morning—when I get up. By the way, I met the pastor of the church that partners with Beacon of Hope. I told him we were planning to visit next week."

"Oh, yeah? Nice guy?"

"Yeah. Nice-looking guy. And very compassionate. He knew that little girl I told you about. Her name is Maya. He was taking her to the shelter."

"Small world," said Kerry. "Well, be off with ya. Get some rest. I'm eager to hear the results."

Pretense bit her lower lip. "If you don't see me first thing in the morning, that means the test is positive. I may need time alone to process everything."

Kerry took Pretense in her arms and held her tight, then drew away. "I'm here for you—whatever the outcome."

For the first time, Pretense didn't pull away from another human's touch. There was a sense of completeness and serenity that flowed from Kerry's embrace. Something natural and good. Something unfamiliar.

———

The next morning, Pretense followed the instructions, then sat back and waited. She got up and paced the floor, chewing her fingernails and watching the clock. She hadn't thought through what she would do if she were pregnant. Her mind wasn't ready to go there.

When the time had passed, she picked up the testing stick with trembling hands. The plus sign was clearly visible. She walked over to the window and held it up to the light. Her shoulders caved. She went to the bed, curling into a fetal position, tears streaming down her face. *This can't be happening.* Choking sobs racked her body. This changed everything. She lay for hours, unwilling to move.

The knock on the door was soft. "Claire? It's me, Kerry. Can I come in?"

"I need to be alone," Pretense murmured.

"Please. Let me in."

Pretense drew herself from bed and unlocked the door. Kerry's face crumpled, her eyes shining with tears, as she pulled Pretense close and held her for several minutes before letting go.

"I don't know what to do," said Pretense, shredding a tissue in her hands and sinking on the bed. "I guess I'll have an abortion."

"A baby is a gift," said Kerry. "Why don't you contact the father? Things may work out for you two."

"That's not an option," she said sharply. "I'm in this alone."

Kerry grabbed a chair and dragged it to the bed and sat, taking Pretense's hands, her eyes weighing into Pretense. "What I wouldn't give to have a baby of my own. Do you know how lucky you are? Denzel and I have tried, but we haven't been successful." She looked off. "Funny how life works. Oh, Claire, you need to think this through. If you decide to stay on as a partner, I could help with the baby."

A steady stream of tears rolled down Pretense's cheeks, her face granite. How could she explain that night to Kerry—the seed forced into her limp body? "Thank you. I'd like to be alone now."

Kerry stood. "Of course. Take the rest of the day off—think things through. And let me know if you want the number to my gynecologist. You should see a doctor—to be sure." Kerry placed a hand on Pretense's shoulder. "I'm here for you if you need me."

After embracing Kerry, Pretense closed the door. Alone with her thoughts, she flopped on the bed, fighting back tears. Her hand went to her belly, stroking the taut skin where the seed hid. She wasn't even sure who the father was. Her guess was Jack Moore, the hotel owner in the British Virgin Islands, the last person she remembered at the bar before she blacked out. But it could have been anyone, for that matter. Maybe the test was wrong. Perhaps things aren't as buttoned up here in Thailand, and maybe they sold second-hand pregnancy test kits.

She got out of bed and took a shower, then called Kerry, asking for the number to her gynecologist. She made an appointment for later that week. Once she received confirmation, she'd decide what to do. Until then, life would go on.

CHAPTER 39

The doctor confirmed her worst fears. Pretense was eight weeks pregnant. During the visit, she broached the subject of abortion and learned the practice was illegal in Thailand, except in the case of rape. But Pretense had no proof of the rape. No police report had been filed, nor would one ever be. And since she wasn't willing to put her health at risk by seeking an illegal abortion in Thailand, she'd need to leave the country. There was also the option of adoption, if she were willing to endure the pregnancy. A decision would need to be made.

"So, how are you feeling about everything?" Kerry asked, after Pretense revealed the doctor's report.

"I have mixed emotions. I think about this child growing inside of me—wondering if it's a boy or a girl—and I find myself getting excited. But when I consider raising the child as a single parent, I freak out."

Kerry scrutinized her. "You know where I stand. And you know we will help you. I'll support you whatever you decide. And I won't bring it up again until you are ready to talk." Kerry pulled out a ledger and set it on the desk. "Are you up to doing some work today? I need a second set of eyes to go through the numbers."

"Sure," said Pretense. "Thanks for being there for me. It means a lot."

"Of course," said Kerry. "By the way, I'm going to Beacon of Hope tomorrow. Would you like to join me?"

"I'd like that."

———

Beacon of Hope/Crossroads Church. The rusted sign was obscured by a patch of overgrown foliage along the unpaved road. "There it is," said Pretense. "Turn here." With Pretense clinging to Kerry's waist, Kerry steered the scooter down a sandy path, sloshing through puddles leftover from last night's rainfall. Before long, they reached a humble brick building, with several smaller outbuildings scattered around the property. A group of children played out front, squeals of laughter cutting through the sticky air.

Pretense climbed off the scooter shaking her skirt to create airflow, a layer of sweat coating her face and arms.

"Looks like the place is in need of some major remodeling," said Kerry, glancing around.

In the distance, a door creaked open. Pedro bounded down the steps and came toward them. "Hello, Claire. Good to see you again. This must be your friend."

She felt herself flush. "Hello, Pedro. This is Kerry."

"Nice to meet you," said Kerry, shaking his outstretched hand, her other hand pinching Pretense on the backside. "Claire tells me you are the pastor. Thank you for the wonderful work you are doing on the island."

"I couldn't do it without the support of others. Do you ladies live on the island?"

"I've lived here twenty years," said Kerry. "My husband and I own Moonbeam Bungalows on Maenam Beach."

"I know it well. I've often thought if I could get some free time, I'd book a room there and just hang out and do nothing. What about you, Claire? Local or visitor?"

"Visitor now, but I'm considering moving here. I'm staying at Moonbeam Bungalows while I decide, which is how I met Kerry."

Kerry nudged Pretense. "And we are trying to convince her to stay."

"It's a beautiful place to live," said Pedro. "Why don't I show you ladies around the property?"

They followed Pedro into the main building and down a dingy hallway. He stopped in the doorway of a simple, wood-paneled room with a cross hanging above a raised step. "This is the church where Sunday services are held. When we opened five years ago, we were lucky to have ten people in attendance. Now we have close to seventy-five regulars, thanks be to God."

"Interesting," said Kerry. "Especially given that ninety-five percent of Thais are Buddhists."

"Yes, that's true," said Pedro. "We focus on the lost and forgotten souls. Our goal is rescuing children and adults from human trafficking and drugs and equipping them with an education, medical care, and life skills."

Pretense reflected on her childhood and wondered what impact an organization like this could have had on her life. But no one ever seemed to notice—or to care. A lump formed in her throat as her hand drifted to her belly, slowly caressing the small bump. "The children playing out front, have they been trafficked?" Pretense asked.

Pedro's eyes scanned the cluster of boys and girls playing nearby. "Some have. Others are here because their parents are drug addicts." His brows knitted thoughtfully, sadness clouding his face. "Let me show you the rest of the property."

Pedro took them to a classroom, a meeting room, a kitchen, a small pantry stocked with canned food and medical supplies, and the living quarters for the staff. "Besides me, we have two other people on staff. Beacon of Hope is located in the building behind us. That is where visitors stay—like missionaries. It's basically an administrative office and a dormitory."

"Do you have family here?" asked Kerry.

Pedro smiled and spread his arms wide. "This is my family." He turned and headed for the front door. "One last area to show you."

They followed him across the yard to a small outbuilding with a striped, scalloped awning, the words *Bread of Life* written across the front. "This is our bakery," said Pedro. "We teach men and women everything they need to know to run a business. And we sell our products here and in town. The money helps fund our organization." He hooked his hands on his hips. "I hope the tour gave you a sense of our mission."

"Yes, it did," said Kerry. "I had no idea." She pulled out her wallet. "My husband and I have been meaning to donate for some time. I'm glad I finally came by." She handed Pedro a thousand-baht banknote. "Thank you for all you do."

"You are very generous," said Pedro, clasping both of her hands. "The money will be put to good use."

"I didn't bring my wallet," said Pretense. "I'll stop by again. Are you here most days?"

"Any day is good. Why don't you come to our nine o'clock service on Sunday?" said Pedro, his dark eyes settling on Pretense.

Church wasn't her thing, but then again, how would she know. She'd never been to church. She wasn't interested in the service, only in the speaker. "Maybe I'll do that."

"Great," said Pedro.

A little boy ran across the play area toward Pedro. He stooped and opened his arms, the child plowing into Pedro's chest. He picked up the boy and stood. "This is Somboon. He's been staying with us for a few weeks." The boy buried his face in Pedro's neck. "As you can see, he's very shy."

"He's adorable," said Pretense, patting the child's back, her eyes lingering. "Well, we should be going. Maybe I'll see you Sunday."

Once they had settled on the scooter, Kerry turned around to Pretense, a thick smile plastered on her face. "I think he has eyes for you. I caught him checking you out when you weren't looking. And he didn't allude to family, so he's likely single."

"Well, wouldn't that be my luck," said Pretense. "I get pregnant, then meet someone interesting. It's supposed to be the other way around."

"Ahh, but you're missing something, mate. That spunk seems to love those little ankle biters. Didn't you see the way his face lit up when that little boy ran into his arms?"

"Spunk?" asked Pretense.

"You know, a hunk of spunk."

———

Pretense slipped on her nightgown and crawled into bed, her mind consumed by the growing seed in her belly. Maybe this wasn't the worst thing that could happen. She had enough money to support a child, and she had always wanted a family of her own. But she would need to give up her independence. And then there was *her* mother. What if she had inherited her mother's lack of maternal instincts? It wouldn't work. She would find a country where she could get a legal abortion and be done with it.

She felt worthless. An inexpressible gloom passed over her, squeezing her brain. It wasn't just the abortion. It was the money. Who was she kidding? And Pedro. She found him attractive, but a pastor no less. It seemed to be a cruel joke. *Oh, Pedro. There's something I need to tell you. I got knocked up after being raped in a foreign country while setting up a phony company to stash the millions I embezzled from two senior citizens. And oh, by the way, my name isn't Claire.*

The money didn't solve her problems; it had created more.

She got out of bed and stepped onto the patio, breathing in the night air. *I've made such a mess of everything.* A torrent of tears spilled down her cheeks, her body racked with persistent sobs. Images of those trapped in Simon's office played on her mind like a three-dimensional slide show. They were in his office because of her—and yet, *she* made it out alive. Why?

She stepped off the patio and walked to the water's edge and stood, digging her toes into the damp sand, the gentle waves lapping her feet, drawing her forward. The cool water chilled her ankles, then traveled to the hem of her nightgown before encircling her collarbone. She pushed off the sea floor, her arms reaching forward toward the twinkling lights of neighboring Koh Pha-Ngan. Saline water caressed her face, the motion of the waves carrying her farther from shore. She glided across the blackened sea, stroke upon stroke, until her arms grew heavy. The cold water reached up and pulled her into its depth. It felt peaceful when she let herself go, like falling into outstretched arms. She willed her lungs to drink in the briny water—to wash away the guilt and pain. But instead, she felt her body propelled upward. As she rose to the surface, her arms and legs thrashed frantically. She flailed in the deep. Hungry for air. Hungry for life. Raw panic flooded her veins, the sound of her rattling teeth piercing the night air. *Stay calm.* She recalled the breathing exercises from her scuba lesson: *Stop, Breathe, Think, Act.* Her eyes locked on the shoreline—farther than she remembered. She rolled onto her back, floating to regain strength, but the waves pulled her farther out. She turned over onto her belly, positioning her body perpendicular to the tide, and with smooth, determined strokes, began the fight for life. Two feet forward. Five feet back. She kept at it, drawing stamina from somewhere unknown, moving like a machine with preprogrammed perfection. From her peripheral vision, she spotted a lone wave rolling toward her—a rescue wave—its swell opening like an enormous blowfish. The wave seized her body and carried her high above the water's surface, burping her out close to shore.

CHAPTER 40

Pretense stumbled out of the water and dropped to the sand, shivering and gasping for air. Her nightgown had been torn from her body. She wrapped her arms around herself and looked around. Illuminated beneath the glow of a full moon, she spotted her bungalow several hundred feet down the shore. Too exhausted to move, she fell back and stared at the midnight sky. A stream of hot tears mingled with sea water warmed her face. Her hand moved to her belly. *I should have died tonight. I should have died in the towers. Why am I alive?*

There was no forethought in what she had done. It was as though a magnetic force drew her into the water, then set her free. She lay motionless, trying to make sense of it all.

After a time, she crept down the beach toward the bungalow, her hands strategically covering her nudity. A young couple in the cottage next to hers lazed on their patio, a bottle of wine between them. They waved, seemingly unfazed by her naked-ness. *They must be from Germany.* Pretense waved back and entered her room. Depleted of energy, she sank into bed, the mind-boggling event worming through her brain.

The cell phone droned on the nightstand, jerking her from sleep.

"Hey, Claire. It's Kerry. Is everything okay?"

"Yeah." Pretense rubbed her eyes. "What time is it?"

"It's ten o'clock. We were going to shop for linens today —remember?"

"I'll be right there." Pretense sprang from bed, threw on a mismatched outfit, brushed her teeth and hair, then left the room.

"Rough night last night?" asked Kerry, standing behind the front desk when Pretense burst through the lobby.

"You could say that," said Pretense, recalling the perplexing event. "But once I fell asleep, it was the best sleep I've had in ages."

"Good morning, Claire," said Denzel, appearing from the back room. "You ladies have fun shopping today. I've got it under control."

Kerry smirked and leaned into Denzel. "I'll make it up to you tonight."

Kerry led the way to the parking lot. "We'll take the car in case we have a big load. I thought we'd go to the west coast. You can see where the locals hang out."

"I'm always up for something new," said Pretense, as she settled into the passenger seat. Something about this day seemed different. She felt more alive, like a simmering euphoria primed to erupt.

As they motored along, Pretense leaned out the open window gulping in the tropical air, a feeling of gratitude soaking her mind. The island colors seemed more vibrant; the polished sapphire sea sparkled against a glimmering-gold seashore, emerald, feather-shaped palm fronds fanning a topaz sky. They drove along the coastline, the wind whipping through their hair, the song "Drops of Jupiter" blaring through the speakers.

Kerry slapped the steering wheel and hollered, "I love this song." She cranked the volume full blast, her voice booming as her fist punched the air, her head snapping to the beat.

Pretense looked over at her friend and grinned. The more time she spent with Kerry, the more her spirit soared.

Kerry pulled off the main road in the village of Lipa Noi and parked near a string of outdoor markets. They got out and strolled along the sidewalk, entering several open-air shops, pawing over fabrics and textures, before selecting several sets of cotton bedsheets. "I've been wanting to replace the sheets but never found the time," said Kerry, as they finished loading the trunk. "Hey, let's celebrate. I know a great place for lunch."

"You read my mind."

Kerry pulled into the dusty lot of a funky retro café fashioned from recycled shipping containers. They went inside and sat at a table on the beach, facing the lagoon.

"Denzel and I used to eat here often—before we got busy with the resort. We love this area."

"So, are things better between you and Denzel?" asked Pretense after the waitress took their order.

"Yes, and it's because of you. Your being here has made our lives easier." She reached across the table and patted Pretense's hand. "Even if the partnering option doesn't work, you could apply for the proper permits and stay on as an employee. If you decide to keep the baby, we have a two-bedroom bungalow you could move into—right near Aunty Kerry and Uncle Denzel." She smirked. "Just something to think about."

"I'll keep that in mind." The waitress set their meals before them. "This looks incredible," said Pretense. She took a bite and rolled her head back, closing her eyes. "Wow. I love the explosion of flavors. It's like a symphony on my tongue."

"Ghang Phed Ped Yang—my favorite Thai dish," said Kerry, taking a bite. "Hey, what did you decide about Sunday? Are you going to church?"

"I'm thinking about it. Why don't you come with me?"

"Maybe another Sunday. Denzel's parents are coming for brunch."

They lingered over lunch, catching up on personal and business issues. "Well, we should head back," said Kerry. "Denzel will wonder what happened to us."

As they walked toward the car, they passed a woman searching for something on the ground while balancing an infant on her hip. "Did you lose something?" Kerry asked.

"My car keys," said the woman in broken English. "I dropped them." Suddenly, her face went eerily blank and her arms straightened like rigid boards, her fists clenching. The infant tumbled to the ground as the woman fell backward, her body jerking violently.

"She's having a seizure!" Kerry yelled. She crouched beside the woman, struggling to position the woman's body on her side, while Pretense ran over and picked up the wailing baby, cradling the child to her chest and rocking back and forth. She watched Kerry stroking the woman's shuddering head.

"Is she going to be okay?" asked Pretense, biting her lip.

"I think so," said Kerry. After a moment, the woman's limbs relaxed. Kerry turned her on her back. "Are you okay, ma'am?"

The woman looked around, her mouth slightly open and loose. She blinked, as though trying to refocus. Then she bolted upright, her eyes darting. "My baby! Where's my baby!"

"It's okay," said Kerry. "The baby is here."

Pretense rocked the child, her hand bracing its head as she whispered in its ear. The baby's cries turned to muffled hiccups as the infant burrowed its head into the crook of Pretense's neck.

Kerry helped the woman to her feet. "Is there anyone I can call?"

"My husband," said the woman, rattling off a number while holding her arms out to Pretense. "I take her now."

Pretense shifted the child into its mother's waiting arms. "What is her name?"

"Preeda," said the woman, clinging to the child and kissing her forehead.

While they waited for the woman's husband to arrive, Kerry

searched around the car and spotted the keys lying next to the front tire. "Found them."

The woman expelled a sigh. "Thank you. We live just around the corner. My husband, he'll be here any minute."

"How did you know what to do for that woman?" asked Pretense on the drive back.

"A childhood friend of mine had epilepsy. Her mother taught me to roll her on her side to keep her from choking." She glanced over at Pretense. "And how did you know what to do with the baby?"

Pretense paused, the feel of the child still with her. "I don't know. It just felt natural." Her open hand moved in slow strokes across her tummy, as she gazed out the car window.

"Do you ever feel like things happen for a reason?" Kerry asked. "I mean, we just happened to be in the right place at the right time. And what would have happened to Preeda if we hadn't been around?" Kerry shuddered. "Anyway, mate, if you ask me, today was an ace day."

Pretense reached over and touched Kerry's arm. "Yes, today was a special day."

CHAPTER 41

I t was Sunday morning, and Pedro filled her mind. But as much as she wanted to see him, church just wasn't her thing. She'd seen some whacky stuff on TV before; snake charmers, innocent worshippers being drowned in a baptism tank. She decided to pass and stop by during the week to drop off a donation.

A day of sightseeing seemed more to her liking. And since Denzel's Uncle Sunan would handle the front desk while Kerry and Denzel entertained his parents, there was nothing to keep her busy at the resort. After changing into an airy, knee-length skirt and a sleeveless button-down blouse, she left the bungalow and hopped on a scooter. With no particular route in mind, she traversed the road along the seashore and came upon a colorful thatched roof cart selling fruit smoothies. She ordered a strawberry mango blend, then sat at an empty picnic table, soaking in the vivid scenery. When she finished the drink, she got back on the scooter and pulled away, taking in the unfamiliar landscape. Before she knew it, she found herself pulling into the church parking lot, the sound of harmonious voices wafting through the open doors of the building. Her stomach pitched as she eased off the scooter, contemplating her next move. Then her legs started to walk, her body along for the ride. When she reached the church entrance, she peered inside, gawking at the backsides of animated parishioners, their hands held high as though awaiting droppings from the sky. No one noticed her. She crept in and took a seat in the back row.

When the singing ended, Pedro took the stage, dressed in frayed blue jeans, a buff white t-shirt, and flip-flops—not exactly the getup she had imagined. He motioned for everyone to be seated. "Good morning, brothers and sisters." A man stood off to the side, translating in Thai. "My name is Pedro Garcia, pastor of Crossroads Church. Welcome. If you're visiting us for the first time, please stand and introduce yourself."

Holy crap. Pretense tried shrinking into her chair, but it was too late. Like a pack of sniffer dogs tracking her scent, the entire congregation craned their necks, urging her onto her feet.

Pedro leaned sideways, his eyes locking on hers. "I see we have a visitor today. Claire, please stand so everyone can see you."

Pretense unrolled, feeling like a giant in a sea of little people. She offered an awkward half-wave. "Sawasdee ka. My name is Claire Voyant." She plopped into her seat.

"Thanks for joining us, Claire. I hope you stay after the service." He opened the large leather-bound book on the podium and scanned the crowd. "Today, we will continue our discussion on sin and forgiveness. Please turn in your Bibles to Luke, chapter twenty-three, verses forty-two and forty-three. We will learn about one of two thieves crucified alongside Jesus." The sound of rustling pages filled the room.

Pedro read aloud, "Then he said, 'Jesus, remember me when you come into your kingdom.' Jesus answered him, 'Truly I tell you, today you will be with me in paradise.'" Pedro held the book high in the air. "This is the word of God."

"Praise God," shouted a man in the front row. "Hallelujah," said a young woman, springing from her seat, her arms raised.

Sweat poked at Pretense, her eyes wild and darting as she

gawked at the worshippers performing like spring-operated puppets. She thought about running before things really got out of hand, but she wanted to hear Pedro speak.

Pedro seemed unfazed by the sudden outbursts. He set the book aside and walked to the front of the stage, his head down, drawing his hand over his chin. Then he looked up, his smiling eyes scanning the crowd, comfortable in his skin. "Sometimes bad guys finish first," he said. "Like the thief on the cross. This man did nothing in his life that was good. Nothing. And yet," he raised his forefinger in the air, "his belief in the Savior was enough to rescue him from the depths of Hell. This passage hits close to home because I, too, was a bad guy." He paused and looked off, a wounded expression on his face. "I was born to a single mom, a drug-addicted woman in Barcelona, Spain. At the age of twelve, I was taken from the street and sold into a sex-trafficking ring. My mother never looked for me. Six months later, I escaped and joined a street gang in order to survive. The gang terrorized the small town where we operated, stealing from the innocent, selling drugs to the lost." He reached for a glass, taking several long swallows. "Late one summer night, an elderly gentleman was locking up his small meat market on a darkened side street. I knew he was carrying cash, so I waited until no one was around, then I attacked the man, knocking him to the ground. I held a knife to his throat and demanded money. But that man just looked me in the eye—in a way that I've never been looked at before—and he told me Jesus loved me. There was no hate in his gaze. No judgment. Only a soul-piercing kind-ness that stripped me of all the pent-up anger I had carried with me for years. I dropped the knife and ran until there was no breath left in me. From that day on, God picked me up and carried me on His shoulders. My life was not the same." He paced the small stage, looking out at the crowd. "Many of you here today are broken. But there is good news. There is no brokenness that cannot be healed and no sin that cannot be forgiven."

Pretense sat cemented to her chair, tears streaming down her cheeks. The magnitude of her sin pierced her sole with a rare force. She wanted to flee, but where could she go to escape her loathsome self?

When she looked around, the service had ended. People were greeting one another and filing into an adjacent room. A couple in front of her coaxed her to follow. She smiled and waved them off. A blurry reflection came toward her, his smile penetrating. "Hey, are you joining us?" Pedro asked. He tilted his head as he reached for her, his long fingers settling on her upper arm. "Is everything okay?"

She answered with a nod, her throat void of sound.

"I'd like to talk," he said.

With her stare fixed to the ground, she shook her head, then turned and left, rushing across the dusty lot to her scooter. As she pulled away, she looked back. He stood by the door, watching.

She drove aimlessly for some time before stopping at a deserted stretch of beach. She kicked off her sandals and walked toward the water as tears trickled down her face. She thought about Pedro's sermon. Despite his past a spirit of joy seemed to live inside him—the same joy Daphne had shown. She wanted that for herself. The money hadn't brought the happiness she'd anticipated. Living in Thailand and working for Kerry and Denzel had given her so much more.

She no longer wanted the money. She loathed the money. It was a curse. Somehow, she would figure out a way to return the funds to the Rothschilds. She could never become Pretense again, but at least she'd rid herself of the guilt gnawing at her. It was a partial way back.

———

After work on Monday, she went back to her bungalow and waited. New York was eleven hours behind. At 9 p.m., she dialed the Rothschilds' number, her hands trembling. The sweet sound of Edna's frail voice tore through her heart. Pretense closed her eyes to the emotion and worked her mouth into a high-pitched British accent. "Hello, Mrs. Rothschild. This is Kate Spencer from C Katz Investments."

"Hello, Kate," said Edna. "I've been trying to get a hold of you, but the number was disconnected."

"Yes. I'm very sorry. How are you doing?"

"Not too good. Our son, Baron, is missing and presumed dead. According to his wife, he had a business meeting at the World Trade Center on September 11. And Hyman suffered a stroke a week ago." Edna blew her nose. "He's now confined to a wheelchair."

A searing fire rose in her throat, the result of her actions spreading like cancer. "I am so sorry, Mrs. Rothschild."

"We haven't heard from anyone at Crawford Spectrum, either. Have you? I know Pretense would have called by now—if she were alive." She sniffed. "She was one special lady."

A black mist settled, dampening her core. She wanted to bare her soul to Edna—to tell her she was sorry for all she had done. But how much more pain could this woman endure? "No, I have not heard from anyone at Crawford Spectrum."

Edna let out a long sigh. "Before Hyman's stroke, we talked about moving all our money out of Crawford Spectrum and into C Katz Investments."

Pretense took in a sharp breath. "I see. However, the reason for this call is to inform you that C Katz Investments is facing turbulent waters ahead, and I wanted to forewarn you before it's too late. That's why I'm calling you on my personal line. I'm proposing that I wire back your entire investment, including all interest to date." There was no response. "Mrs. Rothschild?"

"What do you mean 'turbulent waters'?"

"I'm not at liberty to say," Pretense responded. "I shouldn't even be calling you, but I know Pretense was very fond of you both. I think she would have wanted me to caution you. Please trust me."

"Where would you wire the money to?"

"I'm hoping you can provide a personal bank account number, since we don't want to send it to the Crawford Spectrum account. I can set up a wire transfer tomorrow."

There was a long pause. "I'm not comfortable with this conversation," said Edna. "And I certainly don't feel comfortable giving you my personal information. How do I know this isn't a scam call?"

"I understand. But I'm just looking out for your best interests. I don't want to see you suffer any more than you already have. Would you feel more at ease if I ordered a bank draft sent to the home address we have on file?"

"Yes, that would be fine. When should I expect it?"

"I'll make sure it goes out first thing tomorrow. You have my word."

"How will I get in touch with you?" Edna asked. "I see that your number is blocked."

"I will call you in a few days. I must be going now. Again, I'm sorry for your loss and saddened to hear about Hyman. Please relay my condolences to Baron's wife, Vanka." She ended the call and ran to the bathroom, heaving into the toilet until there was nothing left to hurl. She wiped the vomit from her mouth and splashed her face with water before sagging into a chair, depleted of all energy.

———

Letting go of the money brought no regret.

Pretense phoned Lan Chan at the bank in Singapore to obtain the balance in the personal and business account. Then she asked her to move all but her own money—plus any money she had spent—into the business account and create a bank draft for over $2.5 million and send it to the Rothschilds. Once the check cleared, Lan would close both accounts and send Pretense a check for $10,000—her life savings from her years at Crawford Spectrum.

It wouldn't leave her much, but she didn't care. She felt rich. She felt free.

CHAPTER 42

The ice cubes clanked against the Waterford crystal glass as Edna Rothschild finished her midafternoon cocktail, gin and Dubonnet. She looked over at Hyman, slumped in his wheelchair parked in front of the television set. Reruns of his favorite show, *All in the Family*, held the screen, his usual laughter trumped by a blank stare.

She wanted to tell Hyman about the phone call from Kate Spencer, but what would it matter? She ran her feeble hand over his thinning hair. A tear dribbled down her cheek. Husband and son now gone, and no one left in the world but her high-society "friends" ... women she never really liked but tolerated as part of the money game.

A silver-framed photo of Baron Rothschild at eight years old smirked from across the room. Memories of joyful times flashed through her brain. They would never mend their broken relationship.

She thought about the phone call from Kate Spencer. Something felt off. Why would Kate be concerned with their well-being and offer to send their money back? She ruminated on Kate's words. *I'm calling on my personal line ... I wanted to forewarn you before it was too late.* None of it made sense. For several minutes, she tapped her finger on the arm of the chair, rehashing. Then a spark lit Edna's sharp mind. *Kate had said to give her condolences to Baron's wife, Vanka. How did she know Baron's wife's name? I never mentioned her name to Kate. Is there a connection between Vanka and Kate?*

Edna stood and paced the room. She recalled thinking at the time of the conversation that Kate's voice didn't sound as "British" as it had previously. She wondered if Kate had been tired. Perhaps British people take on an American accent when they are fatigued. Nonsense. The whole thing smelled fishy.

The time had come to have a conversation with Vanka. She dialed her number and scheduled lunch for the following day. It was just a hunch, but what else did she have to do? Better than playing Bridge at the club with a bunch of Botox faces.

––––––

The lacquered mannequin strolled into the restaurant sheathed in a white St. John suit with a red Prada handbag dangling from its forearm, its wrist drooping like a dead flower. Edna smiled and waved Vanka over to her table.

"How lovely to see you," said Edna, offering a double cheek air-kiss. "You look fabulous."

"And so do you. How is Hyman doing?" she asked, placing her well-toned butt in the chair.

"Not good. I don't know if he'll ever fully recover."

Vanka shook her head, a wind gust blowing through her over-plump lips. "It's so incredibly sad."

Conversation felt bumpy until the second glass of wine kicked in. After they finished their entrées, Edna pounced. "Have you ever heard of C Katz Investments?" She studied Vanka's face, looking for a sign of uneasiness.

"Funny you should ask," Vanka responded. "I was cleaning out Baron's desk yesterday, and I found a C Katz Investment brochure. I'd never seen it before, nor did he ever mention it. Why do you ask?"

Edna pursed her lips. "Hyman had spoken to Baron about the company. I believe Baron's meeting in the World Trade Center had something to do with C Katz. I've wondered if that's why Baron was there on nine-eleven."

"Baron mentioned he had a meeting with a man named Griffin at the World Trade Center."

"Do you know anything about this Griffin character?"

"No, Baron didn't often share his business dealings with me. Maybe I'll come across something." Vanka's eyes narrowed. "What is this about?"

Edna waved her hand. "Oh, it's nothing really." She thought about Baron's short life ending in the tower and of their strained relationship. A wave of sadness gripped her, her eyes welling with tears. She pulled a handkerchief from her purse and dabbed her lids. "Forgive me. I'm just trying to piece together Baron's last moments."

Vanka reached over and took Edna's hand. "It's just the two of us now. I've never said this before, but you are like a mother to me. If there is anything you need—anything—please don't hesitate to call. I want us to remain close. We only have each other."

Edna pulled her hand away and blew into a handkerchief. *She must think I'm senile.* "Thank you. I should be going. I don't like leaving Hyman with Rafaela too long. If you find out anything about Griffin, will you let me know? I need to have closure."

"Of course."

Later that afternoon, Vanka called to tell her she had found a business card for a Griffin McCoy, Private Investigator. She gave Edna the phone number. Edna thanked her and hung up, then dialed the number.

"McCoy Private Investigation. How may I help you?"

"Hello. May I speak to Griffin McCoy?"

There was a pause. "I'm sorry. Whom may I ask is calling?"

"This is Edna Rothschild."

"Hello, Edna. I'm sorry, but Griffin McCoy is not available. Would you like to speak to his associate, Gary Marion?"

"Yes, that would be fine." When Gary came on the line, Edna explained that her son, Baron, had been working with Griffin on a case and that Baron was presumed dead as a result of the attack on 9-11. The reason for the call was to resume the case on Baron's behalf.

"I'm so sorry to hear about your son. Unfortunately, Griffin McCoy is also presumed dead. He had a meeting with your son at the World Trade Center on nine-eleven. If you are available tomorrow, we can meet at my office to review Griffin's findings."

———

Gary Marion met Edna in the lobby and escorted her into his office. He opened a manila folder on his desk. "I went through the file that Griffin had been working on. We had discussed the case, but not in great detail. Your son, Baron Rothschild, hired Griffin to investigate a financial adviser who he believed was mismanaging his parents' funds. Your funds." He glanced down and drew his finger over the typewritten page. "A Ms. Pretense Abdicator. I presume you know her."

Edna sputtered and clutched her throat. "Pretense? She's a lovely woman. Why would Baron be suspicious of Pretense?"

"I'm not sure what triggered his suspicions, but after reading through the case file there is compelling evidence that Pretense had set up a counterfeit company called C Katz Investments in order to embezzle money from you and Mr. Rothschild."

"No, it can't be. We worked with a woman named Kate Spencer from C Katz, not Pretense."

He put his reading glasses on and scanned the page. "It says here that Pretense Abdicator and Kate Spencer were one and the same."

Edna fell back against the chair with her hand on her heart, gasping for breath.

Gary's eyes popped. "Are you okay? Can I get you some water?"

"I ... I'm fine." She thought back to the recent conversation with Kate. She was suspicious at the time ... for good reason.

Gary pulled off his glasses. "It is my understanding that Griffin and Baron were meeting with Pretense, along with a Simon Crawford, and FBI agent, Dick Birchwood in the offices of Crawford Spectrum. No one has heard from any of the others that were in that meeting. It's highly likely that Pretense also perished on nine-eleven. As far as the money, Griffin was unable to track it down."

Edna retrieved a handkerchief from her purse and dabbed her face. "May I get a copy of that file?"

"Yes. I'll make you a copy."

———

After feeding Hyman and settling him in front of the TV, Edna sat at the desk and opened the folder. She read through the contents and discovered that Pretense had lied about growing up in foster homes. She had lived in a trailer park in New Mexico with her mother. And she read about the connection between Kate Spencer and another name, Claire Voyant, likely all the same person.

Edna put the paper down and pinched the bridge of her nose. It was too much to take in. Edna had always admired Pretense, and, at the same time, she felt sorry for her. But everything about her was a lie. If it was Pretense who called the other night—and she was convinced it was—then she was alive. But why would she send the money back? Since she is presumed dead, her chances of getting caught were scarce. Nothing made sense.

She picked up the phone and dialed Gary Marion's number. "I'd like for you take on the Pretense Abdicator case, but with very specific charges. I want you to go to New Mexico and do some digging on her background. When you get back, we can discuss next steps."

———

The following week, Edna's phone rang. A woman identifying herself as Kate Spencer came on the line. Her thick British accent appeared more pronounced this time. Edna listened intently and thought she heard the inflection of Pretense's voice.

"Hello, Mrs. Rothschild. Kate Spencer here. I have good news."

"Hello, Kate. I was wondering if you were going to call. Where are you calling from?"

There was a pause. "I'm calling from Connecticut. Why?"

"Oh, just curious. You sound a world away."

"Perhaps it's the connection. I'm calling to see if you received the bank draft."

"Yes, I did," Edna responded. "It has already been deposited. I noticed the bank that created the draft is located in Singapore."

"Yes, that is correct. I just wanted to follow up. I hate to cut you short, but I'm running late for an appointment. It was nice working with both you and Mr. Rothschild. Take care of yourselves."

"Perhaps we can meet in person one day. Thank you for your call." Edna hung up the phone and looked over at Hyman. "Darling, I think I just spoke to Pretense Abdicator." His dead eyes were fixed to the TV screen.

CHAPTER 43

The phone call with Edna felt odd. Pretense dragged her hand through her hair, then got up and paced the room, chewing on her thumbnail. Lan Chan had assured her that Claire Voyant would never be tied to the bank account in Singapore. And without that connection, the chances of being discovered were slim. She tossed her worries aside, grabbed her purse, and headed out the door.

Kerry's face lit when she saw Pretense entering the lobby. "Well? Did you go to church Sunday?"

"Yes. And I'm glad I did. I don't know what changed, but I haven't felt the same since."

Kerry rolled her eyes. "Did Pastor Pedro winnow you on the threshing floor?"

"I'm serious. We didn't really talk, but his sermon was incredible."

"Maybe I'll go with you next Sunday." Kerry pulled an envelope from her desk drawer. "Do you mind going to the bank today?"

"Sure. I'll go at the end of the day. I'd like to drop off a donation at the church and talk to Pedro, if he's around."

———

After making the deposit, she drove to the church, still pondering the phone call with Edna. Her spirit lifted when she saw Pedro out front, kicking around a soccer ball with a group of youngsters. He smiled and waved, then tossed the ball to an older boy and walked toward her.

Beads of sweat trickled down his neck and arms. He lifted his t-shirt and wiped his forehead. "It's good to see you. To what do I owe the pleasure?" he asked, his dark eyes teasing.

Pretense pulled a few cash banknotes from her purse and handed them to him. "I wanted to drop this off."

He took the money. "Thank you. Can you stay for dinner?"

"I'd like that," said Pretense.

They walked across the yard, several children chasing after them. A small boy clung to Pedro's leg, curbing his stride. Pedro bent down and lifted the youngster in the air. "Somboon, why don't you go into the dining hall. I'll be there in a few minutes."

As they entered the building, a middle-aged woman came forward, clasping her hands together and bowing. "My name is Solada."

Pretense returned the *wai* gesture and introduced herself.

"Solada and her husband, Udom, work and live at the church," Pedro explained. "I couldn't manage without them." He held a chair for Pretense, while the children clamored around the oblong dining table, fighting for a seat nearest Pedro. He walked around settling the youngsters, then he took a seat next to Pretense.

A young girl slid out of her chair and inched toward her, a shy smile forming. She recognized the child she'd seen selling flowers on the street. When the girl tried climbing onto Pretense's lap, Pedro leaned over, coaxing her down.

"I don't mind if she sits with me," said Pretense.

Pedro smiled and ruffled Maya's hair. "Maya would like that. She's the youngest in the group. We tend to spoil her."

While Pedro introduced Udom to Pretense, Solada fluttered around the table setting out bowls of sticky rice, sautéed vegetables, and curried chicken. After Solada took a seat, everyone bowed heads. Pedro's hand took hers, then he said grace, his words flowing unencumbered, stroking her mind, reminding her of the meal in Daphne's home when she had felt that same odd sense of peace. *Sweet Daphne, where are you now?*

After everyone had eaten and the plates were cleared, Solada came to take Maya. "It's time for a bath, little one." Maya reached for Solada, as Udom corralled the other children and led them into another room.

"Do you have to leave right away?" Pedro asked Pretense.

"Not really, but definitely before dark. I don't know my way around the island that well."

"I'll make sure you are home before dark, or I will personally escort you back. Let's go for a walk."

Pedro led Pretense along a riverside path behind the church, the sound of rushing water intensifying with each step. They reached a clearing where the river tumbled over an orange-hued rock ledge and into a plunge pool below. "This is where I come to think." He climbed a moss-covered hill on the edge of the river and motioned for Pretense to follow.

"It's gorgeous here," said Pretense. She sat down beside him. "What do you think about when you come here?"

He looked off. "I think about the children, and I pray that each one will be safe and find peace with God."

"Like you have?"

He turned to her, his eyes studying. "Yes, like I have. So, tell me about you. You seemed emotional after the sermon."

She looked down, toying with a strand of hair. "I'm pregnant," she blurted. She waited for his reaction, but he seemed unfazed.

"Congratulations. And the father?"

"He's not in the picture."

"Is that why you came to Thailand? To begin a new life?"

"I found out about the baby after I arrived."

He paused and picked up a stone, tossing it into the river. "What are you going to do?"

"I'm not sure." She turned away, tears burning her eyes. She felt his steady gaze.

"Do you have family back home?" he asked. "A support system?"

"No." She swiped a tear from her cheek. "My life is a mess. I'm a mess. It's complicated." He nodded and looked away. She regarded him closely; the set line of his jaw, the low ponytail trailing down his back, his hands slung loosely between propped knees. He seemed adrift in thought. "I'm sorry for being curt," she said, touching his arm.

He placed his hand over hers, his face taut. "Don't apologize. Life is never perfect."

She glimpsed the image of his hand on hers and then it moved away. "How did you get that?" she asked, reaching out tentatively and touching the scar on his face with her finger.

He looked at her. "A knife fight with a rival street gang. When I was young and reckless."

She studied him. "Where did you learn to speak English?"

"After I was saved, I lived with an American couple in Spain. They were missionaries. Not only did they guide me deeper in my faith, they taught me to read and write in English."

"Are you still in contact with them?"

Pedro looked off. "No. They both passed away. They were the parents I never had." He turned to her. "Let's talk about you."

She felt her body go tense. She picked at the hem of her skirt. "I'm not comfortable talking about myself."

"But you're comfortable asking me about myself. I think we come from similar backgrounds. Your anger on the street the day you saw me with Maya. Your emotion on Sunday when I shared my past. Am I wrong?"

She flinched and reeled back, startled by his insight. Her eyes shimmered as she fought for control, but the tears spilled as memories sawed through her, rusty-edged cans, each slice a festering wound. She had been laid bare. Her trembling hands covered her face to escape his probing eyes.

As she curled into herself, she felt the warmth of his arms. She let go of the pain and sank into him. They sat in silence, lulled by the hum of rushing water. After some time, she withdrew, her head hung low. "I've never spoken of my past to anyone."

He raised her chin with his finger. "Sometimes it helps to talk."

She nodded and turned away, her eyes squeezed shut. Then the words she thought she'd never share came out, spoken with eerie indifference. She told him about the men who came on a regular basis—the known pedophiles. Her mother told her it was the only way they could make a living. Either that or she would be given up for adoption. She wasn't sure which was worse. She was six when the nightmare began. Her only escape being school—her ticket to freedom.

His expression was resolute. "What about your father?"

"I never met my father."

"Is your mother still alive?"

"I think so, but I don't care. We don't talk."

His eyes found the swell in her belly and lingered.

She stroked the small bump. "I was drugged and raped. It happened in the Caribbean. I was there on business. I never reported it. I'm not even sure who the father is." Her eyes captured his gaze. "Now you understand. I'm a mess."

He smiled patiently. "The world is full of messy people. Sometimes we create our own mess, other times it's created for us. Take what has been given and make the most of your life. Never lose hope."

"But there is so much more. Things I can't even begin to tell you. I'm too ashamed."

His hand stroked her back, his face compassionate. "When

you are ready to talk about the rest, you know where to find me."

A fine mist began to fall. He stood and held out his hand. "It's almost dark and the roads will be slippery," he said, helping her to her feet. "I'll drive you home. You can pick up the scooter tomorrow."

He helped her down the hill. When she neared the bottom, his hand tightened over hers, their fingers intertwined. He led the way along the sodden path, as she followed close behind, comforted by the warmth of his skin.

When they reached the Jeep, he opened her door, then got in on the other side, pulling a dry towel from the backseat and handing it to her. "In case you want to dry off."

She took the towel and shook it through her flattened hair, then pulled down the visor and looked in the mirror. Her hair rumpled in an unruly heap. "I look awful," she said, dragging her fingers through the mass.

He started the car and glanced over at her. "I like it," he said.

She stared straight ahead.

He glanced her way. "You don't like yourself, do you?"

She considered the question and then flipped subjects. "Do you ever feel lonely?"

"Sometimes. I have my church family and the children, but I would like a family of my own one day—before I'm too old." He paused, his eyes fixed to the road. "I was engaged once. My fiancée decided that being a pastor's wife and living in Thailand was too much to handle. We came from very different worlds. She had a life of privilege. And you know my past. We were like oil and water." His expression dulled.

"I guess it was better to find out before you married."

He nodded and pulled the car into the parking lot of Moon-beam Bungalows. "Which room is yours?"

"I'm in the back, along the beach."

He got out and opened her door and took her hand. "I'll walk you. It's dark outside."

When they reached the door of her cottage, she hesitated. "Do you want to come inside?"

"I do, but I won't."

She flushed. "I'll ask Kerry to drive me to the church tomorrow to pick up the scooter."

"Call me if you want me to come and get you." He handed her a card. "Here's my number. Have a good night." He turned and left.

She looked after him as he walked away, each step further opening her void.

CHAPTER 44

n the front office, Pretense found Kerry sitting in the back room going over a stack of receipts. Kerry looked up. "There you are. I need your eyes. Do you mind?"

"Sure," said Pretense, closing the door. "Do you have a minute to talk?"

Kerry pulled down her reading glasses. "Is everything okay?"

Pretense nibbled at her bottom lip and looked down. "I don't know where to start, so I'll just come out with it." Her eyes met Kerry's anxious stare. "I haven't been totally honest with you and Denzel. Not because I wanted to deceive you. But because of problems in my past. I won't go into all the details, but I will tell you as much as I can … to set the record straight."

Concern blanketed Kerry's face. "I'm listening."

Pretense shoved her damp hands in her lap, her fingers crossing and uncrossing. She told Kerry that her parents didn't die when she was young and that her mother was still living, as far as she knew. She told her about the abuse she had suffered under her mother's care, and that the pregnancy was the result of an unreported rape. And finally, the nest egg she had spoken of no longer existed.

When she finished speaking, Kerry swallowed hard, her eyes brimming with tears. "Oh, Claire, I'm so sorry. Why did you feel you needed to be untruthful?"

"Shame, among other things. Fear of being judged. It's complicated. I had a long talk with Pedro and was able to deal with some things in my past. I wish I could explain why I lied, but I would need to reveal more than I'm willing—at least for now." Tears raced down her face. She dropped her head and hugged herself. "I'm trying to make things right, but it's so hard."

Kerry sat motionless. "The partnership we spoke of—were you really interested?"

"Yes, when I had the money."

Kerry rubbed her temples. "I'm having a hard time processing everything."

"I understand if you want me to leave. It seems I've spent my whole life trying to deny my past. Lying became my code of behavior. It was easier than telling the truth. But I'm trying to change. Having you in my life has made me realize the importance of friendship and honesty."

Kerry sank in her seat. "I can't even begin to understand what you've gone through."

"Can you forgive me?"

"Yes, of course. I'm just a little startled. You've thrown a lot at me."

"I'm sorry for everything. I just wanted you to know." Pretense rose from her seat. "I'll go through those receipts for you. One more thing. I left the scooter at the church yesterday. It was late, and it was raining, so Pedro drove me home. He said if I couldn't get a ride back he'd come and get me."

"I'll drive you," said Kerry. She stood and walked toward Pretense, stopping in front of her. She opened her arms, and they embraced. It was some time before either was willing to let go.

After Kerry left, Pretense sat down. With tears obscuring her vision, she tallied the pile of papers on the desk. Visions of the stunned look on Kerry's face surfaced, a painful reminder of her deceitful behavior … another victim of her pathetic life.

When she finished going over the receipts, she spent the afternoon going about her other chores, mindlessly drifting from task to task. She thought about her disjointed life and the innocent child she carried. What would become of them? And she wondered if her friendship with Kerry had been ruined.

After fluffing the bed pillows and arranging fresh orchids in a vase, she stood back, visualizing a guest's first impression—the way Kerry had taught her. Pleased, she opened the door and found Kerry on the porch, about to enter.

"You ready?" Kerry asked. "I can take you to the church now."

"Let me grab my purse."

The drive along the winding road was quiet. Then Kerry spoke. "I talked to Denzel. We agreed our lives have changed for the better since you've been here." She slowed the car and turned off into a pullout along the shore. With tears trickling down her cheeks, she stared straight ahead, her fingers gripping the steering wheel. "All I could think about today is the horrific abuse you've suffered. Please don't ever feel you can't be honest with me. That's what friends are for."

Pretense lowered her head. "I would never intentionally hurt you or Denzel. You mean so much to me."

"You have your reasons," said Kerry. "I don't fully understand, but going forward, let's not keep secrets." She started the car and drove away.

After Kerry dropped her off, Pedro came out of a building and jogged toward Pretense. His eyebrows furrowed. "Is everything okay?"

"Yes." She swiped a tear from her cheek. "Everything is fine. How was your day?"

"Busy. One of our partner churches in the U.S. is sending a mission team to Beacon of Hope. This happens a few times each year. I'm preparing for the group's arrival next week."

"What will they do when they arrive?"

"They help with the street children, lead Bible studies, and do general repairs on our buildings. Some of them work in the bakery. You should stop by next week and meet them."

She weighed the invitation. "I might do that. Maybe you can put me to work."

"Be careful what you ask for." The corners of his eyes crinkled. "Hey, I need your opinion. I'm planning a leisure day for the mission team and I'd like to take them sightseeing and then to lunch—somewhere different—but not sure where. Any thoughts?"

"Hmm. Kerry once took me to a funky café in Lipa Noi on the beach. Great food and atmosphere."

"I know that place. That's a great idea."

Pretense looked around. "Where are the children?"

"Udom and Solada are playing a game with them. Do you have to leave right away? I thought we'd go for a drive. I can show you one of the sightseeing spots I had in mind for the team."

She thought it best to decline, but she didn't. "I'd like that."

After a short drive, Pedro turned down a muddy road. As the Jeep churned through the sludge and climbed the side of a dense, forested mountain, Pretense gripped the door handle.

Pedro turned to her. "The view is worth the pain."

"I hope I don't vomit in your car."'

"Are you feeling sick?"

"Just a little dizzy. I'll be okay."

Pedro reached the top and pulled into a clearing, then opened her door and led her to a grassy spot overlooking the forested hills rimmed by the turquoise sea. The sun had washed the sky with bold streaks of golden orange, casting an ethereal glow.

She sat beside him on a patch of grass, taking in the sweeping vista. "Do you ever look at something so incredibly beautiful but don't quite know what to do with that feeling?"

He turned to her. "Like a taste of something longed for but never quite fulfilled. Like a taste of heaven." His eyes loitered then he looked away. "Do you think you'll stay in Thailand?"

"I'm trying to figure that out."

"Have you decided what to do about the baby?"

She drew in a slow breath. "Sometimes I want it gone, because of how it came to be. But when I run my hand over my stomach, I marvel at the miracle of life. I'm torn." She studied his profile, his tightening jaw stirring the muscles in his face.

He picked up a loose twig and dragged it across the ground. "My mother was raped. I suppose that's why she got into drugs. And why she never wanted me. It took me a long time to accept that. But looking back, I'm convinced it was my gift." He lifted his eyes from beneath dark brows. "Our past, no matter how ugly, can be a light. If my mother had aborted me, I wouldn't be here now, helping these children. Only you can decide what to do. But I wanted you to have a different perspective—from someone who was given a chance at life."

A lump rose in her throat. She peered into his eyes and swallowed deep. "Pedro, I'm so sorry."

"Don't be sorry." He took her hand and drew it to his lips, kissing her open palm, his breath warm on her skin. With their fingers knit together, his hand moved to the swell in her belly. "God gave me purpose. I didn't choose to be born, but I'm grateful I was." He looked away and released her hand, then stood. "We should get back before it gets dark." He reached for her arm and helped her to her feet.

She brushed the loose debris from her skirt. "Thank you for sharing your story, and for helping me realize that something good can come from evil."

"I'll pray you make the right decision."

She wondered if he would remember to pray, or was it just something religious people said out of habit. She didn't understand his world or his God, but he had a peace about him that she craved, like warm water soaking into her soul.

On the ride back, Pedro talked about the increase in child sex trafficking cases on the island. "These criminals are becoming more aggressive. There is a gentleman coming with the mission team next week. He's an expert on fighting the spread of this crime. While he is here, we plan to host an event to enlighten the community so that everyone is aware and involved in the fight."

"I'd like to attend the event."

"I'd like for you to be there." He turned into the church lot and parked. "Are you okay to drive back?"

"I'm fine."

He helped her get settled on the scooter. "When will I see you again?"

"I'm coming to church on Sunday. And I'm serious about helping prepare for the mission team."

"I can always use help. If you're free on Saturday, come by."

"I'll do that."

CHAPTER 45

Solada came out of the kitchen, wiping her hands on her apron. "Claire, I understand you are volunteering today. Do you mind chopping vegetables? I'm trying to get as much done as possible before the mission team arrives on Monday."

"Of course," said Pretense, glancing around expectantly.

Solada set bundles of baby bok choy on the counter along with several heads of garlic. "I need you to slice the heads of the bok choy and finely mince the garlic." She set several containers on the counter. "When you're done, put them in here." Solada smiled and patted Pretense on the back before resuming her position at the stove.

Pretense picked up a chopping knife and went to work. Soon after, Maya appeared from the corner of her eye, skootching a chair next to Pretense and climbing onto the seat, her eyes following Pretense.

"You can help me," said Pretense. After washing Maya's hands, she demonstrated how to gather the cut vegetables and place them into the containers. Maya dutifully obliged, working alongside Pretense all morning until Solada approached with a container of Pad Thai and two empty bowls.

"Why don't you two break for lunch?" asked Solada.

Pretense thanked her and took Maya's hand. On the way outside, she grabbed a children's picture book. Maya skipped alongside Pretense, babbling in Thai, while Pretense nodded and smiled. When they reached the picnic table, Pretense lifted Maya's slender body onto the bench and portioned the food into the bowls. Pretense picked up a utensil and started to eat, while Maya sat perfectly still, her head bowed. Pretense turned to her. "Grace?" She clasped her hands together. "You want me to say grace?"

Maya beamed. "Chai."

Pretense nodded. She looked around and took several deep breaths, then took Maya's hand and bowed her head. "Dear God. Thank you for this food, and thank you for Maya. May your shield of protection follow her all the days of her life. Amen." She raised her head, startled by the words that seemed to flow effortlessly from her lips. She looked at Maya. Maya's hazel eyes gazed up at her, her tiny hand reaching toward Pretense's face and patting her on the cheek. "Suay."

Pretense recalled their first meeting. "Yes, she is very pretty," Pedro had said when Maya had spoken that word. Pretense reached over and stroked Maya's cheek and moved her face closer to Maya. "Suay," said Pretense, pointing her finger at Maya. "You suay."

They ate in silence, Maya's eyes tracking Pretense. When Pretense dabbed her mouth with a napkin, Maya patted her lips with her fingers. Pretense ran her hand through her hair. Maya clawed at her dark hair, her fingers snagging in a butterfly barrette. Pretense reached over and hugged her. "Are you mocking me, you silly girl?" Maya giggled and leaned closer, running her petite hands across Pretense's skirt.

A sudden swell of protectiveness came over her. Maya was so tiny. So defenseless. What would become of her? Without warning, a flashback invaded; scratchy whiskers jabbing her slender throat, leathery hands groping her fragile body, as she lay helpless, drowning in the stench of whiskey and sweat. She struggled to breathe. She glanced over at Maya. Maya was watching Pretense and making exaggerated gasping sounds, gulping at the air. She reached for Maya and ran her hand over her head. "Let's fix your hair," said Pretense. She pulled Maya onto her lap and removed the barrette, her dark glossy hair falling over tiny rounded shoulders. "I think we should braid your hair." Maya sat unmoving as Pretense sectioned her mane, crossing each piece over the other, then clasped the tail end with the barrette. "There you go."

The child ran her hand over her hair and grinned. Pretense kissed her cheek, then opened the children's storybook and read as Maya followed along, pressing her finger onto each word.

"My two favorite girls," said Pedro, walking toward them. "I was wondering where you were."

Maya jumped off Pretense's lap and twirled before Pedro, running her hand along the braid. Pedro smiled and swept Maya into his arms. He looked at Pretense, his expression uneasy. "Maya's mother, Kwang, is here to take her home."

Pretense stood, fear gripping her face. "She can't take her. You said her mother is a drug addict. What if she tries selling her into the sex-trafficking ring?"

Pedro let out a long exhale. "I can't stop a mother from taking her own child. We can only pray that she is safe." He touched her arm, then turned and walked away carrying Maya.

"Wait," said Pretense, walking after Pedro and grabbing his shirt. "What if we tell Kwang she's not here? I can take Maya to the resort with me. Kwang won't look for her there."

Pedro's chocolate eyes melted into hers, his expression firm. "We will pray." Pedro turned and left.

Pretense followed him into the church foyer. A young Thai woman with lifeless eyes sat on a bench. When she saw Pedro with Maya, the woman got up and held her arms open. Maya tightened her grip around Pedro and buried her face in his neck.

Pedro bent and tried setting Maya on the ground, but she started crying, her tiny hands clinging to Pedro's t-shirt.

Pretense rushed forward. "She doesn't want to go with you. Can't you see that?"

Kwang gawked at Pretense, a confused look on her face.

"Claire, don't," whispered Pedro. "Kwang doesn't understand English. Let me handle this."

"How can you let her go with that woman?"

Maya's face blistered crimson, as her cries echoed through the hall. Solada rushed into the foyer and steered Pretense away from the scene and into the kitchen.

Pretense shielded her eyes, as a steady stream of tears dribbled down her cheeks. She fell limp into Solada's arms, as Maya's screams tore through her heart.

"We must leave it in God's hands," said Solada. "Perhaps Maya will come back to us again. She often does."

Pretense nodded, the knob in her throat choking back words. Solada led her to the kitchen table and poured a glass of water. Pretense drank deliberately, the water soothing her misery. When she looked up, Pedro was standing at the kitchen door.

"Let's walk," he said to Pretense, his hand outstretched.

He led her outside. They walked along the road in silence. Then Pedro stopped and placed his hands on her shoulders. "Claire, Kwang is Maya's mother. We cannot keep her away from Maya. As much as it hurts—and it hurts me, too—we must trust in God."

Pretense hung her head. "When I see Maya, I see myself. And I think about the dysfunctional woman I became. If someone would have rescued me, maybe I wouldn't be the way I am now. I only want what's right for Maya. Is that wrong?"

"No, it's not wrong." He pulled her into him.

His breath felt warm against her neck. His heartbeat pulsated through her trembling body as his arms tightened around her. She buried her face in his chest, surrendering to the shelter of his protection, her worries drifting like a cloud across a pale blue sky.

He pulled away and looked at her, his eyes steady. His hands took her face and drew her nearer until his parted lips pressed against hers. Instinctively, she drew back and looked down.

He shifted backward. "I didn't mean for that to happen."

A sinking, yielding sensation edged in. She met his gaze, then stepped into him, their mouths meeting once again. His lips were intent, descending down her neck, his breath caressing her skin. She ran her hands down the length of his back, his body pressing against hers, their mouths willing as the world slipped away.

He broke away, his hands dropping to his sides. "Claire, I want to be with you but not like this. I want us to be right with God."

She folded her arms across her chest and stared up at him, her guilty eyes laced with shame. "I'm not who you think I am."

He studied her face. "Then tell me who you are."

"I am a bad person." She turned away, tears pricking her eyes.

He moved into her space and raised her chin, his penetrating gaze tunneling into her soul. "I don't believe that. I see how your heart aches for Maya and the other children. I think you are a good person, but you've been broken. And you are trying to put yourself back together, but something is holding you back." His hand stroked her face. "What is it?"

She felt consumed by his existence. "I ... I'm not ..." She squeezed her eyes shut, blocking his gaze, and willed the words to come. But an inner voice took over. *Don't do it.* She stopped and yanked his hand from her face. "You won't understand. I have to go." She turned and ran toward the church, the sound of his distant voice calling after her, stabbing her heart.

When she returned to the resort, she parked the motorbike and walked to the water's edge, her mind drowning in a swirl of hopelessness. Her mother was right. She was never meant for anything good. The last glint of sunshine poked the twilight sky, illuminating her wretched existence. A trail of tears ran down her cheeks like Satan's claws. Snapshots of Maya's terrified face and Pedro's persistent eyes flashed beneath her eyelids. She looked toward heaven and contemplated the invisible God. Pedro's God. Daphne's God. The gentle placement of a palm against her back roused her to the present.

"Claire? Are you okay?" asked Kerry.

Pretense brushed her tears with a quick swipe. "I'm fine."

"Pedro called the resort looking for you. He's worried. He said you left your cell phone at the church. He wants you to call him."

Pretense nodded then covered her face with her hands.

Kerry stopped in front of her and pulled Pretense's hands away. "What's going on?"

"I'm in love with Pedro."

Kerry's eyes popped. "Wow. Is that a bad thing?"

"It is for someone like me. He's a pastor. And I don't even know if I believe in God, not to mention that I'm pregnant. How's that going to work?"

A soft smile creased Kerry's face. She tucked a strand of Pretense's hair behind her ear. "If it's meant to be, it'll work out. Go call him? Use the phone in the lobby."

Pretense scrunched the sand with her bare toes. "I guess you're right."

She flicked on the light in the lobby and went into the office and dialed Pedro's number. He answered on the first ring. "Claire. I was worried about you. Are you okay?"

"Yes, I'm okay. I'm sorry for running off like that."

He inhaled deep, then let out a long sigh. "Claire … we need to talk … about us. Are you free for dinner tomorrow night?"

Her heart stumbled in her chest. After a bloated pause, she answered. "Yes, I'd love to have dinner with you."

CHAPTER 46

After returning from New Mexico, Private Investigator, Gary Marion, met with Edna Rothschild in his New York office. "I had a very productive trip," Gary said, opening a manila folder. "What I learned is heart wrenching."

"I'm anxious to hear," Edna responded.

Gary leaned forward. "I located the mother of Pretense Abdicator. She lives in a dilapidated trailer in a cluster of mobile homes off of Route 66 in Gallup, New Mexico. Her name is Wanda Abdicator. I did some digging. Wanda has lived there for over forty years. Pretense lived there also until she went away to college. There were numerous police reports filed against the mother, but no formal charges were ever issued. Why, I don't know." Gary slipped on his reading glasses. "In 1977, police were called to the home when five-year-old Pretense was seen running around the property, naked and crying. The mother explained she was sleeping when the child let herself out of the trailer. However, neighbors in the area told of a man—one of her mother's visitors—chasing the child through the yard while the mother sat on the porch laughing."

Edna threw her hand to her open mouth and gasped.

Gary paused, glancing over his glasses. "There's more. In

1979, a teacher noticed rope burns on the child's wrists and ankles. She contacted Child Protective Services. They went to the home, but again, nothing was done." Gary flipped through several sheets of paper. "In 1980, there were numerous sightings of a young Pretense standing on a street corner peddling flowers in downtown Gallup while dressed in suggestive clothing and wearing makeup. Her mother would watch from a nearby location, then the two would get into a car and drive off, only to return to the same corner later in the day. Then the cycle would repeat. Again, in 1980..."

"Stop." Edna reached in her purse and drew out a handkerchief, dabbing her eyes. "I've heard enough."

Gary collected the papers and tapped them on his desk. "I do have some good news if you are interested."

Edna fanned her face with her hand. "Only if it's positive."

"I was able to go through Pretense's school records. She has an impressive IQ and maintained a 4.0 average throughout her years in middle school and high school. As a result, she received a full-ride scholarship to Harvard. I did some checking into her years at Harvard. No one knew much about her, other than she kept to herself, buried in her studies and working side jobs, taking on the maximum hours allowed. One staff member described her as oddly intelligent but overlooked by everyone."

"I heard about the scholarship. I'm pleased to hear the claim was truthful." Edna took in a long breath. "How she managed to maintain her grades while suffering through that hellish life is beyond me." With a shaky hand, she drew a checkbook from her purse and wrote a check, slipping it across the desk. "This has been most informative. I have another request. I'd like you to find Pretense, and I don't care what it costs."

Gary frowned. "Mrs. Rothschild, there is overwhelming evidence that no one who attended the meeting with Baron on nine-eleven made it out of the tower alive."

"I don't believe that. I believe Pretense is alive." Edna explained the call from Kate Spencer and the return of the money. "I think she left the country. I want you to locate her and find out everything you can—where she is staying, what she is doing, et cetera."

"I'm happy to do that, but I'm curious why you wouldn't go to the FBI. According to Griffin's file, he was working very closely with an FBI agent."

"I don't want them involved. I have my reasons. If you are willing to look for her, you will be paid very handsomely for your services. And the sooner you provide results, the more lucrative your compensation. Time is of the essence. As you can see, I'm not getting any younger."

Gary nodded. "I will move my current workload to one of my colleagues and dedicate the next few months to this case."

———

After Edna left his office, Gary raked his fingers through his copper hair. The money couldn't have come at a better time. He didn't have a single case in the hopper, and his 1991 Chevrolet Cavalier was fighting to stay alive. He buzzed Helen at the front desk and asked her to bring everything she could find related to the Baron Rothschild file. It was Friday, but he didn't mind working late; however, the wife would be none too pleased. For the second week in a row, he would miss their Samba dance lesson and dinner with the in-laws. A snarky grin cracked his face.

After breaking the news to Carol, he removed his sport jacket, loosened his tie, and ordered a large, deep-dish pizza—heavy on the anchovies. When dinner arrived, he shoved a wedge of cardboard crust into his mouth, as he rummaged through the *Rothschild* Bankers Box, setting the documents aside. At the bottom of the pile was a stack of scribbled notes. A tinge of sadness washed over him as he read Griffin's telltale chicken scratch. Griffin was one of the brightest men he'd ever known. "Here's to you, good buddy, wherever you are," he said, raising a bottle of Bud Light into the air. He shook off the bluesy feeling and homed in on a clue written in bold, block letters. *SHELL COMPANY—BVI-GCS?* Griffin must have been onto something. Gary knew the British Virgin Islands was a mecca for legitimate shell company incorporators, but what or who was GCS? He searched online for a list of all BVI incorporators. An hour later, he came across Global Corporate Solutions. He leaned back in his chair and propped his feet on the desk, then dialed the number.

"Global Corporate Solutions, Justin Moore speaking."

"Hello, Justin. My name is Gary Marion, and I'm interested in setting up a shell company and an offshore bank account."

"Absolutely. My company handles the registration of the shell company in the British Virgin Islands. As far as the offshore bank account, we assist you in setting up an account through our banking partner in Singapore."

"I've done research on banking in Singapore," said Gary. "That particular location appears to be a very safe and stable option for my money. Can I ask the name of the bank you partner with?"

"We work exclusively with PTS Bank. They are known for their sound reputation."

Gary stiffened. Edna had said the bank draft came from PTS Bank in Singapore. "Would it be possible to speak directly to your contact at PTS Bank? I have specific questions."

"I'm sorry, but PTS prefers to work directly through me. Once you've registered a shell company with GCS and your banking application is approved, then you can speak directly with our contact. Maybe I can help answer your questions."

Gary drummed his fingers on the desk. "As it so happens, I'm going to be in the Virgin Islands next week on business. Why don't we schedule an in-person meeting? Does Monday work for you?"

After confirming the meeting schedule, he spent the remainder of the evening concocting details for a phony shell company. Before leaving the office, he booked a flight to the British Virgin Islands.

———

Gary was stunned by how easy it was to set up a shell company in the British Virgin Islands. But he needed that one critical piece of information—the contact name at PTS Bank. Rather than fly back to the states and wait for a call from the bank, he decided to hang around the islands and work on his Coppertone tan.

Three days later, his cell phone buzzed as he lounged beachside in a hammock sucking down a Banana Daiquiri.

"Hello, Mr. Marion. This is Lan Chan calling from PTS Bank in Singapore. I'm calling to inform you that a bank account has been set up for your company, Griffin Rocks." She went on to explain the particulars.

After asking a number of semi-intelligent financial questions, Gary spun the conversation. It was a longshot, but he gave it a try. "My good friend Claire Voyant mentioned that she worked with you to set up an account for her company, C Katz Investments. She had nothing but great things to say about your professionalism and your attention to detail."

There was a brief pause. "You are a friend of Claire's?"

"Yes, we went to school together. She is quite an adventurous woman. It's hard keeping up with her. She's always traveling to some exotic location. We are planning to meet up soon."

"Well, tell Claire I said hello."

"I will," said Gary. "The last time we spoke, she mentioned going to … gosh, I can't remember. It's hard keeping track."

"Thailand. She went to Koh Samui. It is very beautiful there."

Gary thanked Lan Chan for her time and ended the call, then sprang from the hammock and sprinted down the beach. "Wow, did that just happen?" he said aloud. It seemed too easy, like a crime fiction novel where the convoluted plot miraculously comes together.

CHAPTER 47

P retense slid the chartreuse dress over her shoulders; the creamy stroke of silk brushing her bare skin. She tousled her hair, then fingered the simple diamond pendant dangling from a gold chain. "A little pop of bling will send ripples down his spine," Kerry had said when she lent Pretense the necklace.

She glanced at her watch. Pedro would be here any minute. Her stomach pitched and rolled, as she slipped into a pair of sandals and dabbed gloss on her lips. The soft knock startled her. She fluffed her hair again, took two deep breaths, and opened the door. Pedro stood before her, clad in black pants and a white linen shirt, unbuttoned at the collar, the sleeves rolled just above his wrists. She swallowed deep.

He handed her a bouquet of white roses. "Good evening, Claire," he said, his playful eyes traveling over her. "You look enchanting."

Her heart fluttered as she took the flowers and inhaled the scent. "Thank you. They are beautiful. Would you like to come in while I put these in water?"

"I'll wait outside and enjoy the view."

She went inside and assembled the roses in a glass vase. It was the first time she had been given flowers. She felt frozen in time, a princess holding court. Gathering her wits, she dabbed at her eyes and stepped outside.

He turned to her, his dark eyes lingering. "I hope you're hungry."

"I'm starving," she replied. He took her by the hand and led her to his car. Her thumb traced his skin in an absent manner as she ingested the nearness of his body.

When they passed by the front lobby window, Pretense noticed Kerry's face peeking between the fronds of an artificial kangaroo paw fern. Her hand appeared, delivering a thumbs-up. Pretense smirked.

"Where are we going?" she asked, when Pedro pulled the Jeep out of the parking lot.

"To one of the nicer restaurants on the island. One of my parishioners gave me a gift card awhile back. I've never had the opportunity to use it. I heard the food is fantastic." He looked at her and winked before turning his attention to the road.

Conversation came easy, as they drove along the coastal lane leading to the northern tip of Koh Samui. Pedro slowed the car and pulled to the front entrance of an exclusive-looking restaurant. He handed his keys to the valet and led Pretense inside a darkened room, the warm glow of tiki torches casting a halo of light across a wood plank floor.

They were led outside to a private, weathered teak and bamboo terrace that faced the Gulf of Thailand. The host held a chair for Pretense. "Your waiter will be here shortly," he said.

Pretense looked around. "Do we have this whole section to ourselves?"

"Yes. I wanted to make this evening special." He reached across the table, his hand covering hers.

A tingling awareness spread through her body. She looked down to hide the reddish glow covering her face. He squeezed her hand. Her eyes hung on his, then she looked away.

"Would you like something to drink?" the waiter asked.

Pedro looked at Pretense. "How about lime tea?"

"Lime tea is fine."

"We'll have two Cha Manaos and Kao Yum to start," said Pedro.

When the waiter left, she turned to him. "Any word on Maya?"

"Udom paid a visit to Kwang's house, but no one was home. Solada thinks she may have seen Maya selling flowers on a street corner when she drove by. But by the time Solada parked the car, Maya was gone. I'm planning to go to their house soon."

"I'd like to go with you. I would love to see Maya."

His jaw tightened. "It's best if you didn't. Not because I don't want you to go, but because it's too emotional—for you and for Maya. I hope you understand."

She forced a smile. "I understand." She looked off, blinking back tears.

"Hey, look," he said, "the minute I hear something, I'll let you know." He stroked her arm. "You have a good heart, Claire."

"No one has ever accused me of having a good heart."

He looked intently at her. "You have many fine qualities. I felt it the first moment I met you—when you badgered me on the street about Maya. Something stirred inside of me that day. And it hasn't stopped stirring since."

She held his gaze. "There are so many good women deserving of a man like you. Godly women. Why me?"

He stood up and moved his chair closer to hers, then sat down, their arms touching. "When I was young and living with the missionary couple, the woman, Elizabeth, sat me down one day and told me all the reasons why she loved me. She must have given me ten reasons. But I couldn't think of one reason why anybody would love me. I remember looking at her, totally baffled—like the way you just looked at me. And then she said something I'll never forget. She said, 'Pedro, you'll never experience the depth of genuine love unless you first learn to love yourself.' For those of us who have struggled with an abusive past, it's hard to let go of our self-hatred. It's what we were taught. But I'm blessed that I was able to scale that mountain." He reached out and took her hand. "God created us for relationships. I can't answer your question, *Why me?* It's like a force, drawing me to you. I can't explain. I only know how I feel."

She gazed steadily at him, her eyes soft. "I'd be lying if I said I didn't share the same feelings as you. I do. When I'm with you, I feel worthy, and when I'm not with you, my heart hurts. It's as though I've been searching for you all of my life. And now that you are here, I'm frightened."

"What are you afraid of?"

She looked out at the ocean. "I'm afraid you'll discover who I really am."

"Then tell me who you really are. Let me decide." He took her chin and turned her face to him.

"I am a damaged woman who desperately wishes she were someone else. Someone you could be proud of."

The waiter returned with their tea and mixed rice salad.

"It looks delicious," said Pretense.

Pedro took a sip of tea. "Let's lighten up this conversation and enjoy our dinner."

They dined on steamed sea bass in a lime and chili marinade, jasmine rice, and an assortment of mini Thai desserts. When they finished eating, she sat back in her chair and heaved a sigh. "That was the best meal I've ever had. Thank you—for everything."

"I'm glad you enjoyed it. Let's take a walk down the beach," he said, after settling the bill.

Pretense removed her sandals and took Pedro's outstretched hand. He led her down the steps to the water's edge. A gentle breeze wafted in off the ocean, as palm fronds waved lazily against the night sky. They walked along in silence, content in each other's company.

He stopped and wrapped his arms around her waist, lifting

her up against him. His lips were on hers for what seemed an endless time, and then he drew back, his eyes searching her face. "I'm in love with you, Claire. Marry me. I know it's only been a few weeks since we met, but your baby needs a father, and I need you."

CHAPTER 48

Pretense tossed in bed, her mind fixated on Pedro's marriage proposal. She sat up and pulled her knees to her chest. Moonlight streamed through the window, illuminating silvery roses on the nightstand—his gift to her. She felt undone by an aching desire.

Although everything inside of her said yes, she didn't give him an answer. When he kissed her goodnight, he told her to take her time and think it over. But what was there to think about? It would never work. When her tears subsided, she drifted into a fitful sleep.

———

"Are you all right?" asked Kerry, when Pretense arrived for work the following morning.

"I didn't sleep well." She held out the diamond pendant. "Thanks for letting me borrow your necklace."

"No worries." Kerry took the chain and tapped her foot on the floor, her hands slung on her hips. "Is that all you have to say? I'm dying to know. Did he spend the night?"

"Kerry, he's a pastor. He's not like other men."

"Well, I'm sure he's functional. Don't you think?"

Pretense laughed and sank into a chair. "Oh, Kerry. It was the most magical night of my life, and I'm helplessly in love with him. He asked me to marry him."

Kerry's mouth dropped like a slack-jawed puppet. "Get out! I'm flabbergasted. You said yes, right?"

"I didn't give him an answer." Pretense gnawed her lower lip. "How can someone with my baggage marry a pastor?"

"But you told him about the baby and about your upbringing. He's obviously not fazed. And you said you love him. What's the problem?"

"Good things aren't meant for people like me." She turned away. "I'll get started on the rooms. I told Pedro I would stop by the church after work. A team of missionaries is arriving from the U.S. today. I'm going to help."

"Claire, don't you want to talk this through? It's the chance of a lifetime. He's willing to be the father of your baby. Don't be a dingbat."

"There is nothing to talk about." Pretense picked up the printed room roster. "I'll get to work now."

When she had finished her chores, Pretense drove to the church and found Solada in the kitchen, sweat beading on her face.

"Oh, thank God you're here," said Solada. "I could use your help."

Pretense felt relieved Pedro wasn't around. She'd have to face him at some point, but she dreaded the conversation. And he had enough on his mind today. After setting the dining table and washing a sink full of dirty pots and pans, Solada asked her to fetch a few loaves of bread from the bakery across the yard. Pretense grabbed a wicker basket and headed outside. As she neared the bakery, she spotted Pedro on the playground giving a group of people a tour of the grounds. He waved to her and resumed his discussion with the missionary team.

She opened the wooden door of the bakery and went inside. Freshly baked loaves were stacked on the countertop. After loading the bread into the basket, she stood at the small window gazing at the man she loved. He appeared so comfortable around people—children and adults alike. Easy in his own skin. She left the bakery and walked toward the church. As she passed the cluster of people, Pedro turned and winked. He said something to the group and jogged toward her. When he caught up to her, he kissed her openly on the cheek.

"I thought we'd be able to talk later—you know—about last night. But it looks like I'll be busy the rest of the day. Will you be at the community event tomorrow night? The gentleman I told you about—the authority on child sex trafficking—will be speaking. We can talk after the meeting."

"Yes, of course.

He tucked a strand of hair behind her ear. "I'll see you tomorrow night." He squeezed her hand and rejoined the group.

She clutched the wicker basket to her chest and went inside to find Solada at the chopping block, slicing a stack of carrots, the stainless-steel knife a blur in her hand.

Solada looked up. "There you are. I saw you outside with Pedro. He kissed your cheek. I think that man is in love with you."

A faltering smile formed on her lips. "He's a good man. Any woman would be lucky to have him."

Solada went over and placed her hands on Pretense's arms. "I think you are that lucky woman." She wiped her hands on her apron. "Come sit with me. I need a break." Solada poured steaming water from a kettle into two teacups and set it on the table between them. "I've known Pedro for over five years. Did he tell you he was engaged?"

"Yes, he did mention it."

"I'm glad it didn't work out. Her name was Sofia. She was

very beautiful, but a little too … how you say … highfalutin. She didn't like the heat, so she spent a lot of time shielding her head under an umbrella. Very pale, she was, for a Spaniard. And very delicate. Pedro met her in Spain, and she came shortly after he arrived in Thailand. They were supposed to be married soon after, but I think when she got here, he realized he had made a mistake. So, they parted ways. Pedro seemed very sad at first, but I think deep down he was relieved. And so was I." She patted Pretense on the hand. "I think you are perfect for Pedro."

Pretense looked down. "Pedro is such a godly man, and I've never had a relationship with his God, or any god."

"But you are searching. That's why you are here today, and why you met Pedro. Sometimes I think Pedro can look into someone's heart and see what others cannot."

"I don't feel I'm good enough for Pedro, or for Pedro's God."

"God's grace is not something you achieve—it's something you receive. It's realizing that you are not good enough, and therein lies the reason you need God."

Pretense looked away and stood. "Thank you for your encouragement. It means a lot to me. I should get back to work. What do you need me to do next?"

———

When she returned to the resort, she went out onto the patio. The last glint of sunlight danced off the turquoise waves of the ocean like cut diamonds spilling from a jeweler's velvet bag. She leaned her head back and closed her eyes, rehashing her conversation with Solada. *Maybe things really do happen for a reason.*

CHAPTER 49

Before leaving the British Virgin Islands, Gary Marion contacted Edna Rothschild, informing her of the lead. Then he reached out to a private investigator in Thailand to expedite the process of locating Claire Voyant. According to the gentleman he spoke to, David Omni, a local like himself would have access to databases and connections to the right people—something that Gary lacked. Convinced David was the right man, Gary provided him the information he had and emailed a photo of Pretense Abdicator.

Samui International Airport appeared through an opening in the clouds as the plane approached the northern tip of the island. Once on terra firma, Gary collected his bag and stepped out of the open-air terminal and into a wall of tropical heat. He hailed a taxi and gave the driver a slip of paper with David's office address written across the front.

The driver dropped him off in front of a run-down building in the city of Chaweng. Gary looked around. The place seemed deserted. He tried opening the door, but it was locked. He cupped his hands over his eyes and looked through a grimy window, then he knocked. A smallish man appeared from behind a metal filing cabinet, clad in a pair of billowing black trousers and a powder-blue smock resembling a chef's jacket.

"You must be Gary Marion," said the man in perfect English, after unlocking the door. "I'm David Omni."

Gary shook his hand and stepped inside. David led him into a room behind the filing cabinet. A wire, cage-like fan sat atop a window sill, its whirring blades sending wind squalls across the room, causing David's toupee to flap like a piece of cardboard in a tropical cyclone. David rolled a swivel chair across the floor toward Gary.

"Take a seat. You must be thirsty. How about a beer?"

I'm starting to like this guy. "I would love one." Gary pulled out a notepad and fanned himself, waiting for David's return.

"Here you go," said David, setting down two ice-filled glasses and a bowl brimming with caramel-colored, crispy snacks. After pouring a bottle of Singha over ice, he tipped his glass to Gary.

Gary returned the gesture and took a hearty swallow of ale. "Thank you. I needed that." Low on fuel, he popped a handful of treats in his mouth. "These are great," he said, smacking his lips and reaching for more. "What are these?"

"They are called Nhon Mhai Tod," said David. "Better known as deep-fried silkworms."

A stream of bile rose in Gary's throat. He fought back a gag and reached for his glass, draining the liquid.

David's eyes puckered, then he doubled over and let out a high-pitched squeal followed by choking laughter. Several minutes passed, then he wiped his eyes with a handkerchief. "Welcome to Thailand. I'll get you another beer. Then we get to work."

Gary thought about leaving but remembered Edna's words … "The sooner you provide results, the more lucrative your compensation." He took five deep breaths and chalked it up to a bad bout of culture shock.

David returned with two more beers and a stack of papers.

He slipped on a pair of turquoise-rimmed reading glasses and spread the documents on a wobbly pedestal table. "I was able to uncover information regarding your subject." He revealed the exact date that a woman by the name of Claire Voyant had cleared Customs in Thailand and the name of the resort where she currently stayed. Then he produced a stack of black and white photos and handed them to Gary.

Gary shuffled through the images. The woman resembled the snapshot Gary had of Pretense Abdicator, although the hair appeared lighter, and the nose definitely different—more refined. Edna had also mentioned something about a chipped front tooth. He went back and studied a close-up photo of Claire smiling, her teeth flawless.

"This is great work," said Gary. He paid David the agreed upon amount. "Thank you. I believe I have everything I need to get started. I'll try to book a room where the woman is staying."

"If you need anything else, please contact me." He slid a business card across the table.

———

It was after 5 p.m. when Gary checked into the last available room at Moonbeam Bungalows. He set aside his bag and stepped onto the patio, taking in the view. Squinting against the glare, he scanned the string of cottages lining the beach. No sign of Pretense.

He went inside his room and called home, wishing Carol could be here with him. They never had a proper honeymoon. The in-laws had gifted them with an all-inclusive getaway to the Mall of America, including two nights in the honeymoon suite at the Best Western and two free meals at Buffalo Wild Wings. Not exactly the romantic honeymoon he had in mind. He would make it up to Carol once he received the lucrative payout from Edna.

After ending the call, he took a shower, then removed the

short-sleeved silk Tommy Bahama shirt from his bag and held it up to his chest. The wispy green palm fronds and yellow hibiscus pattern complemented his orange tan and hair. He put it on, then threw on a pair of aviator-mirrored sunglasses and stood in front of the mirror, shifting from side to side, an unlit cigar clamped between his teeth. He looked like a typical tourist. He gave his reflection a thumbs-up, then grabbed his Panama hat and left the bungalow, heading in the direction of the front lobby.

The woman who had checked him in earlier was at the front desk. "Kerry, right?" asked Gary. "I'm looking for a place to eat. Any recommendations?"

"We have a lovely restaurant on the grounds," said Kerry. "But if you want something more casual," she said, eyeing his ensemble, "then I'd suggest taking a cab to Chaweng Beach and eating at one of the local food stalls. If you're looking for nightlife, many of our guests have raved about the Cha-Cha Dance Club." She wrote the address on a business card and handed it to him.

After thanking Kerry, Gary took a cab to the heart of the beach town. He wandered the food stalls and ordered a meal from a small stand with a neon sign that read THE BEST BBQ IN THAILAND. With his stomach full, he wiped his mouth with the back of his hand, then adjusted his hat and swaggered toward the thumping music. His Samba dance moves just may come in handy tonight.

The ground shook as he neared the Cha-Cha Moon Dance Club, an open-air pavilion with thousands of fairy lights strung across the ceiling. He stepped inside and took in the electrifying scene. A DJ spun tunes from inside a gargantuan makeshift martini glass, while fire dancers twirled from the rafters. Throngs of partygoers crowded the dance floor, their glistening bodies cavorting to the music.

Gary stood off to the side, bobbing his head and sipping a scotch on the rocks.

"Would you like to dance?" A twentysomething Thai woman smiled up at him, her slender body stuffed into a black, low-cut Saran Wrap dress, her elfin feet adorned with towering, red high heels.

"I'd love to," Gary answered, surprised by his stroke of luck.

She took his hand and led him to the dance floor.

———

When Gary regained consciousness, he was lying next to a trash dumpster, a multi-colored rooster pecking his loafers. He sat up, his head whirring like a washing machine on the agitation cycle. He touched the back of his skull and felt something sticky. Remnants of his hat were scattered across the concrete, a mass of shredded straw. He stood up and kicked at the striking chicken, then felt in his back pocket. His wallet was gone. *What the hell happened?* The last thing he remembered was leaving the bar alone.

When he found his way back to the dance club, he reached inside his shirt pocket and pulled out the card from Moonbeam Bungalows. He asked to use the phone and dialed the number. After Gary explained his dilemma, Denzel told him someone would be there shortly to bring him back to the resort. Gary waited near the front entrance, his mind in a tailspin. Thankfully, he had left his passport in the room, but without a credit card and identification, his undercover work would be stalled.

Minutes later, a car pulled up in front. A woman in the driver's seat waved him over. Gary peered in, his mouth opening like a window. The woman he'd seen in David Omni's photos was smiling up at him. "Are you from Moonbeam Bungalows?" Gary asked.

"Yes. You must be Gary Marion. Hop in."

He nodded and opened the door.

They eyed each other, then the woman held out her hand. "I'm Claire Voyant."

CHAPTER 50

When she dropped Gary off at the resort, Pretense returned to her room. Something about the copper-headed man made her uneasy. He barely uttered two words during the drive. And those darting eyes flicking a peek when he didn't think she'd noticed. Her flesh crawled. She shook off the feeling and changed into a nightgown.

Her focus turned to the upcoming community event. Pedro said they would talk afterward. He was waiting for an answer. A weighty sigh escaped, as her hand drifted to the place where the baby slept. She pulled her nightgown tight across her midsection. The bump felt a tad more prominent. Perhaps a girl—like Maya. But a boy would be just fine, too.

She didn't know at what point in her mind she had accepted Pedro's proposal, but a sea change had occurred. They would love this child with the love denied them and live happily ever after. And when the timing seemed right, she would one day tell Pedro everything. She stretched her body out on the bed and freed a soft yawn. Sleep came without delay.

***

After being dropped off, Gary went to his bungalow, dumbstruck by the chance encounter with Claire ... or Pretense ... or whoever she was. He paced his room, unable to sleep. Being so close to her in the car had rattled his otherwise chill demeanor. Griffin had always told him, "Expect the unexpected." He should have seized the opportunity to grill her with questions, but his tongue had tangled. And now there was the problem of his wallet. Without a credit card and identification, he was at a standstill. Desperate, he called David Omni.

"Sawasdee krub, David Omni."

"David. This is Gary Marion. Sorry for calling at this late hour."

"Hello, Gary. No problem. I was just rehearsing a song for a wedding this weekend. It's a side job. Would you like to hear it? It's an American Elvis song."

This guy is a nut job. "Sure, why not?"

David sparked up what sounded to be a 2000-watt Karaoke sound system and began singing like a wounded whippoorwill. "This is the moment ..."

"David, I hate to interrupt, but I need your help."

David's voice echoed through the phone. "What do you need?"

"Maybe you could turn off the loudspeaker."

"Oh, sorry." His voice quieted. "What do you need?"

Gary explained that he had gotten rolled and asked if David could help find his wallet.

"Ahh. The Cha-Cha Moon Dance Club. Notorious for pickpockets. You called the right man. We will go there tonight and find your wallet. I will pick you up in ten minutes."

"Tonight?"

There was no answer.

Gary left the bungalow and walked to the front of the resort. David's dwarfish vehicle was idling out front. He climbed into the passenger seat. "That was quick."

"Sleuth Dawg never sleeps." The car lurched forward and left the parking lot at an alarming rate of speed, gravel spitting from the donut-sized tires. Within seconds, they were pulling up to the entrance of the club. David leapt out. "Follow me."

Gary half trotted to keep pace with the little man's gait. He watched, as David shot onto the dance floor, boogying through the crowd, weaving his way in and out of pulsating twosomes, occasionally pausing to cavort with a duo. Then he waved toward Gary and pointed.

Gary followed David outside and onto the beach. David's powder-blue chef jacket glowed against the moon-lit sky as he sprinted toward a threesome standing under a palm tree. He heard David shouting. The men looked up.

What happened next defied the laws of gravity. David left the ground, his body twirling mid-air, his legs opening like a pair of gardening sheers swathed in billowing, black fabric. With scissor-like precision, his ankles snapped together around one man's neck, and they tumbled to the ground and rolled down the beach. Suddenly, David sprang to his feet, barking like a dog, as he ran toward another man. David pushed his body off the sand and launched into a series of full-frontal body flips down the beach toward the running man. David's toupee escaped from his head and landed in the bay. The running man tossed Gary's wallet and scurried up a palm tree. The third man disappeared into the night. David planted himself at the base of the tree, shouting something in Thai and shaking his fist.

Gary emerged from his hiding place, his mouth ajar.

David jogged toward him, a halo of moonlight luminous on his bald head. He handed Gary his wallet. "Check to make sure everything is there."

Gary fingered the contents. "Everything appears to be in order. That was amazing. How did you learn to do that?"

"Side job. I teach Thai boxing. Maybe you would like some lessons?"

Gary smiled. "Maybe another time."

———

After a restless night, Pretense dragged her body from bed and staggered to the shower, visions of the cagey guest played on her mind. After changing, she left the bungalow and went into the front lobby.

"Good morning," said Kerry. "Did you make a decision regarding Pedro?"

"I think so. I'm supposed to give him an answer tonight."

"Maybe you should practice with me. Pretend I'm Pedro." Kerry invaded her space and took Pretense's face. "Will you marry me?"

Pretense laughed and pushed her away. "Hey, you know that guy that checked in yesterday—Gary Marion? What do you know about him?"

"I know he's a bad dresser."

"Seriously. He gives me the creeps." She told Kerry about last night.

Kerry found his check-in card. "Let's see. His home address is listed as West 44th Street, New York, New York."

Pretense gulped back a slug of acid, churning in her throat.

"He paid for a week with a credit card." Kerry skimmed the copy of his passport. "He was born in New York in 1965. Not much else." She put the card away. "Hey, you look stressed out. If you are uncomfortable, don't bother cleaning his room today. I can do it."

"That's okay. I can take care of it."

———

Pretense waited until she saw Gary in the parking lot straddling a scooter, then she pushed her cleaning cart to his cottage and entered his room, closing the door behind her. *Clean first, spy later.* She ripped the sheets from the bed, snapping them in the air. A flock of papers fluttered, sailing from a side table unto the floor. She hurriedly gathered the documents and returned them to their spot. A single sheet had escaped and sailed under the bed. On her hands and knees, she reached under the bed. From the corner of her eye, she glimpsed an off-white folder wedged into the underside of the box spring. She looked around then pulled it out. As she read the marking stamped across the front —DAVID OMNI, PRIVATE INVESTIGATOR, KOH SAMUI—the packet quivered in her hands. She could hear her breath, as she stumbled backward and plunked down on the bed, saliva pooling in her mouth. The sound of footsteps derailed her attention. She jammed the folder back in its hiding place and grabbed the floor duster, then heard a tug on the door handle.

"Claire, its Kerry. Let me in."

Pretense jolted the door open, fanning herself with her hand.

"Good grief. You look like you saw a dead body. Did you?"

Pretense feigned a smile. "There's nothing here. I overreacted." She gathered her cleaning articles and shoved them into the cart. "Let's get out of here before Ralph Lauren comes back."

CHAPTER 51

On the drive to the community event, Pretense stopped at the church to help Solada, then took a detour to the town where Solada had last spotted Maya. She parked the car and walked along the crowded street, strolling in and out of shops and food stalls, hoping for a sign of her little friend. About to give up, she noticed the hem of a tattered yellow dress beneath a flowering shrub, two soiled feet sticking out. Pretense walked over and peeked under the foliage. Maya sat in the dirt with a crumpled Styrofoam container in her lap, picking hardened rice pebbles from the carton and stuffing the grains into her mouth.

"Maya, sweetheart, come here." Pretense held her arms out.

Maya blinked a few times, then dropped the container and scrambled to her feet, falling into Pretense's embrace.

Pretense squeezed the child then pressed her face against Maya's cheek. When she pulled away, Maya reached out to Pretense and stroked her face. Pretense smiled and pulled a tissue from her purse, wiping the grime from Maya's lips.

"You must be hungry," she said, pointing to her mouth. "Hiu mai ka?"

Maya nodded. Pretense took her hand and led her to a

nearby food stall. After paying the food vendor, she steered Maya to a bench and watched with sad eyes as Maya scooped the Pad Thai into her mouth, making sucking sounds as the noodles slapped her face.

A voice yelled out, "Maya!" Startled, Maya looked up and flinched. Kwang, her mother, ran toward them, yelling, "Ma ni si." Maya slid off the bench, her food container falling to the ground.

Pretense stood and took Maya's hand. "Your child is hungry," Pretense said, stepping forward. "You need to take better care of your daughter."

Kwang yanked Maya's hand from Pretense, shouting in Thai, her eyes wild and glassy. She grabbed Maya by the arm and left, Maya half-running as she tried to keep pace.

Pretense stared after them as they disappeared around a corner, then walked to her car and slid into the driver's seat, fighting back tears of rage and frustration. After pulling herself together, she drove to the town of Lipa Noi. When she pulled into the lot of the Koh Samui Municipality Office, Pedro was standing out front. He waved then walked to her car and planted a lingering kiss on her cheek.

"I didn't think you were coming," he said, his warm hand on her bare arm. "You look beautiful. It looks like we have a good turnout. The room is practically full. I saved you a seat up front."

"I'm sorry I'm late. I saw Maya in town. She was filthy and starving. I bought her something to eat, then Kwang came and took her away. Oh, Pedro, we need to do something."

He ran his hand over her hair, his soft eyes holding hers. "We are doing all we can."

"But it's not enough. Do we just sit back and wait for her to be sold off to some pimp? Then it will be too late. We have to do something now."

He squeezed her hand. "Claire, you need to trust me."

She folded into him, as his arms tightened around her, his hand caressing her back.

"I'm sorry." She looked up and kissed his lips. "I often think about the day before you came—when my life held little meaning. I'm so grateful for you."

His gaze lingered, then he kissed her forehead. "Let's go inside."

He ushered Pretense to her seat, then walked to the front of the room with Udom. Pedro stood before the crowd and summarized the purpose of the meeting, while Udom translated in Thai. He then introduced Finn Gallagher, an expert on child sex trafficking.

Finn spoke of his background as a 25-year veteran lieutenant with the Los Angeles Police department, investigating over 3,500 cases involving trafficking, pimping, and other sex-related crimes. He was now responsible for organizing training courses throughout the world. "We have found that once the community is involved, we begin to notice a sharp decline in the number of cases. Fortunately for all of you, you have a warrior in your midst—someone who is willing to lead this charge. Pedro Garcia has agreed to sponsor a program to bring greater awareness to the cause. I have provided him with the necessary tools, and now he needs you … committed volunteers who are willing to help. Every member of this community can play a role in protecting our children. Please, join in the fight and give every child hope for a better future. Thank you."

After a lively round of applause, several individuals gathered around Pedro and Finn. Pedro caught Pretense's eye and held up his forefinger. She nodded.

While she waited, she skimmed the faces in the crowd searching for Solada. She found her standing by the front entrance. As Pretense made her way over, she caught a glint of coppery hair. She shoved her way through the crowd, her heart galloping in her chest. When she reached the door and stepped outside, she spotted Gary Marion in the parking lot climbing onto a scooter.

"There you are," said Solada, patting her arm. "I was looking for you."

Pretense whirled. "Yes … yes. Good meeting," she said, her tongue tripping over words. She followed Solada back inside. Had Gary followed her there?

When she looked around, Pedro and Finn were walking toward them. "Claire, I'd like you to meet Finn." Pedro put his arm around Pretense's waist. "Claire is also from California."

She drew a breath, trying to steady her voice. "It's nice to meet you, Finn. Your speech was very moving."

"Thank you. Whereabouts you from in California?"

"Palm Springs." She turned to Pedro. "I hate to run, but I need to get back to the resort."

"Is everything okay?"

"Yes, everything is fine, but Kerry needs me to handle something urgent. Nice meeting you, Finn."

"I'll walk you out," said Pedro.

"Oh, don't bother. You have guests to attend to. I'll see you tomorrow."

Pedro kissed her cheek. As she walked away, she felt his steely gaze following her. *Don't look back.* She steadied her gait, counting the steps to her car. When she was safely planted on the front seat, she exhaled a spurt of air, her juddering fingers wrestling with the ignition key. *Think. Think. Why was Gary at the meeting? And Finn, a former police lieutenant from California? Is he working with Gary?* The drive back to the resort was fuzzy. The world was squeezing her into a corner.

When she reached the resort, she parked the car and snuck past the lobby. She flicked on the lights in her room and stood, her bones rattling, as a tear jerked itself free. *How could I be so naïve, believing I could actually get away with this?* She flung herself across the bed, hopelessness sweeping her thoughts. Minutes became hours. She lay in wait for the hammer to strike.

CHAPTER 52

Edna Rothschild sat opposite Gary Marion, her foot tapping anxiously on the linoleum floor.

"Thank you for coming in today," said Gary. "Can I get you anything to drink, coffee —"

"Let's cut to the chase. I'm eager to hear what you found out."

Gary pulled a stack of photographs from a leather-bound portfolio and arranged them along his desk. "The woman in these pictures goes by the name of Claire Voyant."

Edna reached for a close-up photo, her finger skating across the glossy image, tracing the hair and facial features.

"Does she resemble Pretense Abdicator?" asked Gary.

Edna's face scrunched. "Somewhat. The woman in this photo is much more attractive. Pretense wasn't what you'd call a looker. She had a chipped front tooth and an awkward nose."

"Perhaps she had some work done."

"Perhaps." Edna returned the photo to the lineup. "So, what did you find out about this woman, Claire?"

"In late September, Claire arrived on Koh Samui, an island off the coast of Thailand. She currently resides in a resort cottage, where she also works. In her off hours, she spends time at a small church. While I was there, the church was hosting a group of missionaries. I've included snapshots of Claire working at the church. And it appears she may be having a romantic relationship with the pastor of that church, a Mr. Pedro Garcia." Gary handed Edna several images of Claire and Pedro together.

Edna nodded, as she shuffled through the stack. "They make a beautiful couple."

"I worked with a private investigator on the island to help cut through some of the red tape. A guy by the name of David Omni. He told me about the upsurge in child sex crimes on Koh Samui. It seems the pastor is working to get rid of this problem."

Gary retrieved another stack of photos. "These were taken a few days ago."

Edna took the photos and studied each one; images of Claire embracing a little girl next to an overgrown shrub, Claire buying lunch at a food stall and the two sitting at a bench while the child ate. And another photo of an altercation with a woman who was whisking the child away. Edna set the photos aside, her eyes cloudy. She opened her purse and withdrew a leather checkbook. Without pause, she scribbled across the paper and tore it free, sliding it across the desk. "Excellent work. I trust the amount is satisfactory."

Gary took the check. "Thank you. It's very generous."

"It goes without saying that our discussion is strictly confidential."

"Of course," said Gary. He gathered the photos and placed them into the portfolio, then handed it to Edna. "Claire's contact information and everything else I discovered is in the portfolio. Don't hesitate to call if you have questions."

———

Rafaela greeted Edna at the door and took her coat. "Mr. Rothschild is in the study. Your cocktail is poured and waiting for you."

"You are such a dear, Rafaela," said Edna.

Hyman's wheelchair was parked in front of the windows overlooking Central Park. Edna came up behind him and kissed the top of his head. She cradled her cocktail glass and sat down before him. Several lingering sips later, she set the crystal aside. "Hyman, darling, I need to go away for a while. I won't be gone long. Rafaela will look after you." She searched for a flicker in his dead, coal eyes, but nothing sparked.

She got up and slid open the top drawer of the mahogany desk, pulling out a stack of sympathy cards received after Baron's disappearance on 9-11. She untied the black ribbon and flicked through each one, searching for the simple white card with the poignant message written inside—the one from Daphne Duke. Edna remembered the receptionist at Crawford Spectrum —the woman with the kind demeanor. She found the card and read the last paragraph. *If there is anything you need, or if you ever just want to talk, please call me. It is only by the grace of God I made it out alive on 9-11. My heart grieves deeply for those who did not. With Deepest Sympathy, Daphne Duke.*

Edna took a swallow of gin and Dubonnet, then dialed the number. When she hung up, she found Rafaela in the kitchen preparing dinner. "I'd like for you to put together a simple luncheon for tomorrow. I'm having a special guest." She wasn't sure if her plan would work, but it was worth a shot.

———

Edna was seated in the drawing room when Rafaela escorted Daphne in. Daphne came forward in a rush, binding Edna in a ferocious hug. "It's so good to see you, Mrs. Rothschild."

Edna shrank from the onslaught, her hand smoothing her

perfectly coiffed hair. "How good of you to come. Please, have a seat. Would you like a glass of wine before lunch?"

"No, thank you," said Daphne, taking a seat and smoothing her skirt over her knees. "You have a lovely home. It's not often I'm invited to lunch in a penthouse overlooking Central Park."

"You are always welcome here." Edna patted Daphne's shoulder, then sat opposite her, cradling her wine glass before taking a sip. "I didn't realize you were in the tower on nine-eleven. Not until I received your card."

Daphne unsnapped her purse and withdrew a tissue, wiping her eyes. "It's hard to talk about that day. So many lives lost—your son, Baron, Pretense, Mr. Crawford. I still have nightmares."

Edna nodded, her heart weakening. "If it's not too difficult, do you mind telling me how you made it out?"

Daphne looked away as though ashamed, fondling the tissue in her lap. "Ariana—I'm not sure you knew her—asked me to go upstairs to get a coffee and a donut. It's funny. We weren't really friends. I remember being surprised and excited by the unexpected invitation. On my way to Ariana's office, I stopped by Pretense's office to ask if she wanted to go with us, but she said she was busy. When I went to get Ariana, I mentioned that I had asked Pretense to join us. Ariana told me that Pretense had a meeting with Baron and Mr. Crawford. That's when I remembered the copies I had made the night before for Mr. Crawford's meeting. I had them in my briefcase when I came to work that morning, but I used the lavatory on the first floor. I realized then I had left my briefcase in the restroom. I told Ariana to go ahead without me, then I went down to the lobby and that's when the plane hit." A mound of shredded tissue lay in her lap. "The café was on the ninety-third floor."

Edna drained her glass. "I can't imagine the torment you must be feeling."

Rafaela came into the room and announced lunch. Edna stood and escorted Daphne into the dining room. Lunch was a somber affair. Daphne picked at a chicken salad croissant, while Edna sipped a few spoonfuls of tomato-basil soup before setting her silverware aside.

"You mentioned making copies for the meeting," said Edna. "Do you happen to know what that meeting was about?"

"I don't," said Daphne. "I never read documents I'm copying. It wouldn't be right, unless Mr. Crawford asked me to."

Edna nodded. "You mentioned Baron, Pretense, and Mr. Crawford. How can we be certain that one or all of them didn't make it out alive?"

Daphne looked confused. "Certainly, someone would know by now." Her lips curled in. "I wanted to spare you the grim details; however, I don't want you to cling to false hope. I've kept in touch with some of the employees at Crawford Spectrum. One of those individuals recalls seeing several other people in Mr. Crawford's office that morning—our HR Director, Thelma Barnes, and two other unidentified gentlemen. This employee said that when the plane hit the tower, the door to Mr. Crawford's office had jammed and people were screaming, trying to get out." She looked away. "That employee stopped to help, but the door was hopelessly stuck, and he couldn't find anyone willing to assist. People were running for their lives."

Edna pictured Baron's last desperate moments. *If Pretense was in that meeting, how did she make it out alive? Or did she?* "Thank you for sharing that story with me." She looked away, lost in thought. "I recall you were very involved in mission work," said Edna, after an uncomfortable silence. "Is that something you still do?"

Daphne seemed relieved by the diversion. "Oh, yes. Especially now that I'm not working. My fiancé, Andrew, is a youth pastor. We've been praying about another mission trip."

"Would you be interested in helping me organize a mission trip to Thailand? I've learned about a church on the island of Koh Samui that is seeking missionaries to help in their fight against child sex trafficking. The church is doing wonderful work there. I'd like to go and see for myself. If this appeals to you, I would pay travel expenses for the entire mission team."

Daphne shot from her seat and whirled in a circle, clapping her hands. "Mrs. Rothschild! I'm taken aback. Truly. Once again, God has answered our prayers." She took flight at Edna, her arms a six-foot wingspan, swooping in for the hug.

CHAPTER 53

Pretense breathed easy when Gary checked out of his room at Moonbeam Bungalows. According to Kerry, he returned to New York earlier than expected. But why was he here? She recalled the name on the folder she had found under his bed, *David Omni, Private Investigator.* The label listed an address on Koh Samui. It was time to pay David a visit.

After running errands, Pretense drove to the town of Chaweng and located the office of Omni Private Investigators. She knocked on the locked door. A small, bald-headed man greeted her.

"Good afternoon," he said with a jeering smirk. "I'm David Omni. What can I do for you?"

The way he looked at her made her uneasy, as though he were anticipating her arrival. "Hello. My name is Claire Voyant and I need some information on a client of yours."

"Please come in. Which client, and what information do you need?"

She stepped inside the dark office. "His name is Gary Marion. I want to know what type of work you were doing for him. I'm willing to pay for this information."

He chortled. "I'm sorry, but that information is confidential."

312

"What if I were to hire you to provide a rundown of Gary Marion's activities on the island?"

His brows arched. "Isn't that the same thing?"

"Not necessarily. You don't need to tell me about the work *you* did for him. Just tell me what Gary did while he was here, including what the two of you talked about. And you don't need to follow him. He left this morning for New York. The way I see it, it's easy money. I'll pay you ten-thousand baht."

David pursed his lips and stroked his chin. "Fifteen-thousand baht. No less."

Pretense estimated the amount in dollars. "Twelve-thousand baht. No more."

"You have a deal. When do you need the information?"

"Right now."

———

An hour later, Pretense sat in her car, her brain swirling in a funnel of perfect bliss. Her suspicions were just that—suspicions. Gary wasn't following her after all. He was pursuing a child sex trafficker for a couple from New York whose daughter had been abducted and presumed to be in Thailand. Now it made sense why Gary had attended the community event.

She rolled her head back against the car seat and closed her eyes. Her thoughts turned to Pedro and her unborn child. Maybe the marriage would work out after all. Everything seemed to be falling into place, and Pedro wanted an answer.

As she pulled into the resort, her cell phone rang.

"I need to see you," said Pedro. "We didn't talk last night."

"I know, and I'm sorry I left so quickly. I want to see you, too. Do you want me to come to the church?"

"No. I want to be alone with you—uninterrupted. The mission team is still here. I just took Finn to the airport. I can be at your place in ten minutes. Have you eaten?"

"No. We could go to the restaurant here on the property."

"Why don't I pick up carryout and bring it to your place?"

After she parked the car, she flew into the lobby and dropped off the supplies she'd purchased.

Kerry emerged from the back office. "You look flushed. Are you in a hurry?"

"Pedro is on his way over. We didn't get to talk last night."

"You are saying *yes*, right?"

"I think so."

"Oh, Claire. This is so damned exciting. Do you mind if I hang out under your window? I could play Denzel's khlui. It has a flute-like timbre. It might add a nice romantic flair to the evening."

"I'll pass." Pretense threw her arms around Kerry. "Oh, Kerry. I am so happy. And I'm so grateful to have you as a friend." She pulled away. "Now, leave me alone so I can get ready."

After tidying her room and freshening up, she sat on the patio and waited. Restless, she got up and walked to the water's edge, tilting her head toward heaven. *More than anything in the world, I want to be a good wife and mother. If you are listening, show me the way, God. Help me make the right decision.*

Her thoughts were waylaid by the familiar physique pressing into her from behind, thick arms circling her waist. "Alone at last," Pedro whispered, his lips brushing her neck.

She rested her head back against his chest, inhaling his scent. "I missed you—so much."

He turned her around and kissed her mouth. "I missed you, too. We have unfinished business to discuss, but before things get too serious, let's eat." He took her hand and steered her to the patio.

They sat at the small table, enjoying the meal and each other's company, the inevitable talk hanging in the air. When they finished eating, Pretense gathered the empty containers and took them inside, stalling for time—searching for direction.

"Are you coming out?" he asked through the door.

She went outside and sat down next to him, her eyes drawn into the depths of his soulful gaze.

He took her hand in his, and kissed her fingers. "Claire, will you marry me?"

She took his hand and held it to her cheek, then she kissed his palm. "I love you, and I want to be your wife, but ..." A cold sweat seized, as her heart thumped violently against her chest. The words stuck in her throat. She looked away.

He tilted his head, his probing eyes dragging her under. "What is it?"

"You don't know me. And I'm not good for you."

"Claire, there are no perfect people in this world. I want to spend my life with you and to be the father of your baby. If there are things you need to tell me, then tell me. I won't judge." He put his arm around her and pulled her close. "I sense you've done something that you feel is unforgiveable. Am I right?"

She nodded. "I'm not ready to talk about it—at least not now."

He sighed and leaned his head back. "Claire, we can't go into a marriage with secrets between us."

She pushed her chair back and stood, a dull feeling of dread burning in the pit of her stomach. "I need something to drink. Do you want anything?"

"No, thank you."

She went inside and took several deep swallows from a bottled water, the moisture soothing her parched throat. She gazed out onto the patio, a pool of tears forming in her eyes. Inside the bathroom, she shut the door and splashed her face with cold water, stalling for time. When she came out, he was standing by her bed, a look of defeat etched on his face.

"Come here," he said.

She drifted into his embrace, nuzzling her face in his neck.

His lips brushed the top of her head. "I don't think there is anything you could say that would make me stop loving you." His arms tightened around her, as he eased her down onto the bed. "There is nothing I want more than to wake up beside you each morning—to spend my life with you. But I need you to be honest with me. And the sooner the better." He kissed her forehead. "You are three months pregnant."

His heart pulsed against her cheek, as she dragged her fingers over his bare arm, wondering what it would feel like to be with him. "I've never been intimate with a man in a way that wasn't forced. I don't know how it feels to be loved by a man in that way."

He sighed, then turned to her, his eyes shimmering like a sun-soaked sea. He pulled her face to his, his lips soft against her mouth. They fell back against the mattress, their bodies woven like mesh. "I want to be with you, Claire." His lips brushed her ear. "I want you to be my wife."

She could feel his passion, as he gripped her tighter, his kisses determined. She stirred beneath him, her body dissolving into his.

"Claire, please be still," he whispered, dropping his forehead against hers. "I'm sorry. This is my fault. We need to stop." He rolled off the bed and stood over her, dragging his hand over his hair. "I should leave now."

She looked up at him, breathless.

His dark eyes held hers captive, as though he were searching for clarity. "We will marry when the time is right."

CHAPTER 54

Pedro left Pretense alone on the bed, his scent still lingering. He told her he would be patient, but he was also firm. There would be no marriage with secrets between them.

She pondered the goodness of Pedro in her heart—the goodness she craved for herself. If only she had faith like his, then perhaps God would listen to her pleas. But when she had sought His direction, no answer came. Or did it? Pedro had given her the opportunity to come clean. Was she expected to tell him everything, no matter the consequences? Is that how faith worked? She had once heard Pedro say that trust in God comes not in knowing the path ahead but in knowing the one who walks it with you. She meditated on his words and fell asleep in the warm embrace of something not seen.

———

"I'm dying to know," said Kerry when Pretense came through the lobby door. "When is the wedding?"

"We have some things to work through."

Kerry's face crumpled. "Things? I thought everything was

317

settled. Maybe some things are better left unspoken. Unless you murdered someone, does it really matter? I mean, you didn't murder someone, did you?"

Pretense grinned. "No, but I understand where he is coming from, especially given his position."

Kerry came around from behind the desk and took Pretense in her arms. "I wish there was something I could say, but without knowing what is troubling you, I can't help. Do you want to talk about it?"

"Thank you. I'll figure it out." She pulled away and took Kerry's hands. "You always have my best interests at heart."

"When will you see him again?"

"I'm not sure. I need time to think."

Pretense left the lobby and went about her chores, her mind playing havoc with her. One minute, she was committed to bearing her soul to Pedro. The next, she was returning to New York to turn herself in. But one thing she was sure of, she was tired of living a lie.

The phone vibrated in her pocket. Her heart skipped when she heard Pedro's calm voice asking to meet later. He assured her there was no pressure, unless she was ready to talk. He simply wanted to be with her.

When she arrived at the church, Pedro stood out front holding a blanket and a picnic basket. "I told Solada you were coming. She insisted on packing a meal for us." He took her hand and kissed her cheek, his lips lingering. "I thought we'd go to my favorite spot."

"I'm glad you called. I miss *us*."

Pedro pressed her fingers in his as they walked. When they reached the clearing, he spread the blanket on the moss-covered ground and pulled her down beside him. After they finished eating, he drew his knees to his chest and looked out over the river. "I have some good news. Another mission team is arriving next week. It was unexpected. Apparently, they heard about the work we are doing and decided to send a small group to help out."

"That's great news. Where are they from?"

"Brookside Bible Church. Somewhere in the U.S."

Had she heard that name before? She pushed the thought aside. "I'd like to help when they arrive. I'll talk to Solada when we get back. Have you heard anything more about Maya?"

Pedro told her about his visit to Maya's home. Tears formed, as she listened with remorse to the dreary discourse. She felt his arm around her shoulders, pulling her close. She sank into him, his hand stroking her head.

She picked at his shirt. "Pedro, thank you for being patient with me. I want to tell you everything, but I'm just not there yet."

"What will get you there?"

She looked up, taking him in. "When I realize that the freedom truth offers is greater than the fear of losing you forever."

He kissed her forehead. "I love you, Claire. More than you know."

CHAPTER 55

Gary Marion scratched his head and immediately rang Edna Rothschild. "I just had an interesting call from the private investigator in Thailand, David Omni. It seems that a woman by the name of Claire Voyant—the same woman in the photos—paid David a visit, asking about the purpose of my recent trip. David fabricated a story to throw her off. I thought you might want to know before leaving for Koh Samui."

After Edna hung up, she sat on the edge of her bed, her heart pattering. She was certain there was a connection. Having Daphne with her on the trip would help confirm her suspicions.

———

Edna felt awkward sitting in a first-class while the mission team was crammed three-abreast in coach. She flagged down the flight attendant and asked to trade seats with the serviceman seated next to Daphne and her sister, Sarah.

"I'm so glad you are sitting with us," said Daphne, when Edna took the seat next to her. "This is my sister, Sarah. It's her first mission trip, too. And her first time on an airplane. My fiancé, Andrew, is sitting three rows up. I'll introduce you to him later."

Sarah leaned forward from the window seat. "Hello, Mrs. Edna. Do you want me to draw your picture?"

Edna smiled. "Sure. You must like to draw."

"Not really. But my sister said I need to behave. She thinks if I'm busy, I can't get into trouble." She threw her head back and laughed raucously. Then she curled her arm protectively around her paper and began doodling.

Daphne turned to Edna. "I can't begin to express how appreciative the team is by your generosity."

Edna waved away the compliment. "It is my pleasure. And thank you for pulling this trip together on such short notice. It sounds like you have a lot of experience organizing mission trips. It must give you some lasting level of satisfaction."

"Yes, it is hard to explain. I always return home with a broader perspective and a rejuvenated mind. After nine-eleven, I realized just how short life can be. That was when Andrew and I decided to become full-time missionaries. We are waiting for the right opportunity."

"Here is your picture, Mrs. Edna," said Sarah, pitching the sheet across Daphne's lap.

"Thank you." Edna studied the drawing. The stick figure depicted a woman with sweeping eyelashes, her hands primly folded in her lap. On her left finger, an enormous diamond jutted out, half the size of the figure itself, with sunburst lines radiating outward.

"Oh, my," said Edna, fondling her gemstone. "You must think my ring is rather large."

"It's almost as big as your head," said Sarah.

Daphne shushed her and turned to Edna. "I wouldn't want anything to happen to your lovely ring. When we arrive in Thailand, you should keep it somewhere safe and out of sight."

"You are probably right." Edna slid the rock over her knuckle and slipped it inside her purse. "Were you and Pretense close?"

Daphne's eyes drifted. "I don't think anyone got too close to Pretense. But I like to believe we were making headway. My heart ached for her. She had a difficult life. Did you know she had been raised in several foster homes?"

Edna thought about the stories Pretense had fabricated. "I had heard that. Hyman and I were both very fond of her."

"Me too," said Sarah, flinging herself over Daphne. "I loved her. We were best friends."

Daphne absently stroked Sarah's head. "Pretense had a special bond with children. I think deep down she had a good heart, but no one ever taught her how to use it. I had hoped to be that person, but it's too late now." A tear meandered down her cheek. She tilted her head back against the headrest and closed her eyes. "The day the towers were hit, I tried to go back up—to look for Pretense. But they wouldn't let me. I felt so helpless. I had always believed that God put me in her life to save her. Maybe in some way I did."

Edna patted Daphne's hand then turned away, struggling to tame a rising swell in her throat. She leaned back, studying the humble faces of those around her, their smiles and laughter bringing peace to her heart. Who was she that so much had been given her? And what had she done with her eighty-plus years on this earth? Hosted a few charity events for the mega-rich? Raised a greedy son, then wondered why he coveted their money? She felt a vague feeling of regret. Something left undone. She wanted her life to have meaning, but the years were slipping away, like a passing breeze that doesn't return. She stirred uneasily.

———

After the grueling thirty-two-hour flight, the plane touched down on the tropical island of Koh Samui. The team gathered their luggage, then waited outside in the stifling heat. Thirty minutes later, they were ascending the steps of a rusted out, multicolored bus with the words BEACON OF HOPE spray-painted on both sides. The driver, Udom, introduced himself and explained that he would be taking the team to the nonprofit center on the property of Crossroads Church, where they would stay in dorm-like rooms. The pastor, Pedro Garcia, would meet the team after they were settled.

Edna made her way down the narrow aisle of the bus and settled into a seat, gripping the worn vinyl cushion in front of her. Sweat slid down her body and slicked her neck, her linen trousers clinging to her limbs like wet Kleenex. *Oh, if Hyman could see me now.* Her thumb plunged into a gash on the seat, popping an acrylic fingernail off its bed. Could this be a sign; stripped of her ring, then her nails, next her dignity?

The bus left the airport grounds, limping along the pitted road, rocking from side to side. Daphne reached across the narrow aisle and patted Edna's arm. "Don't you just love the adventure of it all? I can picture myself living here." Her head whirled. "Andrew, can't you see us living here?"

"Yes, love. Maybe we will raise our family here."

Edna looked around, the sweet chatter of voices rose and blended together like a symphony, lulling her into a state of blithe assurance. She relaxed, taking in coastal lowlands cloaked in virgin rainforest, waves lapping lazily along a palm-fringed shoreline. If only Hyman were here to experience the untouched beauty of the island, so unlike the manicured properties they had so often frequented.

The bus turned down an unpaved road, overgrown foliage scraping the metal, a sign leaning against a gnarly tree—*Beacon of Hope/Crossroads Church.* The van groaned to a stop in front of the building. So, this could be where Pretense spent her days. A far cry from the professional environment of Crawford Spectrum. Edna gazed out the window, watching a group of young boys jostling one another in a cloud of dust, their toes tapping a soccer ball. A middle-aged Thai woman chased after younger children clamoring for a seat on a weathered swing set. And off in the distance, her eyes beheld a different scene. A tall, attractive woman leaned freely against a man, her arms slung loosely around his neck as they looked intently at each other. She studied the woman's mannerisms, as she climbed onto a scooter and drove away. Edna inhaled a tunnel of air and glanced across the aisle at Daphne twisting sideways in her seat, both hands pressed against the bus window. Sarah tugged at Daphne's shirt, vying for attention. Daphne turned from the window, her eyes sprung wide, then she sank into her seat, her face as white as a cracked coconut.

CHAPTER 56

Pretense lingered on the patio of her bungalow watching a young couple playing with a chubby, tow-headed toddler. A pang of jealously gripped. She had it in her mind to tell Pedro everything today, but then the subject of Maya had come up, derailing her good intentions. Or, was it just another convenient excuse. And now with the recent mission team's arrival, their time alone would be compromised.

When Pedro spoke about his unannounced visit to Maya's house, her heart sank. According to Pedro, Kwang said her daughter was asleep when he asked to see her. But Pedro heard Maya's cries through an open window. He asked if he could come inside to talk, but Kwang shook her head, her unkempt hair falling over listless eyes, her skin luridly pale. Pedro glanced through the partially opened door and noticed a scruffy man dozing on a beaten sofa. Drug paraphernalia lay strewn across a table and open Styrofoam containers baited flies with scraps of half-eaten food. Unsettled, Pedro left the house, determined to return.

Upon hearing the account, her soul ached for Maya. She knew firsthand the infinite helplessness of abuse and the terrifying knowledge that whatever had happened would happen

325

again and again. Visions of her childhood slithered into her mind. What had caused her mother to do the things she did? Had she also been abused? Wanda never spoke of her upbringing. There were no grandparents, aunts or uncles, or cousins. It seemed as though Wanda had been dropped from the sky, a seed germinating in dirt until her roots took hold. Pretense shuddered, as if some venomous thing were twining around her torso, the air suddenly thin, her heart squeezing tight.

Her dark thoughts were abandoned when Kerry walked toward her from the beach, waving her toned arms, her blond hair lifting off her shoulders and scattering in the breeze. "Do you feel like going into town with me?"

———

They strolled arm-in-arm through the Walking Street Market in Chaweng, swept along in a riot of colors, sounds and scents, taking turns trying on beach dresses in a small souvenir shop, wearing sunglasses upside down, and parading around in colorful sarongs. After Pretense knocked over a display table and stumbled into dozens of hanging bamboo wood chimes, an angry shop owner ordered them to leave. They staggered out of the store, their howls of laughter attracting curious stares.

A few blocks down, they wandered into a shop selling children's clothing. "Oh, Claire, look how small these booties are," said Kerry, holding up a pair of pink knitted socks with pompoms. "I'm buying these for the baby."

"What if it's a boy?" asked Pretense, smoothing her hand over a swaddling blanket, imagining herself clutching a bundled infant in her arms.

"Then I'll buy another pair." She paused and studied Pretense. "Don't you look all clucky. Motherhood certainly suits you." After purchasing the booties, Kerry grabbed Pretense's arm and pulled her out of the shop. "Let's get something to eat."

As they moseyed along the street, Kerry stopped in front of a newsstand and reached for a magazine. The cover photo displayed two towers engulfed in black smoke, orange flames licking a vivid blue sky. "It is so horrifying to imagine what those people went through that day," she said, shaking her head and flipping through the pages.

Pretense glanced at the images as the blood ran from her face. She struggled to breathe and tottered backward, her arms pinwheeling at the air, searching for support.

"Claire, are you okay?" asked Kerry, dropping the magazine and grabbing Pretense's arm.

"I think so," she answered, her breaths shallow and shaky, as she steadied herself against Kerry. "Maybe we should get something to eat. I'm feeling a little lightheaded."

The carefree day turned dour, as Pretense picked at her meal, reliving memories of that fateful day. As much as she tried to forget, something would spark a flashback—the smell of fuel; flickering lights; a cloudless, blue sky. It seemed like yesterday. It seemed like forever.

Kerry observed Pretense, then took her hand. "You look like you are a million miles away. I know I said I wouldn't probe, but I can't stop myself. Did you have 'the *talk*' with Pedro?"

Pretense inhaled and looked away, shaking her head.

"I'm assuming that whatever happened in your past is something you feel he needs to know, and you are worried he will withdraw his proposal."

"Something like that."

Kerry nodded. "Then maybe it wasn't meant to be. Perhaps one day you'll meet another man."

Tears bloomed in Pretense's eyes. "I don't want another man. Pedro is everything I want."

"Then dammit, Claire, either shit or get off the pot. I don't mean to be harsh, but it's not fair to you, and it's not fair to Pedro." She scooched her chair closer. "And it's not fair to me. I hate seeing you in such turmoil. Just spit it out and be done with it. Pastors are used to hearing all kinds of wacky things. It can't be that bad."

———

That night, she lay in bed brooding over her conversation with Kerry. Kerry was right. After the mission team left, she would tell him everything and face the consequences. She stroked her belly, her fingers probing the seed within. *I am so sorry you ended up with someone like me.*

CHAPTER 57

Pretense finished her chores, then headed for the church, stopping along the way to Maya's house, hoping to catch a glimpse of the child outside. The sky-blue corrugated metal hut with a sagging roof looked ready to fold into itself. Kwang was slumped sideways in a plastic lawn chair out front, a cigarette burning between her fingers. There was no sign of Maya. Tempted to approach Kwang, she stopped, remembering the promise she had made to Pedro. She drove away, her thoughts drowning in unbearable sadness.

When she reached the church, she spotted Pedro alongside a small group armed with paint brushes and ladders, working tirelessly in the blistering sun. He waved when he saw her and trotted over, kissing her cheek. "Solada is inside with some of the women from the mission team."

"I'll go in and see if she needs help." She paused and looked away. "I drove by Maya's house on my way over."

"Claire, you shouldn't get involved." He put his finger under her chin, turning her face to his. "We talked about this."

"I know. And I'm sorry. Kwang was outside. It looked like she had passed out. Oh, Pedro, who is taking care of Maya? We need to do something." She felt his strong arms surround her, his sweat cool against her body.

"We are working on it." He pulled back. "Why don't you help Solada? Maybe collect the loaves of bread from the bakery?"

They strolled back to the building hand in hand. Pretense smiled and waved to the working men, one in particular catching her eye. He looked vaguely familiar, but she couldn't place his face.

———

As Edna was preparing to head over to the church with Daphne and Sarah, she glimpsed the "mystery" woman from her dorm-room window holding Pastor Pedro's hand. Her heart bounced. After running a comb through her hair, she readied her mind for the surprise reunion.

Sarah skipped ahead, as Daphne and Edna strolled over to the church. Once inside, they were greeted by Solada and escorted to a long table containing several binders and stacks of multi-colored paper. After the other women from the mission team arrived, Solada gave instructions to the group.

Edna kept watch, the anticipation overwhelming. She glanced over at Daphne and Sarah, seated at one end of the long table. Suddenly, Sarah looked up, her eyes boinging in their sockets as she rushed to the window, her small frame stretching over the ledge. Like an atomic vortex, she spun and knocked over a small desk, then flung open the door and ran outside. Daphne pushed away from the table and chased after Sarah.

Edna stood and looked beyond the open door. Then she saw her.

———

Pretense lingered by the church entrance, gazing up at Pedro as he pounded a clay tile onto the roof. As she turned away and headed toward the bakery, a child's voice called out behind her, its tone familiar.

"Pretense. Wait up, Pretense."

Oh, God. Decay crept into her bones. *Don't react.* She kept walking, struggling to temper her pace. The sound of shuffling feet grew nearer, then a tug at her skirt. When she turned and looked down, two almond-shaped eyes peered up at her—the unmistakable eyes of Sarah, Daphne's sister. Her heart cannonballed in her chest. She flicked a glimpse toward Pedro. His eyes sat on her like a dead weight. Averting his stare, she crouched, working her shuddering lips into a crooked smile. "Hello, young lady. What is your name?"

"You know me," Sarah shouted, opening her arms wide.

Pretense embraced Sarah, then held her at arm's length. "I'm sorry. I'm afraid I don't know you. My name is Claire."

From her peripheral vision, a figure came toward Pretense bearing the distinctive gait of Daphne Duke. *Daphne is alive!* Sudden joy turned to blind terror.

"Sarah, come here," said Daphne, stopping in front of Pretense, her face ashen, the grooves in her forehead like Death Valley. "Pretense? Is that you?"

Pretense extended a shaky hand, straining to keep her voice level. "Hello. I'm Claire Voyant." She offered a nervous laugh. "It seems as though I have a double."

Daphne took her hand in a robot-like gesture, her eyes unblinking. "It's uncanny. You resemble someone I once knew."

"No, it's Pretense," said Sarah, her arms wrapped around Pretense's legs. "Remember? I made you a card."

Before she could regain her composure, she recognized an elderly woman in the doorway of the church. The woman stepped down the porch and came toward them. *Oh my God, it's Edna Rothschild! What is happening? It's a sting operation.* In that moment, she remembered the man working with Pedro—Andrew, Daphne's friend.

Daphne tried prying Sarah's hands away as Edna joined the group.

"What is all the ruckus about?" asked Edna.

Daphne turned to Edna. "Sarah believes this is Pretense Abdicator. I thought the same thing when I saw her."

Pretense held out her hand. "Hello. I'm Claire Voyant."

Edna took her hand, her eyes calm and penetrating. "Yes, she does bear a striking resemblance to Pretense. I'm Edna Rothschild. It's nice to meet you, Claire."

Pedro climbed down the ladder and walked toward the group wearing a puzzled look. He stopped next to Pretense, his arm encircling her waist. "What's going on? Do you know each other?"

Pretense felt the air vibrating off her rattling body. "Apparently, I remind them of someone they know." She patted Sarah's head and smiled at Daphne and Edna.

Pedro's eyes bounced from Edna to Daphne. "So, Claire has a twin?"

Daphne's tongue tripped over her words. "It's ... I'm ...," she gurgled, "in shock. The resemblance is uncanny. But the person I knew—Pretense Abdicator—is missing."

"Yes," Edna interjected, "Pretense was in the World Trade Center in New York on nine-eleven."

Sarah bobbled and sprang in place. "But she didn't die, because she is right here, right now."

Pedro looked at Pretense, his arm tightening around her middle as though trying to restrain her.

"I've never been to New York," said Pretense. "I'm from California." *Stop talking.*

The color slipped into Daphne's face. "Well, it was nice meeting you. We should get back inside. Solada will wonder what happened to her volunteers. I'm sorry for the confusion."

She grasped Sarah's shoulders. "Come, Sarah, and let the nice lady get back to her work."

Sarah smiled. "Bye, Pretense."

"Her name is Claire," Daphne said to Sarah, then turned to Pretense. "I hope to see you again, Claire."

When the threesome moved a safe distance away, she felt Pedro's hand slide from her midsection.

"I should get back to work," he said. He regarded her cautiously. "Don't leave without saying goodbye." He kissed her cheek and walked away.

Panic clawed up Pretense's throat. She wanted to run, but her feet were pinned to the ground. Then a shadow appeared in the corner of her eye—Pedro walking toward her.

He studied her evenly, then took her in his arms, his mannerisms slow and calculating. The sound of his labored breaths filled the air as his lips brushed her ear. "Is there something you want to tell me?"

Her heart stopped. She pushed him away and answered in a strangled voice. "I am a mistake." She turned and ran toward her car, feeling the heaviness of his glare against her skin. His voice called after her, but she didn't look back.

CHAPTER 58

After stopping at the bank and making a withdrawal, Pretense returned to her bungalow and flung her suitcase on the bed, tossing her belongings into the open bag. She put her passport into her purse and counted out the money. Just under ten thousand dollars. She didn't know where she was going, but she had to flee.

An incoming call lit her phone screen. *Pedro*. Her heart stuttered. She waited for the buzzing to stop, then called a taxi. As she scooped toiletries into her makeup bag, a shadow passed by her front window. Then a knock.

"Claire? It's me, Kerry."

She opened the door a crack and peeked through the gap. "What's up?"

"Pedro called the front desk. He wants you to call him right away. He said you didn't answer your phone." Kerry glanced past Pretense, her eyes bouncing around the room. "Are you going somewhere? It looks like you're packing."

"Something came up. I need to leave right away."

"Were you going to tell me, or were you just going to leave?"

"Of course I was going to tell you."

Kerry regarded her carefully. "What about Pedro? Does he know?"

Pretense dragged her fingers through her hair and looked down, fighting back tears.

Kerry's eyes sliced into Pretense. "You weren't going to tell me, and you weren't going to tell Pedro. What's going on?" Kerry pushed open the door and went inside.

Pretense stepped back and dropped her head in her hands.

"Claire, talk to me."

She tried mouthing words, but no sound came. Then she felt Kerry's arms around her, pulling her close.

"I love you, Kerry." She held Kerry tight, not wanting to let go. "Thank you for all you've done for me, but I need to leave. I'm so sorry." She pulled away and slammed her suitcase shut, dragging it off the bed as tears spilled down her cheeks.

"Are you coming back?"

Without answering, Pretense brushed past her and opened the door and left. The taxi idled in the parking lot. Pretense jumped into the backseat and ordered the driver to leave. As the cab sped away, she turned around and looked out the rear window, the blurred image of Kerry growing smaller, fading from her life.

She scribbled down Maya's address and handed the scratch of paper to the driver. Minutes later, they pulled in front of Maya's house. Pretense held up a forefinger, then walked toward the porch. Kwang hadn't moved. Her body still listing sideways in the plastic chair. Pretense inched near the motionless figure. The stench of burnt flesh and cigarette smoke assaulted her nostrils. She bent down and put her face next to Kwang's. Then she lifted Kwang's chin and placed her fingertips on the side of her neck. She stepped back, her hand covering her mouth, then ran inside the house.

Maya sprang off the sofa and ran toward her, whimpering and burying her face in Pretense's skirt. Pretense knelt down and dried Maya's eyes with her fingers. "Do you want to come with

335

me? Rot?" She pointed to the yellow and maroon cab out front. The driver appeared to be napping, oblivious to the unfolding events.

Maya nodded and laced her fingers inside Pretense's hand, steering her to a small closet with a cot inside. Maya reached under the blanket and pulled out a disfigured doll with a mop of tangled, black hair and a missing arm. Maya clutched the doll to her chest, her eyes questioning. Pretense smiled. "Of course, you can take her." She led Maya outside and into the waiting cab. The driver sat up straight and yawned. Pretense directed the man to drive to Nathon Pier. A ferry would be departing for mainland Thailand in less than an hour.

Maya snuggled next to Pretense, her tiny body trembling. Pretense wrapped her arm around her and pulled her close, stroking her hair as tears raced down her cheeks. "I won't let anyone ever hurt you again."

When the ferry pulled up to the dock in the port city of Surat Thani, Pretense got off with Maya and purchased two bus tickets for the nine-hour journey to Bangkok. It was the cheapest option and the most difficult to track.

With over an hour before departure, they stopped at a street vendor and purchased snacks for the trip. Then Pretense took Maya into a restroom and scrubbed her face and hands, washing the buildup of grime from her body. Afterward, they found a small shop where Pretense purchased clothing items and sunglasses for Maya, and a baseball cap for each of them.

Once on board the bus, they worked their way toward the rear. After settling Maya in a window seat, she placed a jacket over her and took the aisle seat. The sun was disappearing by the time the bus set out for the long journey. She looked down at Maya, her eyelids drooping, her head bobbing up and down.

Pretense pulled her onto her lap and before long, Maya drifted off to sleep. She stroked Maya's hair and ran a finger over her soft cheek, wondering what would become of them in the days and weeks ahead. Tears spilled down her face. She thought about what she had done and the people she had left behind. It all happened so fast, she hadn't had time to think or to piece together why Edna and Daphne were traveling together. She recalled the warmth and sweetness of Daphne's smile, and the split-second spark of joy she felt upon seeing her alive. She thought about Kerry, the best friend she'd ever had. But most of all, she thought about Pedro and the baby growing inside, her dream of a family now crushed. Surely by now, Edna and Daphne had told Pedro everything. As she pictured his reaction to her unforgiveable betrayal, her body writhed in disgust. It would have been easier had she told him herself, but instead he would hear the truth from two strangers. Her life's one hope a fading mist.

She leaned back against the head rest and closed her eyes. *God, if you can hear me, please help. I know I deserve nothing good, but I'm not asking for me. I'm asking for Maya and my unborn child. Give them a good life. I vow to do everything I can to keep them safe for as long as You let me. Please God, hear my prayer.*

She looked out the window, the passing dark shadows a blur as the movement of wheels against the unlit road lulled her to sleep. Several hours later she awoke when the bus pulled into the first rest stop. Maya squirmed and groaned, then repositioned her head in Pretense's lap, falling back to sleep. Pretense looked down and studied Maya's face. She looked so peaceful with her one-armed doll in her clutched arm. Pretense wrapped her jacket around Maya's tiny body and stroked her silky hair, watching her even breaths. She would wait to stretch her legs at the next stop.

The morning light crawled into the tinted window. Pretense stirred and looked around, surprised to see the bus pulling into the Sai Tai Mai Bus Station in southern Bangkok. Had she slept through every rest stop? She ran her hand through her hair then gently shook Maya.

Maya squirmed, then sat up, looking around and smiling. She reached her hand to Pretense's face. "Chan rak khun," she said softly.

Pretense kissed the top of Maya's head, remembering the words Pedro had taught her. "I love you, too," she responded. She removed a bristle brush from her purse and ran it through Maya's hair, then placed the baseball cap on her head and the sunglasses over her eyes. "Let's go find someplace to stay."

They gathered their belongings and stepped off the bus and into the Bang Khae section of Bangkok—their new home for now. Pretense glanced around the bustling town, second-guessing her rash decision, until she looked down at Maya's petite frame, her hand clutching Pretense's hand as she gaped up at her with a small, toothy smile. "You are safe now."

CHAPTER 59

Daphne grabbed Edna by the arm when they moved out of earshot. "I would swear on my life that woman is Pretense Abdicator. Everything about her reminds me of Pretense. Sarah thought the same thing. Is it possible she is alive after all? And if so, why is she pretending to be someone else?"

"I do believe Claire resembles Pretense, but I've often heard that everyone has a double."

"Aside from her nose and front tooth, they could be twins." Daphne fanned herself with her hand, then stopped abruptly. "I just thought of something. Pretense was a foster child. She may have an identical twin somewhere that she knew nothing about. I bet that's it. Claire is Pretense Abdicator's identical twin!"

Edna's eyes spun like a forty-five vinyl. "Land sakes alive. You could be onto something. What are the chances?"

———

Pedro hung up with Kerry and waited for Claire to return his call. When the phone rang, Kerry's voice cried out, breathless and in tears.

"She left. She packed up everything and called a cab. When I asked if she was coming back, she didn't answer."

He drew in a long breath. "Did she say where she was going?"

"No. Did something happen between you two? I'm worried."

"I'll call you back. I need to figure out what's going on."

Pedro stared blankly, unnerved by the curious encounter between Claire and the women from the mission team. They said she resembled someone they knew. And now Claire was gone. A chill rippled down his spine, as he sank into a chair and dragged his hand over his chin. He dropped his head in his hands and prayed for God's guidance. Then he got up and walked across the church yard.

He spotted the older woman, Edna, sitting at a picnic table watching Sarah play on a swing set. Pedro went over.

"Would you like some company?" Pedro asked.

"Please, sit down."

"I understand this is your first mission trip. We are blessed to have you here with us."

"I feel privileged to be here. Thank you for the wonderful work you are doing."

"We couldn't do it without the support of people like you." He laced his fingers on the table in front of him and leaned in. "The woman you met earlier—Claire—it sounds like she resembles someone you know. Do you mind if I ask you a few questions?"

"Ask me anything you like. I'm probably more anxious to talk to you than you realize."

He stared for a minute and drew in a long breath. "What exactly is it about Claire that reminds you of your acquaintance, Pretense?"

"Aside from a few minor differences, like her hair color and nose, her facial features are strikingly similar, and she has the same mannerisms and the same tone of voice."

Pedro took in a sharp breath. "What about height?"

"Same height. Same physique."

His shoulders slumped. "I have a vested interest in Claire. I've asked her to be my wife."

Edna nodded. "Congratulations. I imagine this conversation is quite startling for you." She patted his hand. "Before today, did you have doubts about Claire's character?"

"I knew she had a troubled past. And that she had kept something hidden inside. We agreed to have a heart-to-heart after you and the others returned home. But something spooked her today. Now she has disappeared—packed her bags and left." He took Edna's hands in his. "If you know something … anything … please tell me. I want to help her."

Edna gazed hard into Pedro's pleading eyes, then looked off. "I don't know where to begin." So, she began at the beginning and ended with the return of the money and the private investigator's findings. "I've always had a soft spot in my heart for Pretense, and I thought she felt the same about my husband and me. As you can imagine, I was devastated when I learned about the scheme. I had hoped that coming here would prove me wrong. But when I saw her, I knew." She reached into her shirt pocket and pulled out a tissue, dabbing her eyes and honking into the hankie.

Pedro leaned his forehead against clenched fists. A nameless dread had been gnawing at him all day. His mind became numb with shock. After several minutes, he looked at Edna with compassion. "It must have been hard for you, confronting your suspicions. Thank you for sharing everything with me. The other woman—Daphne—does she know?"

"No. I wanted Daphne with me to get her reaction. She was very close to Pretense and she is heavily involved in mission work. It was a win-win situation."

Pedro nodded. "Your son, Baron, you must blame Pretense for his presumed death. He would not have been in the building that day had it not been for her actions."

Edna rolled her lips in. "Baron discovered Pretense's plan

while conspiring to siphon money from our account. The private investigator I worked with, Gary Marion, learned of his plot while going through the files of the former lead on the case. Baron was in the building that day because he was trying to stop Pretense from doing what he had planned to do. He would have inherited everything from us in due time. I guess we weren't dying fast enough." She blew her nose into the tissue.

"I'm so sorry. The love of money can cause people to do horrible things." He reflected on Pretense's actions. "Now that your suspicions about Pretense have been confirmed, what do you plan to do with this information?"

She paused for a long minute. "Nothing. She gave the money back. I came here because I needed to know, and I wanted to confront Pretense … to understand why. However, I am not sure I will have that opportunity." She leaned forward. "Tell me about Claire, the woman you know. You must love her."

The statement made him pause. "I do. Very much. We come from similar backgrounds, so we understand each other." Pedro told Edna about their first meeting on the street when captivated by her beauty, then by her passion for children. Then he told her of his own dysfunctional past. "The only difference between us is I had someone who cared enough to help me. She never did." He bit his lip, his lower lids welling. "God never wastes our pain. Only we do that. I believe He has given both of us a purpose. To share our stories in order to help others. I was hoping to spend our lives doing that together."

"You are a good man, Pedro. And despite her mistakes, I believe Pretense is a good woman who finally found what she was searching for—a place where she belonged."

A spray of spitting gravel stole their attention. Udom jumped out of the car and ran toward them, panting. "I just went to check on Maya. Kwang is dead. An overdose. And no one knows where Maya is."

CHAPTER 60

Pedro shot to his feet, panic taking his body. He turned to Edna. "I need to find Claire. She may be with Maya."

Edna stood, her face ashen. "What do you mean?"

Pedro placed his hands on Edna's shoulders. "We believe Maya was being trafficked for sex. We were working to get her removed from her home, and Claire was frustrated by the slow process. She may have taken matters into her own hands."

"Are you going to call the police?"

"If I do, they will arrest Claire for kidnapping. And who knows what will happen to Maya."

"I think I know someone who can help find Claire. My private investigator worked with an investigator here on the island. His name is David Omni. You should contact him. And don't worry about the cost. I will pay for everything."

———

After David Omni agreed to look for Claire, Pedro called Kerry. "I need your help. Do you recall the name of the cab company that picked up Claire?"

"What's going on?" Kerry asked, after she gave Pedro the information.

"I'm not sure. I'll call you when I know more."

"What can I do?"

"Pray."

Pedro called David with the cab information, then slumped into a chair. His mind skittered. He got up and paced the floor, then picked up his Bible. He sat down again, trying to calm his frenzied mind. He read through Psalms, but had trouble focusing. And then eight simple words seemed to rise off the page: *Be still and know that I am God.* He closed the book and meditated on the verse.

When he opened his eyes, Daphne was sitting across from him, her hands folded in her lap. "I'm sorry to bother you, Pastor Pedro. Do you have a minute?"

"Yes, of course. And call me Pedro. Edna tells me you are interested in becoming a full-time missionary."

"I am. When I go on short-term mission trips, I don't go because I feel called. I feel called because I go. And after each trip, I know I've made the right choice. So, my fiancé, Andrew, and I are ready to take the next step."

Pedro studied Daphne in silence for a moment. "I admire your conviction. Is that what you wanted to talk about—missionary work?"

"I always want to talk about God's work, but I came to ask you about Claire. Do you know if she is coming back? I'd like to speak with her."

"I don't know when she will be back."

Daphne shifted in her seat. "Forgive me for being forward, but I saw the two of you together." Her faced bloomed crimson. "You looked to be more than just acquaintances."

Pedro nodded slowly. "Why do you want to speak with her?"

"As you heard, Claire reminds me of someone. I know this sounds crazy, but I'm convinced that Claire could be her identical twin. My acquaintance, Pretense, grew up in foster care, so she never knew her biological mother. I wanted to ask Claire about her background. Perhaps you know."

Pedro squirmed. "From what Claire has told me, she lived with her biological mother. She had no siblings and never met her father." All true, as far as he knew. "This person, Pretense, was she a good friend of yours?"

"She was very special to me." Her eyes swept the room. "It was hard to get close to Pretense. She was incredibly smart, but somewhat detached. She didn't let people in. I think she wanted to, but she didn't know how. She came to my house for dinner one day and for the first time, I saw her as she really was—a vulnerable woman who seemed to want nothing more than to fit in somewhere." Daphne swiped a tear from her cheek. "We believe Pretense died on nine-eleven."

Pedro reached for Daphne's hand. "I'm sorry to hear that. You were very fond of Pretense."

Sarah blew into the room like a gale and flung herself on the floor at Daphne's feet. "Did you find Pretense?"

Daphne leaned forward and stroked Sarah's hair. "We talked about this—remember? That other lady just looks like Pretense."

Sarah turned to Pedro. "Pretense is my friend. We have private talks."

"Your sister told me about Pretense," said Pedro. "She sounds like a nice lady."

Somboon inched into the room and cowered behind Pedro's chair. Pedro felt behind his chair and took hold of his arm, guiding him around front. The child buried his face on Pedro's thighs. "I told Somboon we would practice soccer today. Sarah, would you like to come watch?"

"Yes," said Sarah, leaping to her feet.

"It looks like I'm being called." Pedro stood and took the children's hands, one on either side. He turned to Daphne. "I'm glad we talked."

Daphne smiled. "I will pray things work out between you and Claire." She touched his arm, then turned and left the room.

Pedro led the children outside, grateful for the diversion. But he couldn't calm his racing mind. Visions of Claire and Maya lingered.

———

It had been a few days since Claire's disappearance, and there was no sign of her or Maya. Tired of the endless wait, Pedro wrapped up his duties at the church, then went for an evening drive to clear his head. Before long, he found himself in front of Moonbeam Bungalows. He parked the car and walked to the shore, stalling in front of her room along the way. Thoughts of their time together left him with a crushing emptiness that cried to be filled. He stood on the seashore, watching the moonbeam ripple across the inky water, the vastness of God's creation weighing down. Movement appeared from the corner of his eye.

"I thought it was you," said Kerry. She placed her hand on his back. "How are you doing?"

He looked at her face, illuminated in a lunar glow. "I'm trying to be patient. What about you?"

"I'm worried sick. I don't know why she left, but I suspect you might. Claire talked about things in her past—things she was afraid to share with you. Do you think that is why she ran away?"

Pedro rubbed his forehead, then looked at Kerry. "It's highly likely."

"You obviously know something. How bad is it? Is it bad enough to make you stop loving her?"

"I'll never stop loving her. But I don't know if we have a future together."

A soft whimper escaped her lips. "You are a pastor. Don't you believe in forgiveness?"

He looked out across the ocean, the moonlight glistening off the water. "I have forgiven Claire. We all make mistakes. But forgiveness is not the same as trust."

CHAPTER 61

After dropping the mission team off at the airport, Pedro felt empty, like a piece of Claire had left with them. He sat in the van and examined the business card Edna had slipped into his hand. "Call me if you find her," she'd whispered, embracing him curbside, her frail body bound with intent. "She may need help." Her spindly finger wagged in his face. "Everyone deserves a happy ending."

———

It was two a.m. Pedro stirred in bed, his eyes fixed on the ceiling fan while visions of Claire whirled in his mind. The drone of the cell phone vibrated on the nightstand, shaking his thoughts. He bolted from bed.

"I found her," said David Omni. "She is with the young girl at a hotel in the Bang Khae section of Bangkok."

Pedro sighed, dragging his hand through his hair and pacing the room. "Does she know you're following her?"

"No. I'm very unassuming. I blend into scenery. Do you want me to apprehend her?"

"No, please. Just give me the address. I will come for her."

"Okay. I'll continue to monitor her movements until you get here. When will you arrive?"

He glanced at the clock. "Sometime this afternoon. Thank you for your help."

At the break of dawn, Pedro informed Udom and Solada that he would be gone for a few days. He drove to the Lipa Noi Pier and took the car ferry to mainland Thailand, then set out in his Jeep for the long drive to Bang Khae.

Eight hours later, he pulled into the hotel parking lot of the address David had provided. A pocket-sized man approached his car and knocked on the glass. Pedro rolled down the window.

"Are you Pedro Garcia? I'm David Omni, private investigator."

Pedro reached through the open window and shook his hand. "Yes. Is she here?"

"Yes. And, she is with the girl. They are in the pool. Do you need me to stand by?" His beady eyes jackhammered right and center.

"I'll be okay. I appreciate all you've done."

Pedro parked the car and walked around to the back of the hotel. His jaw clenched when he saw them alone in the pool. Maya lay prostrate, floating atop the water, while Pretense braced her midsection, steering her around the pool. They splashed in the water, Maya's squeals of laughter echoing through the air. Pedro stopped and took in the scene from a distance, the image melting his heart.

He leaned against a pillar, delaying the inevitable. Before long, Maya's eyes found him. "Pedro," she screamed, her face lit with excitement, her hand flapping in the air.

Pretense turned and pulled Maya to her chest, her eyes wild with panic.

Pedro strolled to the edge of the pool and crouched, dragging his fingers through the crystalline water. His face broke into a weak smile. "Hello, Claire. Hello, Maya."

Pretense felt her knees crumple beneath her, as she gripped Maya and worked her way toward the concrete steps. When they emerged from the water, Maya broke free and ran into Pedro's outstretched arms. Pretense stood off to the side, a half-naked, drenched soldier shivering and awaiting punishment.

Pedro rose and took Maya's hand, then walked toward her. Without speaking, he pulled her trembling body into his arms and drew her head to his chest.

"You know," she whispered, her tears soaking his shirt. "I wanted to tell you. I'm sorry you found out the way you did. And Maya—I only wanted to protect her. They would have taken her."

"I understand," he said, holding her tight. After a time, he pulled away and held her face. "I love you—with all that I have. But everything has changed. I came to take Maya back with me." He took the beach towel hanging on a nearby lawn chair and wrapped it around Pretense, then he kissed her forehead. "I'd like to get Maya's things and get her changed into dry clothes."

She gulped back tears, trying to tame a choking mass forming in her throat. "What will you do with her?"

"I'll take her to the church. She will live there until we find her a good home."

Hot tears rushed down her cheeks. With trembling hands, she handed Pedro the hotel key. "Her clothes are in the room," she managed to say. "And her doll—don't forget her doll."

He took the key, then bent down and said something in Thai to Maya. Maya looked confused, then wrapped her arms around Pretense's legs.

"Chan rak khun," said Maya.

Pretense knelt and held Maya's face in her hands, a briny mix burning her eyes. "I love you, too, my little darling." She kissed her cheek, then she stood and placed her palm against Pedro's face, her eyes fastened on his.

He pressed her open hand to his mouth, his lips gentle against her fingers. Then he dried her eyes with his thumbs and handed her Edna's business card. "She said she can help you. Find out who you are and make things right." His eyes shimmered as he took Maya's hand and turned away.

She studied his back as they faded out of her life, hand in hand—a reminder of the day they had first met. The greatest treasure she'd ever known, ripped from her hand. And God stood by silently.

Hours passed as she sat alone staring at the pool with vacant eyes. A young family appeared with two children, their idle chatter and laughter filling her with deep and sombrous melancholy. Several more hours and the sun dipped low, a sudden breeze whipping the air and striking a chill in her heart. She rose from her chair and drifted back to the empty room—the empty life.

She fell back on the bed and ran her hand over her rounded belly, wondering about the future of her unborn child. Her chance for the family she had always dreamt of now gone forever. Her finger caught the edge of the card she'd tucked into the bottom of her swimsuit. She pulled it out and stared at the black letters embossed across the front: *Edna Rothschild*.

CHAPTER 62

After hours of solemn deliberation, Pretense reached for the phone with juddering fingers. What little confidence she had had faltered when she heard Edna's voice. Like a babbling five-year-old, Pretense managed to mutter her name and a senseless opening line.

"I've been waiting for you," said Edna, calmly. "I'm glad you called."

"Oh, Edna, I am so very sorry for everything."

"I know you are, dear."

"And Hyman? He must hate me."

Pretense wept openly after learning about Hyman's stroke, the consequence of her sins relentless. But Edna's soothing words helped ease the guilt. The conversation turned to the events leading up to the embezzlement and why Pretense returned the money and how she had finally found what she had been searching for. She spoke about the rape and the baby she carried, and Pedro's willingness to raise the child as his own. "That is…" She trailed off. "Pedro came for Maya and left. It's over between us."

"You poor dear," said Edna. "But you cannot continue living a lie and pretending to be someone you are not. Sooner or later it

was bound to catch up with you. Really, what were you thinking, taking that child?"

"I wasn't thinking. Everything happened so fast. I worried
the traffickers would come for her. Had I been thinking ratio-
nally, I would have called Pedro. But nothing in my life is
rational."

Edna sighed. "What about your baby?"

"With Pedro out of the picture, I'll probably put the baby up
for adoption—to give it a normal life with a loving family." She
blew her nose. "I want to make things right, but I don't know
where to start."

"Let me help you, Pretense. I've been thinking this through,
and I have an idea. If you were to fly back to the U.S. using the
passport you left with—the one for Claire—there shouldn't be
any alarms raised. Once you return, destroy the documents
related to Claire Voyant and resume your true identity."

"You make it sound so easy. What if I get stopped by
Customs?"

"I have some of the best lawyers around."

"Edna, why do you want to help me after all I've put you
through? You have enough to worry about, given Hyman's
condition. And because of me, your son Baron is gone."

Edna told Pretense about Baron's plan to steal money from
their account. "So, you see, Baron was in the tower that day due
to his own deceitful intentions."

"I'm so sorry."

"Yes, I am too. But that is in the past." She heard a sniffle,
then Edna cleared her throat. "Do you still have your old passport and driver's license?"

Pretense thought for a minute. Her old passport had been in
the apartment in New York. She never went back after 9-11. And
her license, still in her purse, likely destroyed when the tower
fell. "I don't. And if I applied for new documents, wouldn't that
alert the authorities? A man from the FBI was in the meeting that

day, along with Baron. If he didn't make it out, I'm sure there is a record of my case."

"I'm aware of the FBI's involvement. If they were to be notified, my lawyers would handle everything. Why don't you book a flight to New York as soon as possible? You can stay with me until the baby is born. And if you still choose to, you can put the child up for adoption in the U.S."

"Edna, I still don't understand. Why are you doing this for me?"

There came a slight pause. "Because I can. I remember the first day we met at Crawford Spectrum. I immediately took a liking to you. You weren't like the others, putting on airs, talking yourself up. You were just you—quietly brilliant, but in a wounded sort of way. When I found out you had lied about being a foster child, I felt betrayed. That is until I learned that your truth was uglier than your lies. It was your way of coping with the garbage life threw at you. Pretense, I know you are trying to be a better person, and I admire that. I want you to be that person. I'm getting on in my years, and I'd like to do something meaningful in my life. Please, let me help you."

"You are so very kind," she said, her voice cracking. Years of pent-up emotions came gushing out, and for the first time in her life she felt exposed. But instead of shame, she felt set free from a burden she could no longer carry.

"Pretense, get yourself well. I have a therapist in New York who can help you. You have so much to offer others who have suffered like you. Don't throw your priceless gift away."

She recalled something Pedro once said. *Our past, no matter how ugly, can be a light.* "Thank you, Edna, for all you've done for me."

———

Seated in the terminal with her meager belongings, Pretense waited to board the plane bound for New York. An unhappy ending to a life that had held so much promise—a land and a people she had grown to love. With tears pooling in her eyes, she made one last call before leaving Thailand.

"Oh my God," said Kerry. "Where are you?"

"I'm at the airport. I'm going to New York."

"Why?"

"Kerry, I need to be upfront with you." The sentences came out in quick spurts and gulps of air until nothing remained unsaid. An uncomfortable silence loomed. "Kerry, did you hear me? Say something."

"I can't believe your mother named you Pretense Abdicator. No wonder you were screwed up." She heard ripples of sobbing, muddled with Kerry's familiar laugh. "Oh, Claire—I refuse to call you Pretense—will I ever see you again?"

"You can visit me in New York. And, who knows, maybe one day I'll come back."

"I hope so," Kerry said, sniveling. "You always have a place with me and Denzel. What about the baby?"

"I'm leaning toward adoption."

"And Pedro?"

"I don't think he will ever trust me again."

"But now he knows everything. And you love each other. Doesn't that count for anything?"

"Kerry, I have to go. My plane is boarding. We'll talk once I'm settled." She clenched her teeth, trying to tame the groundswell of emotion. "I love you, Kerry. You mean so much to me." With tears soaking her face, she pressed the END CALL button and boarded the plane bound for New York City.

CHAPTER 63

Four weeks had passed since her uneventful arrival in the U.S. Pretense moved in with Edna and a special bond formed that seemed to further strengthen after Hyman's passing two weeks earlier. Edna became the mother she had always hoped for and never thought she'd have. They spent long hours together, talking about their lives, the birth of her unborn child, the progress she'd been making with the therapist, and her future goal of one day opening an orphanage for abused children.

"With my experience in nonprofits, I can help you get the orphanage started," said Edna one afternoon.

Rafaela came into the room and announced dinner. "Edna tells me you were born in Spain," said Pretense, reflecting on Pedro's roots.

"Yes. I haven't been back since I was a little girl, but would love to return one day." Rafaela set a plate of roast beef on the dining room table. "Have you been to Spain?"

"No, but I would love to go one day."

"Rafaela, why don't you join us for dinner?" asked Edna, patting the seat next to her.

"Why, Mrs. Rothschild, I couldn't do that."

"Why not? Go mix yourself a cocktail and come sit down. And by the way, you can start calling me Edna."

Rafaela beamed. "Thank you, Mrs. Rothschild, er … Edna. I would be flattered to join you."

Pretense leaned over to Edna after Rafaela left the room. "That was very gracious of you."

Edna waved her hand dismissively. "Hyman would roll over in his grave if he ever saw me mingling with the staff. Even though we both came from money, my parents were very different than Hyman's. My mother taught us to treat everyone with respect. Hyman was raised with a golden chalice lodged in his butt. But I still loved that man."

After Rafaela returned, Edna and Pretense shared stories about their time in Thailand while Edna and Rafaela sipped cocktails. By the end of the evening, Rafaela rose unsteadily and put on her coat.

"You know, I never asked you where you live," said Edna. "Is it far from here?"

"Not too far," said Rafaela. "It's about an hour by subway into Queens."

"Nonsense. You will sleep in the spare bedroom tonight. Do you need to call anyone to let them know?"

"I live alone. It's just me."

From that day forward, Rafaela became a member of the makeshift family, spending most nights at the Rothschild residence. Pretense took note of the shift in Edna's personality since Hyman's passing—a softening of the heart. The three began attending Redeemer Presbyterian Church on Sundays, and Pretense enrolled in a woman's Bible study that met during the week.

As they were sitting on the balcony one evening, Pretense turned to Edna. "I tried to get ahold of Daphne today using the number you gave me, but the phone had been disconnected. I wanted to tell her everything. I hope to one day get that chance."

"That's odd," said Edna. "I'll check with one of the people

that went on the mission trip. Maybe they know what's going on."

Pretense reached over and squeezed Edna's hand. "I'd appreciate that. Thank you. I spoke to my therapist the other day about legally changing my name to Claire. She thought it was a positive move. What do you think?"

"I think it would give you freedom from your past. Did your mother tell you why she named you Pretense?"

"She liked the sound of the word." She looked down, picking her fingernails. "So many bad memories are associated with my name."

Edna nodded. "Do you ever think about getting in touch with your mother?"

"Not until lately. It seems I've spent my entire life hating her, but I never tried to understand why she did the things she did. We never talked like you and I do."

"You should think about calling her. Maybe it will help you heal." She patted Pretense's hand. "Are you nervous about the meeting at the adoption agency tomorrow?"

Pretense touched her belly, her words trapped inside the lump in her throat. She swallowed and nodded.

"Are you sure this is what you want?" asked Edna.

"I want my baby to have a normal life—with normal people. I'm not normal. Sometimes when the dark clouds come, I go insane—or at least it feels that way. I go back to that room in my mother's house and there are times I can't get out. When I was a child, I used to think I had died and that I was living in Hell."

Edna took in a sharp breath. "I can't imagine. But you are getting stronger each day. And you said you were willing to keep the baby with Pedro. Are you afraid of being a single parent?"

"Pedro was my rock. He kept my dark thoughts away. I'm not sure I can be that person without him."

Edna took her hand. "Of course you can. You cannot rely on other people. They may not always be there for you—they die, they move away. I learned that long ago. Hyman—bless his heart—wanted to control every aspect of my life. It was his way of protecting me. If I would have allowed that, I would be a lonely, frightened widow today. Go to the meeting tomorrow and gather the information, but don't commit yourself. If it is something you are meant to do, the prompting will come."

"Edna, you always make me feel better."

———

Pretense left the penthouse for the meeting at the adoption agency, while Rafaela went shopping. Edna sat relaxing in the study when she heard the lobby buzzer.

"Chris Decker and Walt Thumper are here to see you," announced the doorman. "They said they are from the FBI. Should I send them up?"

Edna fanned herself with her hand and patted her hair. She looked at the mantel clock. Pretense would be back in a few hours. "Send them up, please."

After the men introduced themselves and were seated in the drawing room, the tall, thin man, Chris, apologized for the unannounced visit.

"I don't have much time," said Edna. "What can I do for you?"

Chris leaned forward while Walt scribbled notes on a small pad. "We are here to talk to you about Pretense Abdicator. We understand she was your financial adviser."

"Yes, that is correct," said Edna.

Chris shifted in his seat. "One of our agents, Dick Birchwood, was assigned a case looking into an embezzlement scheme involving your funds at Crawford Spectrum. We believe Pretense Abdicator was involved in that scheme." Chris stalled, awaiting Edna's reaction. A deadpan expression lingered. "Until recently, we had reason to believe that Pretense Abdicator perished on nine-eleven, along with our agent, Dick, and your son, Baron. To be sure, we put a tracer on her credit card, passport, driver's license, et cetera, looking for any activity that might prove otherwise. This past week, we were alerted that someone applied for all three documents. Before I go further, I should ask if you were aware of the embezzlement scheme."

The front door opened and closed. Edna leaned forward in her seat. "Rafaela, is that you?"

Rafaela came into the room. "Yes, Edna. Do you need something?"

"Can you make some coffee for these nice gentlemen? Oh, and bring some of those French macarons you picked up at the bakery yesterday, those pastel pink-and-green ones."

After Rafaela left the room, Edna scooched her chair forward and smoothed her skirt. "Gentlemen, my late husband, Hyman, and I asked Pretense Abdicator to quietly move money in large increments out of our account and into an offshore bank account in order to hide money from our son, Baron. So, yes, I was aware of her actions. Baron was trying to gain access to our trust by claiming we were unfit to handle our funds. I'm not sure why the FBI is involved, but I assume Baron was the instigator. Perhaps to try to get Pretense out of the way." She yanked a tissue from a gold-plated cube and patted her eyes. "I guess I will never know."

Rafaela returned and set a silver platter of pastel confections and a carafe of coffee on a side table.

Edna thanked her. "Gentlemen, please," she said, splaying her hand toward the tray.

They rose, helping themselves before sitting down. Walt scratched his head with the tip of his pen, then slurped his coffee and bit into a macaron. "These are delicious. So airy and light." He took another bite. "So, are you claiming that Pretense worked for you and there was no misconduct on her part?"

Edna pursed her lips. "Walt, let me be very clear. I'm stating a fact. Pretense was and is working for me."

Chris and Walt looked at each other. "So, Pretense Abdicator is alive?" asked Chris. "You've seen her?"

"Yes, of course. Pretense lives here with me." Edna's eyes bounced from Walt to Chris with an actor-worthy expression of alarm stamped on her face. "Do I need to involve my lawyers?"

Chris rolled his shoulders and adjusted his necktie. "Mrs. Rothschild, we would like to talk to Pretense. Is she available?"

"She is out, and I don't expect her back soon. You must excuse me, gentlemen, but I have an appointment."

Chris held up a forefinger. "One last question. Do you know a woman by the name of Claire Voyant?"

"Yes, I do. Pretense worked with Claire to set up the offshore bank account and a shell company. It is all perfectly legal, according to my lawyers. Now, if you'll excuse me." Edna rose from her chair, and the men did likewise. "Rafaela will show you out. And if you are determined to interview Pretense, I will insist that my attorneys are present. Thank you for your time."

Rafaela came into the room. "This way, gentlemen." Walt grabbed two cookies and stuffed them into his pocket before following Rafaela to the front door.

———

On the elevator ride down to the lobby, Chris looked at Walt noshing on a macaron. "I guess we should let the boss know that the case against Pretense Abdicator can be closed."

CHAPTER 64

"What if they come back?" asked Pretense after returning home from the adoption agency and learning of the unexpected visit.

"I don't think they will," said Edna. "Now, stop worrying and tell me about the meeting. How did it go?"

Pretense dropped to the sofa. "They were wonderful—very professional. We talked at length about my vision of the perfect family. I would be able to meet the potential parents before signing anything. And once the baby is born, I have seventy-two hours before I legally consent to the adoption."

Edna studied her face. "You don't want to do this, do you?"

Tears squirrelled down her cheeks. "No, but I want what is best for my baby, despite how it came to be." She revealed to Edna that Pedro's mother had been raped. "Pedro has accomplished so much in his life. It gives me hope for my child. I worry I'm making the wrong decision by giving my baby up for adoption."

"It is remarkable what a fine man Pedro turned into. He seems so well grounded. If you decide to keep the baby, I can help you."

"Oh, Edna. As it is, I can never repay you."

"You repay me every day you are here. I always wanted a daughter, but after Baron was born, we learned we couldn't have more children. And now that Baron and Hyman are gone, you are all that I have. You and Rafaela."

Pretense cupped Edna's face. "You mean everything to me." She wrapped her arms around Edna's frail body. "When I think about what I had done to you, it sickens me. I could say I'm sorry a thousand times, but it would never be enough."

"Then don't ever say it again. Think about the good that has come out of this. Things happen for a reason."

Pretense went to her room that night, mulling over her complex, ever-changing life. Edna had it right. Her world had changed—tenfold. And even though she had lost the people she'd grown to love, she was left with a treasure trove of precious memories, dearer than all the money in the world. She rested in the unshakeable knowledge of a future steeped in hope.

———

The following morning, Pretense made the long overdue call to Kerry in Thailand. Her heart leapt at the sound of Kerry's voice.

"Claire," she squealed. "Denzel and I have been so worried. You promised to call right away. Are you okay?"

"Yes, I am fine. I'm staying with Edna Rothschild."

"Edna? The woman you stole money from—then gave it back? How is that working out?"

"It couldn't be more perfect. Edna has been so gracious and forgiving. I can't even begin to describe our relationship."

They talked for over an hour, as though she had never left, about all that had transpired over the last four weeks.

"I have good news," said Kerry. "I'm pregnant."

"Oh, Kerry. That's wonderful. I'm so happy. Promise you'll fly out to New York while you can still travel. I spoke to Edna, and she said you are welcome to stay here anytime."

"I will definitely do that. Hey, have you spoken to Pedro?"

The sound of his name sparked her heart. "No. I doubt I'll ever hear from him again."

"You don't know that. He loves you, Claire. He came by with Maya the other day, asking if I'd heard from you. He looks broken. Why don't you call him?"

"I can't. The day he came to take Maya from me, there was something different about him. Like a wall had gone up between us."

"Claire! Can you blame him? The poor man falls in love and asks for your hand in marriage, then he learns you are not who you say you are, and you are running from a criminal past. And, as if that's not enough, you kidnap a child and run off to another part of the country. You probably scared the crap out of him. But he's had time to reflect."

Pretense sighed. "Then why hasn't he called me?"

"Maybe he's waiting for you to find yourself."

"I love him so much. And I miss Maya." She blew into a Kleenex. "But I'm not ready to call him. Please don't tell him you spoke to me."

"You have my word. But don't wait too long. Time dulls pain, and we all move on."

———

She wrapped the shawl around her shivering shoulders, the chilled air still, as she sat alone on the balcony. Just when she felt herself gaining balance, Pedro swooped in and stole her thoughts away.

The French doors opened, freeing a blast of warm air. "You must be freezing," said Edna. "Why don't you come inside?"

Pretense turned and smiled. "I'm enjoying the beautiful view. It's so peaceful. Come join me."

Edna grabbed a sweater from inside and sat next to Pretense. "Hyman and I used to spend hours out here, just sitting and talking. I miss him. He was the only man I ever loved." She shook her head as though denying the pain. "Did you call Kerry?"

"Yes. She said she would love to come to New York. And she's pregnant. I'm so happy for her. I can't wait for you to meet her."

"That's wonderful. I would love to meet her. Any news from Pedro?"

She pulled the shawl tight and looked off toward the sky-high buildings surrounding Central Park. "Kerry said he came by her place with Maya, asking about me. But I've not heard from him."

"You miss him, don't you?"

"Yes, very much. And I miss Maya."

"What do you propose to do about it?"

She looked up at the sky with a wistful expression. "I think it's best if I stay out of their lives."

Edna studied her for a long moment, then reached over and squeezed her hand. "Let's go inside before we catch cold."

After dinner, Pretense retired to her room. Her mind traveled back to her years at Crawford Spectrum and her once lonely, angry life. So much had changed. She had changed. It felt so gradual—almost unnoticeable. She lay across the bed and thought about the dinner in Daphne's home, Daphne on one side of her and Sarah on the other. They had said grace—the first glint of a feeling longed for, like a secret signature scrawled across her soul. She slowly inhaled life, her story playing like golden threads twining their way through a rich tapestry of interconnected lives. It was clear. God was moving in her life, breaking down barriers she had built. She let go and moved with Him, her eyelids growing heavy.

She woke to a haunting sound that seemed to be in the room —a shrill voice calling out to her. Slicked with sweat, she sat upright, her breaths churning in heavy pants. It was only 7:00 p.m. It seemed later. She rose from bed and swayed uneasily, making her way into the bathroom and cupping her hands under the faucet, drinking the cool water trapped in her hands, then splashing her face. When she looked in the mirror, an elderly woman with a mountain of graying hair and a deeply lined face glared back at her. She gasped and stumbled back, turning away. As though she had no control over her movements, she floated toward the nightstand and watched as her fingers reached for the phone. An unfamiliar voice answered.

"Mom? It's Pretense."

"Pretense? This is Lola, your mom's neighbor. They just took her away. How did you know? I found her on the floor—stiff as a board."

"She's dead?"

"Yes. Hey, do you mind if I go through some of her stuff before they condemn the trailer? We was good friends, ya know."

"Take what you want," she said, before the phone slipped from her hand. She sank onto the bed, the shock gripping in bitter clutches. There were no tears; only a feeling of something left undone. A tacit tension.

CHAPTER 65

The mile-long procession of freight trains clattered along rusty wrought-iron tracks, sending plumes of dust across the rugged terrain of Gallup, New Mexico. This was where her life began and where Pretense vowed to never return. But here she was, standing in a barren cemetery expressing gratitude to a handful of mourners as they returned to their cars.

Lola hung back until the last person left, then handed Pretense an envelope. "I found this when I was goin through Wanda's things. I still can't believe she's gone. She was in pretty bad shape these last months, always wondering if you was alive…what with those towers falling and all."

Pretense took the envelope and stuffed it into her pocket. "I appreciate everything you've done these past few days … cleaning out the trailer, contacting her friends. I couldn't have done it without you."

"It was my pleasure, honey. I've known your mother for many years. I was there the day you was born. She was just a kid herself. A real fighter, she was. What, with the life she had and no one to help her. Hey, do you plan on sticking around? Maybe we can go for a drink somewhere and chat."

"I would love to, but I need to leave shortly."

"Too bad. She always talked you up like you was some sort of big-shot genius. She said you was goin places and one day you'd come back for her. Too late for that now. Well, I should let you alone to properly mourn her passing. Call if you need anything. It was good seeing you."

After Lola left, she hung back, bracing against an icy east wind whipping hair across her stoic face. She pulled her coat tightly around herself and pondered Lola's words—words she had never heard before. She looked down, eyeing the unpretentious gravestone. A slice of sun cut through the overcast sky, casting a spotlight on the freshly laid slab, the etching, *Mother*, radiant, as if by some cruel joke. As she lingered over the grave marker, she searched her mind for a few kind words, but a void of nothingness dwelled.

Pretense hesitated before reaching into her pocket and pulling out the envelope, her mother's childlike scrawl painted across the front. She toyed with the packet for some time before sliding her thumbnail under the flap and withdrawing a handwritten letter, the stench of stale cigarette smoke wafting upwards. She unfolded the paper and began reading her mother's declaration of guilt.

Dear Pretense. If your reeding this I'm probly dead witch is a good thing. I wasnt werth much as a person. You probly wonder bout your famly. We never spoke bout it. I want you to no. You should no. There was only you and me. I was born sumtime in Febury 1956. I dont no the day. They said I was left in a garbidge bag in a dumstir. The man who found me took me and hid me. He gave me a made-up name. Wanda after his goldfish and Abdicator after some king who gave up his royal crown. I member sumtimes women came by. I grew up in his house. Sumtimes women teach me reeding and riting but most times I worked to make men happy. When I was 16 you came so they made me go. I tried to be a good mother but I dont no how so I raised you how I was raised and made a livin for us. I never treeted you nice. I dont no why but the day you said you never want to talk to me agin that was the werst day of my life. I didnt no then but you were the only thing I loved. I looked at other kids then I felt bad you ended up with me. I dont no who decided that but you was cheeted. I dont no why I never said nice things to you. Maybe cause saying nice things would stop you from trying to be sumbody. But I was always prowd of you I wanted you to make sumthing better of yerself. I hope one day you meet a nice man who loves you the way I never could. I hope one day you will think bout me and fergive me for being your mother. Im sorry I was born. Wanda.

Her face crumpled as a stream of tears fell, tracing a path through the thin layer of dust coating her cheeks. She reread the letter and stuck it in her pocket as sobs wracked her body. Every bad choice her mother had made was a foretaste of the pain she carried in herself. If only they would have had the chance to talk. If only time turned back.

She stood there with a faraway look in her eyes, reflecting on her past and the hardships she had overcome. She thought about the grace and love of those who appeared in her life; people she needed at exactly the right time. It didn't seem possible, yet only by a miracle. A blustery wind blew in, then an eerie calm arose wrapping its arms around her. A calm she'd never known, but familiar still; that flicker of something longed for, teasing just beyond her grasp. She wasn't alone. The One who had always been there watching over her was with her now. He had been with her all along, clearing a path forward.

Her attention turned to the sound of tires crunching along the gravel road. A car stopped. A door opened and closed. Footsteps rustled in the grass. Perhaps a late mourner. She didn't turn. The steps ceased behind her and a familiar scent filled the air. She froze, her heart charging at full speed.

"Claire."

She spun.

Pedro stood before her, his radiant, dark eyes burning into her soul. "I'm so sorry about your mother." His hands smoothed the hair away from her upturned face, then he pulled her into him, cradling her head against his chest.

She felt her body go limp as she dissolved into him, too afraid to move lest it was a dream. After several silent moments, she pulled back, her eyes glistening. "I can't believe you're here." She searched his face, taking him in. "How... how did you find me?"

"Edna. I had planned to fly to New York, but Edna said you needed me here." He leaned forward, his lips brushing her ear. "I love you, Claire. I can't live without you. I should have never let you go."

She pulled back and looked up at him. "But you needed to let me go. Do you remember the last thing you said to me? You said to figure out who I am and make things right. I finally found who I am." She reached into her coat pocket and took out the note, handing it to Pedro. "My mother left this for me."

Pedro slid a glance at her and paused before opening the letter. After he finished reading it, he reached for her. "I wish she were here so I could tell her you found the man who would always love you. Claire, marry me."

She laid a hand against the side of his face. "You are the only man I ever loved. But my past will always be with me."

His breath fell out in a heavy sigh. "And my past will always be with me. It's who we are. It's time for us, Claire." He searched her eyes then leaned down and found her mouth with his own, his kiss eager with intention. He drew her up against him with such force, her breath caught, as the heat of his lips burned through her body.

When he pulled away, her head dropped to his chest, her arms reaching around his waist, incapable of letting go. "I love you, Pedro. And I'll never stop loving you."

"Is that a yes?"

"Yes. I will marry you."

He took her face in his hands. "I can't wait to bring you back. And I have good news. Daphne and Andrew are moving to Koh

369

Samui. They have agreed to run Beacon of Hope as full-time missionaries."

"Oh, Pedro, that's wonderful news. This is the happiest day of my life. I only wish my mother had met you. And that she and I had made amends. But it's too late."

He pulled her into his arms and kissed her, then his hand moved down to the swell of her belly, lingering. "We've wasted too much time. Let's go home. Maya is waiting for us."

EPILOGUE

The familiar sound of a child's cries echoed in Claire's ears. She stopped and brushed the dirt from her hands and looked over at Pedro, smiling.

"Sounds like somebody is hungry," he said. "I'll keep an eye on the girls while you go feed Daniel."

She climbed the worn wooden steps to their living quarters and entered the small room where Daniel lay. "Mama's here, sweetheart." Daniel's wailing subsided upon hearing his mother's voice, his little arms and legs flailing about. She reached in the crib and pulled him to her chest, her lips brushing his soft face in butterfly kisses. He breathed in sharply and let out a long, shuddering sigh, his body settling against her. She rocked him back and forth as she stood before the open window and gazed out at her family: Maya seated alongside her little sister, Angela, their fingers intertwined, listening raptly as Daphne read a Bible story to the children's group, Pedro tilling the soil with a shovel, his vigilant glance at his two girls warming her insides. Her heart surged with inexpressible thankfulness.

After changing Daniel's diaper, she sat in the rocking chair, the child's mouth feeding at her breast. She gazed down and stroked his olive skin with her finger, tracing the line of his nose and marveling at the resemblance he bore to Pedro at just nine months. In these quiet moments, she reflected upon God for the gift of His countless blessings. And for the mending of her soul, something she'd never felt possible.

Her thoughts were interrupted when Pedro came into the room and crouched beside the chair, running his hand over his son's dark, feathery hair as he looked anxiously into her eyes. "There is bad news. Rafaela just called. Edna has passed away." He handed her an envelope. "And this came by express mail."

An unbroken stream of tears ran down her face. Her voice cracked. "She never got a chance to meet Daniel. She said she was coming next month with Rafaela. Oh, Pedro." Her shoulders quaked as she tried forcing out words between hiccupping sobs. Sensing a change in mood, Daniel stirred against her breast, then turned from her nipple and began to cry.

Pedro reached out and gathered Daniel in his arms while Claire buttoned her blouse and tore open the envelope. Her face turned ashen as the letter slipped from her fingers and fluttered to the ground. "Edna has left everything to us—everything. To use as we see fit. Her only request is that Rafaela be provided for until her death."

Pedro's dark eyes shimmered against the Koh Samui sun shining through the open window, his son's head nestled in the crook of his neck. He moved toward Claire, his lips brushing her hair, the child they had made together tucked between them. "Edna was a special lady with a heart of gold. We will bring Rafaela here to live with us. She loves the girls. And she can teach the children Spanish."

"Yes. And we will honor Edna's legacy and use the money to expand the orphanage. This is truly a blessing."

The sound of thunderous footsteps clattered on the stairs, the children's laughter growing louder with each passing second. Maya and Angela burst in the doorway, behind them a breath-less Kerry clinging to her son's hand. "They beat me," said

Kerry, gasping for air. Her expression turned serious when she noted the look on their faces. "Hey, is everything all right?"

Claire went to the girls and stooped down, wrapping her arms around them, reveling in the closeness of their bodies. She looked up at her dear friend, her eyes shining as she reflected on her life path, an unwritten slate that started wrong. She turned toward Pedro, taking in the image of their son secure in his father's arms and wondering how she ended up in this life. But she knew. "Yes, Kerry, everything is *all* right."

AN AUTHOR'S REQUEST

Thank you for taking the time to read *Escaping Pretense*. I sincerely appreciate your interest in my second novel and hope you enjoyed the story.

While book reviews matter, reader book reviews are golden! However, only 1 percent to 3 percent of readers leave a review. May I humbly ask that you consider posting feedback on your favorite review site? It doesn't need to be a lengthy summary— although I would love that if you have the time. A sentence or two will do.

Feel free to send me an email at djmfiction@gmail.com. I look forward to hearing from you.

ACKNOWLEDGMENTS

My deepest gratitude to all the early readers: Jackie Atchison (a multiple-round reader), my sisters Karen Hill and Sherry O'Brien, my ninety-three-year-old mother Evelyn Cioccio, Paula Ford, Debi Harmount, Paulette Morgan, Lisa Schultz, Nancy Yonkman, and June Reznich for her feedback on the culture and language of Thailand. And to my incredible husband, Bill Miller, whose undying patience and support keep me sane.

I would also like to thank my editor, Michael McConnell, for his depth of experience and insightful guidance. Your positive feedback put an extra bounce in my step.

Seeing the book cover come to life was an awe-inspiring experience. Thank you, Emilie Hendryx Haney, for going to great lengths to make my vision a reality. You are a creative genius! Once again, it was a pleasure working with you.

And lastly, a huge debt of gratitude to my brother, Gary Murrell, my tireless cheerleader. I honestly don't believe I would continue to write if it weren't for your ongoing encouragement and interest in the stories I dream up. Our time together is priceless. I am eternally grateful for all you do.

ABOUT THE AUTHOR

Deborah Jean Miller grew up in Southeast Michigan and never left. Prior to writing her first novel, *The Essence of Shade*, Deborah was a meat wrapper, accountant, quality control analyst, and a director of operations. After retiring, she wrote the stories that have plagued her brain for over fifteen years. When not holed up in her writing cave, Deborah spends time in the kitchen, daydreaming that she is the next Food Network star. To learn more about Deborah, go to her website and check out some of her favorite recipes. You can find her at www.deborahjean-miller.com